THE AMBASSADOR · URSUN'S TEETH

KASPAR VON VELTEN has grown older but the wars never cease. His will may be strong but his career as a general is over. Although far more comfortable with a sword in his hand than dealing with the intrigues of court, he is pressed into service of the Emperor as an ambassador in the far-off, frozen wastes of Kislev.

No sooner does he arrive than his position is thrown into peril. Someone definitely does not want him there. The people are restless, the intricacies of the Kislev court (and its mysterious Tzarina) seem ambiguous and sinister and, to make matters worse, there is a brutal killer on the loose in the city.

The Ambassador Chronicles follows Kaspar as he struggles to protect the city from the monsters outside the walls and the traitors within. Collected for the first time in one edition, this volume contains both of Graham McNeill's fantasy novels *The Ambassador* and *Ursun's Teeth*.

More Graham McNeill from the Black Library

The Ultramarines novels

NIGHTBRINGER
WARRIORS OF ULTRAMAR
DEAD SKY, BLACK SUN

More Warhammer 40,000

STORM OF IRON

A WARHAMMER OMNIBUS

The Ambassador Chronicles

GRAHAM McNEILL

A Black Library Publication

This omnibus edition published in Great Britain in 2005 by
BL Publishing,
Games Workshop Ltd.,
Willow Road, Nottingham,
NG7 2WS, UK.

10 9 8 7 6 5 4 3 2 1

Cover illustration by Sam Hadley.
Map by Nuala Kinrade.

A CIP record for this book is available from the British Library.

ISBN 13: 978 1 84416 199 7
ISBN 10: 1 84416 199 4

Distributed in the US by Simon & Schuster
1230 Avenue of the Americas, New York, NY 10020, US.

Printed and bound in Great Britain by
Bookmarque, Surrey, UK.

THIS IS A DARK age, a bloody age, an age of daemons and of sorcery. It is an age of battle and death, and of the world's ending. Amidst all of the fire, flame and fury it is a time, too, of mighty heroes, of bold deeds and great courage.

AT THE HEART of the Old World sprawls the Empire, the largest and most powerful of the human realms. Known for its engineers, sorcerers, traders and soldiers, it is a land of great mountains, mighty rivers, dark forests and vast cities. And from his throne in Altdorf reigns the Emperor Karl-Franz, sacred descendant of the founder of these lands, Sigmar, and wielder of his magical warhammer.

BUT THESE ARE far from civilised times. Across the length and breadth of the Old World, from the knightly palaces of Bretonnia to ice-bound Kislev in the far north, come rumblings of war. In the towering World's Edge Mountains, the orc tribes are gathering for another assault. Bandits and renegades harry the wild southern lands of the Border Princes. There are rumours of rat-things, the skaven, emerging from the sewers and swamps across the land. And from the northern wildernesses there is the ever-present threat of Chaos, of daemons and beastmen corrupted by the foul powers of the Dark Gods. As the time of battle draws ever near, the Empire needs heroes like never before.

Norsca
Sea of Chaos...
L'Anguille.
Couronne.
The Wasteland.
Marienburg.
Arden forest.
Gisoreux.
Bordeleaux
Bretonnia
Brionne.
Quenelles.
Loren forest

North of Here Lie The
Dreaded Chaos Wastes.
Erengrad.
Here Be Trolls...
Praag.
middle mountains.
Kislev
Kislev.
Wolfenburg.
Talabheim
Altdorf.
The Empire
Sylvania.
Nuln.
The
Moot.
Dracken
-hof.
Zhufbar.
Averheim.
Black
Water.
Black fire Pass.
Karak
Norn.

CONTENTS

Introduction

I ALWAYS FIND introductions hard to do. You see what others have written before you in other anthologies and you want to sound as witty, urbane and slyly intelligent as them. You carefully hone your off-the-cuff wit, refine your spontaneous remarks and read your carefully scripted ad-libs over and over again to make sure they have the right blend of humour and gravitas, thus leaving your readers in no doubt as to your genius...

Stuff that. Sounds too much like hard work to me.

So I'm going to just write this as it occurs to me and if it rambles off on a few tangents that don't seem to be going anywhere, don't worry, it will all make sense by the end. Hopefully. You have in your hands, *The Ambassador Chronicles*, a two-part Warhammer story set in the cold, eastern land of Kislev, full of intrigue, scheming, blackmail and, of course, battles. Because, let's not forget, the Black Library novels are set in the world of Warhammer Fantasy *Battle*...

Part of the idea behind writing the Ambassador books was that I fancied a break from the hack and slash of the 41st millennium to see if I could write stories where the suspension of disbelief wasn't so great, where there was a more obvious connection to the *kinds* of characters we'd meet in a fantasy novel. Writing stories set in the dark, gothic worlds of the far future is great, but it's easy to fall into the trap of thinking that your characters don't need to act believably simply because they live in the most insane universe imaginable. I wanted to write a story set in a world which, though fantastical, was much more accessible to the reader, where recognisable human characters could exist – and to see if I could write them in a believable way.

Though, truth be told, my first steps along the road that led me to writing a fantasy novel began with the purchase of the Fighting Fantasy book, *The Warlock of Firetop Mountain*, a dog-eared copy of which still sits on my bookshelf as a fond, nostalgic reminder of more innocent times, when all we wanted out of a fantasy book was to kick open the door, kill the goblin and steal his 10gp. Of course it wasn't as simple as that, but we've all grown up a little since then and now we want something with a little more meat to it. The times where the heroes wore white hats and the bad guys wore black hats are behind us and we know now that people can't be defined so simply. Good people are capable of terrible acts and those we think of as evil can surprise us with acts of great heroism. I wanted to challenge what we thought we knew about the characters, to invest in flawed heroes who face uncertain choices in a dangerous world. I wanted the reader to cheer for heroes with all-too-human weaknesses and see if they'd still embrace them if they fail, because I don't believe that to portray them as flawed creations weakens them: instead it strengthens them.

Out of all this weighty pontificating came the characters of Kaspar von Velten and Sasha Kajetan, who, once you've read the two books, represent the culmination of that thinking. To an extent they all do, because I wanted to turn the dynamic of most of the characters around from what you expected. The relationship between Kaspar and Pavel develops beyond the usual 'hero and sidekick'. The relationship between Chekatilo and Kaspar also changes to become more than just protagonist/antagonist. This all sounds pretty grand, but don't get me wrong, I'm not trying to write 'Great Literature' that kids will be forced to read in school, I want to tell a ripping yarn with good characters, interesting plots, a truckload of battles and to really bring home the dark, twisted world that is Warhammer.

These were fun books to write, though they were almost just the one book. When planning the book out with the Black Library, it became abundantly clear that there was more plot than could be squeezed into one novel and, rather than cutting out loads of bits to get it all to fit in, I decided to write two books, back to back, in a Matrix kind of way (though hopefully without the disappointment factor the sequels to that movie engendered). The plan was to finish *The Ambassador* then plunge straight into *Ursun's Teeth*. Of course 'the best-laid schemes o' mice an men gang aft agley' and that didn't quite happen, with me taking a rather too long break between finishing one book and starting the next. But deadlines have a wonderful habit of focussing the mind when they are set to drop on you like a lead weight, and *Ursun's Teeth* was written in a flurry of stabbing at the keyboard, late nights and enough coffee to keep the Columbian economy afloat for years to come.

Once they were finished, and I read the manuscript in its entirety, I saw that they veered towards a darkness that almost went too far in some parts. But as anyone who's ever read any of my books can probably testify, they all take that road for a little while. Bits of the book shocked and horrified me – and I wrote them! – but I didn't ever feel that they were gratuitous. If I'd felt that, I'd have cut them out. Upon publication, the books got some pretty good word of mouth and seemed to sell well enough (helped immeasurably by stunning Paul Dainton cover art). I'm very proud of them and my first foray into fantasy has proven to be an overwhelmingly positive experience for me. So much so that I returned once again to the Old World to write *Guardians of the Forest*, the project that occupies most of my time at the moment.

Ok, well, that's about all I've got to say, though of course as soon I send this to the Black Library I'm sure I'll think of all those cunning linguistic puns that elude me at the moment. Oh well.

Enjoy.

Graham McNeill,
25 November, 2004

BOOK ONE
THE AMBASSADOR

Now...
Spring 2522

I

DAWN WAS MINUTES old and already men were dying. From where he knelt by a smouldering campfire, Kaspar could hear their screams of pain, carried on the cold wind that blew from the valley mouth and silently commended their souls to Sigmar. Or Ursun. Or Olric. Or whatever deity, if any, might happen to be watching over them this bleak morning.

Scraps of mist clung to the ground as the sun weakly climbed through the pale sky, replacing the descending full moon and casting its watery light on the valley as two armies greeted the new day and prepared to slaughter one another. Kaspar stood stiffly, massaging his swollen knee and wincing as his aged bones cracked. He was too old to be sleeping on the ground again and he ached all over from the cold.

Thousands of men filled the valley: pikemen from Ostland, halberdiers from the Ostermark, archers from Stirland, Kossars from Erengrad, swordsmen from Praag and scraps of bloodied regiments trapped in Kislev following the massacre at Zhedevka. They roused themselves from their blankets and stirred smouldering fires to life. From where Kaspar stood, he could see perhaps two-thirds of the army, some seven thousand men from the Empire and a further nine thousand from the city of Kislev and its surrounding stanistas. The mist and slope of the land conspired to conceal another six or seven thousand warriors from his sight.

It had been many years since he had commanded soldiers in battle and the thought of sending these brave men to their deaths, many of them barely old enough to shave, brought a familiar sadness and humility.

Hundreds of horses whinnied and stamped their hooves, aggravated by the presence of so many soldiers and the smell of cooking meat around them. Squires calmed their masters' steeds with soft words while Kislevite lancers painted their own mounts' coats with the colours of war and secured feathered banners to the saddles. Black-robed members of the Kislevite priesthood circulated through the army, blessing axes, lances and swords as they went, while priests of Sigmar read aloud from the *Canticle of the Heldenhammer*. Some men claimed to have seen a twin-tailed comet during the night and, while no one was quite sure what kind of an omen it was, the priests were taking it as a sign that the patron deity of the Empire was with them.

Kaspar himself had dreamed of the comet, watching it blaze across the heavens and bathe the land in its divine light. He had dreamed of the Empire wracked by war, its mighty cities cast down and its people exterminated: Altdorf burned in the fires of conquest and the northern fastness of Middenheim drowned in blood, its inhabitants hung by their entrails from the top of the Fauschlag. Barbarous northmen and monstrous beasts that walked on two legs rampaged through the ancient streets of his beloved Nuln, ravaging and burning everything in their path while a young, golden-haired youth, hefting his father's blacksmith's hammers, rose to fight them.

He shook off such melancholy thoughts and made his way through the army. He had slept apart from his comrades, unable to relinquish his guilt and unwilling to share his grief after what he had done at the foot of the *Gora Geroyev* the previous week.

Drays laden with bags of powder and shot plied their way across the muddy ground, sweating muleteers and muscled teamsters struggling to keep them from becoming bogged down. They lurched towards the higher ground where the banners of the Imperial Gunnery School fluttered above massed lines of heavy cannon. Braziers smoked where the gunners waited for the order to fire, and engineers in the blue and red livery of Altdorf plotted ranges for the mortars dug into gabion-edged artillery pits behind the cannon.

Kaspar moved around a dray carrying halberds, billhooks and pike shafts and made his way to where his black and gold banner billowed next to the purple gonfalon of the Knights Panther. His own horse was corralled with those of the knights and was being fed and watered by Kurt Bremen's squire. Kurt himself knelt in prayer with the rest of his knights and Kaspar did not interrupt their devotions, helping himself to a mug of hot tea from a pot steaming above a nearby fire.

Pavel snored beside the fire, his massive frame wrapped in furs, and despite everything that had transpired over the past months, Kaspar felt a surge of affection for his old friend. He sipped the hot tea, wishing that he had some honey to sweeten it with, but smiling at the ridiculousness of such a notion here and feeling the dregs of sleep fade from his head. He cast his gaze north, towards the mouth of the valley where forty thousand northern tribesmen of High Zar Aelfric Cyenwulf's horde also prepared for battle.

'Just like old days, eh?' said Pavel, finally emerging from his bedroll and reaching for a hide skin of kvas. He took a mighty swig and held it up to Kaspar.

'Aye,' agreed Kaspar, swallowing a mouthful of the strong liquor. 'Except we're both twenty years older.'

'Older, yes. Wiser, well, Pavel not know about that.'

'You'll get no argument from me on that score.'

'Do they come at us yet?'

'No,' said Kaspar, 'not yet. But soon they will.'

'And we send them back north without their balls!'

Kaspar chuckled. 'I certainly hope so, Pavel.'

Silence fell between the old comrades before Pavel said, 'You think we can beat them?'

Kaspar considered the question for several seconds before saying, 'No, I do not think we can. There's just too many of them.'

'Ice Queen say we will win,' said Pavel.

Kaspar looked towards the top of the valley sides as the mournful bray of a tribal horn sounded from far away, desperately wanting to believe that the Ice Queen was correct. The mist and smoke from the campsite obscured all but one of the great standing stones that gave this valley its name.

Urszebya. Ursun's Teeth.

A swelling roar built from the mouth of the valley, guttural chanting from the High Zar's warriors that echoed in time with the clash of their swords and axes on iron-bossed shields.

The Ice Queen claimed these stones were worth fighting for.

Kaspar just hoped they were worth dying for.

CHAPTER ONE
Six Months Ago

I

'Neither the climate, manners nor diversions of the place suit either my health or temper and the only pleasures I may indulge in are eating and drinking – yet Sigmar knows I have scarce tasted much worse in my time as an ambassador of our noble Emperor than I found here.'

– Letter to Altdorf, Andreas Teugenheim,
former ambassador to the court of the Tzarina Katarin

Kaspar von Velten reined in his bay gelding and stared up at the great walled city of Kislev, unwinding a woollen scarf from around his face. Autumn was barely a month old, yet the day was bracingly chill and his breath misted in the air before him. He knew that winter came early in Kislev and it wouldn't be long before the hillside the capital sprawled across was locked in its icy grip. A fine, wind-blown rain drizzled from the sullen sky and Kaspar could well understand the dislike of this country's climate that Ambassador Teugenheim had expressed in his letters.

His deep-set blue eyes had lost none of the brightness of youth, but were set in an expression of tense anticipation, his skin tanned and leather-tough from years of campaigning across the Old World. Beneath his wide brimmed hat, he wore his thinning silver hair close cropped, his beard similarly neat and trimmed. A faded tattoo from his youthful days in the ranks snaked its way from behind his left ear and down his neck.

Sunlight glittered from the spear points and armour of soldiers walking the ramparts of the massive wall, their fur-lined cloaks flapping in the wind. Kaspar smiled as he remembered Teugenheim's description of the first time he had seen the city in his letters home to Altdorf…

The city rises from the oblast like a jagged spike on the landscape, dominating the countryside around it in a vulgar fashion that is only to be expected of this rude nation. The walls are high and impressive to be sure, but how high must a wall be before it becomes unnecessary? It seems that these Kislevites have built their walls higher than any I have ever seen, and the effect is, though impressive, somewhat gauche for my taste.

Kaspar's trained eye swept the length of the wall and took in the lethal nature of the defences. Machicolations were cunningly wrought within the decorative gargoyles at the wall head and smoke curled lazily upwards from prepared braziers on the ramparts. The precise construction of the protruding towers and gatehouse ensured that every yard of rocky ground before the walls was a killing zone, covered by crossbows and cannon fire.

Teugenheim's descriptions scarce did the scale of the fortifications any justice and Kaspar knew from bitter experience that an attacker would pay a fearsome toll in blood to breach these walls.

A cobbled roadway wound up the *Gora Geroyev*, the Hill of Heroes, to a wide bridge that crossed a deep ditch and led to a studded timber gate banded with black iron and protected by murder holes in the stone roof.

Though he had fought and led armies in Kislev before, Kaspar had never had occasion to visit the capital city before, but knew good fortifications when he saw them. These walls were amongst the most steadfast defences he had ever laid eyes upon, at least the equal of Nuln or Altdorf. However, unlike either of those cities, Kislev's walls had a smooth, glassy look to them, as though the stone had vitrified under some intense heat.

Perhaps the most common tale sung by the more prosaic bards and troubadours of the Empire was of the Great War against Chaos, a mythic epic which told that in times past, hordes of the northern tribes had laid siege to this mighty city before being routed by an alliance of elves, dwarfs and men. It was a rousing tale of heroism and sacrifice, which had been embellished wildly over the years. The most common embroidery of the tale, added by its more imaginative tellers, was that the mutating powers of the dark gods had caused the solid stone of the walls to run like molten wax. Most scholars dismissed this as pure fancy, but looking at the walls of this city, Kaspar could only too readily believe every one of those embellishments.

'Sir?' came a voice from behind him and Kaspar snapped out of his reverie.

Behind him stood a black, mud-spattered carriage, emblazoned with the golden crest of Nuln. A scowling old man, his skin like a craggy mountainside, was seated on the cushioned buckboard holding the horse teams' reins loosely in his one good hand. Further back were four covered wagons, their contents and passengers protected by oiled canvas. The drivers shivered in the cold and the horses impatiently stamped the muddy roadway. Huddled miserably on the back of the last two wagons were sixteen young men, the lance carriers and squires of the giant knights in shining plate armour who ringed the small convoy. The knights rode wide-chested Averland steeds, each dressed in embroidered caparisons and not one beast less than sixteen hands high. The armoured warriors wore the threat of their power like a cloak; a potent manifestation of the might of the Empire's armies. They held their heavy lances proudly aloft, purple, gold and lilac pennons attached below the iron tips fluttering in the breeze.

Grilled helmet visors obscured their faces, but there was no doubting the regal bearing of each and every knight. Damp panther pelts were draped across their shoulder guards and both the Imperial standard and Kaspar's personal heraldry flapped noisily in the stiff breeze from a knight's banner pole.

'My apologies, Stefan,' said Kaspar, 'I was admiring the fortifications.'

'Aye, well we should get inside the walls,' said Stefan Reiger, Kaspar's oldest and most trusted friend. 'I'm chilled to the marrow and your old bones don't take well to this cold neither. Why you insist on riding out here when there's a perfectly good carriage is beyond me. Waste of bloody time bringing it, if you ask me.'

The knight riding alongside the carriage turned his head, his displeasure at Stefan's familiarity obvious despite the lowered visor. Many an Empire noble would have had a servant flogged for speaking in such a familiar tone, but Stefan had fought alongside Kaspar for too many years for either of them to put up with such formal nonsense.

'Less of the "old", Stefan, you'll be in the temple of Morr before I.'

'Aye, that's as maybe, but I'm much better preserved. I'm more like a fine Tilean wine – I improve with age.'

'If you mean you become more like sour vinegar, old man, then I'm in total agreement with you. But you're right, we should get inside, it won't be long before it's dark.'

Kaspar dug his heels into the horse's flanks and dragged the reins in the direction of the city gates. The lead knight also spurred his horse, riding alongside Kaspar as they crossed the wide, stone bridge and approached the gate. He raised his helmet guard, revealing a chiselled, patrician face, lined with concern and experience. Kaspar slapped a gloved hand on the knight's shoulder plate.

'I know what you're thinking, Kurt,' said Kaspar.

Kurt Bremen, the leader of the knights, scanned the warriors on the battlements seeing several had trained bows on them, and his frown deepened.

'All I am hoping,' replied Bremen in his clipped Altdorf accent, 'is that none of the soldiers up there have loose bow fingers. How you permit the lower orders to address you is none of my concern. My only priority, Ambassador von Velten, is to see you safely to your post.'

Kaspar nodded, ignoring Bremen's oblique disdain for his current task, and followed his stare. 'You don't think highly of the Kislev soldiery, Kurt? I commanded many of them in battle. They are wild, it's true, but they are men of courage and honour. The winged lancers are the equal of any Empire knightly order...'

Bremen's head snapped round, his lip twisted in a sneer before he realised he was being baited. He returned his gaze to the walls and nodded grudgingly.

'Perhaps,' he allowed. 'I have heard that their lancers and horse archers are fierce, if reckless, warriors, but the rest are lazy Gospodar scum. I'd sooner entrust my flank to a free company.'

'Then you have a lot to learn about the Kislevites,' snapped Kaspar and pulled ahead of the knight. The gates swung wide on well-oiled hinges and Kaspar found himself confronting a man with the longest, bushiest moustache he had ever seen. He wore a threadbare surcoat depicting the bear rampant over a rusted mail shirt and chewed messily on a chicken leg. Behind him stood a detachment of armoured soldiers with crossbows and spears. He cast an appraising eye over Kaspar before sliding his gaze across to the carriage and wagons behind him.

'Nya, doyest vha?' he finally barked, obviously drunk.

'Nya Kislevarin,' said Kaspar, shaking his head.

'Who you?' said the man finally, his Reikspiel mangled and barely intelligible.

Bremen opened his mouth to speak, but Kaspar silenced him with a gesture, dismounting to stand before the gatekeeper. The man's eyes were bleary and red and he had trouble focusing on Kaspar. His breath was foetid and stale.

'My name is Kaspar von Velten, the new ambassador to the court of the Ice Queen of Kislev. I demand you and your men stand back from the gateway and allow my party to enter the city.'

Kaspar pulled a scroll bearing the Imperial eagle pressed into a wax seal from within his doublet and waved it beneath the gatekeeper's veined nose. He said, 'Do you understand me?'

In a brief moment of clarity, the man noticed the knights and the flapping banner and stumbled backwards. He waved a hand vaguely in the direction of the soldiers behind him who gratefully retreated into the warmth of the gatehouse. Kaspar replaced the scroll and swiftly swung back into the saddle. The gatekeeper sketched a drunken salute to him and Kaspar smiled as the man said, 'Good welcome to Kislev.'

II

KASPAR BLINKED AS he emerged from the darkness of the gateway into Kislev. A cobbled esplanade filled with market stalls and shouting traders lay before him, the air thick with the smell of fish and sound of cursing voices. Three streets led deeper into the centre, each one similarly choked with people and pack animals. Kaspar inhaled the pungent aroma of the bustling city. The buildings here were well constructed of stone with tiled roofs of clay. The clatter of wagon wheels sounded behind him and he pulled his horse to one side as Stefan drove through the gate.

'So this is Kislev,' said Stefan, unimpressed. 'Reminds me of Marienburg. Too cramped, too noisy and it smells of fish.'

'You can moan about this posting later, Stefan. I want to get to the embassy before our intoxicated friend sends word ahead.'

'Pah! That drunken fool probably doesn't even remember us by now.'

'Probably not, but it won't hurt to be sure,' said Kaspar. He turned in the saddle to address Kurt Bremen and waved his hand at the three streets ahead.

'You've been here before, Kurt. Which is the quickest way to the embassy?'

The leader of the knights pointed up the central street, 'There. The Goromadny Prospekt leads through the city to Geroyev Square. The embassy is behind the high temple to the wolf god.'

Kaspar laughed. 'Even in their town planning they thumb their noses at us, putting a Sigmarite nation's embassy behind Ulric's temple. Oh, they are sly these Kislevites. Come, let us be on our way. I'm sure Ambassador Teugenheim will be only too happy to see us.'

The wagons and carriage began forcing their way slowly along the Goromadny Prospekt. The streets were thronged with people hurrying about their business, well dressed in warm fur cloaks and woollen colbacks. They were a fierce looking people, saw Kaspar, shorter than most folk of the Empire, but they carried themselves proudly. Here and there he could see grim, swaggering figures clad in armour and furs, reminiscent of the Norse raiders who plagued the coastal settlements on the Sea of Claws. Bremen and the knight with the banner pole parted the sea of scowling Kislevites with their giant destriers, Kaspar and the others following behind.

Lining the gutters and street corners limbless beggars were pleading for a few kopecks, and painted whores hawked their wares with weary resignation. The city reeked of desperation and hopelessness. Much like any city in the Old World these days, reflected Kaspar.

The wars of the past year had brought hardship to all corners of the world and forever changed the landscapes of the Empire and Kislev. Whole swathes of the Ostermark, Ostland and southern Kislev had been laid waste by the march of armies, and famine stalked the land like a hungry killer. Following the calamitous defeat at Aachden, tens of thousands of blood-soaked tribesmen had invested the Empire city of Wolfenburg. The hopes of Kaspar's nation now rested on this grand northern city holding out until winter when the enemy army would freeze and starve. Should it fall before then, the road south to Altdorf would be wide open.

Hordes of refugees, thousands strong, were fleeing south from the armies of the northmen and entire communities were now little more than ghost towns. These were harsh times to be sure, but there was something else as well – an undeniable tension that had nothing to do with the drums of war, as though people did not wish to linger outside any longer than they must. Strange...

A flash of colour further up the street drew his gaze and he saw a gleaming dark green carriage coming from the opposite direction. The design was old fashioned but regal and Kaspar noticed that the Kislevites happily moved clear of this vehicle's path without the grumbling that accompanied his own passage. The lacquered door bore a crest depicting a crown encircling a heart and as the carriage passed, Kaspar caught a glimpse of a woman with raven black hair through the open window. She nodded towards Kaspar and he craned his neck to follow her carriage as it travelled the way they had just come. Soon it was lost to sight, turning a corner to follow the line of the city walls.

He turned his attention back to the street, wondering at the identity of the woman, and sharply pulled back on the horse's reins as a black-robed figure leapt in front of him. The man's garb marked him as one of the Kislev priesthood and his face was lit with an expression of lunacy that Kaspar liked not at all. He touched the brim of his hat respectfully and pulled the horse left to move round the man, but he stepped into Kaspar's way once more. Not wanting any trouble with the local church, Kaspar forced a smile and pulled his horse away again. Once more the priest moved to block his path.

'You will be judged!' he yelled hoarsely. 'The wrath of the Butcherman shall fall upon you! He will cut out your heart for a sweetmeat and your organs will be a banquet for his delight!'

'Ho there, fellow,' snapped Kurt Bremen, riding in front of Kaspar. 'Be about your business. We don't have time to dally with the likes of you. Go on now!'

The priest pointed a long, dirt-encrusted finger at the knight. 'Templar of Sigmar, your god cannot help you here,' he sneered. 'The Butcherman's blade will open your belly just as easily and his teeth will tear the flesh from your bones!'

Bremen drew his sword partly from its scabbard, showing the dirty-faced priest the gleaming blade meaningfully. The man spat on the ground in front of Bremen and turned tail, sprinting nimbly away from the knight. The crowd soon swallowed him up and Bremen let his sword slide back into the scabbard. 'Mad,' he said.

'Mad,' agreed Kaspar and rode on.

The Goromadny Prospekt was a long street, running through the city for almost half a mile, an industrious place where all manner of business was conducted. Stallholders yelled at passers-by as footpads sprinted from their pursuing victims and fur clad citizens travelled back and forth. Most of the men sported shaven heads with some form of elaborate topknot and long, drooping moustache, while the women wore simple woollen dresses with richly embroidered shawls and furred colbacks.

Eventually the street widened into a tavern-lined boulevard, thronged with carousing men who sang martial songs and waved long axes. As Kaspar and his entourage passed, the songs swelled to new heights, the axes brandished threateningly towards the knights. The boulevard continued to widen until it opened into the granite-flagged centre of the city, Geroyev Square. Hulking iron statues of long-dead tzars edged its perimeter, and forming the square were ornate buildings of red stone with high peaked roofs crowned with onion domed towers and narrow windows.

But as spectacular as the buildings around the edge of the square were, they were but pale shadows of the mighty structure that dominated the far side, the palace of the Tzarina, the Ice Queen Katarin the Great. The mighty fortress rose in tier upon tier of white stone towers and colourfully festooned battlements that reached their pinnacle as a great golden dome. Its beauty was breathtaking, like a vast ice sculpture rising from the ground, and Kaspar felt a new respect for the Kislevites. Surely a people that could build such beauty could not all be savages?

Dragging his attention back down to earth, he guided his horse towards the temple of Ulric, a massive edifice of white stone adorned with statues of fierce wolves that flanked the black wooden doors. Knots of bearded, black robed priests stared at them with quizzical glances from its steps.

In the grassed centre of the square a wide corral had been set up with scores of ponies being walked in circles before a baying crowd of prospective buyers. These were plains ponies, sturdy beasts that thrived in the harsh climate of Kislev, but were slower on the gallop than the grain fed horses of the Empire. Even at this distance Kaspar could see that many were sway-backed. He gave none more than six months of useful life.

A narrow street ran along the side of the wolf god's temple, the buildings to either side shrouding it in darkness.

Kaspar waited until his carriage and wagons caught up to him before heading down the deserted looking street. It led into a wide courtyard with a bronze fountain at its centre, a patina of green covering its every surface. A dirty brown liquid gurgled from a small angel's cup, filling the fountain's bowl.

Behind the aged fountain and a rusted iron fence was the embassy of the Empire.

Having read Ambassador Teugenheim's letters on the journey from Nuln, Kaspar had expected the embassy to appear somewhat run down, but nothing had prepared him for the state of neglect and air of abandonment he saw before him now. The building's windows were boarded up with lengths of timber, the stonework cracked and broken, and illegible Kislevite graffiti was daubed across the doors. Were it not for the two guards lounging on halberds, Kaspar would have thought the building deserted.

'Sigmar's hammer!' swore Bremen, appalled at the embassy's appearance. Kaspar could feel his fury mounting towards Andreas Teugenheim, the man he was to replace. To have allowed an outpost of the Emperor to fall into such a state of disrepair was unforgivable. He rode through the sagging, open gate and as he approached the building, he saw the guards finally register his presence. Kaspar took no small amount of satisfaction from the look of alarm on their faces as they saw the Knights Panther and the Imperial banner fluttering behind him.

Had he not been so angry, he would have laughed at their pathetic attempts to straighten their threadbare uniforms and come to attention. They probably wouldn't yet realise who he was, but must know that anyone distinguished enough to merit an Imperial banner and sixteen Knights Panther for an entourage was clearly a man not to be trifled with.

He halted before the door and nodded towards Kurt Bremen who dismounted and approached the fearful guards. The knight's face was set in a granite-hard expression as he cast his critical eye over the two men.

'You should be ashamed of yourselves,' he began. 'Look at the state of your weapons and armour. I should put you on a charge right now!'

Bremen snatched one of the halberds and tested its nicked and dull edge with his thumb. Blunt.

He held the weapon in front of the guard and shook his head.

'If I were to try and enter this building, how would you stop me?' he bellowed. 'With this? You couldn't cut your way through an Altdorf fog with this edge! And you, look at the rust on that breastplate!'

Bremen spun the halberd and jabbed the butt of the weapon hard against the man's chest. The breastplate was rusted through and cracked like an eggshell.

'You men are a disgrace to the Empire! I shall be having words with your commanding officer. I am relieving you of duty as of this moment.'

The guards withered under his verbal assault, eyes cast down. Bremen turned to his knights and said, 'Werner, Ostwald, guard the door. No one enters until I say so.'

Kaspar dismounted and stood beside Bremen. He jabbed a finger at one of the guards and said, 'You. Take me to Ambassador Teugenheim immediately!'

The man nodded hurriedly and opened the embassy door. As he scurried through, Kaspar turned to Kurt Bremen and said, 'You and Valdhaas come with me. Leave the rest of the men here with the wagons. We have work to do.'

Bremen relayed the orders to his knights and followed Kaspar and the guard inside.

III

THE INTERIOR POSITIVELY reeked of abandonment, the embassy's air of neglect and emptiness even stronger now they were inside. The timber-panelled walls were bare of hangings and the floorboards were discoloured where carpeting had obviously been ripped up. The guard reluctantly ascended a wide staircase that led to the next storey with Kaspar, Bremen and Valdhaas following behind. The man was sweating profusely. Kaspar noted, his every movement furtive and nervous. Like the ground floor, the second level of the embassy had been stripped of furnishings and decoration. They walked along a wide corridor, footsteps loud on the bare boards until finally arriving at an ornately carved door.

The guard pointed at the door and stammered, 'This is the ambassador's study. But he... well, he has a guest. I'm sure he'd rather not be disturbed.'

'Then this really isn't his day,' snapped Kaspar, twisting the handle and pushing the door open. He entered a room as plushly furnished as the rest of the building was empty. One wall was dominated by a huge oaken desk and drinks cabinet while on another, a log fire blazed in a marble fireplace before two expansive leather chairs. Seated in the chairs were two men, one of whom was obviously a Kislevite, with a drooping moustache and swarthy complexion. He was enjoying a snifter of brandy and a cigar and regarded Kaspar and the knights with only mild interest. The second man, whip-thin and dressed in a red and blue doublet sprang from his seat, his face a mask of forced bluster.

'Who in the name of Sigmar are you?' he demanded in a reed-thin voice. 'What the devil are you doing in my private chambers? Get out, damn your eyes, or I shall call for my guards!'

'Go ahead, Teugenheim,' said Kaspar calmly, 'for all the good it will do you. I doubt one in ten of them has a weapon that wouldn't shatter on the armour of these knights here.'

Bremen stepped forward, resting his hand on his sword hilt. Ambassador Teugenheim blanched at the sight of the two fully armoured knights and the pelts over their shoulders. He stole a glance at the seated man and licked his lips.

'Who are you?'

'I'm glad you asked,' said Kaspar, holding out the same wax sealed scroll he had earlier shown to the gatekeeper. 'My name is Kaspar von Velten and this will explain everything.'

Teugenheim took the scroll and broke open the seal, quickly scanning the contents of the document. He shook his head as he read, his lips moving soundlessly.

'I can go home?' he wheezed slowly, sinking into the leather seat.

'Yes. You've been recalled to Altdorf and should leave as soon as your effects can be gathered together. There are dark times coming, Andreas, and I don't think you're up to facing them.'

'No,' agreed Teugenheim, sadly. 'But I tried, I really did...'

Kaspar noticed that Teugenheim kept throwing mournful glances towards the seated figure and turned his attention to the large man, asking, 'Sir, would you be so good as to give me the pleasure of your name?'

The man rose from the chair and Kaspar suddenly realised how huge he was. The man was a bear, broad shouldered and slab muscled. His gut was running to flab, but his physical presence was undeniable. Bremen moved closer to Kaspar and stared threateningly at the man, who grinned indulgently at the knight.

'Certainly. I am Vassily Chekatilo, a personal friend of ambassador.'

'I am the ambassador now and I have never heard of you, Chekatilo. So unless you have some business with me, then I'm afraid I'll have to ask you to leave.'

'You talk big for a little man,' rumbled Chekatilo. 'Especially when you have shiny soldiers with you.'

'And you are a fat man who doesn't understand simple requests.'

'Now you are insulting me,' laughed Chekatilo.

'Yes,' said Kaspar, 'I am. Do you have a problem with that?'

Chekatilo grinned and leaned in closer, 'I am not man who forgets insults, von Velten. I can be good friend to those who remember that. It would be foolish of you to make enemy of me.'

'Are you threatening me in my own embassy?'

'Not at all... ambassador,' smiled Chekatilo, draining the last of his brandy and taking a huge draw on his cigar. He blew the smoke into Bremen's face and laughed as the knight spluttered in the blue cloud. He dropped the cigar butt and crushed it into the carpet with his boot.

Kaspar stepped closer to Chekatilo and hissed, 'Get out of my embassy. Now!'

'As you wish,' said Chekatilo. 'But I warn you, I am powerful man in Kislev. You do well not to forget that.'

Chekatilo pushed past Kurt Bremen towards the door and sketched a mocking salute to him before departing with a derisory laugh. Kaspar fought down his anger and turned to Valdhaas, pointing at Teugenheim.

'Escort Ambassador Teugenheim to his chambers and have your squires assist him in packing his effects. He will remain here until we can arrange his transport back to Altdorf.'

The knight saluted and indicated that Teugenheim should follow him.

Teugenheim rose from his chair and said, 'I don't envy you this posting, von Velten. This place is a haven for beggars and thieves, and there are so many excesses and disorders that after sunset nobody dares venture abroad without sufficient company.'

Kaspar nodded and said, 'It is time for you to go, Andreas.'

Teugenheim smiled weakly, 'As the lord Sigmar wills it,' and followed the Knight Panther from the room.

Kaspar slumped down in one of the chairs and rubbed his forehead with both hands. Bremen stood beside the fireplace and removed his helm, tucking it in the crook of his arm.

'Now what, ambassador?'

'We get this place back on its feet and make it a post worthy of the Empire. War is coming and we must be ready for it.'

'Not an easy task.'

'No,' agreed Kaspar, 'but that's why they sent me here.'

IV

NIGHT WAS FALLING as Kaspar put aside his quill and carefully reread the words he had just written. Judging the tone to be erring on the correct side of caution he dusted sand over the ink before folding the letter carefully and sealing it with a blob of red wax. He pressed a stamp with the imprint of a twin-tailed comet into the soft wax and set the letter to one side.

He pushed back the chair, rising stiffly from behind the desk and walking to the window to stare down into the street below. Tomorrow one of the Knights Panther would deliver his missive to the Winter Palace, requesting an audience with the Ice Queen and the opportunity to present himself with a formal introduction. He just hoped that whatever damage Teugenheim had done in his time as ambassador would not prejudice the Tzarina against him.

His exact knowledge of what had gone on in Kislev was limited, though, given the state of the embassy and its emptied coffers, it seemed clear that Chekatilo had been extorting Teugenheim or otherwise blackmailing him. Andreas Teugenheim should never have been appointed to Kislev, it was a war posting and the man had neither the temperament nor the strength for such a position.

With armies on the move throughout the Old World, men of courage and steel were needed to fight the coming battles, and the powers that be in the court of Altdorf had decided that Teugenheim had neither. The first blow of any real invasion of the Empire would have to come through Kislev and thousands of his countrymen would soon be marching north towards this desolate, wind-blown country. Men who understood war would be needed to ensure that they were able to fight alongside the Kislevites and Kaspar knew his years of service in the armies of Karl-Franz made him an ideal candidate for this posting. Or at least he hoped he did. The art of war he could understand, but the subtleties and etiquette of courtly life were a mystery to him.

Years before, Kaspar's wife, Madeline, had made sure he was a regular visitor to the royal court at Nuln. She understood better than he the value of the Countess-Elector Emmanuelle von Liebewitz's patronage and, despite his protestations, dragged him to every one of her legendary masked balls and parties. His tales of battle and life on the campaign trail always thrilled the effete courtiers and made him a popular, if reluctant, guest at the palace.

After Madeline's death he'd withdrawn from court society, spending more and more time alone in a house that suddenly seemed much bigger and emptier than before. Invites to the palace continued to arrive at his door, but Kaspar attended only those functions he absolutely had to.

But his reputation had spread further than he knew, and when the summons to the countess's palace had come, and the courtiers from Altdorf had offered him this posting, he knew he could not refuse it.

Kaspar had left for Kislev within the week.

He sighed and drew the heavy curtains across the window, moving towards the crackling fire in the hearth.

The tremendous crash of the door slamming open startled him from his melancholic reverie and he spun, reaching for his sword. A hulking figure with an enormous grey beard filled the doorframe, carrying a bottle of clear liquid in one hand. He stepped into the room and placed the bottle on the table next to the leather chairs.

'By Tor!' he rumbled, 'I am told that we have new ambassador here, but no one tells me he is so ugly!'

'Pavel!' laughed Kaspar, as the man strode towards him. The giant pulled him into a crushing bear hug and laughed heartily.

Kaspar slapped his old friend's back and felt immense relief wash through him. Pavel Korovic, a fellow campaigner from his days in the army, released him from the embrace and cast his gaze over Kaspar. A savage warrior, Pavel had been a great friend to Kaspar during the northern wars and had saved his life more times than he could remember.

'Perhaps you look less ugly when I am drunk, yes?'

'You're already drunk, Pavel.'

'Not true,' protested the giant. 'I only drink two bottles today!'

'But you'll drink more won't you?' pointed out Kaspar.

'So? When I rode into battle I had drunk many bottles before we fight!'

'I remember,' said Kaspar, picking up the bottle. 'Did your lancers ever fight sober?'

'Fight sober! Don't be foolish, man!' roared Pavel, snatching the bottle back from Kaspar. 'No Dolgan ever went into battle sober! Now we drink kvas together, like old times!'

He yanked the cork free with his teeth, spitting it into the fire, and took a mighty swig of its contents. He passed the bottle to Kaspar.

'It is good to see you again, old friend!'

Kaspar took a more restrained swig and handed the bottle back, coughing.

'Ha!' laughed Pavel. 'You go soft now you not soldier! You cannot drink like old Pavel, eh?'

Kaspar nodded between coughs. 'Perhaps, but at least I'll never be as fat as old Pavel. No horse would take your weight now.'

Pavel patted his round belly and nodded sagely. 'That I give you. But Pavel does not mind. Now Pavel carries the horse instead. But enough! We will go now and drink. You and I have much catching up to do.'

'Very well,' said Kaspar, knowing that he would be in for a night of serious drinking. 'It's not as though there's much I can do here tonight. And anyway, what in Sigmar's name are you doing here? I thought you were going home to the Yemovia stanista to breed horses.'

'Pah! My people, they say I am *lichnostyob*, a lout, and do not want me back! Pavel comes to the city and his uncle Drostya gets him job in the embassy as reward for his years of loyal service in army. They call me the Kislevite liaison to Imperial ambassador. Sounds impressive, yes?'

'Oh yes, very impressive. What does it actually mean?'

Pavel sneered. 'With that spineless fool Teugenheim, it means I can drink most of the day and get to fall asleep in office rather than smelly tent on steppe. Come! We go and drink at my house. You will be guest until you are rid of Teugenheim!'

Kaspar could see that his old comrade in arms would not take no for an answer. He smiled; perhaps it would be good to catch up with Pavel and relive the old days. Besides, until Teugenheim was gone he had no wish to stay in the embassy and did not relish the prospect of staying in a tavern. He put his arm across Pavel's shoulder.

'Let's go then, old friend. I hope you have more of that kvas at home.'

'Have no fear of that,' Pavel assured him.

V

KASPAR SIPPED HIS kvas as Pavel threw back another glass of the powerful spirit. The lancer's fondness for kvas was legendary and it appeared that the years had not lessened his capacity for the drink. Kaspar could feel the effects of the alcohol already and had been nursing the glass in his hand for the past hour. Two bottles had been emptied and his companion was now roaringly drunk. They sat before the fireplace in Pavel's kitchen, barely five hundred yards from the embassy, the wagons and carriage safely tethered within the courtyard of the townhouse. Stefan had declined Pavel's offer of lodgings, preferring to stay at the embassy where he could begin assessing what needed to be done to make it more presentable. With the exception of Valdhaas, who stood guard outside, the Knights Panther had taken quarters at the embassy. Kaspar did not envy the slovenly soldiers billeted there the wrath of Kurt Bremen.

Pavel grinned as he poured another drink and belched. Despite all outward appearances, Kaspar knew that Pavel was a shrewd man indeed. The limited correspondence they had traded in the last few years had indicated that a number of highly lucrative contracts to provide mounts for the Kislevite army had made Pavel Korovic a very wealthy man.

'So, who is this Chekatilo?' asked Kaspar.

Pavel hiccupped and scowled at Kaspar. 'Very bad man,' he said finally. 'Is *nekulturny*, no honour. Is killer and thief, run everything illegal in Kislev. Has many fingers in many things. All must pay his "taxes" or suffer. Fires, beatings. Killed his own brother they say.'

'So what was he doing with Teugenheim then? Were the two of them in league together?'

'With Chekatilo, nothing surprise me. Teugenheim was probably selling off embassy to him to pay off debts. Perhaps ambassador has expensive taste in whores,' suggested Pavel. 'Who knows, maybe Kislev get lucky and the Butcherman will take Chekatilo?'

Kaspar's interest was suddenly piqued. He'd heard the name already. 'Butcherman? Who is he anyway? I had some mad priest raving about him earlier.'

'Another bad one. A madman,' said Pavel darkly. He lit a pipe with a taper from the fire and passed it to Kaspar. 'No one know who the Butcherman is or even if he is man at all. He kills men, women and children then vanishes into shadows. He cuts out victim's heart and eats their flesh. Some say he is an altered, that bodies have flesh melted from bone. He kill many and *Chekist* cannot catch him. A bad one indeed. People are afraid.'

Kaspar nodded, remembering a similar spate of killings in Altdorf some years ago, the so-called 'Beast' murders. But that murderer had eventually been caught and killed by the watchman Kleindeinst.

'How many people have been killed?'

Pavel shrugged. 'Hard to say. Dozens probably, maybe more. But people die all the time in Kislev. Who can say if all are the work of the Butcherman? You should forget about him. He is crazy and will be caught and hanged soon.'

Kaspar drained his glass and slid it across the table towards Pavel. He stood and stretched, saying, 'I don't doubt you're right. Anyway, I'm exhausted and the days ahead are sure to be busy. I have to meet the rest of the embassy staff tomorrow and I would prefer to do that without a hangover. I think I'll call it a night.'

'You do not want to stay up till dawn and sing songs of war! You are soft now, Kaspar von Velten!' laughed Pavel, gulping down his kvas.

'Maybe, Pavel, but we're not the young men we were,' said Kaspar.

'Speak for yourself, Empire man. Pavel will drink the rest of bottle and sleep beside the fire.'

'Goodnight Pavel,' said Kaspar.

CHAPTER TWO

I

KASPAR SHOOK HIS head in exasperation at the sight before him. Thirty soldiers dressed in the blue and red livery of Altdorf stumbled, staggered and lurched towards him, their breath ragged and uneven.

Despite the chill air, their faces were streaked with sweat, red and burning as they completed their fifth circuit of the walls of Kislev. The Knights Panther had finished almost a full hour earlier and stood to attention beside Kaspar and Pavel's horses, barely having even broken a sweat.

'Not an impressive sight,' commented Pavel needlessly.

'No,' agreed Kaspar, his voice low and threatening. 'These soldiers wouldn't last half a day in the ranks. One skirmish and they would be food for the crows.'

Pavel nodded and took a huge draw on an evil-smelling cheroot, blowing a filthy blue cloud of smoke skyward. 'Not like before, eh?'

Kaspar allowed himself a tight smile. 'No, Pavel, not like before. The men we fought alongside were ten feet tall and could smite an army with one blow of a halberd! These sorry specimens would have a hard job lifting a halberd, let alone swinging one.'

'Aye,' laughed Pavel, taking a swig from a leather canteen. 'Often I wonder what became of those men. Do you see anyone from the old days?'

'I exchanged a few letters with Tannhaus for a time, but I heard later that he got himself killed when he joined a mercenary company that set off for Araby.'

Pavel took another drink. 'That is shame. I liked Tannhaus, he could fight like a devil and knew how to take drink.'

'The damn fool was in his fifties,' snapped Kaspar. 'He should have bloody well known better than to go off glory hunting at his age. War is a young man's game, Pavel. It's not for the likes of us now.'

'By Olric, you are in a sour mood today, Empire man!' muttered Pavel, offering the canteen to Kaspar. 'Here, take a drink.'

Without taking his eyes from the exhausted soldiers, Kaspar took the proffered canteen and took a swig. He'd swallowed a huge mouthful before he realised the canteen contained kvas and was bent almost double by the powerful spirit. His gullet burned with liquid fire and he coughed, his eyes watering.

'Damn it, Pavel!' swore Kaspar. 'What the hell are you doing? It's not even midday!'

'So? In Kislev is good to drink early. It make rest of day not seem so bad.'

Scowling, Kaspar wiped the back of his hand across his mouth and said, 'As a favour to me, try and keep sober, yes?'

Pavel shrugged and took back the canteen, but said nothing as the embassy soldiers finally reached them, collapsing in utter exhaustion. Kaspar could feel his already foul mood darkening even more. That his predecessor could have allowed his soldiery to lapse into such a disgraceful state was unbelievable and, given the choice, Kaspar would have sent every one of them back to the Empire.

However, under the circumstances that was not an option. Kurt Bremen had assured him that he could whip them into shape and had spent the week since they had arrived in Kislev doing just that. Resplendent in his shining plate armour, panther pelt draped impressively around his shoulders, Bremen strode through the panting guards, his face like thunder.

'Call yourselves soldiers!' he roared. 'I've known serving wenches with more stamina than you lot! An hour in the battleline and you'd be begging the enemy to gut you!'

At least the soldiers had the decency to look ashamed, noted Kaspar. Perhaps there were still some amongst them who might yet be worthy of the Emperor's uniform.

'My knights completed this jaunt in full armour and not one of them has a face as red as a Tilean's arse.'

'We ain't done any training in nigh on a year,' complained a reedy voice from amongst the soldiers.

'That's plain to see,' snapped Bremen. 'Well, that laziness stops now. I'm in charge of you and I swear that you men are going to hate me more than you've ever hated anyone before.'

'We're already there,' came another voice.

Bremen smiled, but there was nothing reassuring in his expression.

'Good,' he snarled. 'Then we've begun. I will break you down to nothing, cause you pain until you plead with me to kill you just to put you out of your misery. But I won't. I'll break you and then build you back up into the best damn soldiers under the Emperor's command.'

Kaspar turned his attention to the city walls as he heard laughter drift down from the ramparts looking out over the hillside. Groups of Kislevite soldiers lounged on the wall head and clustered around smoking braziers, laughing and pointing at the Empire soldiers' exertions.

Kaspar was damned if he would allow this mockery to go unanswered. He raked his spurs back, startling the gelding, and cantered forward past Bremen then pointed towards the walled city of Kislev.

He unwound the scarf from around his neck, his breath feathering in the air as he spoke. 'You see those men on the walls?' Kaspar began. He did not raise his voice, but every one of the soldiers recognised the years of authority it contained. He swept his hand in a gesture along the length of the wall saying, 'These Kislevites are warriors! They live in a land constantly threatened by creatures from your worst nightmares. They must be ready at a moment's notice to fight and win. And right now they are laughing at you!'

Kaspar wheeled his horse, walking the beast through the mob of soldiers. 'And they are right to laugh, because you are all pathetic, worthless pieces of shit that I wouldn't piss on even if you were on fire! You are the worst soldiers that I have ever commanded and as Sigmar is my witness, I will not be shown up by your shortcomings.'

Angry scowls met Kaspar's words, but the new ambassador was not finished yet. 'You are all this and more,' continued Kaspar, 'but that is what you are *now*. What you will *become* is something much more than that. You are soldiers of the Emperor Karl-Franz and you are my men, and together we will become something to be proud of. Ambassador Teugenheim allowed you to forget that you are soldiers of the Emperor. But he is gone now, and I am in charge. I will not let you forget!'

Kaspar turned his horse again as a coarse, heavily accented voice sneered, 'Things was just fine 'till you showed your face.'

He looked down to see a man whose muscle had long since been replaced by flab and whose features bore all the hallmarks of a lifetime's abuse of alcohol. His bearded face was twisted in an ugly mask of contempt, hands planted confrontationally on his hips. Kaspar knew his type; he'd met countless variations of the same personality in his life as a soldier.

He swung smoothly from the saddle and landed lightly on the muddy ground, handing the reins to Kurt Bremen and walking coolly towards the man. More of the soldiers rose to their feet, some placing themselves close to the bearded man, others deliberately keeping their distance. Kaspar recognised the criticality of this moment; he could win or lose the men here in an instant. Kurt Bremen also realised this and moved to stand behind Kaspar, but the ambassador waved him back. He must do this alone.

'What's your name?' hissed Kaspar, taking the measure of the man before him.

He was a big man, but out of shape, with great, meaty hands that Kaspar knew would hit like anvils.

'Marius Loeb,' replied the man, breath sour with last night's rotgut.

Loeb folded his arms across his chest. Kaspar could see that the man was confident in the support of the soldiers at his back. They had it easy here at the embassy and he'd be damned if this old man was going to get in the way of that.

'Loeb....' mused Kaspar, casting his gaze across the rest of the soldiers. 'Yes, Herr Korovic has told me of you.'

Pavel smiled and raised his canteen in a friendly gesture as his name was mentioned and Kaspar continued, 'You are a drunk, a thief, a bully and a lazy, good-for-nothing piece of horse dung. You will be gone from here by morning.'

Loeb's face flushed and his eyes blazed in self-righteous fury. Kaspar saw the punch coming before it was halfway. He stepped forward and pistoned his fist into Loeb's face, a short, hard, economical boxer's punch, and Loeb's nose cracked audibly under the impact. The big man reeled, blood pouring from the centre of his face, but to Kaspar's astonishment, he remained on his feet. Snarling, he launched himself forwards, his massive rock-like fists swinging. Kaspar sidestepped and launched a jab into Loeb's gut before delivering a thunderous right cross to his jaw.

The big man staggered, but kept coming, aiming a wild punch at Kaspar's head. The blow was poorly aimed, but caught Kaspar across the temple. Lights exploded before his eyes. He rolled with the punch and moved in close, thundering a vicious series of jabs to Loeb's mashed features. Blood and teeth flew from the man's jaw as soldiers gathered round the combatants, shouting encouragement to both fighters equally.

Kaspar was tiring and he knew that this was getting out of hand. He had hoped to put Loeb down with one well-aimed punch, but the man just wouldn't give up. Under other circumstances that would have been an admirable trait in a soldier, but now...

Loeb's eye was swollen and blood poured down his face. He was practically blind now, but that didn't seem to impair him much. He roared and aimed a kick between Kaspar's legs. The ambassador stepped aside and hammered his elbow into the man's cheek, feeling bone break under the impact. Loeb's eyes glazed over and he collapsed to his knees before falling face first to the mud.

Kaspar stepped back and massaged his knuckles where the skin had broken.

He stared directly at the few men who had stood behind Loeb and said, 'Get that fat piece of filth back to the embassy and stitch his wounds. He goes back to the Empire tomorrow.'

As his compatriots bent to pick up the unconscious Loeb, a young soldier stepped forward and said, 'Sir?'

Kaspar placed his hands behind his back and marched to stand before the young man who had spoken. He was perhaps twenty, slim with an unruly shock of dark hair and finely chiselled features.

'Who are you then? Another troublemaker?' asked Kaspar.

'Leopold Dietz, sir, from Talabecland,' replied the young soldier, staring at a point over Kaspar's shoulder. 'And no, sir, I ain't no troublemaker. I just wanted you to know that we ain't all like Loeb. There's some good lads here, and we can be better than we's been so far. A lot better.'

'Well, Leopold Dietz, I hope you're correct. It would be a shame if I had to crack some more skulls today.'

'That it would, sir,' agreed Leopold with a wry grin. 'Not all of us have got glass jaws like big Loeb.'

Kaspar laughed and said, 'I'm glad to hear that, son. Because I need tough soldiers doing their best.'

He turned away from Dietz and pointed towards the soldiers struggling towards the gates with the giant Loeb.

'That man...' began Kaspar, 'was a cancer. He infected every man here with the desire to do less than he was capable of, less than his duty demanded. That cancer has been cut out and from now on, things will be done in a proper manner, as befits a garrison of the Emperor's soldiers. I am a hard man, but a fair one and if you prove to me that you are worthy of this post, then I shall see you rewarded for that.'

Kaspar turned back to the scowling Kurt Bremen. He could see the Knight Panther did not approve of his methods, but having come from the ranks himself, he knew there was only one way to earn the respect of the common soldiers. He took the gelding's reins from Bremen and, hooking his foot into the stirrup, swung onto its back.

Pavel leaned in close and whispered, 'Your first punch was good, but you go too easy on him I think. You forget all Pavel teach you about gutter fighting? Eyes and groin. Go for his, protect your own.'

Kaspar smiled weakly, clenching and unclenching his fist. Already he could feel his fingers stiffening and knew that the skin would soon be colourfully bruised.

'Big man almost had you with punch to head,' commented Pavel. 'Perhaps you are right. Perhaps you are too old for soldiering.'

'Aye, he was a tough one alright,' acknowledged Kaspar. He pulled on his black leather riding gloves as Pavel tapped him on the shoulder and nodded in the direction of the city gates, where a trio of horsemen silently observed them.

Kaspar shielded his eyes from the sun and watched the small group as it wound its way down the road towards them. Two bronze-armoured knights with bearskin cloaks flanked a thin, ascetic featured man shrouded in a blue cape with a leather colback planted firmly on his head.

'Who's that?'

'Trouble,' grunted Pavel.

Kaspar glanced at Pavel's normally laconic features, apprehensive at the look of hostility that flickered briefly across his face. He indicated to Bremen that he should continue with the soldiers' training and kicked back his spurs.

'Come on then, Pavel. Let's meet trouble head on.'

'The Gospodars have saying, my friend: "Do not seek out trouble. It find you quick enough",' muttered the giant Kislevite as he pulled his overburdened horse after Kaspar's.

The thin man reined in his mount, a bay gelding from the Empire rather than a smaller Kislevite plains pony, which immediately marked him out as a man of means. Unusually for a Kislevite, he was clean-shaven and his lips curled in distaste as his eyes flickered to the unconscious Loeb, telling Kaspar that he had seen the brawl.

The man gave a perfunctory bow to Kaspar, ignoring Pavel, and inquired, 'Do I have the pleasure of addressing Ambassador von Velten?'

Kaspar nodded. 'You do indeed, though you have me at a disadvantage. You are…?'

The man seemed to swell within his voluminous cloak before he answered. He drew himself up and said, 'I am Pjotr Ivanovich Losov, chief advisor to Tzarina Katarin the Great, and I bid you welcome to her land.'

'Thank you, Herr Losov. Now how may I be of service to you?'

Losov produced a vellum envelope, wax-sealed with the crest of the Ice Queen herself, from his cloak and handed it to Kaspar.

'I bring you this,' he said, 'and hope you will be available to attend.'

Kaspar took the envelope and broke the seal, withdrawing an invitation, sumptuously scripted and printed on heavy paper with the royal cipher as a watermark. In gold embossed lettering, Kaspar read that he was cordially invited to be presented to the Tzarina at the Winter Palace tonight.

Kaspar replaced the invitation in the envelope and said, 'Please convey my thanks to the Tzarina and inform her that we will, of course, be honoured to attend.'

Pjotr Losov's brow furrowed in confusion. 'We?' he began, but before he could say any more, Kaspar continued: 'Excellent. My Kislevite liaison and captain of the guards will no doubt enjoy the evening also. I have heard many fabulous tales regarding the splendour of the Winter Palace.'

Losov frowned, but said nothing, realising that to deny Kaspar guests would be a breach of protocol.

'Of course,' replied Losov, casting a look of distaste towards Pavel. 'The Tzarina will be most pleased to receive them also I'm sure.'

Kaspar smiled at the barely concealed sarcasm and said, 'My thanks for your delivery of this invitation, Herr Losov. I look forward to meeting you again this evening.'

'As do I,' replied Losov, doffing his colback to Kaspar and hauling on his horse's reins. He and his escort rode back up the hillside, joining a caravan of wagons and fur-wrapped peasants as they made their way to the city.

Kaspar watched Losov's retreating back and turned to Pavel. 'I take it you two know each other then?'

'We have dealings in past, yes,' confirmed Pavel neutrally, but said no more. Kaspar filed that nugget away for later and raised his eyes to the low autumn sun. It was still bright, but he knew it was already several hours past noon.

'A reception tonight! She might have given us bit more bloody notice. I've been waiting all week for an audience with her!'

Pavel shrugged, his usual enthusiasm returning as Losov vanished from sight. 'It is the Tzarina's way, my friend. Come, we must return to the embassy and prepare. Pavel must make sure you are presentable for Ice Queen.'

Kaspar plucked at his plain grey shirt and cloak and mud-stained boots, realising what a backward peasant he must have looked to the Tzarina's envoy.

'I take it that it would have been bad form to decline this?' asked Kaspar, waving the envelope.

The very idea seemed to horrify Pavel and he nodded vigorously.

'Very bad, yes, very bad. You cannot decline. Etiquette demand that the Ice Queen's invitations take precedence over all other previous engagements. Even duty to the dead must be set aside, for mourning does not release a guest from appearing at a court ceremony.'

'And the prospect of free food and drink has nothing to do with your steadfast desire that we attend this damned thing...'

'Not at all!' laughed Pavel. 'Pavel just wishes to make sure you do not offend Ice Queen in some way. Were it not already silver, Pavel could turn your hair white with tale of last man who displeased the Tzarina. All I say is that it was as well he and his wife already had children!'

'Then let us go, my friend,' grinned Kaspar, walking his horse towards the city gates. 'I have no wish to suffer a similar fate.'

Kaspar glanced back at the soldiers, who had begun jogging around the city walls once more. He noted that Leopold Dietz led from the front, keeping pace with Kurt Bremen and exhorting the others to push harder. He hoped that the young soldier's optimistic words were not so much hot air. He would need soldiers to be proud of in the coming months if his ambassadorship was to be taken seriously.

II

KASPAR PULLED ON his long coat and admired himself in the full-length mirror. He wore black britches tucked into grey leather boots and an embroidered white cotton shirt with a severely cut, black frock-coat. Every inch a servant of the Empire, he considered. Despite his fifty-four years, he had tried to keep himself in shape and his body was wiry and lean.

Since the departure of Teugenheim earlier in the week, Kaspar had taken the previous ambassador's quarters as his own, refurnishing it at his own expense. He was not living in the manner to which he was accustomed, but it would do for now.

Returning from the cold outside the city walls two hours ago, he had bathed using a Kislevite herbal soap that had a strange, but not unpleasant aroma, and then shaved, twice nicking the edge of his chin with the knife. It was typical, thought Kaspar, that he could shave most mornings while half asleep and not cut himself, but the moment an important function came up, it was as though he hacked at his skin with a rusty axe blade.

A knock came at his door and before he could respond, Stefan entered the room, a colourful bundle of fabric draped over his good arm. His left arm ended at the wrist, a beastman's axe blade having taken his hand a decade ago.

'What do you think?' asked Kaspar.

'Oh no, no, no!' retorted Stefan, casting a scornful gaze over Kaspar's apparel and rolling his eyes. 'You're not going to a funeral, you damn fool, you're going to be presented to a queen.'

'What's wrong with what I'm wearing?' asked Kaspar, raising his arms and turning to face the mirror again.

'You look like a schoolmaster,' commented Stefan, dropping the bundle of fabric on a chair by the window.

'This is Kislev,' continued Stefan. 'They're a dour enough race without everyone going about in black all the time. Royal events are an excuse for the Kislevites to dress up like peacocks and strut around in all their finery.'

As if to underscore Stefan's words, the door slammed open and Pavel strode into Kaspar's chambers, grinning like a fool and dressed in a riotous mix of silks and velvet. He wore a cobalt-blue doublet and hose, stretched across his wobbling belly, patterned with silver stitching and sequined with glittering stones sewn into the lining. An ermine trimmed cape hung to his knees and his boots were fashioned from a ridiculously impractical white velvet. To complete the ensemble, Pavel had waxed his long grey moustache into extravagant spirals that reached below his chin.

Kaspar's jaw dropped at the sight of his comrade as Stefan nodded in approval.

'That's more like it,' he commented. 'That's how you dress for court in Kislev.'

'Please tell me you're joking,' growled Kaspar. 'He looks like a court jester!'

Pavel's face fell and he folded his arms. 'Better a jester than a priest of Morr, Empire man! I will be most handsome man tonight. Women will weep when they see Pavel!'

'Of that I have no doubt,' commented Kaspar dryly.

Pavel smiled, missing Kaspar's ironic tone, and the next twenty minutes were spent in heated debate as Stefan and Pavel attempted to persuade the ambassador to consider a more colourful selection of clothes. Eventually, a compromise was reached and Kaspar changed into an emerald green pair of britches and, as a concession to his Kislevite hosts, a short scarlet dolman, slashed with gold and trimmed with a border of sable. The short cape hung loosely about his shoulders and felt completely impractical to Kaspar. Too small to provide any warmth and just awkward enough to get in the way while walking, it was typical of the Kislevite aristocracy to design a garment with no practical purpose whatsoever.

At last Kaspar and Pavel descended to the main doors of the embassy to find Kurt Bremen waiting for them, his armour shining like polished silver. The knight was without his sword belt and Kaspar could see how much it chafed him to be unarmed. Bremen looked up at the sound of their approach and Kaspar saw him visibly fight to restrain a smirk at their outlandish attire.

'Not a word,' warned Kaspar as Bremen opened the thick wooden door.

The sky was dark as they emerged into the cold of a Kislev night. It was still early evening, but night had fallen with its customary northern swiftness and the chill cut through Kaspar.

'By Sigmar, these clothes don't hold a scrap of heat,' he growled. He stamped his feet on the cobbles to work in some warmth and set off down the steps to the embassy gates where a lacquered and open-topped carriage awaited them. On the tiny coach-box sat a huge driver with a long beard, wrapped in a vast greatcoat and wearing a square red velvet cap. He clambered down and opened the door and saluted as Kaspar, Pavel and Bremen climbed aboard. He returned to his coach-box and cracked his whip, expertly guiding the carriage back towards Geroyev Square.

III

THE DRIVER MANAGED the trotting horses with a practiced ease, the thread-thin reins held tightly in his hands, and Kaspar had to admit that the carriage was a fine method of travel indeed. The harness, made from a few strips of leather, was scarcely visible, and gave a wonderful look of elegance to the steed, which seemed to run without any restraint beneath the great arched piece of wood above the carriage's collar. Had she still lived, Madeline would have loved to travel like this and for a wistful moment he pictured her riding alongside him through this night.

The carriage streaked across the centre of the square, and their speed slowed as the ground became steeper. The carriage carried them smoothly along the Urskoy Prospekt, the great triumphal road, that took its name from the monastery at its beginning, the Reliquary of St. Alexei Urskoy. This massive stone edifice was a sanctuary consecrated to the heroes of Kislev, and the burial-place of the Ice Queen's father, the great Tzar, Radii Bokha himself.

All the way along, the thoroughfare presented a most animated scene. On either side of the road, more humble vehicles plied for hire, drawn by thick-set cart-ponies and driven by rough-coated peasants who had flocked from the surrounding steppe to escape the advancing armies of the northmen.

The ground grew less steep and before them, upon the crest of the *Gora Geroyev*, stood the palace of the Ice Queen. Kaspar had seen the palace several times in the past week and had been overwhelmed by its majesty, but at night, lit from below by vast, Cathayan lanterns, its beauty was spellbinding.

'It's magnificent,' whispered Kaspar as the driver expertly guided the carriage through the wrought iron gates of the palace grounds, passing between rows of armoured knights with helms crafted in the shape of snarling bears. The sheer scale of the royal palace became even more apparent as they neared, its defences every bit as formidable as the city walls themselves.

Scores of sleds and carriages filed along before them, discharging their fur-wrapped charges at the black wooden gates of the palace and swiftly moving on to make room for others following them. Knights on white horses stood motionless at the entrance, watching as the empty carriages slipped back through the gates and formed a line on the square, their coachmen gathering about huge fires burning in braziers provided for the occasion.

Their driver once again climbed down from his coach-box and silently opened the carriage door. Kaspar and Bremen stepped down, lost in admiration at the palace architect's skill. Pavel pressed a few brass kopecks into the driver's outstretched palm and stood alongside the two men from the Empire, following their gaze around the intricately carved columns and pediment that formed the entrance to the Winter Palace.

'You both look like you have never seen palace before. Let us get inside before we are mistaken for ignorant peasants,' said Pavel, striding towards the palace.

Kaspar and Bremen hurriedly caught up with Pavel, the wooden doors swinging open as they approached, and they stepped through into the palace of the Tzarina of Kislev. No sooner were they inside the marble-floored vestibule than the doors closed behind them.

The vast hall was packed with people, brightly chatting young women and bawdily laughing men.

The great majority of the men were soldiers, young moustachioed officers of every corps, haggard faces grim testimony to the fierce battles being fought in the northern oblast against the hordes of Kurgan warriors. They wore bright surcoats and fur-edged dolmans, their armour obviously hastily repaired, and all carried feathered helmets surmounted by a silver bear with spread paws. Scattered here and there were the commanders of regiments of lancers and horse archers with red breastplates and green tunics, as well as hand gunners wrapped in their long tunics and bristling with silver cartridge cases.

Passing quietly to and fro among the crowd were the Tzarina's liveried pages and maids of honour, dressed in long, ice-blue coats, divesting the guests of their heavy pelisses and carrying silver trays laden with flutes of sparkling Bretonnian wine. Pavel reached out and stopped one of the tray carrying servants, procuring a trio of glasses.

Kaspar accepted one from Pavel and sipped the wine, enjoying the refreshing crispness of the beverage.

'It's like something from a child's fairy tale,' said Kaspar in wonderment.

'This?' scoffed Pavel, with a grin. 'This nothing. Wait until you see Gallery of Heroes, my friend.'

Kaspar smiled, and despite his reservations, found himself caught up in the ebullient mood that appeared to infuse the assembled guests of the Tzarina as they made their way slowly towards a gracefully curved marble staircase.

The procession ascended the long, flower garlanded staircase, lace trains sweeping past the porphyry pillars, gems and diamonds gleaming in the light of gently spinning lanterns wreathed in silk. Many-coloured uniforms passed through the vestibule, the click of sabres and spurs loud on the floor. Slowly the guests ascended between ranks of Kislevite knights chosen from among the most handsome men of the Palace Guard, grand-looking giants, who stood expressionless in their burnished armour of bronze.

A mammoth painting of the Tzarina's father on the back of a monstrous white-furred bear dominated the wall at the head of the stairs and beneath it, Kaspar saw the elegantly dressed form of Pjotr Losov. He wore a long, crimson robe, decorated with swirls of yellow leather and hung with silver tassels.

The Tzarina's advisor spotted him and raised his hand in welcome.

'Be wary of that one,' warned Pavel as they reached the top of the stairs. 'He is snake and not to be trusted.'

Before Kaspar could question Pavel further, Losov swept towards them and shook Kaspar's hand. He smiled and said, 'Welcome to the Winter Palace, Ambassador von Velten. It is good to see you once again.'

'I am honoured to be invited, Herr Losov. The palace is magnificent, I have never seen its like before. Truly it is a marvel.'

Losov nodded, accepting the compliment gracefully as Kaspar said, 'Allow me to present my companions to you, sir. This is my captain of the guard, Kurt Bremen of the Knights Panther.'

'Honoured, sir knight,' answered Losov as Bremen bowed curtly and clicked his heels together.

'And this,' said Kaspar, indicating Pavel, 'is the Kislevite liaison to the Imperial ambassador, Pavel Korovic. Pavel and I served in the Emperor's armies many years ago. He is an old and trusted friend.'

Barely even bothering to mask his contempt, Losov briefly inclined his head in Pavel's direction before saying, 'If you would permit me, I should like to escort you to the Gallery of

Heroes. There are many people here tonight I believe it would be to your advantage to meet, Herr Ambassador, should you wish your post here to be a profitable one.'

'So long as the Emperor's views are expressed at court, then I consider that my time here will have been spent profitably,' replied Kaspar.

'My meaning entirely, Herr Ambassador.'

The white doors below the massive portrait were held open by more of the blue-liveried servants as Losov escorted them through into the Gallery of Heroes, and once again, Kaspar found himself lost for words at the opulence of the scene before him.

IV

The Gallery of Heroes was one segment of a great three-part hall composed of what Kaspar at first took to be glass, before realising that it was in fact solid ice. This first part of the gallery made up the southern wing of the palace and glittered dazzlingly with pinpoints of reflected light from the hundreds of silver candelabras. On one side, it opened through a single, great arch and arcade of ice columns, into a massive semi-circular room filled with tables and set for dining.

On the opposite side, a series of small arches led from the gallery into another, equally impressive space where clapping observers watched a group of bare chested warriors sparring with long, curved swords.

Kaspar halted to watch, grotesquely fascinated by the warriors, each with blades sheathed through cauterised flaps of skin on their heavily muscled chests and stomachs. Long topknots dangled from their shaven skulls and azure sashes were bound around their narrow waists. A handsome warrior with a long waxed moustache and oiled topknot bounced lightly on the balls of his feet in the centre of a circle of warriors. He had a lithe, dancer's physique together with the narrow hips and powerful shoulders of a swordsman. He carried two exquisite blades and wore loose fitting scarlet cavalry troos. His body was freshly oiled and his sculpted muscles gleamed in the torchlight.

Four similarly attired warriors surrounded the man and bowed to him before raising their swords. Kaspar watched with a practiced eye as the lone man dropped to a fighting crouch, one blade pointed at his nearest opponent, the other curled above his head.

'Who is that warrior?' asked Kaspar as Pjotr Losov appeared at his side.

'That,' said Losov proudly, 'is Sasha Fjodorovich Kajetan. He commands one of the Tzarina's most glorious squadrons of the Gryphon Legion. His family have estates at a wondrously picturesque part of the Tobol and many say he will command the legion within the year.'

Kaspar nodded, suitably impressed as the four swordsmen closed on Kajetan.

'This hardly seems fair.'

'I know,' agreed Losov, 'but Kajetan is *Droyaska*, a blademaster. Were he to take on any more opponents it would appear as though he were showing off.'

Kaspar cast a puzzled glance at Losov before returning his attention to the fight. Kajetan's cold features betrayed little apprehension at the thought of facing four armed opponents and Kaspar could not decide whether it was arrogance or courage he was seeing.

The fight began and it was over so quickly that Kaspar had trouble believing what he had just seen. As the first of Kajetan's foes lunged towards him, he leapt and spun through the air to land between two of the swordsmen and slam the pommels of his swords against their foreheads. Even as they fell, he was in motion, swaying aside from the slash of another opponent's blade and rolling beneath a high cut that Kaspar felt would surely decapitate him. He rolled to his knees and swept his leg out in a long slash that scythed another swordsman's legs out from under him. He hammered his elbow into the fallen man's neck before arching his back and bringing his swords together above his head to block a downward cut. He somersaulted backwards, delivering a thunderous kick to his last opponent's jaw as he spun through the air before landing gracefully with his swords crossed before him.

Rapturous applause filled the hall and Kaspar found himself joining in, amazed at this warrior's sublime skill. His opponents groggily picked themselves up as the applause swelled.

'Where in the name of all the gods did that man learn to fight?' he asked.

'I'm given to understand that he took instruction from a warrior order far to the east,' said Losov vaguely. 'On one of the Cathayan islands, I believe.'

Kaspar nodded, still in awe at Kajetan's dazzling display and allowed himself to be led from the contest of arms into the main gallery once more. Its great vaulted ceiling was filled with a vast mosaic depicting the coronation of Igor the Terrible and a great chandelier from the time of Tzar Alexis hung from its centre. Great columns formed from sepia-tinted ice, veined with subtle golden threads and capped with fluted, hand-carved capitals supported the ceiling. The walls were smooth and translucent and numerous rugs from Bretonnia, Estalia and Tilea were strewn across the cold floor.

Kaspar was amazed; he had visited the Imperial Palace in Altdorf many years ago, when receiving his general's baton, but its splendour paled next to this opulence.

He could see that Bremen was similarly in awe of his surroundings as Pavel accosted another servant to replenish their empty glasses. Losov guided Kaspar into the hall, pointing out particularly impressive paintings and features of the room.

'The Gallery of Heroes takes its name from the collection of paintings of the Kislevite Tzars that hang here. It is a living history of Kislev's ancient rulers, with portraits of Tzar Alexis, Radii Bokha, Alexander, his children and, of course, the Khan Queens Miska and Anastasia.'

Kaspar nodded in time with Losov's words, lost in the wonder of his surroundings.

Losov continued his narration. 'The furniture is mostly Bretonnian, and includes a number of pieces by Eugene Fosse, which were brought to the Winter Palace from Bordeleaux in 2071.'

As Losov began talking about the portraits of the Khan Queens, Kaspar found his gaze and attention straying to a raven-haired woman dressed in an ivory gown who moved behind the throng of guests. Whilst giving the appearance of listening to Losov, he attempted to get a good look at her face, but she remained frustratingly out of plain sight. As he caught a glimpse of her mischievous smile, a faint memory fluttered, but remained elusive.

Kaspar realised Losov had moved on and stepped after him, cannoning into another guest and spilling his wine down the man's furred dolman.

Horrified, Kaspar said, 'My apologies, sir. My fault entirely...'

A string of unintelligible Kislevite assaulted him and though his knowledge of the language was rudimentary, he could tell he was being horribly insulted. The man was broad and powerful, his thick furs and armour obviously expensive. He wore a peaked helmet edged with gold that marked him as a boyarin, one of the Kislevite nobility, and his ruddy, bearded features spoke of a hard life spent outdoors. The collision had almost knocked him from his feet and Kaspar could see the boyarin was stinkingly drunk, his bleary eyes ugly and hostile.

'You Empire man?' asked the man in thickly accented Reikspiel.

'I am, yes,' answered Kaspar. 'I am–'

'Bastard Empire,' slurred the man. 'Kept safe with Kislev blood. You and your land be dead but for us. Kislev's sons die to keep your lands safe and only when Empire burns do you come to fight.'

Kaspar fought to hold his temper as the drunken boyarin jabbed his thick finger into Kaspar's chest. 'What here for, huh? Want Kislev warriors fight for you? Ha! Treat us like dogs then expect us to die for you?'

'That's not–'

'Shit on you, Empire man. I hope your lands burn in hell,' growled the boyarin and Kaspar bunched his fists, feeling his temper fray even more. He grabbed the boyarin's tunic and pulled his face down to his own.

'Now listen to me, you piece of–'

'Come now, Alexei Kovovich,' said Pjotr Losov smoothly, appearing once more at Kaspar's side and separating the two men. 'There's no need for all this. Ambassador von Velten is to be presented to the Tzarina tonight and I'm sure you wouldn't want to bruise him before then, would you?'

Alexei Kovovich focussed on Losov before spitting on the floor in front of Kaspar and turning away to stagger towards the martial displays in the previous hall. Heads throughout the hall had turned to watch the altercation and Kaspar felt his skin redden.

'My apologies, ambassador,' said Losov. 'Boyarin Kovovich can be a little uncouth when in his cups, though he is a great warrior if he can stay sober. A common factor amongst some of our aristocracy, I regret to say.'

'That's alright,' said Kaspar, ashamed at his loss of temper. What sort of impression would that make on the Kislevites? The tension slowly drained from him as Losov ushered him into a line of guests extending from a set of beaten gold double doors at the far end of the hall. It seemed he was not the only person to be presented to the Tzarina tonight, and judging by his position in the line, not even the most noteworthy.

An ornate clock above the doors began chiming and at the ninth chime, the double doors of the inner apartments were flung open. Immediately the silence of death fell upon the gallery. A voice announced: 'The Tzarina, Katarin the Great, Queen of all Kislev!' and Kaspar had his first glimpse of the infamous Ice Queen herself.

Tall and majestic, with the beauty of a sculpted work of art, the Tzarina wore a long, pale blue dress with a lace train that glittered with icy shards. Her hair was the colour of a clear winter sky, confined beneath a crescent of azure velvet and set with pearls, from which hung a long white veil.

The Ice Queen was followed by her many retainers and close family. As she greeted those closest to her apartment doors, Kaspar watched the effect her entry had on the faces of those within the hall. Every countenance had assumed the same expression, by turns serious and smiling, as though everyone present was afraid to catch the eye of their queen, while at the same time afraid not to try.

The Tzarina had almost reached him and he was reminded of the Ice Queen's status as a powerful sorceress whose powers were said to come from the icy land of Kislev itself as the air around him grew colder. He shivered as his gaze was drawn to the Tzarina's waist where a long bladed sword was buckled. Waves of icy chill radiated from the weapon and Kaspar knew he looked upon the mighty war-blade, Fearfrost. The magical sword had been forged in ancient times by the Khan Queen Miska and wielded by her when she had conquered whole swathes of the Empire.

Not only was it highly unusual for the Tzarina to be armed on an occasion such as this, but Kaspar understood that it was a calculated insult for her to wear a weapon that had killed so many Empire nobles in the past.

At last the Tzarina reached Kaspar and he could feel the chill of her nearness deep in his bones as he bowed deeply towards her. The Ice Queen offered her hand, palm down, to Kaspar and he lifted it to his mouth, kissing it lightly. His lips burned with cold, as though he had kissed a block of ice. He straightened and met the Ice Queen's gaze as she pulled the lace veil back from her face. Her skin was pale and translucent, a mocking smile playing about her lips. Her eyes were like chips of cold sapphire.

'Ambassador von Velten. We are pleased you could attend. I hope we did not drag you from some pressing business to attend our little soiree.'

'Not at all, your majesty. I wouldn't have missed this for all the gold in the Grey Mountains.'

'Quite,' agreed the Tzarina, her milky eyes drifting to the other guests in the line.

'My compliments on your palace, truly it is magnificent.'

'Thank you for your kind words, Ambassador von Velten. I am, of course, always pleased to welcome our cousin in the Empire's representatives to Kislev and hope that you enjoy more success than your predecessor.'

'I endeavour only to serve, your majesty.'

'What a wonderful philosophy you have, ambassador,' said the Tzarina playfully before moving on to the next guest and Kaspar felt the chill air depart with her.

V

As the opening chords of a marching tune were struck to polite applause, the Tzarina, along with her current favourite, led the way into the centre of the long hall. The fine rugs from foreign lands had been removed and the polished floor could now serve for dancing. Other couples followed the Ice Queen and Kaspar caught sight of Pavel offering his hand to a grey haired woman old enough to be his grandmother, smiling indulgently as he strutted along like a Tzar himself. He laughed as he saw a young girl of no more than sixteen summers grab Kurt Bremen's hand and all but drag him onto the floor. The crowd clapped in time to the Tzarina's steps and Kaspar joined in, the smile freezing on his face as a delicate hand slipped into his own and pulled him away from the dance floor.

He opened his mouth to protest, then shut it just as quickly as he recognised the dark haired woman he had been searching for earlier. Kaspar guessed she was perhaps in her mid thirties, and when she smiled at him her savage beauty struck him like a comet. Jet-black hair spilled from a crescent of jewelled silk and gathered around her shoulders like iridescent oil, framing her full lips and jade green eyes perfectly. Her ivory dress flirted with decency, with a golden pendant hanging in her ample cleavage.

Crafted in the shape of a crown encircling a heart, Kaspar's eyes were drawn to it as he recognised the heraldry on the coach that had passed him when he arrived through the gates of Kislev. The elusive memory he had grasped for earlier swam to the surface of his mind as he remembered her face passing by him on the Goromadny Prospekt. He felt her eyes on him and blushed as he realised what she must think he was looking at.

She chuckled playfully and as they passed a series of arches in the eastern wall of the gallery, she inclined her head in the direction of an adjacent gallery.

Kaspar nodded, quickly checking to see that Bremen and Pavel were still occupied behind him and followed the woman into the next hall.

Smaller than the Gallery of Heroes, it was nonetheless still impressive. To Kaspar's left, wide stairs led down to sets of double doors that opened into a shimmering garden of white trees and ice sculptures. A massive painting depicting the final battle of the Great War against Chaos at the gates of Kislev dominated the hall and, hand in hand, Kaspar and the woman made their way to stand before it.

She stared at the picture as though enraptured, still holding Kaspar's hand, and he followed her gaze. The picture was a work of grand scale and he was impressed by its passion, if not its bias.

In the painting, the city of Kislev was in flames, her noble warriors painted with bold brush strokes and noble countenance. The dwarfs and warriors of the Empire who had also fought to defeat the forces of Chaos were painted with smaller, less confident strokes, their faces in shadow. He had to hunt before he could even find Magnus the Pious, the Empire hero who had led the combined armies to ultimate victory. As far as revisionist pieces of artwork went, it was a classic.

He threw a quick glance over his shoulder into the Gallery of Heroes as the dancing began in earnest. He recognised the first measures of the *mazurka,* a passionate military dance of Kislev and smiled as he watched a young warrior of the Gryphon Legion beat time to the music with the sole of his spurred boot. The man swept a redheaded woman into his arms and threw himself forward, leaping across the room with long strides. He spun the laughing girl and fell on his knees before her. Kaspar's heart surged as he remembered dancing the *mazurka* with Madeline in Nuln. It was a dance from the old days of gallantry, full of suggestions of passionate and romantic love.

He felt the woman's eyes on him and turned from the energetic dancing, lifting her hand and planting a kiss upon its warmth.

'You are gallant indeed, Kaspar von Velten.'

'One must always be gallant in the presence of beauty, milady,' replied Kaspar, not relinquishing his hold on her hand.

'If only all men thought as you do,' smiled the woman. 'But unfortunately that is not always the case.'

'Sadly true, milady,' agreed Kaspar. He wanted to ask her name or how she knew his, but felt that to do so would break the spell that held them here in this moment.

'I am Anastasia Vilkova,' she said, solving his dilemma.

'The Khan Queen,' whispered Kaspar, inwardly cursing himself for his clumsiness. He was supposed to be a diplomat and here he was tongue tied, blurting the first thing that came into his head.

Anastasia laughed, saying, 'Yes, I was named after her, but to put your mind at ease, I have no intention of mounting your head on a chariot spike.'

'Well that's a relief,' replied Kaspar, a measure of his composure returning.

'Though I am told I have a wicked streak, I think that would be a bit much.'

'At best it would be impolitic given my position here in Kislev,' agreed Kaspar.

Anastasia's eyes darted over his shoulder and Kaspar turned to see the man who had given the stunning display of swordsmanship approach with the confident stride of a natural warrior. He wore an embroidered green tunic with a scarlet sash tied crosswise across his chest and his twin blades sheathed in hide scabbards across his back. His topknot was freshly oiled and hung around his neck like glistening snake. His violet eyes were the cold steel of a warrior about to go into battle, and Kaspar had to resist the urge to take a backward step.

The man bowed curtly to Anastasia, ignoring Kaspar and said something in the thick tongue of Kislev. Anastasia's features wrinkled in annoyance and she shook her head impatiently, casting a wary glance in Kaspar's direction.

'Kaspar, have you been introduced to Sasha Kajetan?' she asked.

'Not yet,' replied Kaspar, turning to address Kajetan and offering his hand. 'A pleasure, sir.'

'What are you doing?' said Kajetan, ignoring Kaspar's outstretched hand. 'Why are you talking to Anastasia like this?'

'I'm sorry?' said Kaspar, nonplussed. 'I don't follow...'

'Well I do!' snapped the swordsman. 'Don't think I don't understand what you were trying to do here. Anastasia is mine, not yours.'

'Oh, come now,' protested Anastasia, 'that's hardly the kind of conversation we should be having here.'

'Are you trying to tell me he wasn't kissing your hand a second ago?'

'As a gentleman should,' said Anastasia haughtily, though Kaspar caught a hint of excitement in her tone and realised she was enjoying having two men argue over her.

He could see colour building on Kajetan's neck and, knowing that he was not a man to antagonise, said, 'I assure you, Herr Kajetan, that my intentions were strictly honourable. Had I known you and Madam Vilkova were a couple, I would have never have acted in such an inappropriate manner.'

Anastasia giggled. 'Sasha and I are old friends. We aren't a couple.'

Kaspar saw a flicker of emotion pass across Kajetan's cold features and wondered if he knew that. He heard the music from the main hall peter out and his irritation with Kajetan grew as the swordsman impulsively grabbed Anastasia's arm.

Kaspar said, 'I was privileged to witness your fighting skills earlier, Herr Kajetan. I have never seen their like.'

Kajetan nodded, momentarily distracted, and said, 'Thank you.'

'Truly inspiring,' said Kaspar, picking a fragment of lint from his collar. 'Though it is never quite the same when there is no risk involved and the fighters are comrades.'

Kajetan flushed red and snarled, 'I would be only too happy to try my blade against yours and show you what happens when the fighters are not comrades.'

'That won't be necessary,' said Anastasia hurriedly, stepping between the two men. Out of sight from Kajetan, she pulled a folded piece of paper from her décolletage and crushed it into Kaspar's hand. As a collective gasp of dismay sounded from the main hall she leaned forward and whispered, 'These are directions to my home. Call upon me,' before linking her arm with Kajetan's and leading him away.

Kaspar nodded and slipped the paper into the breast pocket of his shirt as he caught sight of Kurt Bremen approaching, his face grim.

'What's happened?' said Kaspar, looking past the knight and seeing anxious faces in the main hall.

'Wolfenburg has fallen,' said Bremen.

CHAPTER THREE

I

HE WATCHED THE *boyarin lean against the side of the alley to let the evening's kvas pour from his body in a stream of hot urine. He watched him sway in his drunkenness and, once he had finished, watched him button up his britches with some difficulty. The boyarin staggered off down the street, and his thoughts turned sour as he pictured her face once again. He ghosted down the alley, naked as the beasts of the dark forests, and following the zigzagging boyarin as he made his way through the foggy darkness of the city towards his lodgings.*

As he watched the boyarin's swaying back, he felt the familiar bitterness swell within his breast. Not content with beating his mother half to death with a poker, his father had turned the long length of black iron on the boy, thrashing obedience and devotion into him in equal measure.

He whimpered as he remembered the pain and humiliation. The powerlessness that had gripped him until the moment he had been elevated to his trueself. In their ignorance, the people of this city called him the Butcherman and he laughed at the inappropriateness of the name.

The boyarin spun and stumbled against a wall, hearing the laughter behind him. He froze in his hunt, blending into the brickwork of the wall and holding his breath lest the drunken fool somehow see him.

He knew it was unlikely. The little light cast by the moon just made the fog glow a spectral white and the torches of the palace were but a distant memory. The boyarin's lurching footsteps were louder now and he could easily make out the bulky, fur-clad figure moving unsteadily through the soupy fog. A familiar word sprang to mind.

Hunted.

He pictured her face again, bruised, bloody and with one eye swollen shut with weeping contusions. His teeth ground together with a rage and love that had not dimmed with time, and his fists bunched as he thought of ending the life of the pathetic specimen of humanity that stumbled and belched ahead of him. He promised himself that this time he would enjoy what he must do. His otherself would wail and cry, but what was he but the otherself's secret face? That weakness was tucked away in a corner of his mind and would only be released when this task was completed.

He pictured what would happen next, seeing once more the green field where he had taken the first, faltering steps on the road that had led here, the first emergence of his trueself. The blood, the axe and the taste of warm meat ripped from the bones of a living body.

The boyarin even wore the same form of peaked helmet, the same colour of dolman as…

He took a deep breath to calm himself, feeling the familiar excitement of the hunt build in his breast at the thought of pleasing her again. He slid the long, thin bladed knife his mother had given him from his flesh and padded soundlessly forward.

There. He saw the boyarin steady himself on the corner of a sagging redbrick building, the moonlight illuminating his hateful features. Alexei Kovovich's face was flushed with alcohol and self-righteous indignation. He could well imagine the satisfaction the boyarin had gotten insulting the new ambassador from the Empire. He bit his lip hard to stop from screaming as his anger built to incandescent levels. He leapt forward and grabbed the boyarin's arm, spinning him around and hammering the knife into his ugly face.

The man roared in pain and dropped to his knees, his head lolling back on slack muscles. Moonlight glinted on the descending blade as he stabbed again and again. The boyarin's throat geysered and he was upon him, the knife forgotten as he tore flesh with his bare hands. Spittle flew and blood steamed in the cold night.

He swallowed lumps of gristly meat as he bit them from the man's face.

He vomited onto the boyarin's chest as he stabbed his thumbs through the jelly of the man's eyes.

He bled and his otherself wept as he took yet another life.

He could not enjoy this.

He hated this almost as much as he hated himself.

II

KASPAR SIGNED HIS name on a promissory note and handed it to Stefan with a growl of displeasure. It felt foolish to be spending money, his own money no less, on refurnishing the embassy and returning it to its former grandeur when hordes of northmen were massing to smash it to ruins. But standards had to be maintained and it would take time for more money to arrive from Altdorf.

Outside, he could hear tradesmen cleaning the walls of the embassy of the Kislevite graffiti while glaziers tore off the wooden boards covering the windows and replaced them with new-blown glass.

'We're getting there, slowly but surely,' said Stefan. 'Soon this embassy will be an outpost for the Emperor to be proud of.'

'But it will take time, Stefan. Time I'm not sure we have any more.'

'Perhaps,' said Stefan, casting a scathing look at Pavel, who lounged in the corner of the room, smoking a long and evil-smelling pipe. 'But we can't have these Kislevites thinking they're better than us, can we?'

Pavel winked and said, 'Already know,' before blowing a smoke ring.

'That's not it,' said Kaspar. 'I'd just be happier knowing that I wasn't wasting my money.'

'Is there any further news from the Empire?' asked Stefan. The question was asked lightly, but Kaspar could sense the anxiety behind it.

The news that Wolfenburg had fallen had been a harsh blow to morale, made all the more so by the lack of any further reliable information.

Riders and messengers arrived at sporadic intervals, each bearing wildly contradictory rumours from the Empire.

'Nothing reliable, no,' said Kaspar, shaking his head.

'I was speaking to some arquebusiers from Wissenland yesterday,' said Stefan. 'Their regiment was destroyed at Zhedevka and they've been living hand-to-mouth since then. They said that they'd heard the Kurgans had pressed south and are camped outside Talabheim.'

'Aye,' said Kaspar, arching his eyebrows. 'And *I've* heard that the Kurgans are in the west of the Empire, somewhere around Middenheim.'

'You don't believe that?'

Kaspar shook his head. 'Of course not, no army can cover those kinds of distances in so short a time. You should know better than that. For what it's worth, I think that with winter coming, the Kurgans will turn northwards and march back to Kislev.'

'Rumour has it a pulk gathers in fringes of oblast. Many soldiers,' said Pavel.

'Is that true?' asked Kaspar.

'Damned if I know. Tzarina not exactly share information with me.'

'Oh, well thank you for your insight,' said Stefan.

Kaspar ignored their bickering and leafed through a stack of papers on his desk and steepled his fingers before him. He was tired and the stress of the last few days was beginning to take its toll. Requests for an audience with the Tzarina to discuss military cooperation were being met by a stone wall, though Pjotr Losov had assured Kaspar that the Ice Queen would grant him an audience as soon as she became available.

'These Wissenland arquebusiers you were talking to?' he asked. 'Where are they billeted?'

'They're not. They're camped just outside the city walls. Them and a few hundred other souls who've come down from the fighting in the north.'

'You said they're living hand-to-mouth?'

'Yes.'

'Find out who commands them and send him to me. And find out what happened to the food that was sent to Kislev to feed these men. I want to know why they've not been supplied properly.'

Stefan nodded and departed as Pavel stood and walked to the window.

'Is bad times coming,' he said sagely.

'Aye,' agreed Kaspar, rubbing his eyes.

'Pavel not seen city like this before now.'

'Like what?'

'You think Kislev so busy all the time?' asked Pavel. 'No, most live on the steppe, in stanistas. You know, small villages? Most only come to city when winter breaks to sell furs, meat and such things.'

'But now they're coming south because of the tribesmen?'

'Aye. Has happened before, but not like this. Kyazak bandits, Kul and Tahmak mostly, ride the steppe to kill and rob, but people are safe behind timber walls. Take more than Kyazak riders to make this many people come to city. Kislev people are people of land, not stone. They not leave steppe unless forced to.'

Kaspar nodded at Pavel's words. The city had felt busy, but no busier than most other cities he had visited. It had not occurred to him that this would not be the normal state of affairs.

'If there is another army gathering in the north, it's only going to get worse before it gets better, Pavel.'

'Is of no matter. Kislev been through hard times before. Survived them, will survive this.'

'You seem very sure.'

'How long you know me?' asked Pavel suddenly.

'I don't know exactly, twenty-five years maybe?'

'And in that time, you ever know me to give up fight?'

'Never,' answered Kaspar instantly.

'That Kislev way. Land all that matters. We may die, but Kislev live on. So long as land go on, so do we. The northmen may kill us all, but they will die eventually or someone else kill them. Is of no matter to land. Kislev is land and land is Kislev.'

Pavel's line of thought was too abstract for Kaspar to follow and he simply nodded, unsure of what exactly his friend meant. He was spared from thinking of a reply by Pavel asking, 'You expecting visitors?'

'No,' replied Kaspar, rising from his chair as the sound of angry voices came from the street beyond.

III

He woke and couldn't open his mouth.

He clawed at his lips, peeling the dead skin mask from his face and hurling it to the floor in revulsion. He sat bolt upright, eyes wide in terror. The low sun shone through the dirty skylight and dimly illuminated the timber-framed attic, motes of dust drifting through stray beams. Flies buzzed around him, settling on his lips and arms where patches of sticky blood clung to him.

Something dangled on a hook behind him, but he didn't want to look at it yet.

He pushed himself to his feet, a terrible sickness building in his stomach as the smell of the attic assailed him: putrefaction and the reek of embalming fluids stolen from the *Chekist* building.

In waking here, he knew that the thing inside him that called itself the trueself had killed again, though he did not remember who it had eaten. All that was certain was that another life had been torn screaming from this world and that it – he – was responsible. He dropped to his knees and retched, tasting raw meat in his mouth. The guilt was overpowering and he wept like a newborn for over an hour, rocking in a foetal position until he remembered the locket, clicking it open and staring at her picture within. A coiled lock of auburn hair nestled inside and he pressed it to his face, inhaling the rich aroma of her scent.

He gulped deep breaths and the shaking subsided to a level where he was able to push himself to his knees. The lingering echoes of the trueself drained from his mind as he picked up a red sash, like that worn by Kislevite boyarin, and wiped his face, feeling his strength and identity returning as he cleaned himself.

Silently he padded to the attic hatch and listened for any noises from below. He was always careful to conceal the activities of the trueself from the others; they would not understand the pain he suffered being torn between his warring selves.

Satisfied that the tack store below was empty, he pulled open the hatch and climbed down to the cold wooden floor. He could sense that, save for the horses in their stalls below, the building was empty and made his way quickly to his billet in the adjacent building. Here, he located fresh clothes, a linen towel and a bar of scented soap, then headed back down into to the exercise yard.

He worked the hand pump, filling the horse trough before the stables with icy water and proceeded to wash his entire body with the soap. As each patch of blood washed from his skin, he repeated the Mantra of Tranquillity, feeling calmer, stronger and more purposeful with each repetition. The trueself was still there, of course, but he could feel it receding to the back of his mind with each breath. He didn't know who it had killed, but knew that whoever it had been would have suffered a truly excruciating death. But he could not be held responsible, could he? When the dreams came and the trueself took hold, he had no power over it. Even as he thought of the trueself, a last fragment of its identity swam to the surface of his mind.

The trueself thought of the locket, feeling the otherself becoming physically aroused at the thought of her. Her touch, her skin, her scent and her lingering kisses.

Only for her could it do these things.

It thought of the eyeless head hanging on the hook in the attic and smiled.

The trueself felt sure she would have approved.

* * *

IV

'WHAT IN THE name of Sigmar is going on down there?' said Kaspar as he watched scores of shouting people filling the courtyard before the embassy. Nearly a hundred people pressed against the iron fence, hurling guttural insults at the building and the Knights Panther who had wisely retreated behind the gates and shut them fast.

The crowd gathered around a wailing woman swathed from head to foot in a black pashmina, her wails piteous and heartfelt.

Kaspar turned from the window and grabbed his black cloak, wrapping it around himself before buckling his twin flintlocks on his right hip.

'You sure that is wise?' asked Pavel.

'Well I'm damned if I'm going to face a mob without a weapon.'

Pavel shrugged and followed the ambassador out onto the hallway, where Kurt Bremen and Valdhaas were descending the stairs to the vestibule. Bremen stopped and turned to address the ambassador as he made his way from his chambers.

'Ambassador, you should stay inside. We'll handle this.'

'No, Kurt. I'll not have others fight my battles for me.'

'Herr von Velten,' explained Bremen patiently, 'that is our job.'

Kaspar started to retort, then realised that Bremen was right. 'Very well, come with me. But stay behind me.'

Bremen nodded, noticing the pistols holstered beneath Kaspar's cloak.

'Pavel,' said Kaspar as he took the stairs two at a time. 'The woman in black, what's her story?'

'I do not know. Dressed for mourning, but I not recognise her.'

'Fine, so we know someone's dead and for some reason they're angry at me. Nobody's killed anyone and not told me, have they?'

'No, ambassador,' said Pavel and Bremen together.

'Very well, let's see what's going on then,' said Kaspar and pushed open the door.

Screams and yells of abuse filled the air and the wailing woman slid down the railings of the iron gate, her arms outstretched in abject grief. She screamed and wept uncontrollably. Three young men, their faces alight with righteous fury shook the gates and roared at Kaspar.

'What are they saying?' said Kaspar, suddenly realising the depth of anger in the crowd.

Pavel pointed to the weeping woman. 'They say her husband is dead.'

'And what has that to do with me?'

'They say you killed him.'

'What? Why?'

'Not sure. Hard to make sense of what they say,' said Pavel, gingerly approaching the gate. Six Knights Panther held it against the press of bodies as he yelled into the crowd, waving his arms and pointing at the woman and Kaspar. After several minutes of confused shouting, he returned to Kaspar's side, his face grim.

'Is bad,' he said.

'Yes,' snapped Kaspar. 'I gathered that, but what's happening?'

'Woman is Natalja Kovovich and her husband is dead. Murdered they say.'

'I've never even heard of her husband,' said Kaspar, though the name was vaguely familiar, 'let alone murdered him.'

'The drunk,' said Bremen suddenly. 'At the reception, the boyarin you spilt your drink over. That's who he was.'

'Damn,' swore Kaspar as the name fell into place. He could picture the drunken boyarin's face now and remembered him saying that the Empire ought to burn in hell. He remembered his anger and that he would have put his fist through Kovovich's face if not for the intervention of Losov.

Surely these people didn't think that he could have killed the man?

This was madness, and he felt the situation slipping beyond control with every passing shout hurled in his direction. He drew one of his pistols and pulled back the flint.

'Ambassador, I don't think that is a very good idea,' warned Bremen.

But it was already too late.

Kaspar strode to the gate. He raised his pistol above his head and, before Bremen or anyone else could stop him, fired the pistol into the air.

The crowd screamed as the pistol boomed and a cloud of powder smoke drifted from the muzzle.

'Pavel!' shouted Kaspar. 'Translate for me.'

'Ursun save us,' muttered Pavel, but stood beside the ambassador.

'Tell them that I am deeply sorry for Madam Kovovich's loss, but that I had nothing to do with her husband's death.'

Pavel shouted into the crowd, but they were in no mood for conciliation and drowned his words with cries for vengeance. The remaining Knights Panther raced from the embassy, their swords drawn and closely followed by fearful looking embassy guards with halberds held loosely before them.

Kaspar holstered his spent pistol and drew the second, but before he could fire it, Kurt Bremen grabbed his arm and said, 'Please, Ambassador von Velten, don't. It will only inflame this situation more.'

Kaspar said, 'I'll not be browbeaten by a mob, Kurt.'

'I know, but do you really want to aggravate these people further? It will not take much more for this situation to turn murderous.'

Cold clarity settled on Kaspar as he realised the gravity of the situation. He was reacting as a man and not a leader. A hundred or more angry people were yelling for his blood, only kept at bay by a fence in serious need of repair.

Bremen was right, it was time to defuse this situation rather than inflame it.

He nodded. 'Very well, Kurt, let's see what we can do to calm these people down.'

Bremen sighed in relief, turning sharply as more pistols boomed and screams echoed from walls. A score of horsemen dressed in black with lacquered leather breastplates and long, bronze-tipped cudgels rode into the street. They fired flintlocks over the heads of the crowd and rode into its midst, their cudgels cracking skulls and breaking bones wherever they struck.

'What the hell?' said Kaspar before Pavel bundled him back towards the embassy. 'Who are they?'

Pavel did not stop, but said, '*Chekist*! Like city watch, but much, much worse.'

Screams and cries rang out as the horsemen circled within the courtyard, bludgeoning those closest to them and dispersing the crowd without mercy. Within seconds, the mob had fled, leaving dozens of its members to bleed on the cobbles before the embassy. Stunned, Kaspar and the Knights Panther watched the horsemen circle the fountain at the centre of the courtyard, making sure that there was no further resistance.

Several horsemen rode off in the direction the bulk of the mob had fled while the others reined in before the embassy gates. The leader, a man wearing a fully enclosed helm of dark iron with a feathered crest, dismounted and approached the gates.

The Knights Panther glanced round at Kaspar and Bremen.

Kaspar nodded and the knights unbarred the gate, allowing the leader of the *Chekist* to enter. He marched towards the building and slung his cudgel from his belt before removing his helmet.

He wore his hair long, pulled back in a long scalp lock, and his moustache was clipped short on his upper lip. His eyes were coal-dark and expressionless, his bearing that of a warrior.

'Ambassador von Velten?' he asked in fluent Reikspiel, utterly devoid of accent.

'Yes.'

'My name is Pashenko. Vladimir Pashenko of the *Chekist*, and I am afraid I must ask you some questions.'

V

STUNNED SILENCE GREETED Pashenko's question.

'Did you not understand the question, ambassador?'

'I understood it well enough, Herr Pashenko, I'm just not sure how you can expect me to take it seriously.'

'Because murder is a serious business, ambassador.'

'I couldn't agree more, but I find it hard to believe that you could think I had anything to do with Boyarin Kovovich's death.'

'Why?' asked Pashenko.

'Because I only met him once for less than a minute.'

'How well did you know the boyarin?' asked Pashenko.

'I just told you,' said Kaspar.

'Had you heard of him before you assaulted him at the Winter Palace?'

'I didn't assault him, he–'

'That's not the information I have, ambassador. I have witnesses who inform me that you grabbed the boyarin and threatened him before the Tzarina's advisor separated you.'

'He insulted me,' snapped Kaspar.

'And that infuriated you.'

'No. Well, it made me angry, yes, but not enough to kill him.'

'So you admit you were angry?'

'I never said I wasn't. He told me that he hoped my nation burned in hell.'

'I see,' said Pashenko, writing in his notebook. 'And when did you leave the Winter Palace?'

'I'm not sure of the exact time, not long after we heard that Wolfenburg had fallen.'

'I also have witnesses who tell me that Boyarin Kovovich left around the same time, giving you ample opportunity to follow him and butcher him.'

'Butcher him? What are you talking about?'

'The boyarin's corpse was found the morning after the reception at the palace, though it took some days to identify him due to the fact that his head was missing and much of his clothing and flesh had been burned, as if by some form of acid.'

'Is that supposed to shock me?'

'Does it?'

'Yes, but no more than you thinking that I did it. Sigmar's hammer, don't you already have a killer in Kislev who does this kind of thing? The Butcherman?'

'We do indeed,' nodded Pashenko. 'Though it is not unknown for other wrongdoers to commit crimes in a similar manner to those of an existing criminal in an attempt to have them accrue the blame for their own violent actions. And let us not forget lunatics and the deranged who attempt to emulate someone they perceive as worthy of imitation.'

Kaspar was speechless. Surely this idiot couldn't seriously believe that he had anything to do with the boyarin's death?

But despite the ridiculousness of the accusation, Pashenko radiated an easy confidence that unsettled Kaspar.

'When did you identify the boyarin's body?' asked Kurt Bremen.

'What has that to do with anything?' said Pashenko.

'Perhaps nothing, but when?' pressed the knight.

'Just this morning. His head was left outside our building on the Urskoy Prospekt.'

'Yet not long after that, an angry mob forms and makes its way here? It seems the people of Kislev are truly great detectives to have spoken to all the witnesses you claim to have, deduce the ambassador's involvement and arrive here before you and your men.'

'What are you suggesting?' said Pashenko.

'Come on, Herr Pashenko,' said Kaspar. 'Don't play games with us. Someone gave you the information you have and told the grieving widow where to go, didn't they?'

'You are mistaken,' replied Pashenko.

'No, sir, it is you who is mistaken if you think I am some ignorant peasant you can browbeat with your pathetic attempt at intimidation,' said Kaspar, rising from his seat and indicating the door. 'Now if you will excuse me, I have urgent ambassadorial duties that require my attention. I'm sure you can see yourself out.'

Pashenko rose from his seat and bowed curtly towards the ambassador.

'Your attitude has been noted, herr ambassador. Good day to you,' said Pashenko.

The *Chekist* turned on his heel and left the room without another word, and as the door shut behind him, a collective sigh of relief followed him.

Kaspar rubbed a hand over his scalp and said, 'Can you believe that? If it wasn't so idiotic it would be funny.'

'Nothing funny about *Chekist*,' said Pavel darkly.

'Oh, come on, Pavel,' laughed Kaspar. 'He didn't have a shred of proof.'

'You not understand, *Chekist* not need proof,' snapped Pavel standing and jabbing his finger at Kaspar. 'You not in Empire now, Kaspar. In Kislev, what *Chekist* say is law, *is* law. They disappear people. You understand? Throw people in gaol and they never seen again, never heard of again. Gone...'

'Even an ambassador of a foreign power?' scoffed Kaspar.

'Even you,' nodded Pavel.

Kaspar saw the seriousness of Pavel's expression, finally understanding Pashenko's easy confidence and realising that perhaps the *Chekist's* threat wasn't as empty as he'd believed.

CHAPTER FOUR

I

SPARKS FLEW WHERE the two heavy broadswords clashed, the ring of steel echoing across the courtyard. Kaspar rolled his wrists and stabbed with the point of his sword, but his opponent easily side-stepped the attack. A sword this heavy wasn't meant for thrusting, it was designed to smash through armour by virtue of its sharp edge and sheer weight. He stepped back as his blade was swept aside and a slashing riposte passed within inches of his chest.

He was sweating profusely and his sword arm burned with fatigue. The wire-wound grip of the sword was slippery with moisture and he switched to a two-handed grip, the blade held straight out before him.

'Had enough yet?' asked his opponent.

'No, are you feeling tired?' he replied.

Bader Valdhaas smiled, holding his own heavy blade as though it weighed nothing at all. Kaspar wasn't surprised, Valdhaas was a knight in his prime and thirty-three years Kaspar's junior. He'd watched in admiration as the Knights Panther trained every day with their heavy swords and lances, maintaining the strength and stamina required to wield such cumbersome weapons with ease.

Kaspar couldn't remember blades being this heavy when he had been a soldier, but then he wasn't a young man any more and the strength and immortality of youth were a distant memory to him now. Valdhaas wore his plate armour, while Kaspar was armoured in an iron breastplate and pauldrons edged with twists of gold with a bronze eagle at its centre. To protect against any accidental injuries during this sparring session, he had also been furnished with a mail shirt normally worn beneath a full suit of armour.

The edges of the swords were dulled, but Kaspar knew that any impact from such heavy weapons would still hurt like a bastard. Knights and guards had gathered to watch their new master from the cloisters and balconies overlooking the courtyard and Kaspar began to question the wisdom of his decision to begin sparring again. He had no wish to be carried off on a pallet in front of his staff if he could avoid it.

'Go easy on him, Valdhaas!' called Pavel from an upper balcony. 'Ambassador is old man now, he don't see good!'

'No, Pavel,' shouted Kaspar. 'It's me who should go easy on him, this old dog still knows a few tricks.'

Valdhaas grinned and launched his attack, the blade sweeping low towards Kaspar's legs. Impulsively, the ambassador stepped to meet the blow, bringing his blade down to block, intending to spin inside Valdhaas's guard and deliver a scoring strike to the knight's side.

But the expected impact never came and Kaspar had a horrified moment of seeing the knight's sword slashing towards his face instead. His rash counterattack had brought him much closer than Valdhaas had expected and the knight's sword was about to smash Kaspar's skull to splinters.

As though handling a lightweight duelling sabre, Valdhaas pulled his stroke in time to avoid decapitating Kaspar, but could not prevent the blade from striking his shoulder. The impact tore the pauldron from his armour, spinning him round and sending him crashing to the stone flags of the courtyard. He heard a gasp from the spectators and felt a sticky wetness on his neck.

'Ambassador!' shouted Valdhaas, dropping his sword and rushing to Kaspar's side.

'I'm fine,' said Kaspar, groggily reaching up to touch his neck.

He looked down and saw the torn padding and split links of his armour, blood leaking from a shallow cut just above his collarbone.

'Ambassador, accept my apologies,' blurted the knight. 'I didn't think you would risk coming in so close to attack.'

'I know, and don't worry. This was my fault, I need to remember I'm not the young man I was.'

'I tried telling you that before you started, but you not listen to me,' laughed Pavel.

'But he's a typical man, and had to nearly get his head caved in to learn that,' added a similarly accented female voice from the cloister below Pavel.

Kaspar smiled and pushed himself to his feet as Valdhaas helped him off with his armour. He turned to face the speaker, a tall woman with auburn hair pulled in a severe bun and pinned behind her head. Her features were lined but handsome, and she wore a long green dress with a white apron and a linen pashmina decorated with colourful needlework along its length.

'I know, Sofia, I know,' said Kaspar, pulling his shirt over his head to allow her to examine the cut. She pushed his head to one side and used the edge of his shirt to wipe away the blood.

'You'll need stitches,' she declared. 'Sit over by the trough.'

The knights and guards drifted away, the excitement over for now, and returned to their duties. Kaspar slapped his palm on the knight's armour and said, 'Well, done, lad, you have a fine sword arm on you there. Strong and, thankfully, fast.'

'Thank you, ambassador,' bowed Valdhaas before withdrawing.

Kaspar sat on a stone bench at the edge of the trough and rested his back against the hand pump as Sofia wetted his ruined shirt in the water and cleaned the cut of blood.

'You're a damn fool. You know that, don't you?' she said.

'Aye, it's been said before.'

'And, I have no doubt, will be said again soon enough,' said Sofia.

Kaspar had been introduced to Sofia Valencik when Stefan had employed her as the ambassador's personal physician. She had presented herself at the gates of the embassy three days ago with some impressive credentials and had begun her tenure by insisting that she be allowed to thoroughly examine Kaspar so that she might learn all about her new responsibility.

Between cursing Stefan for the wretch he was and fending off her attempts to remove his clothing for a full examination, Kaspar had insisted he didn't need some Kislevite sawbones poking around his body. But Stefan and Sofia were insistent and eventually he had been forced to relent.

Sofia Valencik could often be blunt, was frequently disrespectful of his position and often affected an aloof superiority, though Kaspar had discovered that she had an irreverent sense of humour. Her manner was honest and if you didn't like it, then you could go to hell.

Kaspar liked her immensely and the two had hit it off almost immediately.

'A man of your age playing with swords... I don't know,' she said shaking her head and pulling a length of twine and a curved needle from her apron.

'I wasn't playing,' said Kaspar, cursing the fact that he sounded like a scolded schoolboy as Sofia threaded the needle and pressed the point to his skin. He gritted his teeth as she expertly worked the needle through his skin, pulling the stitches tight and snipping the end of the twine with a small pocket knife.

'There,' she smiled, 'good as new.'

'Thank you, Sofia, that was mostly painless.'

'Just be thankful I remembered to pack my small needle today,' she said.

II

Kislev bustled with life, though having heard what Pavel had to say on the subject, he could see that many of the people on the streets and filling its parks were not natives of the city. They had the bemused, awed expressions common to peasants when they came to a large city. Even in the few short weeks he had been in Kislev, Kaspar could already see that there were more and more such people coming to the city every day.

On those occasions when he journeyed beyond the city walls to watch the Knights Panther training his embassy soldiers, the roads were always busy with columns of people with carts and drays heading south. The only traffic coming north was occasional river boats from the Empire riding low in the dark waters of the Urskoy as they brought in much-needed supplies. The grain stores of the city were already under pressure and the situation was only going to get worse if the stream of refugees from the north continued.

He had despatched numerous letters to several Empire merchants trading in Kislev in an attempt to secure supplies for the scattered remnants of Imperial regiments trapped here, but had had no luck thus far in cajoling any aid from them.

As each river boat hurriedly departed, Kaspar would ensure that each captain took sealed letters bound for Altdorf, each asking for news from home, requests for more supplies and information regarding the course of the war.

Tensions were high and several violent skirmishes between hungry people fighting for food had already been broken up the city watch and the *Chekist*. Kislev was filling up and that was not good for a city that would no doubt come under siege when the fighting season began in the spring. Kaspar knew that soon the Tzarina was going to have to bar the gates of her city and deny a great many of her people sanctuary. Kaspar had made that choice before and did not envy her the decision as to when to shut the gates. He could still remember the pleading faces outside the walls of Hauptburg when he had been forced to close the gates to save the mountain town from rampaging tribes of greenskins.

Desperate faces watched him from the streets and tree-lined boulevards, each one looking for some sign of hope, but he had none to give them. Every now and then he would catch a glimpse of a black armoured *Chekist* amongst the throng, and wondered if Pashenko was having him followed. It would not surprise him, but he could do little to prevent it as he and two of his Knights Panther rode slowly down the Urskoy Prospekt, making their way to Anastasia Vilkova's home.

The woman intrigued Kaspar and though he had no wish to antagonise the jealous and fiery Sasha Kajetan any further, he found his thoughts constantly returning to Anastasia, her dark hair, emerald eyes and full lips. There was no doubt he was attracted to her and he believed that even though they had only briefly met, there had been a natural chemistry between them.

Whether that was wishful thinking, he didn't know, but he had resolved to find out and thus he and his knights rode to the wealthier southern quarter of Kislev. In all probability it was a fool's errand, but Kaspar had long ago resolved never to let opportunities, no matter how fleeting, pass him by.

Once Sofia had finished stitching his cut and applied a pleasantly aromatic poultice, they had enjoyed a sweet tisane together and he had asked her about Anastasia Vilkova.

'She's a noblewoman,' had been Sofia's curt response. 'How do you know her?'

'I don't really,' Kaspar had explained. 'I met her at the Winter Palace last week and she bade me call on her.'

'I see,' said Sofia archly. 'Well, be careful. I hear the swordsman, Sasha Kajetan, is fond of her.'

'Aye, I noticed that.'

'I don't know too much about her, well, not any more than anyone else, really. I know she's originally from Praag and that her husband was killed six or seven years ago, supposedly in a random attack by street thugs, and she took over his business interests.'

'Why do you say "supposedly"?' said Kaspar.

'Well, the rumour was that her husband was involved in a few, shall we say, risqué business enterprises that were competing with those of the criminal underclasses.'

'Go on,' said Kaspar.

'Well, they say that one of the gang leaders finally got tired of the competition and had his men follow and murder him as he made his way home from a house of ill repute.'

'The bastard.'

'Who?' chuckled Sofia. 'The husband for visiting a whore-house or the gang leader for having him killed?'

'You know what I meant. Don't try and be clever, it doesn't suit you.'

Sofia stuck out her tongue and continued. 'Like I said, Madam Vilkova took over her husband's businesses and cut out the parts that put her in competition with these men. She's quite a wealthy woman now, and they say she donates a lot of money to various hospices and poorhouses around the city.'

'Quite the philanthropist.'

'Yes, one of our nobles actually worthy of the name,' agreed Sofia. 'So why does she want you to call on her?'

'She didn't really have time to say.'

'Perhaps she is infatuated with you,' laughed Sofia.

'Perhaps she is. Is that so hard to believe?' asked Kaspar, rather more brusquely than he had intended.

'Not at all, Kaspar, you're quite a catch.'

'Now you are mocking me,' said the ambassador, rising from the bench.

'A little,' agreed Sofia with a smile.

Kaspar had left Sofia and retired to his chambers to bathe and change before leaving the embassy to travel to Anastasia's home. He had wanted to travel alone, but Kurt Bremen was unwilling to allow the ambassador to ride unaccompanied after the bloodshed at the gates following the *Chekist's* attack on the grieving mob.

Thinking of the boyarin's murder, Kaspar was still unsure what to make of the circumstances surrounding his death. A practical mindset had taught him not to believe in coincidence and he could not shake the nagging suspicion that the killing would yet prove to have some deeper connection to him. Quite what, he did not know, but Kaspar was not the kind of man to let such things lie unresolved. Pavel was already attempting to find out what, if any, connections Boyarin Kovovich had with any disreputable types and whether that trail led back, as Kaspar believed it would, to Chekatilo.

He turned his horse into a cobbled thoroughfare with a sign fixed to a black stone building that informed him it was known as Magnustrasse, and was momentarily taken aback seeing a street with an Empire name.

'Perhaps they don't hate us after all, eh?' he said.

'No, ambassador,' said Valdhaas, still feeling guilty after cutting his master.

The streets here were less crowded than those nearer the centre of the city and Kaspar could practically feel the wealth around him. Clean plastered walls topped with broken glass embedded in mortar surrounded the homes of the wealthy elite of Kislev, each one high enough to keep out all but the most determined intruders.

He followed the street until he reached a stand of evergreen poplars. According to the scribbled directions on the note, these were directly opposite Anastasia's home.

Her home was behind a high wall of dressed ashlar and an open gateway led within. Beyond the walls, Kaspar could see a tastefully constructed building at the end of a paved avenue with a lush, well-tended garden of herbs, shrubs and vividly coloured flowers before it.

Kaspar saw Anastasia kneeling before a small herb garden, tilling freshly turned dark earth with a small trowel, and was struck by a heart-rending sense of déjà vu. He forced a smile as she saw him and waved as she came towards him.

'I'm so glad you came,' she said.

III

KASPAR SOON REALISED that Sofia had been correct in telling him that Anastasia was a very wealthy woman. Green liveried servants had taken their horses as they rode through the gate and led them to a long stable block set against the interior of the wall, while curtseying maids brought the riders some refreshments.

He and his knights had been handed cool glasses of apple juice with crushed ice, telling Kaspar that Anastasia was wealthy enough to have a chilled room below her home where the air was kept frozen by the enchantments of Kislev's ice wizards.

His knights remained discreetly by the entrance to the town-house while he and Anastasia repaired to an oak-panelled receiving room with a high, alabaster ceiling and a lush carpet patterned with coiling dragons spread over a gleaming hard-wood floor.

The interior of the house spoke of great wealth, though never ostentatiously and always tastefully. Every room was elegantly appointed and none overwhelmed a guest with their expense, unlike the castles of many an Empire noble that did all they could to proclaim their owner's wealth.

He and Anastasia had sat upon a sumptuous divan and chatted like old friends of inconsequential things until the matter of Boyarin Kovovich's death inevitably arose.

'I heard about that frightful business with that fool, Pashenko,' said Anastasia. 'Simply terrible that a man like you should be accused of something so horrible.'

'Yes, it was ridiculous,' agreed Kaspar.

'What made Pashenko think you had anything to do with his death?'

Kaspar shrugged. 'People at the palace saw the boyarin and myself exchange words and he leapt to the wrong conclusion.'

'Pah! Pashenko is *nekulturny* and if he were to arrest every man who'd had words with Kovovich, then half of Kislev should be in the *Chekist* gaol.'

'He wasn't well liked then?' asked Kaspar.

'Not particularly,' said Anastasia. 'He was a boorish man and his wife deserves to be on the stage with the act she put on in front of your embassy. They say he beat her mercilessly, so why she should mourn his passing is beyond me.'

Kaspar shook his head, feeling less sorry for Alexei Kovovich the more he learned about him. The man had been a drunk and, by all accounts, Madam Kovovich would be better off without him. He finished his drink and set it down on a hand-carved walnut table beside the divan.

'But enough of such matters, Kaspar,' said Anastasia brightly. 'Times are grim enough without us adding to them. Tell me of yourself, I am intrigued as to how a man such as you comes to be in Kislev at a time like this.'

'I was sent here by my Emperor,' said Kaspar.

'Oh, come now, there must be more to it than that. Did you upset someone in power to merit such an... inauspicious posting?'

'Inauspicious? Why do you say that?'

'Because a posting here can surely bring you neither great material reward nor prestige, whereas a posting at the heart of diplomatic activity, say in Marienburg or Bordeleaux, might be a useful stepping-stone for a ministerial career. Or Tilea? I'm told that it at least has the benefit of a pleasant climate. But Kislev must surely hold little attraction? So tell me, truthfully mind, why did you come to Kislev?'

'I told you. The Emperor asked me to take the post and I accepted.'

'As simple as that?'

Kaspar nodded. 'I served in the Emperor's armies for nearly four decades, taking the Emperor Luitpold's schilling when I was sixteen years old. I joined a pike regiment and spent the next six years fighting in Averland against one orc warlord after another. We marched and fought throughout the Empire, earning quite a name for ourselves I might add, defeating the beasts that hunt in the dark forests, the tribes of northmen who raid your country and the Ostermark, and any foe that came with murder in their hearts. I rose to command my regiment and fought at the side of the Emperor Karl-Franz himself at the Battle of Norduin. Over the years I earned yet more command until I led entire armies for my Emperor.'

'Oh, this is very heroic,' gushed Anastasia.

Kaspar smiled. 'Perhaps, but my nation is in peril and it needs people who understand war to stand against its enemies if it is to survive. Diplomacy and negotiating can achieve only so much, and there comes a time when a man must be willing to fight for what is right. Kislev may not be the most glamorous posting, but if I can make a difference by coming here and helping our nations' armies resist the coming invasion, then this is where I need to be.'

Anastasia smiled. 'Then you are a true patriot and altruist. Men like you are rare.'

'Not as rare as you think,' smiled Kaspar.

Anastasia laughed and asked, 'Why then did you leave the Emperor's service?'

The smile fell from Kaspar's face. 'My wife, Madeline, had a weak heart and the worry of my absences placed great strain upon her,' he said, his tone melancholy. 'When I returned from campaigning in the Border Princedoms, I purchased an honourable discharge from the army and we retired to Nuln.'

'I see. And your wife... does she await your homecoming?'

'No, ' said Kaspar, shaking his head. 'Madeline died three years ago. She collapsed in our garden while tending to her roses. The priest of Morr said her heart simply gave out, that it had no more life to give. He said she would have felt nothing, which I suppose is a blessing of sorts.'

'Oh, I'm so sorry, Kaspar,' said Anastasia, sliding along the divan and taking his hands in hers. 'That was thoughtless of me. Please forgive me, I didn't mean for you to recall such a painful memory.'

Kaspar said, 'That's alright, Anastasia, you weren't to know.'

'Maybe not, but I should have been more thoughtful. I too know what it is to lose a loved one. Andrej, my husband, was murdered six years ago.'

Kaspar reached up and wiped a burgeoning tear from the corner of Anastasia's eye.

'I'm sorry. Was the murderer ever caught?'

'Pah! The city watch and the *Chekist* did nothing! Andrej, Ursun rest his soul, was in some ways a very sweet man, but in others very naïve. Unbeknownst to me, he had invested some of his money in some rather colourful ventures with a *lichnostyob* called Chekatilo.'

Kaspar had cause already to despise Chekatilo and mentally chalked up another.

'I know of Herr Chekatilo,' he said.

'Well, no one knows for sure, but I was told that Andrej was on his way home from a meeting of the Merchant's Guild when they say he was set upon by some footpads. They robbed him of his purse and beat him to death with an iron bar.'

Kaspar thought of the version of this tale Sofia had told him and gave thanks to whomever had spared Anastasia the truth of from where her husband had actually been returning.

'Of course, nothing was ever done about it, but I knew the truth of the matter. I couldn't prove anything of course, but I knew in my heart that the bastard had a hand in Andrej's death.'

Anastasia's eyes filled with tears and her hands flew to her face. 'I'm so sorry, I apologise for my language, but the thought of that piece of human filth still walking the streets makes me so angry.'

Kaspar leaned close and put his arm around her shoulders, unsure as to what he could say to comfort her. Instead he just pulled her close and let her rest her head on his shoulder, smudging kohl from her teary eyes onto his jerkin.

'Don't worry,' promised Kaspar. 'I won't let him hurt you ever again.'

IV

KASPAR PLACED A coin into the hand of the groom holding his mount, pleased to see that the man had taken the time to brush out the horse's silver mane and tail as well as clearing its hooves of stones. He gripped the saddle horn and swung onto his horse's back, casting a protective glance back at Anastasia's home.

They had taken comfort in each other's arms for some minutes before Anastasia had excused herself and Kaspar decided that he should leave her to her grief and withdraw. The scent of her hair and skin were still in his nostrils as he and the Knights Panther guided their horses back onto the Magnustrasse.

Dusk was drawing in and the sun slowly sinking below the line of buildings in the west. Kaspar saw six riders at the end of the street, silhouetted in the dying rays of the sun and his heart sank as he recognised the spiked coxcomb of Sasha Kajetan. He and five of his muscular, blade-pierced warriors cantered towards them, their leader's face cold and his violet eyes blazing in fury.

'Sigmar's blood, not this,' hissed Kaspar under his breath. The two Knights Panther pushed their horses in front of his, wrapping their mounts' reins around their left hands while gripping their swords threateningly.

Kaspar said, 'Ignore them. We'll try and go around them.'

Valdhaas nodded as the three of them walked their mounts to the edge of the street, keeping their own horses between Kajetan's men and the ambassador.

But the swordsman was having none of it, his warriors spreading out to block the street in a long line. Kaspar slid his hand beneath his cloak and eased back the flint on his pistol.

'What are you doing here?' snapped Kajetan.

Kaspar ignored him, keeping his eyes focussed on the end of the street and sliding his finger around the curved silver trigger. He saw other dark horsemen gathered there, but couldn't make out who they were in the glare of the setting sun. Kaspar and the knights kept moving forwards, but Kajetan and his warriors expertly walked their horses backwards. The swordsman kept his gaze locked with Kaspar.

'I asked you a question, Empire man.'

'And I ignored you.'

Kajetan's sabre was in his hand so quickly Kaspar barely saw it leave its sheath.

'When I ask a question, I expect an answer.'

Valdhaas and his comrade quickly drew their swords and, realising this situation could get out of hand with the slightest spark, Kaspar said, 'I was visiting a friend, if you must know. Madam Vilkova invited me to call upon her and I accepted her gracious invitation.'

Kajetan said, 'I told you to stay away from her.'

'I do as I please, Herr Kajetan, and do not count myself beholden to you in whom I may visit,' replied Kaspar. He saw Kajetan's eyes fasten on the shoulder of his tunic and quickly realised what the swordsman was looking at.

The smudge of kohl from Anastasia's eyelashes.

Kajetan's eyes widened and his jaw tensed.

Kaspar realised what was coming and whipped out his cocked pistol, aiming it square between Kajetan's eyes. The swordsman froze, a tight smile playing around the corner of his mouth.

'You going to shoot me, Empire man?'

'If I have to,' answered Kaspar.

'My men would kill you all for that,' assured Kajetan.

'Yes, they probably would, but you'd still be dead.'

'Is of no matter,' shrugged Kajetan and Kaspar was shocked to see he really meant it.

The frozen moment stretched for long seconds before a clipped voice from behind Kajetan and his men said, 'Ambassador von Velten, Sasha Kajetan. I would appreciate it if you would both lower your weapons. My men have all of you covered with muskets and I assure you, they are all excellent shots.'

Reluctantly, Kaspar broke eye contact with the swordsman, seeing Vladimir Pashenko and ten mounted *Chekist*, all with short-barrelled carbines aimed at them.

'Now, please,' said Pashenko. Ten musket flints cocked with a series of loud clicks.

Kaspar eased down the flintlock of his pistol and slowly holstered it as Kajetan reluctantly sheathed his curved cavalry sabre.

The leader of the *Chekist* walked his horse forward, interposing it between Kaspar and the swordsman.

'It seems you attract trouble, herr ambassador,' said Pashenko.

'Have you had your men following me?' asked Kaspar.

'Of course,' replied the *Chekist* as though it were the most natural thing in the world and Kaspar should not be surprised. 'You are a potential suspect in a murder investigation, why would I not have you watched? And it would appear that you should be glad I did. I am sure this little drama would have ended badly for you had we not intervened.'

Kajetan sneered and Pashenko turned his attention to him. 'Do not think that your reputation protects you from my attentions either, Sasha. Had I allowed you to kill this man, you would have danced a jig on the end of the hangman's rope in Geroyev Square before the week was out.'

'I'd like to have seen you try,' said Kajetan. He spat on the ground before Kaspar, before turning his horse and galloping eastwards, his men close behind.

Kaspar felt the tension drain from him as he watched Kajetan's retreating back, running a hand across his scalp and letting out a breath he hadn't realised he'd been holding.

'If I were you,' advised Pashenko, 'I would steer clear of that one. He is in love with Madam Vilkova and love makes a man do foolish things.'

Though he despised the *Chekist*, Kaspar forced himself to be gracious. 'Thank you, Herr Pashenko, for coming to our aid. This could have got out of hand very quickly.'

'Do not be so quick to thank me, herr ambassador. Part of me wanted to let Sasha kill you, but he is a hero to our people and it would be frowned upon if I were to have him hanged.'

Pashenko turned his horse and said, 'But you do not enjoy such a privileged status, herr ambassador, so I would be mindful of who you point that pistol at.'

CHAPTER FIVE

I

The first snow broke over Kislev as dusk drew in on Mittherbst, a day sacred to Ulric, the god of battle and winter. The priests of Ulric rejoiced as the first flakes drifted from the leaden sky, proclaiming that the favour of the wolf god was with them. Others were less certain: the snows and plummeting temperatures were certain to cause great misery and suffering amongst the thousands of refugees filling the city and dwelling in the sprawling canvas camps beyond its walls.

Daily, the stream of refugees from the north grew until the Tzarina was forced to order the gates of the city shut. Kislev simply could not contain any more people. With the practicality common to the Kislevite peasantry, many of the refugees simply decided to continue south towards the Empire, desperate to put as much distance between themselves and the threat of annihilation. Others formed whatever shelters their meagre belongings allowed them and camped around the walls beside the enclaves of Empire and Kislev soldiery.

As the numbers of people grew, the name of the monster that had driven them from their homes came to be heard more and more. Beginning as a low murmur on the fringes of fire-lit conversations and growing in the telling to assume terrifying proportions, the beast's name took on a power all of its own. Tales abounded of stanistas burned to the ground, women and children put to the sword. All manner of atrocities were attributed to the monster and as each day passed, more and more tales of this barbarian spread from campfire to campfire.

It was said that his warriors had cut open the bellies of every living soul in the Ramaejk stanista and impaled them on the sharpened pine logs of their defensive wall. Carrion birds had feasted on the still-living bodies for days and the macabre scene had been left as a monument to the triumph of the monster.

Who had first given voice to the monster's name was a mystery. Perhaps it was not a name at all, but a misheard battle cry, or a cursed talisman to be passed on by those he spared that they might carry the terror of his name and deeds southwards.

However it came to be spoken, the name of Aelfric Cyenwulf, high chieftain of the northern tribes and favoured lieutenant of the dread Archaon himself, had come to Kislev. War-chiefs of the Kurgan were nothing new and the oldest men and women of the steppe knew of many bloodthirsty barbarian leaders who had come and gone. They knew that northern tribes had raided their land before, but even they understood that this time was different.

This time the tribes did not come for plunder, this time they came to destroy.

II

KASPAR WATCHED THE snow falling from the darkening sky with a mixture of apprehension and relief on the sawtoothed ramparts of the city walls. The snows would slow an army and would, in all likelihood, force it to retreat to its winter quarters or face destruction as its warriors starved and froze to death.

Though the snowfall was light, Kaspar knew that the achingly cold Kislevite winter could be little more than a couple of weeks away at best. It would grip the nation in its frozen embrace and bury the landscape in an endless blanket of snow. The Kislevites called this time 'Raspotitsa', which meant roadlessness, and travel became virtually impossible as every trail and road was hidden beneath the snows.

He turned from the walls and the twisting columns of smoke caught in the harsh winds that blew off the northern oblast. Hundreds of small fires burned from the campsites before the walls as people huddled around them for warmth. The most vulnerable people were already dying, the elderly and the newborn unable to survive the bitter cold and lack of food. The soldiers camped nearby fared little better, bereft of supplies and news from home, their morale was virtually non-existent.

Kaspar knew that it was the simple things in life that kept a soldier well motivated and in high spirits. A rousing speech from a leader might put a fire in his heart, but a warm meal and a drop of alcohol would be far more appreciated. So far, the soldiers of the Empire had neither, though Kaspar was about to remedy that.

He watched as a convoy of fifteen long riverboats plied their stately passage along the Urskoy, sliding through the dark waters towards the portcullis of the western river gate. Boatmen lowered sails on the lead boat as it was swallowed by the shadow of the high walls. Kaspar saw the vessel's name painted on her hull, just above the waterline and followed its progress as it emerged from the water gate and made its way upriver to the docks.

Pavel Korovic and Kurt Bremen climbed the steps to join him on the ramparts.

'Is that them?' asked Bremen.

Kaspar nodded. 'Aye, the lead boat is *Scheerlagen's Maiden*, that's them. Are your men ready?'

'We are,' promised Bremen.

'Then let's go,' said Kaspar.

III

THEY FOLLOWED THE riverboats as they made their way towards the main docks of the city. Kaspar was no sailor, having learned to loathe any form of sea travel as a young man, but even he could tell every boat was running dangerously overfull, the slow waters of the river close to spilling over their gunwales. Several times they lost sight of the convoy as they were forced into frustrating detours to avoid streets choked with people, but it was always easy to find again as the river was empty of traffic, most captains already having taken their boats south to join the Talabec and carry onwards to Altdorf or Nuln.

Passers-by gave them curious looks, a man of obvious quality riding with a bearded Kislevite on a struggling, sway-backed dray horse and accompanied by a group of sixteen knights in gleaming plate armour. The crew of the riverboats did not long remain oblivious to their presence either, shouting over to them with loud ahoys.

Kaspar and the knights ignored them, but Pavel shouted over.

'What news from south?'

'Wolfenburg is no more,' shouted back a sailor.

'A great storm destroyed it,' shouted another. 'Dark magicks they say!'

Kaspar let Pavel converse with the men on the boats, too focussed on the task at hand to bother swapping banter with men he might soon have to confront. He had been waiting for the convoy led by *Scheerlagen's Maiden* since receiving letters from Altdorf four days ago.

Emblazoned with the crest of the Second House of Wilhelm and that of the Imperial Commissariat, the letters demanded to know what actions had been taken to prevent further depredations on their wares. Kaspar had no idea what the letters referred to until he spent a gruelling day examining the records kept by the former ambassador. Taken together, he now knew why the Empire regiments in Kislev were starving and why the grain houses of the city were under so much strain. It also went some way to explaining why the ruler of Kislev had met his requests for an audience thus far with nothing but bureaucratic brick walls and polite rebuffs.

Supplies were, it seemed, arriving in Kislev, they just weren't getting to their intended recipients. For the last twelve months, a merchant from Hochland named Matthias Gerhard had been tasked by the Imperial Commissariat with the job of distributing food and weapons as well as the many and varied sundries required by a nation and her allies in time of war. The Emperor had sent a fortune in supplies to Kislev but very little had ever reached those who desperately needed them.

The letters spoke of frequent thefts from the warehouses of Matthias Gerhard, and though his replies spoke of increased watchfulness, it seemed that nothing could prevent the haemorrhaging of supplies from his warehouses. Gerhard blamed the shiftless Kislevites, and to those in Altdorf it must have seemed as though the barbarous people of their northern neighbour were, through their own laziness and stupidity, cursing themselves to starvation and defeat. But here in the city, where it was clear that no one had enough to survive, it was obvious that the supplies were being stolen, just not by footpads.

Kaspar's fury at Teugenheim grew the more he read of the man's journal. The former ambassador must have known that desperately needed supplies from the Empire were being stolen by those entrusted with their distribution, yet had done nothing to prevent it.

Well, this ambassador would have something to say about that.

IV

THE SCHEERLAGEN'S MAIDEN was in the process of being unloaded by the time they reached the quayside. A few other boats had moored, their crews tying thick ropes to iron bollards while others waited their turn at the quay. The sense of relief in the crew of *Scheerlagen's Maiden* was obvious now that they had finally arrived at their destination, and her captain didn't even seem to mind the exorbitant quayage levied on his ship.

Thick-cloaked Kislevite stevedores hauled scores of crates, barrels and heavy sacks on sturdy pulley mechanisms from the ship's hold and onto the cobbled quay where a number of wide-bodied wagons awaited them. A burly man with a large, bushy beard joked with the ship's captain, who looked like he simply wanted to get his vessels unloaded and depart.

'Spread out,' said Kaspar. 'Don't let any of the wagons leave.'

Bremen nodded and jabbed his mailed fist at the three routes leading from the quayside. The knights walked their horses towards them, forming a line of steel and blocking any passage with their heavy horses. With their visors lowered, they were a fearsome sight and though not one had a weapon drawn, the threat was obvious.

The crews and the struggling stevedores finally noticed their presence and cast bemused looks about the docks as Kaspar, Bremen and Pavel rode up to them. A few of the stevedores surreptitiously reached for knives or cudgels, but the scrape of sixteen wickedly sharp cavalry blades being drawn convinced them not to reach any further. The knights were horribly outnumbered, but even these thugs knew they could not defeat heavily armoured and well-trained knights.

The leader of the Knights Panther and Pavel dismounted while Kaspar retained the advantage of height.

'Those supplies,' he said to the captain, 'what are they?'

'What business is it of yours, fellow?' said the man.

'I am the ambassador of the Emperor Karl-Franz and I will ask the questions.'

Seeing the knights and hearing Kaspar's southern accent, the captain nodded.

'Very well, we're bringing in grain, salt, sword blades, axe heads and wheat. All signed, sealed and delivered. What's your problem?'

Kaspar ignored the question and addressed the Kislevite quaymaster next. 'And where do you take this cargo once it's been unloaded?'

The man didn't answer until Pavel barked Kaspar's question in his native tongue. His gaze switching between the two men, the quaymaster sneered and snarled his reply. Kaspar didn't understand his words, but caught the name Gerhard in the torrent of Kislevite.

'He say supplies for Gerhard's warehouse,' translated Pavel.

'Good,' said Kaspar. 'Tell them to finish emptying the boats and load the wagons.'

'Then what?' said Pavel.

'Then we wait for Herr Gerhard,' said Kaspar.

V

VALERY SHEWCHUK PULLED his wife and two daughters closer, feeling their ribs through the thin blanket that was all that separated them from the bitterly cold night. Snow fell in a drifting rain, but they had a good spot here in one of the many cobbled alleyways of the city, a recessed stairway that led up to a door which had long since been bricked up. Protected from the worst of the thieving winds and snow that stole the heat from your body, it was as close to shelter as he could find for his family. He brushed a strand of hair from his Nicolje's face, wishing she could have provided him with sons.

Cursed with aged parents and no sons to send off to war, he had struggled to find enough food to feed his extended family and even though the people of his stanista had tried to help, they could not neglect their own families for the sake of another.

Three weeks ago, his parents had left the stanista during the night and trudged out into the windswept oblast with no blankets and no food. No one had seen them leave and their frozen bodies had been discovered less than half a league from the gates of the stanista, lying embracing one another in the middle of the road.

Valery had wept for them, appreciating their sacrifice, but secretly relieved that he would no longer have to provide for them. As news of yet more stanistas and larger settlements being attacked reached the stanista's ataman, Valery made the decision to leave their izba and take his family to the capital.

He had laden his wagon with their meagre possessions and left, tearfully embracing his friends and neighbours. It had been a hard ride south and they had lost their youngest daughter on the journey, the infant succumbing to a fever that his Nicolje's herbal remedies could not break. They had buried her on the steppe and continued south.

Upon reaching the capital, he had sold his wagon and pony for a pittance and tried desperately to find some kind of work and lodgings for his family. None were available and they had been forced into this filthy alleyway, surviving on what he could steal or they could purchase with the few copper coins left to them.

Three times he had had to fight away thieves and other miscreants who sought to oust them from their shelter, and though he was desperately hungry and exhausted, Valery Shewchuk was a big man and not easy to put down.

He heard a soft padding on the snow from further up the alleyway and held his breath. Too soft for a booted foot, it might be an animal, a dog or cat or rat and the thought of fresh meat brought saliva to his mouth.

Valery slid his bone-handled knife, his one possession he had refused to sell, from its hide sheath and eased himself from the blanket. As thin as it was, he still felt the cold slice through him. His wife stirred from troubled dreams and groggily opened her eyes.

'Valery?'

'Hush, Nicolje,' he whispered. 'Perhaps food.'

He stood and slid himself up the wall, descending the steps and gripping his knife tightly. He hoped the noise he had heard was a dog. There was good eating on a dog.

He couldn't hear the sound any more and decided he would risk a glance around the edge of the recess to catch sight of his prey.

Valery eased his head around the stonework and his jaw fell open as he saw a naked man crouched in the shadows of the snowy alleyway. The man was obviously a madman, abroad in weather like this without furs or a cloak and, by Ursun, Valery was not about to have this lunatic dislodge them from their shelter.

The man gently rocked and muttered to himself, one hand tucked between his legs as he scraped at the flesh of his arms with ragged fingernails. The snow melted where droplets of blood landed.

'Ho there,' said Valery, raising his knife. 'Find yourself somewhere else to bed for the night.'

The man ignored him, muttering, 'No, no, no. They're just dreams… you are *not* me…'

Valery took a nervous step into the alleyway, keeping the tip of his knife pointed towards the crouched figure.

The man's head snapped up and Valery saw that he was wearing an ill-fitting mask of what appeared to be greyish leather, crudely stitched and curling at the edges. Eyes that glittered with lunacy stared through the mask at him.

The madman grinned saying, 'Wrong. I am the trueself,' and leapt forwards, a glittering knife appearing in his hand. The blade slashed down and Valery dropped, his lifeblood spraying from the severed artery in his thigh. He twisted as he fell and cracked his head on the ground.

'By Tor, leave my family alone!' he cried. 'I love them so much, I don't care that I have no sons. I love them too much to leave them. Please…'

He heard screams and a hissing noise, like meat on a skillet, from the recess of the steps, but couldn't see what was happening. He wept bitter tears, crawling weakly through the stained snow to reach his family.

The screams stopped.

A waterfall of blood spilled down the steps, pooling in the snow at their base.

The man who had murdered his family stepped into the alleyway, his face, chest and belly caked with blood that gleamed black in the moonlight. His eyes were alight, his chest heaving with excitement as the thrill of the kill pulsed through his veins.

Valery tried to reach for him as he felt his vision greying.

'No,' said the man, gently pushing him onto his back and leaning over him.

His bloody jaws opened wide.

The madman vomited a froth of gristly blood over his chest and Valery screamed in agony as the viscous liquid hissed and ate the flesh from his bones.

He died as he felt a hand push deep inside the ruin of his chest.

* * *

VI

SORKA COULD HEAR screaming from somewhere, but ignored it. These days it was stranger when you didn't hear someone suffering. He made his way swiftly down the busy prospekt, still teeming with people despite the darkness and cold. He supposed some people had nowhere to go and feared lying down in the snow lest they not wake up again.

He clutched the metal box tightly within his jerkin, afraid to let it out of his sight, but terrified of holding it too close. Perhaps six inches square, the box was far heavier than something that size had any right to be, and though he had the key to the blackened padlock, the thought of opening the box both horrified and nauseated him. Ever since Chekatilo had given him the box to deliver, he had felt distinctly unwell.

He had been working for the leader of Kislev's criminal empire for nearly six months, spending most of that time enforcing his boss's will through a mixture of beatings, arson and intimidation. He was a big, solid man with little imagination and it thrilled him that his master had entrusted him with a mission of such obvious importance.

'Sorka,' Chekatilo had said, 'this is of great value to me. It must be delivered at midnight precisely at the end of Lime Alley, you know the place?'

Sorka had nodded, having dumped at least three corpses there. 'I won't let you down,' he had promised. He had been told to go to the basement and collect the metal box he now carried and had left immediately. His skin itched and his stomach churned with sickness. Perhaps the fish he had eaten earlier had been off.

He turned from the Goromadny Prospekt and wound his way through the twisting streets, checking his back trail to make sure he wasn't being followed. The fresh snows made it difficult to be sure and the busyness of the streets didn't help much either, but he couldn't see anyone behind him.

At last he came to the entrance of Lime Alley and quickly checked behind him one last time. Satisfied that there was no one nearby, he ghosted into the alley, making his way carefully along its length. Sorka could see that someone had already dumped a body here tonight. The cold had deadened the smell and the dogs had not found it yet, but they would soon enough.

From a pool of shadow ahead a voice called out.

'Do you have it?'

Sorka jumped, startled by the voice. He struggled to remember what he had been ordered to say.

'Yes, if you have the money.'

'I have it,' said the man. 'Put the box down and back away from it.'

That wasn't how this was supposed to happen and Sorka struggled to think of what to say. 'Show me the money and then I'll do it.'

'No.'

Unused to such flat refusals to cooperate, Sorka wasn't sure what to do next. He worked for Chekatilo, therefore when he gave orders they were obeyed quickly. He decided to play along with this fool and wrapped a hand round the hilt of his dagger, sure that he could deal with him if he tried to pull something funny. There was, after all, only one way out of this alley, and that meant going through him.

Not an easy task for anyone, he knew.

'Very well,' he said removing the box from below his jerkin and placing it on the ground. He fished the key from around his neck and dropped it next to the box.

The man moved from the shadows, his face obscured by a hooded cloak and knelt by the box, swiftly unlocking it. Gripping a dark amulet around his neck, he lifted the lid a fraction.

A soft green glow emanated from the box, casting a spectral light over the man and throwing his shadow onto the wall behind him.

To Sorka it looked as though the shadow writhed with a life of its own, no longer mimicking the man it belonged to.

He frowned and blinked to clear his head of the bizarre image, but the mischievous shadow continued in its dance, the darkness of its head swelling as twin horns formed at its brow.

He opened his mouth to comment on this when the kneeling man shot the top of his head off with a wheel-lock pistol.

VII

THE PISTOL SHOT echoed from the mouth of the alleyway and minutes later the dark cloaked man carefully eased his head around the corner. The moon slid from behind the clouds, casting its monochrome light onto the snow-covered street and illuminating his face.

He checked both ways before stepping confidently into the street and making his way back to the centre of the city.

From the opposite side of the street, two men swathed in furs watched him go.

'He shot Sorka,' said the smaller of the two men.

Vassily Chekatilo nodded, rubbing a hand over his chin and tugging at the ends of his moustache. 'Yes, Rejak, I would have done the same thing.'

'We should stop him!' protested Rejak. 'He's trying to cheat you.'

Chekatilo shook his head. 'No, leave him. I am happy to be rid of that damned box and wish I had never agreed to obtain it. And anyway, I think it may profit us more in the long run knowing who we actually obtained it for.'

'But what about Sorka?'

'I will shed no tears over Sorka,' said Chekatilo. 'He followed orders well enough, but there are plenty more like him and he will be no great loss to my organisation.'

'Should we see if he's dead?'

'No, Rejak, leave him. The dogs have to eat too.'

Rejak shrugged. He nodded in the direction of the man making off with the metal box and said, 'What does someone like him want with something that dangerous?'

'What indeed?' agreed Chekatilo, wondering why Pjotr Losov, chief advisor to the Tzarina of Kislev, would want a box containing a fist-sized chunk of warpstone.

* * *

VIII

KASPAR WAS IMPRESSED at how little time it took Matthias Gerhard to come looking for the supplies from the riverboats when they failed to arrive at his warehouses. Once the stevedores had finished unloading the boats, Kaspar had sent them on their way and every one of them had quickly vanished into the night. He ordered the riverboat crews to return to the Empire and, once they had left, the docks became eerily quiet, the water slapping against the stonework of the quayside the only sound save for the occasional scream and a solitary pistol shot.

They had waited at the quayside for a little over two hours before the clatter of carriage wheels and horses' hooves drew close.

The Knights Panther parted as a red and gold troika rattled across the cobbles to the quayside. Of Kislevite origin, the troika was pulled by three horses harnessed abreast of each other, and even in the dim moonlight Kaspar could see it was one of expensive design and elaborate workmanship. It was not hard to guess where the money appropriated by Matthias Gerhard had gone. Six men armoured in heavy hauberks of thick mail links and carrying long spears sat atop the carriage. As it drew to a halt, the Knights Panther gathered in a ring of steel around the troika, cutting off any escape.

The six guards shot each other hurried glances before reluctantly clambering down.

Kaspar relished their obvious discomfort. By now Matthias Gerhard would know that his missing supplies were not the result of some underling's incompetence and Kaspar smiled mirthlessly as the carriage door opened and a tall man of obvious means stepped onto the quay. He wore a gold headband over his shoulder-length blond hair, an expensive crimson doublet slashed with yellow silk and a furred dolman laced with silver threads. Sovereign rings decorated each finger and thick golden chains of office hung around his neck, proving that Matthias Gerhard had wealth, if not taste.

The man's unease was clear and Kaspar decided to attack and put him off balance further before he could rally a defence. He dismounted from his horse and strode towards the merchant.

'Matthias Gerhard, you are a thieving bastard and I should hand you over to the *Chekist* right now for what you've done.'

Despite Kaspar's venomous tone, Gerhard recovered quickly. He was an influential man in a city that did not suffer fools gladly, and no one became as rich as he had without the capacity to keep his wits about him.

'Am I to assume that you are Ambassador von Velten and these are your knights?' he asked.

'You would be correct in that assumption.'

'Then might I enquire as to why you have detained the Emperor's supplies here?' said Gerhard. 'They should be on their way to my warehouses now. There are many in this city who would gladly take the chance to appropriate these goods for their own ends, as I am sure you know.'

'Oh, yes, I know sure enough,' snapped Kaspar. 'Teugenheim's journal and letters I received from Altdorf have told me all I need to know about those kinds of people.'

'Then you will have no objection to my summoning men to have them taken to a place of safe storage,' continued Gerhard smoothly.

'Don't you understand, Gerhard?' said Kaspar, brandishing the letter from the Imperial Commissariat. 'It's over. I know what you've been up to and I'll see you swing from the end of a rope for what you've done.'

'Really?' replied Gerhard. 'What do you think you know?'

'That you've been reporting these supplies as stolen and then selling them on. Tell me how else you can account for the sheer volume of supplies that have gone "missing"?'

'Herr ambassador,' said Gerhard patiently. 'I assure you, the goods the Emperor has sent north are being thieved by parties other than myself. I have all the proper paperwork from the city watch to prove it.'

'I don't need to prove it, I know what you've been doing. I've seen it a hundred times before in the army. Crooked quartermasters keeping back supplies and selling them on to the highest bidder. You're nothing but a common thief!'

'Are you trying to make me angry, ambassador?'

'Aye,' admitted Kaspar, feeling his own temper fray.

'Then you have been a soldier too long, herr ambassador. I am a civilised man, and unlike you, I have learned to control my anger and settle my differences without resorting to violence. Perhaps you should too.'

Kaspar realised that he would get nowhere with Gerhard like this, and grabbed the merchant's tunic, dragging him over to the water's edge. Gerhard's guards stepped forward, but the Knights Panther closed in and prevented them from taking action.

'Really, ambassador!' spluttered Gerhard. 'This is outrageous!'

'I tend to agree with you there, Matthias,' said Kaspar, finally reaching the steps that led down to the dark, icy waters of the Urskoy.

'Herr ambassador!' pleaded Gerhard as he realised what Kaspar intended. 'There is really no need for this.'

'Ah, well, that's where our opinions differ then,' said Kaspar and pushed the merchant from the quayside.

Matthias Gerhard splashed into the water, breaking the surface seconds later and thrashing the river white in his panic. He coughed and screamed, his cries for help gurgling as he swallowed water. The merchant desperately trod water, but his heavy clothes and thick chains conspired to drag him down and his head disappeared beneath the surface of the water again. A torrent of bubbles churned the water as the merchant's head broke through once more.

'Please!' he yelled, finally grasping hold of the stone steps. He wheezed breathlessly, gratefully sucking air into his searing lungs until Kaspar trod on his fingers with the wooden heel of his riding boots. The merchant wailed and slid back under the water.

'Get me one of his guards' spears,' he called up to the quay. He could see Kurt Bremen silhouetted against the brightness of the moon, sensing the knight's displeasure, but he was past caring. Getting the job done was all that mattered now and if he had to resort to violence, well that was too bad.

If Gerhard believed he was a thuggish soldier, then he would behave like one.

'Here,' said Bremen icily.

'Thank you, Kurt,' said the ambassador as Gerhard thrashed his way to the surface once more. Kaspar saw that the merchant was all but spent and held the spear out to him, tantalisingly just out his reach.

The man struggled to grab the wooden shaft of the spear, but each time his fingers brushed it, Kaspar lifted it away.

'Are you ready to talk without feeding me dung now, Matthias?' asked Kaspar.

'Yes!' screamed the merchant, and Kaspar let him grab the spear shaft.

He hauled him close to the steps and gestured for his knights to come and lift the sodden man from the water.

Gerhard rolled onto his side and puked dirty water, his face blue from the freezing temperature of the Urskoy. He wept and as Kaspar knelt beside the gasping merchant, he could smell that Gerhard had soiled himself in terror.

He brushed wet hair from the man's face and said, 'Now that I have your undivided attention, I think we are ready to talk. You have been selling on the Emperor's supplies have you not?'

Gerhard coughed, but nodded slowly.

'Good,' continued Kaspar. 'Now we are getting somewhere. That's over now. Everything you still have and all that arrives from the Empire from now on is going to get to those who desperately need it. Do you understand me?'

'Yes, yes, I do.'

'Now, while you deserve to be thrown in the deepest, darkest cell for what you've done, I still need you to coordinate the distribution of the supplies to the soldiery and people of this city. You will work with my aide, Stefan, and trust me when I say that he *will* know if you fall back on your bad old ways.'

Kaspar stood, massaging his stiff knee and climbed the steps to the quay.

Kurt Bremen awaited him and said quietly, 'Ambassador, may I speak freely?'

'Of course, Kurt.'

'Ambassador, I am uncomfortable with these... brutal methods you seem to favour. Is it really fitting for an emissary of the Emperor to be seen behaving in such a manner.'

Kaspar nodded. 'I understand your objections, Kurt, really I do. It gives me no pleasure to have to resort to such methods, but sometimes a show of force is necessary to get results from those who believe themselves above notions of honesty and duty.'

The knight looked unconvinced and said, 'My knights and I are the instrument by which your will is carried out, Ambassador von Velten, but we must enforce that will in accordance with the vows of our order's code of honour. That is our purpose here and while we are bound to your cause, we cannot perform our duties properly if you insist on behaving like this. You must allow us to do our job without violating our code of honour.'

'Of course, Kurt, but perhaps Gerhard was right,' said Kaspar. 'Perhaps I have been a soldier too long for an ambassadorial position, but such is my lot and this is the only way I know to carry out my duty to the Emperor.'

Bremen nodded curtly, though Kaspar could tell that the knight did not accept what he had just said.

'What do you want done with Gerhard?' asked Bremen, changing the subject.

'Take him back to his lodgings and get him cleaned up. I want some of your men to keep watch on him and make sure he doesn't try to leave the city. I'll send Stefan over in the morning to see what's left of the supplies Gerhard stole so we can begin getting them to our men.'

Bremen turned away and began issuing orders to his men as Kaspar returned to his horse, suddenly feeling the weight of every one of his fifty-four years.

CHAPTER SIX

I

THE SMELL OF cooking meat drifted through the campsite of the Wissenland arquebusiers. Soldiers chewed on fresh baked bread and cheese and washed it down with mugs of Nordland ale. Laughter and the excited babble of conversation surrounded every cookfire and the rekindled spirit evident in the Empire soldiers was a joy to behold, thought Kaspar.

This same scene had been repeated several times over the last five days as Kaspar, Anastasia and wagons driven by the embassy soldiers had delivered much needed supplies to the weary and hungry soldiers of the city. After inventorying Gerhard's warehouses, Stefan had discovered a veritable cornucopia of vital goods and had, together with the disgraced merchant, begun the task of getting them to those who so desperately needed them. Kaspar had asked Sofia to keep a watchful eye on the merchant as well, as he did not want the man to catch a fever from his long immersion in the frozen waters of the Urskoy. No, Gerhard would not escape his punishment *that* easily.

He and Anastasia sat atop the buckboard of an empty wagon, winding their way through the thousands who camped outside the walls, making their way back to the city after yet another trip from the warehouses of Matthias Gerhard. The afternoon's light was deepening to the purple of dusk and Kaspar had no wish to be outside any longer than necessary as the temperature began to drop rapidly. Four mounted Knights Panther rode alongside them, pennons snapping from their silver lance tips in the stiff afternoon breeze and the smiles and the blessings from the crowds of refugees were a refreshing change to the guarded hostility he had encountered in Kislev thus far.

'This is incredible, Kaspar, the difference this has made,' said Anastasia, wrapped tightly in a white cloak edged in snow leopard fur. Her cheeks were red with the cold, but her eyes sparkled as she spoke.

'I know,' smiled Kaspar, pleased at the wholesale change in the demeanour of the soldiers camped around Kislev.

'Where did all this come from?' asked Anastasia.

'A thieving swine from Hochland named Matthias Gerhard,' replied Kaspar. 'He'd been hoarding it all for himself and his warehouses were full to bursting with all manner of stolen goods: weapons, tarpaulins, boots, uniforms, grain, salt beef, black powder, shot, billhooks, pioneer tools and even three cannons from the Imperial Gunnery school.'

'And he had no intention of sharing any of it?'

'No, Anastasia, not one shred of it. Not without payment anyway.'

'I told you already, call me Ana. All my friends do.'

'Very well,' chuckled Kaspar. 'I cannot refuse the word of a lady.'

'Good,' said Anastasia with mock sternness. 'Make sure you remember that, Kaspar von Velten. As to Herr Gerhard, I hope you'll be making sure he'll be punished.'

'Oh yes,' assured Kaspar. 'I'm no quartermaster, and if I didn't need him to help co-ordinating the logistics of this operation I'd have left him in the river with the rest of the scum.'

Anastasia leaned into him as the wagon made its way up the *Gora Geroyev*, and Kaspar enjoyed the feeling of her body next to his. He had been surprised to receive the letter from Anastasia offering to help in whatever way she could in delivering the supplies to the soldiers and refugees until he remembered

Sofia telling him of her patronage of various almshouses and hospices. Her kindness to those less fortunate that herself was renowned throughout Kislev and, truth be told, Kaspar was not sorry to renew his acquaintance with her again. His run-in with Sasha Kajetan notwithstanding, he was determined to see her again, and this just gave him a convenient excuse. The last two days they had spent together helping to distribute food had been just the tonic he had needed to coax him from his growing frustrations.

'But once this war is over, I'll see him swing from the gallows pole in the Königplatz, have no fear of that.'

'What makes a man turn his back on his country and people to do such a thing?' wondered Anastasia.

Kaspar shook his head. 'I don't know, Ana, I really don't. And to be honest, I don't want to know.'

'Well he deserves the very worst punishment that can be meted out for his crimes. I know we are supposed to be forgiving, and Shallya teaches us to be merciful, but Gerhard might have doomed us all.'

Kaspar did not reply immediately, intently watching a troop of horsemen training on the snowy ground further out on the steppe at the base of the hill. Some sixty or so men on lithe, long-limbed horses circled a series of stakes hammered into a square pattern that roughly equated the width and breadth of a massed unit of ranked up soldiers. Head-sized sandbags were tied to each stake and as Kaspar watched, the horsemen circled and darted in close, loosing deadly volleys of red-fletched arrows into their targets.

Each volley was fired with lethal accuracy, thudding through the sandbags or hammering into the wooden stakes just below them. Any men being attacked by these warriors would be suffering terribly under such a punishing barrage, losing dozens of men with each volley. Each warrior fired a short horned bow of laminated strips of seasoned wood whose power belied its size, while guiding their horses with their knees. Kaspar was amazed at the level of control each warrior exercised over their mounts, the entire troop moving as though with a single will.

At the head of the horse archers, a warrior in a baggy white shirt and scarlet cavalry britches fired with incredible speed and accuracy, his horse obeying his commands as though it were an extension of his own flesh, like the beasts of the dark forest that were rumoured to be part man, part horse. His long topknot trailed behind him and he whooped with a savage glee as he sent shaft after shaft through the sandbag 'heads'. Twin curved swords were sheathed at his side and Kaspar easily recognised the warrior, Sasha Kajetan.

'He truly is a magnificent warrior,' said Kaspar.

'Sasha? Yes, he is rather formidable, isn't he? Sweet too, in his own way.'

'Sweet?' said Kaspar, raising an eyebrow. 'Not a word I'd associate with him.'

'Oh, yes…' said Anastasia. 'I heard about that unfortunate altercation outside my home, but you really mustn't trouble yourself over that. While he does have a hopeless infatuation with me, he wouldn't dare hurt you.'

'No? What makes you so sure?' asked Kaspar.

'Because he knows it would displease me, and unfortunately, everything Sasha does he does to please me.'

'I wouldn't be too sure, Ana. When I looked into his eyes, all I saw was the desire to hurt me... or perhaps *be* hurt. Trust me, it is more than infatuation he harbours for you, Ana.'

'Well, that's his own fault. I've told him on several occasions that I don't think of him in that way. Besides, there are others more deserving of my affections, I think.'

Kaspar held the reins loosely in his left hand and felt Anastasia thread her arm through his and hold his wrist. He smiled to himself as he guided the wagon along the rutted roadway that led through the gates of Kislev, enjoying the comfortable silence as Anastasia slid closer to him on the buckboard.

Seeing the white-clad form of Anastasia next to him, the crowds parted before the wagon – her well-known reputation as a friend to the poor ensuring their quick passage along the busy prospekt. There was still a tension on the streets, Kaspar saw, as well there might be. He had heard that the Butcherman had struck again, slaughtering an entire family as they slept within a sheltered alleyway not far from the docks.

The wagon soon ate up the distance between the city gates and the embassy and barely a quarter of an hour had passed before Kaspar tugged on the reins and drove the wagon down the alleyway alongside Ulric's temple.

As he passed the iron railings and circled the fountain at the centre of the courtyard, he reflected that the tradesmen he had employed had done a fine job in restoring the embassy. The graffiti had been washed away and skilled carpenters had fitted new windows and a sturdy new door.

'Well, this certainly looks like an improvement,' noted Anastasia.

'Aye,' agreed Kaspar, sourly. 'So it should be, it's cost me enough, and not a copper pfennig from Altdorf.'

Even the fountain had been scrubbed, the hidden lustre of the bronze shining through in the cherubic angel's face as clear water gurgled from its cup. He stepped down from the buckboard and swiftly made his way around to the other side, offering his hand to Anastasia.

She slid over to the side and reached down, ignoring his proffered hand and reaching out to steady herself on his shoulders. She nimbly hopped down to the cobbles and smiled up at him.

'Shall we?' she said, entwining her arm in his once more.

Seeing the ambassador approach, a pair of guards marched from the embassy towards the gates.

Kaspar noticed a bundle of red cloth sitting before the gates, obscured from the inside by a decorative motif plate at the gate's base. As the guards reached the gate, he knelt beside the bundle and prodded it with his gloved hand.

A terrible smell wafted from the bundle as he began unwrapping it.

As the cloth unwrapped like a long scarf, he recognised it as a crimson sash normally worn by Kislevite boyarins. The stench worsened the more he unwrapped the bundle, but he could not stop now.

A perverse fascination compelled him to complete the task.

At last the contents of the sash lay revealed on the cobbles.

He heard Anastasia scream.

And looked down at a collection of four human hearts.

II

THE LUBJANKO HOSPITAL had been constructed over two hundred years ago against the eastern wall of the city by Tzar Alexis after the Great War against Chaos. Too many men had died needlessly of their wounds following the battles and Alexis had been determined that Kislev would boast the finest facility for the treatment of injuries in all the Old World.

Upon its completion, the priestesses of Shallya had blessed its walls and, for a time, the Lubjanko had indeed served to house those wounded and traumatised by the horrors of war. But before long it had become a dumping ground for the sick, the deranged and the crippled. Entire floors were dedicated to the process of dying, where those too badly injured to live, whether struck down by axe or age, were left to rot away the last miserable hours of their lives.

Rightly it is said that misery loves company and the Lubjanko became a magnet for all manner of the dispossessed. Orphans, homeless, the diseased and the mad came to rest within its walls, and its black stone façade and high, spike-topped walls served as a grim reminder of the fate of those who had fallen between the cracks. Mothers would quiet unruly children by promising to cast them within its brooding, nightmare walls and injured soldiers would pray to the gods to be spared the Lubjanko.

Nightly would the wails of the damned echo from its narrow, barred windows and death stalked its halls like a predator, claiming its nightly toll that would then be taken to the pyres.

Two men made their way along a cold stone corridor, its length dimly illuminated by a dripping torch carried by a limping man whose bulk almost filled the width of the passage. He coughed and spat a phlegmy wad onto the floor, the sound swallowed by the weeping and howling that echoed from the cells to either side of them.

Following behind at a careful distance, Pjotr Losov walked gingerly along the centre of the passageway, his hooded cloak dragging on the dirty flagstones. A trio of rats scurried past him and he chuckled to himself, watching as they sniffed around the first man's wad of spittle.

Grimy, wasted hands reached from between the bars of the cell doors, piteous moans, curses and bodily fluids following close behind. The limping man smashed a bronze-tipped cudgel against those cell doors whose inhabitants thrashed and screamed the loudest.

'Be silent, you filth!' he yelled.

'They are loud tonight, Dimitrji,' observed Losov.

'That they are,' snarled the other man, hammering his cudgel against the bars of another cell. 'It always gets like this as winter comes. I think they sense the darkness and what it hides.'

'Unusually poetic for you, Dimitrji,' said Losov.

Dimitrji shrugged. 'These are unusual times, my friend, but not to worry, I have a clutch of pretties that I think you'll like. Young. Unsullied.' He licked his lips as he spoke.

Losov loathed this sad excuse for a human being. He had no love for many of his fellow species, but Dimitrji was a particularly loathsome example of all that was diseased about humanity. How he longed to draw his wheel-lock, crafted by the master gunsmith Chazate of the eastern kingdoms, and blow Dimitrji's brains out. These walls had seen many horrors in their time, what would one more matter?

He had never told Dimitrji his true name; the gaoler-warden of the Lubjanko believed he was a filth-monger who preferred his sexual conquests to be younger and more easily dominated than those of the common man. The thought that Dimitrji believed this so readily made him sick to his stomach – that one as initiated as he could belong to such a perverted fraternity.

But it was a convenient fiction to maintain, for the truth was far worse.

He had to physically restrain himself from reaching for his pistol when Dimitrji reached a locked door at the end of the passageway and fished a jangling set of keys from beneath his voluminous robes. The lock clicked open and Dimitrji pushed open the door, standing aside to let Losov enter and handing him the torch as he passed.

Unlike every other cell in the Lubjanko, this one was clean and did not stink of shit, death and desperation. Four small cot-beds lined the walls and on each one sat a young child, two boys and two girls. None were older than five or six years.

They looked up nervously as Losov entered and tried to smile at him as they had been told to. They were frightened, but looked at him hopefully, perhaps seeing in him the chance of escape from this dank hellhole.

Losov felt the blood thunder in his veins as he looked at the children.

Dimitrji had been right. They were all unsullied and were perfect.

They had to be innocents. She would know if they were not.

Only the blood of innocents would be good enough.

III

KASPAR HAD BELIEVED his mood could not have worsened after having found the macabre offering left outside the embassy gates.

He could not have been more wrong; this was just the beginning of one of the worst nights of his life. After calming Anastasia down, they had made their way within the embassy to find Pavel awaiting them in the downstairs hallway.

The big Kislevite looked pensive as he said, 'Riders from Altdorf upstairs with letters for you. Important ones, I think.'

'What makes you say that?'

'Heavily armed. Tough men. Ridden hard to get here.'

'I see,' said Kaspar, gingerly passing the gory bundle to Pavel. 'Here, hold this.'

Pavel nodded and peeled back a layer of cloth. 'Ursun's teeth, these are hearts!'

'I know,' said Kaspar, disgustedly as he ascended the newly-carpeted stairs.

Awaiting him within his study were the four riders from Altdorf, their ragged clothes and pinched faces confirming that they had indeed ridden hard for many weeks to get to Kislev. Two knights stood with them and snapped to attention as Kaspar entered.

'Gentlemen,' began Kaspar, moving to stand behind his desk. 'I can see that you have had an arduous journey to get here. Might I offer you some refreshments?'

'No, thank you, herr ambassador,' said a burly man with a face like a mountainside who held out a folded piece of parchment sealed with green wax. 'My name is Pallanz and I bring you letters that come with the greatest urgency. I would see them delivered to you before taking my leave.'

'As you wish, Herr Pallanz,' said Kaspar, accepting the letter. He saw that the wax seal was emblazoned with the crest of the Second House of Wilhelm and his unease grew. He broke the seal and unfolded the thick parchment, taking his time in examining the letter's contents. The script was controlled and angular, and even before he saw the simple signature at the bottom of the letter he knew the handwriting belonged to no less a personage that the Emperor Karl-Franz himself.

Kaspar read the letter twice before letting it slip from his fingers. He slumped into his chair and let the words flow over him, not wanting to believe that they could be true and what it might, nay, *would* mean for his position here in Kislev.

He barely heard the riders ask for permission to retire and waved his hand vaguely in the direction of the door as the request was repeated.

As the riders left his study, Pavel entered, drying his hands on a linen towel.

Pavel pointed at the letter and said, 'Is bad?'

'Is bad,' nodded Kaspar.

IV

'DRINK THE WHOLE lot,' said Sofia. 'It won't do you any good if you don't.'

'Damn you, woman!' snapped Matthias Gerhard. 'It's vile! You are trying to poison me, I know it.'

Sofia Valencik held the glass in front of the merchant and said, 'I assure you, Herr Gerhard, if I had wanted to poison you, then you would already be in no state to complain about it.'

Lamplight glittered through the murky concoction Sofia had mixed together from a multitude of ingredients taken from her canvas satchel. An unhealthy looking remedy, the drink was a leafy liquid that smelled of soured milk. Gerhard sneezed violently and grimaced, but accepted the glass and drained it in a single swallow. He retched and spluttered as he swallowed the herbal medicine, setting the glass down amidst a pile of papers before folding his arms petulantly across his chest.

'It is galling that a man of my standing should be treated in such a manner,' he said.

'You should think yourself lucky, Herr Gerhard,' replied Sofia. 'Many a man would have you thrown in the *Chekist's* deepest gaol for your crimes. Be thankful that Ambassador von Velten still has need of you and has allowed you to remain in your own home.'

'Kept in my study all day under constant guard by armed knights and that old viper!' said the merchant pointing at Stefan, who sat at Gerhard's fabulous oaken desk behind a wall of leather-bound accounts ledgers. Pince-nez glasses were perched on the end of his nose and a goose-feathered quill darted across a long parchment.

'If you ask me, Sofia,' said Stefan, without once looking up from the piles of Gerhard's ledgers, 'you should just let him die of fever. He's certainly earned it.'

'Be quiet, you old fool,' said Sofia, stuffing several jars of herbs and poultices into her satchel. 'The ambassador asked me to make sure this one doesn't die, and I do not intend to let him down.'

'I bet you don't,' said Stefan, the quill twitching across the parchment.

'And what exactly is that supposed to mean?' demanded Sofia, rounding on Stefan.

'Nothing,' said Stefan airily, 'nothing at all.'

'Good, and I'll thank you to keep any such insinuations to yourself in future.'

'I'm just saying that–'

'Well don't,' she said, as the sound of hammering on the front door came from below.

She turned to Gerhard and asked, 'Are you expecting guests?'

V

DARKNESS HAD FALLEN by the time Kaspar and Pavel had changed into clothes more fitting for the palace. Rather than riding, as he normally would have, Kaspar consented to be carried in his carriage to the Winter Palace. Four embassy guards, led by Leopold Dietz, clung to the carriage's running boards and six knights cantered alongside.

The carriage struggled along the crowded streets of the city, pushing its way slowly along the prospekts of Kislev and forcing a path towards the palace hill.

Kaspar sat hunched within, attempting to formulate exactly what he would say to the Tzarina. Assuming that she consented to see him that was, though somehow, he didn't think that would be an issue this time. He had a sick feeling that the brick walls he had met thus far in his attempts to secure an audience with the Tzarina were about to be smashed down from the other side.

'Maybe it not be so bad,' offered Pavel from the seat across from Kaspar. 'Tzarina not stupid, she know Alexander a waste of space and she not like him anyway.'

'There's a difference between not liking your cousin and not caring when he's killed in a foreign city,' pointed out Kaspar.

'Maybe, but it more or less accident.'

'Can you imagine Karl-Franz turning the other cheek if one of his family was murdered "by accident" in Kislev?'

'I suppose not,' said Pavel, folding his arms and looking out the carriage's window. 'Is very bad.'

'Yes,' agreed Kaspar. 'It is.'

Pavel's assessment of the situation could not have been more apt, reflected Kaspar bitterly. The letter from the

Emperor had spoken of an 'unfortunate and most regrettable incident' that had occurred in one of the less salubrious areas of Altdorf some weeks ago.

Unfortunate and most regrettable did not even begin to cover it.

On a foggy night in Brauzeit, a carriage carrying the Tzarina's cousin, Alexander, had been travelling along the Luitpoldstrasse towards the Street of a Hundred Taverns when armed bailiffs acting for one of Altdorf's largest counting houses stopped it outside the notorious Crescent Moon tavern.

An inveterate gambler and infamous libertine, Alexander owed considerable sums to these establishments and their agents were in no mood to listen to his pleas for clemency, hurling him into the nearest debtor's prison.

Upon the morn, when those in power awoke to the previous night's events, there was considerable embarrassment at such a breach of protocol. However, embarrassment was to turn to horror when Alexander's gaolers opened his cell door and found him violated and murdered by his fellow prisoners.

Kaspar could barely imagine the Ice Queen's fury at such ignominy done to her family and the thought of appearing before her in such a frame of mind dumped hot fear into his gut. He would rather confront an army of rampaging greenskins than face the powerful wrath of the enraged sorcereress.

He rested his elbow on the lip of the carriage window and propped his chin on his palm, staring out into the darkness as it emerged into Geroyev Square. Thousands of those people who had been fortunate enough to gain entry to the city before the gates had been shut were camped here, their cookfires burning throughout its length and breadth, and a ragged city of canvas filling the once-spacious square.

'Sigmar's hammer,' cursed Kaspar softly. 'It will be the devil's own task feeding this many when the armies of the north come.'

'Aye,' nodded Pavel. 'How long, you think?'

'As soon as the first snows break,' said Kaspar. 'Late Nachexen, early Jahrdrung at the latest I should imagine.'

'Not long.'

'No.'

The first inkling of trouble came when one of the Knights Panther ordered a knot of people to make way before the ambassador of the Empire. Shouts of abuse and anger were hurled at the coach and Pavel leaned over to look out of the carriage's window.

'Must go faster…' said Pavel.

'What?' asked Kaspar, shaken from his misery-filled reverie.

'Must go faster,' repeated Pavel, pointing through the window.

Kaspar looked outside and saw hundreds of angry faces surrounding the coach, pressing in around the knights and hurling abuse at them. None dared approach them too closely, but Kaspar could see the mood was ugly.

'What are they doing?' said Kaspar, 'And what are they shouting?'

'They know about Alexander,' said Pavel in alarm. 'Not happy about it.'

The yells of the crowd grew louder and the motion of the carriage slowed yet further as more and more angry people pressed in around them. Kaspar now questioned the wisdom of travelling through the city in a carriage liveried with his own personal heraldry and that of the Empire. His knights yelled at the Kislevites to stand back, and even though their words were not understood, their meaning was plain from the way they jabbed their lance butts into the faces of those who got too close to the carriage.

Kaspar saw that they were less than a hundred yards from the palace gates, and there were a score of bronze armoured knights on snorting chargers sitting immobile before the massive building.

Why didn't they advance, wondered Kaspar? Surely they must see that they were in need of assistance?

Then he realised that the knights had probably been ordered not to intervene.

Wood splintered as a cobble torn up from the ground smashed into the carriage.

Kaspar flinched as more missiles rained down on the carriage, thudding against the woodwork and smashing the glass into lethal slivers. Cries of pain and alarm came from his guards on the running boards.

And the crowd surged forwards in anger.

VI

THE DOOR SPLINTERED *under his assault, slamming back on its hinges and cracking the plastered wall behind it. He leapt through the doorway, scenting his prey from the upper levels of the townhouse. The inside of the dwelling was well appointed, obviously that of a wealthy man, though he had no idea of his name.*

He had woken with a face burning in his mind, the early darkness of evening dispelled in the flood of anger and hate that surged through his veins at this latest feast set before him. He neither knew nor cared how these visions came to him to unleash his trueself; that they came and released him from the hellish servitude behind the mask of the beaten and abused otherself.

His trueself would not have suffered the abuse heaped upon the otherself. Had it not in fact ended it?

She had seen beyond the snivelling boy He had made him and awakened his trueself to its full potential. How he had laughed and wept the day he had ended the otherself's suffering, hacking Him into bloody pieces with the axe before setting down to devour the chunks of meat straight from the bone.

Only for her could he have done and continue to do such things.

The hallway was dark and he could see two armoured figures making their way down the stairs towards him, swords raised before them. Knights with panther pelts draped across their shoulder guards stood between him and his prey and that could not be allowed to happen.

Even through their enclosed helms, he could sense their disgust at his naked form and the dead skin mask he wore. How little they understood of him. One of the knights shouted something at him and he saw three figures sprint across the landing above. The scent of prey filled his senses and he roared in fury.

The first knight lunged, swinging his sword towards his midriff, but he rolled beneath the blow, dragging his knife from his flesh and thrusting it through the gap between the cuissart and tace of the knight's armour. The man screamed shrilly as the narrow blade split the links of his mail skirt and sheathed itself in his thigh. A twist of the wrist severed the main artery and he spun to his feet as the warrior fell, blood spraying from the wound.

The other knight stepped towards him and hammered his sword down, but he was no longer there, vaulting backwards over the slashing blade. He landed lightly, pivoting on one leg and thundering his bare foot into the side of the knight's thigh. Metal crumpled under the tremendous force of the blow and he heard the crack of his opponent's thighbone shattering.

The man roared in pain and collapsed. Even before the knight hit the ground, he was sprinting upstairs, taking them three at a time. He leapt to the landing, heading in the direction his prey had taken and smashing through every door between him and his goal.

He was close and shoulder charged the next door, entering a sumptuously appointed bedroom. A thick-timbered four-poster bed, draped in red and gold silks, dominated the room, but he paid it no mind as he saw the three people before him.

He saw their faces twist in terror as he stood before them in all his naked glory.

Their terror of him filled the air with a succulent tang and he laughed.

Then he saw her.

And his world turned upside down.

VII

'DRIVE!' SHOUTED KASPAR through the smashed carriage window.

He heard the crack of a whip, but the carriage could make little headway through the crowd pressed tightly around it. Angry shouts and yells filled the air and Kaspar could hear cries of pain mingled with those of rage as his guards and knights fought to defend him.

He saw that the knights had discarded their lances as too cumbersome to use in such close quarters and had drawn their swords. 'No!' yelled Kaspar. 'No killing.'

He had no way of knowing whether the knights had heard him until he saw that they were setting about themselves with the flats of their blades and pommels.

The embassy guards, still clinging to the carriage's running boards, lashed out with iron-shod boots, breaking limbs and fending off those members of the crowd who got too close to the carriage doors. More cobbles and other missiles rained down on the carriage and Kaspar knew it would not be long before they were totally overrun.

'Damn it, why don't those damned Kislevite knights sally out?' bellowed Kaspar, punching a yelling man's face as he attempted to climb inside the carriage.

'Ice Queen teach us lesson I think,' ventured Pavel, snapping a wrist that reached inside the broken window. There was a scream and the limb was hastily withdrawn.

The Knights Panther circled the carriage, smashing the flats of their blades down into the crowd as their horses stamped with their forelegs and drew sparks from the cobbles. The powerful shoulders of the giant warhorses stood taller than most of the people in the crowd and their great size was as much a deterrent as their lashing hooves.

But there was only so much the knights could do without resorting to lethal force and soon they were surrounded by the angry mob that struck at them with improvised clubs, rocks or whatever came to hand. None of these makeshift weapons stood any chance of penetrating the plate armour of the knights, but as the number of blows increased, they were eventually overwhelmed by sheer weight of numbers.

One was dragged from his horse and the mob descended upon him, raining blows down upon his helmet until blood leaked from his gorget and stained the cobbles. Another knight's horse screamed in pain as some enterprising attacker managed to get behind it and slash the beast's hamstrings. It crashed to the ground, spilling its rider who, miraculously, was able to roll to his feet. He had lost his sword in the fall, but punched out with mailed gauntlets.

Kaspar kicked and punched as the crowd pushed their way in through the doors of his carriage. Pavel kept them at bay from the other door, but it was only a matter of time until they were dragged outside. Kaspar raged at the crowd's mob mentality and cursed the fact that his ambassadorship was likely to end on such a sour note; torn to pieces by the very people he was here to help.

Wood splintered as the crowd punched through the thin timbers of the carriage and began tearing through the walls.

'Pavel!' shouted Kaspar.

'I see!'

A screaming man lunged inside, spittle flying from his lips as he reached for Kaspar. His punch was hampered by the close confines of the carriage and Kaspar was able to roll with the blow. He felt the skin break on his cheek and grabbed the man by the front of his ragged, peasant's tunic, lowering his head and hammering his forehead into the man's face.

The man screamed, bone broke and blood burst from his nose as he tumbled backwards.

A hand reached in and hauled him backwards as others pinned his arms by his side.

'Damn you!' he bellowed as he was struck on the side of the head. Fists and booted feet hammered his side and he felt himself being dragged outside. He thumped down onto the cobbles of the square, catching sight of Pavel on the other side of the coach as he landed. He covered his head with his arms and drew his legs up as blows continued to rain down on him.

Screams and noise filled the air, but even in the confusion, Kaspar could sense a different tenor to them. The people attacking him scattered, running as though the very daemons of Chaos were hot on their heels. He rolled onto his side, wincing as he felt a sharp pain in his ribs, and crawled across the slushy ground to take refuge beneath the smashed remains of his carriage.

Pavel joined him, his face a mask of blood where a kick had opened the skin above his left eye.

'Bastards wait until now…' observed the big Kislevite.

'What?' asked Kaspar, still breathless and dazed.

'There,' said Pavel, pointing to where a score of bronze-armoured knights rode through the crowd, their swords cutting a path through the mob towards them. Their breastplates were emblazoned with a silver bear and their helms were crowned with long-fanged skulls.

They herded the crowd away from the carriage, offering no quarter to anyone who didn't get out of the way quickly enough. Blood stained the cobbles as their swords chopped a path towards them. The six Knights Panther, one helmetless and supported by two of his brethren, formed a line of battle between these armoured giants and the ambassador. The embassy guards stumbled to join them and, seeing from their tattered uniforms and battered appearance that they too had fought tooth and nail with the enraged crowd, Kaspar's heart swelled with pride.

The Kislevite knights reined in their steeds before the Knights Panther, who raised their swords and stood ready to use them.

The lead knight sheathed his bloody blade and said, 'Ambassador von Velten, Ice Queen will see you now.'

Kaspar crawled out from beneath the carriage and pulled himself to his feet using the broken carriage wheel. His knee cracked painfully, and he wiped himself down as best he could, straightening his torn tunic and britches before addressing the knight. He fought to keep his voice even.

'Very well, if this is how she wants to play it, so be it.'

Surrounded by his battered entourage, Kaspar followed the knights through the gates of the Winter Palace.

VIII

THE HALLS OF the Ice Queen had not changed since he had last stood here. The walls of ice still glittered magnificently, the high ceiling's mosaic was still as impressive and the air was still as chill as he remembered. But rather than coming as a reluctant guest, this time he was here as an apologist. The bile rose in his throat at the thought of abasing himself before this haughty woman who had, to his mind, nearly gotten them all killed. As it was, one of his knights had a cracked skull and would likely not see active duty for many weeks. The embassy guards had broken limbs and severe cuts and bruises, and both he and Pavel would be badly bruised for some time to come as well.

Pavel dabbed a cold cloth on his forehead, cleaning the blood from his face as best he could while Kaspar made another futile attempt to make himself look more presentable and less like a filthy peasant.

He had hoped they would have been given time to clean up properly, but it appeared the Ice Queen was not to allow them that luxury either. As soon as they had entered the palace, a harried looking Pjotr Losov had rushed out to meet them, his face lined with concern.

'Ambassador von Velten!' he gushed. 'What times we live in when a man of your standing can be attacked by the mob. It shall not go unpunished I assure you.'

'It wouldn't have happened at all if your damn knights had come to our aid sooner,' snapped Kaspar, his patience worn thin.

'I know, I know, I cannot apologise enough, herr ambassador,' nodded Losov, 'but the palace knights have very specific orders that do not allow them to abandon their posts without express permission from their commander. Unfortunately, it took me some time to locate him.'

'How inconvenient...' said Pavel.

'Indeed so,' smiled Losov, oblivious to or, more likely, ignoring Pavel's sarcasm.

'Some of my men are badly hurt,' said Kaspar. 'They will need water and bandages.'

'I will see to it immediately,' assured Losov, snapping his fingers and barking orders at a blue-liveried servant.

'Your men will be attended to now, herr ambassador, but I'm afraid I must insist that you follow me to the South Hall immediately. The Tzarina awaits your pleasure, and she will not like to be kept waiting any longer than she has already.'

The Tzarina's chief advisor had led them through the main vestibule and up the garland-wreathed staircase they had ascended on their last visit to the palace, though it felt rather less grand than before.

All through the journey, Kaspar had fought for control. The Ice Queen, through Losov, was berating *them* for keeping her waiting! Damn her, but she was testing his patience.

They had entered the main hall where the dancing had taken place during his previous audience and, despite himself, he found himself craning his neck upwards to stare in wonder at the majesty of the Winter Palace.

He caught himself and returned his gaze to the double doors at the end of the hall, understanding the subtlety of the Ice Queen in choosing to hold her audiences in this place, where the incredible display of her sorcererous powers were so obviously demonstrated.

The clock above the doors chimed and they were thrown wide open as the Ice Queen entered the room, together with her bloated retinue of flunkies, favourites, aides, scribes and hangers-on. She was as magnificent as Kaspar remembered, and he could feel the temperature of the hall drop sharply as she neared. Dressed in a long, ivory gown sewn with pearls and shards of ice, she seemed to glide across the floor. Her hair was worn loosely about her shoulders, its hue more icy and cold than Kaspar had remembered it, secured about her forehead by clips of coloured ice. Kaspar saw that once again she was armed with the ancient blade of the Khan Queens, Fearfrost.

Her eyes were like diamonds, hard and sharp, and a painted tear of ice glittered on her cheek.

'She not look happy,' commented Pavel.

'No,' agreed Kaspar as a trio of burly warriors with bare chests, long topknots and waxed moustaches carried a high backed chair of gold and lapis lazuli and deposited it next to their queen before standing behind her with their powerfully muscled arms crossed.

She sat on the throne, not yet deigning to look in their direction as she arranged her scabbarded sword so that it rested upon her lap.

Kaspar shivered, feeling the waves of icy cold that radiated from the queen and her weapon. Before he could say a single word, the Ice Queen crossed her hands across the translucent scabbard and said, 'We have been grievously wounded, Ambassador von Velten. One of Kislev's beloved sons has been taken from us.'

Kaspar knew he had to choose his words carefully and said, 'Your Majesty, on behalf of the Emperor Karl-Franz, may I offer you my nation's most sincere apologies and most fervent condolences upon your loss. It is my understanding that Alexander was a credit to your family.'

The corners of the Ice Queen's mouth twitched as she said, 'Yes, he was a fine figure of a man and his loss will be felt keenly. Tell me, how is it that he died?'

Kaspar hesitated for the briefest second, realising that to lie would be pointless, but knowing that this was not the time to elaborate upon the sordid details of Alexander's death. He saw the veiled threat in the Tzarina's lightly asked question and carefully framed his answer in his head before speaking.

'He... ah, I am told he was killed by ruffians over a matter of some monies owed.'

'Monies? How is it that a noble of Kislev could find himself in such a position? My royal cousin was a man of means. More likely, your usurious clerks of Altdorf hounded him to his death over a matter of a few pfennigs.'

'Your majesty, there is much I do not yet know of the circumstances surrounding Alexander's passing, I am merely here to offer the Emperor's condolences and present to you an offer of reparations for your loss.'

'Reparations?' snapped the Ice Queen. 'What manner of "reparations" can salve the loss of one so dear to me as Alexander. He was a saint amongst men, and your damned officious nation no doubt delighted in seeing him humbled so.'

'I assure you, Majesty, that is not the case,' said Kaspar evenly.

'Don't play games with me, Ambassador von Velten, it is no secret to me how your precious Emperor sees my nation: a vassal state, a convenient buffer between the Empire and the northern barbarian tribes. The deaths of our sons and daughters keep your lands safe. We are nothing more than allies of convenience for you and your people.'

'Your majesty–' began Kaspar, but the Ice Queen was not done yet.

'Every year the tribes of the north raid and plunder our lands, killing hundreds of my people. We bleed for this land and each time we drive them back to their wasteland homes. And what thanks do we get for this great sacrifice?'

Kaspar clenched his fists as the Ice Queen berated him. He couldn't believe she had the gall to suggest such things. Were not men of the Empire dying even now to defend her wretched land? As the Ice Queen berated him further, Kaspar could feel his temper, already frayed by the violence unleashed in Geroyev Square, threatening to get the better of him.

'We call upon your Emperor for aid, but only when you believe your own lands are threatened do you send any warriors.'

'Damn you, woman,' barked Kaspar, his patience finally at an end. He stepped forward, the Tzarina's guards stepping from behind her throne to intercept the enraged Empire general.

'Kaspar, no…' began Pavel, but it was too late.

'How dare you say such things,' shouted Kaspar. 'My countrymen are dying here and now in your miserable country to keep us safe. You know as well as I that our nations have always fought side by side against the tribes of Chaos. Thousands of the Emperor's soldiers are camped outside your walls right now, cold and hungry, but ready to stand before our enemies no matter what. I will not stand to hear these insults heaped on the heads of men of such courage. And if you don't like that, then you can go to hell… your majesty.'

Stunned silence greeted Kaspar's outburst.

Pjotr Losov's face had turned paler than the Ice Queen and her army of flunkies could not have looked more astonished if he had sprouted wings and taken to the air.

Behind him he heard Pavel whisper, 'Ursun save us, Ursun save us…'

The silence stretched and Kaspar felt his anger drain from him as the realisation of what he had just said and to whom he had just said it finally penetrated the fog of his anger.

He looked into the cold, unforgiving eyes of the Ice Queen of Kislev and waited for her to turn him into a frozen statue. Slowly, and with great deliberation, she stood and walked towards him.

She halted before him and leaned forward until the chill of her nearness was almost too much to bear.

The Ice Queen smiled and whispered, 'Very good, Herr von Velten.'

'What?' blurted Kaspar, amazed that he was still alive.

'Walk with me,' she said, linking her burningly cold arm with his and leading him back through to the main stairs, leaving scores of bemused and astonished people behind them. Pjotr Losov tried to follow, but with a single raised hand, the Ice Queen stopped him.

Kaspar passed Pavel, who merely shrugged and rolled his eyes.

He and the Ice Queen walked in silence from the hall until they were out of earshot of those left behind in the hall. The Ice Queen stopped before the gigantic portrait of her father, Radii Bokha, sat astride the monstrous bear, Urskin. She stared up at the portrait and to Kaspar, it seemed as though her expression softened.

'Why aren't you freezing the blood in my veins?' asked Kaspar eventually.

The Ice Queen chuckled. 'As I am sure you know, Alexander was a waster and there are few who will shed tears over his death, save perhaps his creditors and a string of foolish women carrying his bastard children. Why do you think he was sent to the Empire if not to get him from my sight?'

'Then why go through that charade back there?'

'Come now, Herr von Velten, do not play the innocent with me,' said the Tzarina. 'I may have detested my cousin, but I must give the appearance of having been grievously wounded by his death.'

'Well, congratulations. You did an admirable job of making me look like a cantankerous, foul mouthed ruffian,' groused Kaspar.

The Ice Queen laughed at his obvious discomfort and said, 'My father was fond of saying that he would never trust a man who was afraid to lose his temper. As a result, his boyarin were an insufferable band of brutes, always brawling, always arguing and always fighting. But they were loyal, honest and true, and never did a greater band of warriors ever fight shoulder to shoulder. That saying stood my father in good stead, so I see no reason not to trust it also, ambassador.'

'You were trying to make me angry?'

'Of course.'

'Why?'

'I knew your predecessor, Teugenheim,' explained the Ice Queen. 'He was a weasel and a coward and only came to Kislev to advance his own career. I know that this is not an attractive posting compared to some, but it is an important one, one that requires a man of a certain temperament. Andreas Teugenheim was not that man, but I believe that you might just be.'

'A man who loses his temper?'

'No,' said the Ice Queen. 'A man with fire in his heart and the soul of a Kislevite.'

Now it was Kaspar's turn to laugh. 'The soul of a Kislevite? I fear I am too much a son of the Empire for that.'

'You are wrong, Kaspar von Velten. You have fought for Kislev before and you are here in her time of greatest need. The land has called you back here to fight for her and I do not believe you will fail.'

This was too much for Kaspar to take in. 'The land called me here? No, the Emperor sent me here.'

The Ice Queen shook her head. 'No. Whether you believe it or not is irrelevant, you answered the call of the land. Of that I am sure. Come the moment, come the man. You were meant to be here and there is much for you yet to do.'

'Like what?'

'I have no idea,' confessed the Ice Queen with a cold smile. 'That's for you to find out.'

IX

'PAVEL STILL NOT believe we not dead.'

'I'm not so sure I believe it myself,' said Kaspar as they rode down the alleyway leading back to the embassy. The bronze-armoured knights had provided them with safe passage through Kislev, the mob that had attacked them earlier vanishing like morning mist before these fearsome warriors. The wounded members of Kaspar's entourage followed behind in a cushioned wagon, while he rode a fresh horse from the Ice Queen's stables, a dun gelding that was easily the equal of the beast that had been lost in Geroyev Square.

There had been no sign of his battered coach, its smashed timbers no doubt burning on someone's fire, its fine fabrics stuffed inside layers of grubby clothing for extra warmth. Kaspar did not mourn its loss; he had never liked travelling in it anyway.

The ride back had been uneventful, but as he handed the reins of his mount to a waiting stable lad, and limped towards the embassy, he could sense that something was wrong from the tense expressions of the guards at the door.

They opened the door for him and he made his way upstairs to his study.

Inside he found Kurt Bremen and the *Chekist*, Vladimir Pashenko, awaiting him.

Before Pashenko could say anything, Kaspar addressed Bremen. 'What's happened?' he demanded.

'Something bad,' warned Bremen.

'Don't play games, man, whatever it is, spit it out.'

'There was an attack on Matthias Gerhard's home earlier today. One of my knights is dead and another badly wounded,' said Bremen.

The knight took a deep breath and said, 'Stefan is dead.'

Kaspar felt his stomach lurch and his face flushed as he felt a heartbreaking grief well up inside him. Stefan. His oldest comrade from the ranks, the man who had taught him everything he had needed to know to survive as a soldier. Dead. It had to be some kind of mistake. Stefan was too stubborn to be dead.

But as he saw Bremen's solemn face he knew there was no mistake. It was true.

'What about Sofia?' he asked, desperately afraid for her, but afraid of the answer even more. 'What about Sofia, damn it?'

'I don't know,' said Bremen slowly.

'What the hell do you mean, "You don't know"?'

'I mean that there's no sign of her or Matthias Gerhard. They're both gone.'

CHAPTER SEVEN

I

Kaspar knelt beside the blood-spattered bed, twisting the fabric of its red and gold silk sheets in frustration and grief. Broken glass lay strewn about the floor of Matthias Gerhard's bedroom and several pieces of furniture had been overturned and smashed to matchwood. A grand mirror in its carved mahogany frame lay in splinters, each jagged, reflective shard throwing back the faces of the men that gathered in this abattoir and multiple images of the words written in blood upon the walls.

Blood coated almost every surface, the floor, the walls and even the ceiling.

Kaspar looked up at the daubings on the wall opposite the bed. The bloody words had been written in a childlike hand in halting, grammatically incorrect Reikspiel, and Kaspar knew the macabre graffiti must have been written while Stefan lay dying.

It read: 'It all was her for.'

Stefan had died in this room and Sofia had been... what? Abducted? Killed?

The fear of what Sofia might even now be suffering was a physical pain in Kaspar's chest and, while they had only known each other a few months, they had slipped easily into the familiarity of old friends, and the thought of her in pain scared him more than he imagined possible.

Vladimir Pashenko pointed to a huge plum-coloured stain on the expensive carpeting next to Kurt Bremen, its fabric now matted and stinking with blood.

'That is where we found your manservant. It would appear that he died from a single wound to the throat that severed the main artery in his neck.'

'His name was Stefan,' growled Kaspar.

'Indeed,' continued Pashenko. 'Whoever killed him used an exceptionally sharp blade and knew exactly where to strike.'

'Or took them by surprise, which seems unlikely given that the door to the house has been broken down and my knights had made their way downstairs to fight the bastard,' said Kurt Bremen, furious at having two of his warriors defeated with such apparent ease. One knight lay beneath a shroud in the temple of Morr, while the other would probably lose his leg below the knee.

'The wound in his neck is the only injury that was done to the victim,' went on Pashenko, reading from a black leather notebook. 'There were no defensive wounds.'

'Defensive wounds?' asked Kaspar, pulling himself to his feet.

'Yes, when someone is being attacked by a person armed with a knife, they typically raise their hands in front of them to ward off the blows, and they are often found missing fingers or with their forearms slashed to ribbons.'

'But Stefan had none of these?' asked Kaspar.

Pashenko checked his notes. 'No, none at all.'

'Do you have any idea why that might be?'

Pashenko shrugged. 'I do not know. Perhaps the killer was so swift in his attack that his victim had no chance to defend himself.'

Kaspar nodded. 'Have you found anything else that might help you catch this bastard?'

'Not a great deal,' admitted Pashenko.

'But surely someone must have seen something?' said Bremen.

Pashenko shook his head. 'The attack happened in darkness and those few souls who would be abroad at that time are not the sort to come forward and talk to me. Though as soon as your knight is able, I shall of course speak to him. He may be the only person in Kislev who has seen the Butcherman and lived.

'However, we did find some tracks leading both to and from Gerhard's stables. Two of the horses from his troika are missing, so I can only assume that the killer made his escape on one and transported his captives on the other.'

Kaspar paced the room, stopping before the dripping words painted on the wall. 'And what in the name of Sigmar does this mean? "It all was her for." Who is "her"? Have you seen anything like this at previous Butcherman killings?'

'No,' said Pashenko, pointedly. 'Only since you arrived in Kislev has the killer been leaving trophies or messages.'

'And what does that mean?'

'I do not know for certain, but I believe the killer is trying to tell you something.'

'Tell me something? What?'

'Again, I do not know,' said Pashenko, 'but taken together with the hearts left outside the embassy, I believe this message was intended for you. For whatever reason, the Butcherman has fixated on you, Ambassador von Velten.'

II

HER FIRST SENSATION was pain. Then grief. Then terror.

Sofia kept her breathing even and her eyes shut. She could feel that she was seated on a heavy wooden chair, her hands securely bound behind her to the uprights and her wrists chafed bloody by the rough cord. She couldn't tell if there was anyone in the same room as her, so she continued to give the appearance of unconsciousness while she attempted to collect her terrified thoughts. She was cold, but felt that she wasn't outside. Wherever she was smelled bad and she had worked in enough field hospitals to recognise the stench of rotten flesh and blood. She suppressed a disgusted retch as the pain in her head returned with a vengeance.

Tears leaked from beneath her eyelids as she remembered the lightning flash of the knife that had ended Stefan's life, the gouting spray of arterial blood and the look of apology in his eyes as he fell.

A single word entered her head... *Butcherman*.

Gerhard's screams still echoed in her head and she found she could not remember what had happened after that, save an anguished cry that had preceded a blow to her temple.

'You might as well open your eyes,' said a man's voice. 'I know you are awake.'

Sofia sobbed, all self-control lost as she felt her captor's hand slide under her jaw and lift her head.

'I am sorry I hit you,' he said. 'I just didn't expect to see you there. I thought that you were dead.'

Sofia twisted her head from his grip. 'Please don't hurt me, please, please...'

'Shhhh... I'm not going to hurt you, matka,' said the voice. 'How could you think such a thing? After all you did for me. You kept me safe, comforted me, loved me and prepared me for the day when we could finally be rid of Him. How could I hurt you? I love you, I've always loved you.'

Sofia wept softly as he ran his hands through her auburn locks and she felt his nearness. She heard an intake of breath and realised he was smelling her hair.

'Please,' she begged. 'Whatever you want, just don't kill me.'

'Kill you?' laughed the voice. 'Don't you remember? You're already dead, but I kept a piece of you.'

She twisted her head away from the Butcherman as she felt his face press against hers and a moist tongue lick her cheek. His skin felt leathery and hard.

'Why do you pull away?' he asked.

'Because you frighten me,' said Sofia.

'But it's me,' he said, hurt. 'Your little boy, your precious warrior. Look at me.'

'Please, no,' wept Sofia, keeping her eyes screwed shut.

'I said look at me!' her captor bellowed, slapping her hard across the jaw. Sofia felt blood in her mouth and a weight drop across her thighs as he fell against her, wailing in anguish.

'I'm sorry!' he sobbed. 'I'm so sorry. I didn't mean... I would never! Please don't make me hurt you! Don't make me hurt you again. You don't want that.'

She felt him push himself upright to stand before her, and instinctively lashed out with her foot. But he was too quick, and her blow missed its target.

'I told you to open your eyes,' he said, his earlier distress gone. 'I'll cut your eyelids off if you don't.'

Her eyes filled with tears of pain, Sofia obeyed his command.

Naked, the Butcherman stood before her, his flesh slathered in blood, manic eyes staring from behind a mask of crudely stitched skin, a mask of dead human skin. It had obviously once belonged to a man, but the ragged skin was decades dead, preserved and stitched into this grotesque façade. A long, thin bladed knife was sheathed in a cut of flesh on his muscled abdomen.

Behind him, twisting gently on a butcher's hook suspended from the central beam of the roof, was the flayed body of Matthias Gerhard. His face, the only piece of skin his killer had left him was fixed in an expression of eternal agony.

Sofia screamed.

She screamed and screamed until he pressed his dead-fleshed face against hers and kissed her furiously while embracing her tightly to his naked body.

III

'You mustn't fret, Kaspar. We'll get her back,' said Anastasia, holding his hand in hers while massaging the back of his neck with her free hand. They sat in the embassy courtyard, where Kaspar had sparred with Valdhaas and where Sofia had stitched his wounded shoulder. Anastasia wore a crimson gown, edged with silver fur, and had come to the embassy immediately upon hearing of the attack at Matthias Gerhard's. Two days had passed since that awful night and she had come to the embassy each day, bringing hopeful sentiments and the solace of a friend. The bright, cold light of morning made her skin shimmer and Kaspar was grateful for her words of comfort, even though enough time had passed to give them a hollow edge.

'Pashenko thinks she is already dead,' said Kaspar, finally giving voice to the thought that had plagued him these last two days and kept him from sleep. The *Chekist* and the Knights Panther had been searching for Sofia and Gerhard, but in such a packed city, the odds of stumbling across them were astronomical. The knight wounded in the attack on Gerhard's house was unable to shed any useful information on the killer; merely that he was able to easily best them in combat and fought naked.

The only thing that gave Kaspar a glimmer of hope was the fact that they had found no bodies and that there had been no more grisly offerings left for him.

'No, you can't think like that,' said Anastasia. 'Surely if this madman were going to kill her and Gerhard, he would have done it already. At the same time he… he killed Stefan.'

'Perhaps,' said Kaspar unconvinced.

'Have the *Chekist* managed to come up with any idea of what actually happened yet?'

Kaspar sneered. 'No. That fool Pashenko will happily find a convenient scapegoat soon enough, but he knows nothing.'

Anastasia sighed. 'And he has no idea why or where Sofia and Gerhard were taken?'

'If he does, he's not saying.'

Anastasia nodded, chewing her bottom lip as though wrestling with a thorny ethical dilemma. Kaspar caught the look and said, 'What is it?'

'Well, it's… it's that I know you are fond of Sofia,' said Anastasia hesitantly.

'What does that mean?'

'How much do you really know about her?'

'Enough to know that she's a good person and that I trust her.'

'That's what I mean. You trust her, but you don't really *know* her, do you? I know that she used to work for Vassily Chekatilo before she came to work for you.'

'You're joking,' said Kaspar, incredulous.

'I wish I was, Kaspar, but I'm led to believe she worked for him for several years.'

'What are you trying to suggest?'

'Chekatilo is not a man you can just walk away from,' said Anastasia. 'I know. I'm saying that perhaps the Butcherman has not kidnapped Sofia at all. I'm saying that perhaps Chekatilo forcibly took her back himself.'

IV

TIME BLURRED; HER only connection to the outside world a smeared skylight that allowed only the most fitful light to enter. Sofia didn't know how many days had passed since her abduction, only that her pain increased with every moment and that there was a growing realisation that she would, in all likelihood, die in this stinking attic.

She wept tears of bitterness and frustration, her sobs muffled by the blood-stiffened rag stuffed in her mouth and tied in place with a broad leather strap. Her wrists throbbed dully; she could no longer feel her fingertips and even the slightest movement brought fiery agony as the crusted blood split and the rough cord dug further into the meat of her arms.

The days passed. Some as pain-filled boredom, others as unrelenting horror as he would climb into the attic, the dead skin mask stretched tight across his features. On many of those occasions, he would touch her, whisper to her that he loved her or that he had followed her orders and killed again for her, that he had eaten human flesh in honour of their day of liberation from *his* tyranny.

Her eyes were gummed with lack of sleep and tears, her vision blurred with malnutrition and her lips cracked with dehydration. Her mouth felt sticky and her head rolled slackly on her shoulders as she heard the hateful creak of the trapdoor that led into the attic as it opened on rusted hinges.

'Are you there, matka?' he said. Then he laughed. 'Of course you are. Where could you go?'

She squeezed her eyes shut as she heard his footfalls approach and he laid a callused hand on her shoulder. She smelled his nearness and though she tried to be strong, could not help shuddering in naked fear. She felt his hands move across her body and felt him press himself against her.

He moaned and said, 'I am almost done, yes?'

Sofia could not answer, the gag choking any words she might have given voice to. But then she understood that he was not speaking to her at all. She hadn't heard anyone else enter the attic, but another voice, a distant, melodic voice answered, sounding as though it came from the bottom of a very deep well.

'Very nearly, my handsome prince, very nearly. I have just one thing left for you to do. One last tiny thing and we will be done.'

'Anything, matka, anything,' he said.

'I want you to kill me,' said the voice. 'I was dead once before and I do not belong in this world. Morr claims me for his own and I should not be back in your world.'

'No!' he cried. Sofia felt his grip on her body tighten and gave a muffled cry of pain as he roughly turned the chair around so that she was facing him. 'Why would you ask this of me? I only just found you again, I won't let you go. Not again.'

'Trust me, my prince, you must,' said the soft, teasing voice.

Sofia slitted open her eyes, seeing the loathsome masked face before her. A rippling light cast a soft glow over the preserved features of the corpse-mask, her captor's violet eyes wide with adoration beneath it. He stared at something over her shoulder, a firefly light glinting in the darkness of his pupils. Her eyes stung, but for the briefest instant it seemed as though the reflection of a bright face, pale and angelic, ghosted across the surface of his eye.

'I can't,' he wailed, throwing his arms around her and burying his head in her lap.

'Listen to me!' roared the voice, stripped bare of its earlier grace. 'Do it. I demand you do it. Kill me, kill me now. Cast off the shackles of your abused otherself and take out your knife, the knife *I* gave you and cut my throat, you snivelling, pathetic little whoreson. Kill her, cut her into pieces and throw them at von Velten's feet.'

'No... I won't! I love you...' he wept, his voice trailing off into choking sobs.

Sofia felt the fury of whatever was talking to her captor rise to terrifying heights and shut her eyes once more. Even through her swollen lids, she felt a burning light fill the death attic, but just as quickly as it bloomed, it faded and she sensed that whatever had spoken to the man had departed. Its rage left a crackling, actinic tang of magic in the air, but she felt a tiny flutter of hope at his defiance of its murderous desires. It wanted him to kill her, but, for whatever reason, he believed that she was his matka, his mother, and would not.

'I can't kill you...' he said, as though hearing her thoughts. 'Not yet, but I have to cut you. Oh, matka, I have to cut you.'

Sofia felt the blade of his knife against her skin and tried to scream as he sliced the thumb from her left hand.

V

THE BROTHEL WAS housed in a nondescript building of sagging black timbers and random blocks of rough-hewn stone that had once been part of the original city wall. Coloured panes of glass in the upper windows and a crimson sash hanging limply from the roof's finial were the only clue to the building's purpose and Kaspar could practically smell the stench of desperation that saturated its fabric.

'This is the place?' he asked.

'Aye,' nodded Pavel. 'You find Chekatilo here, though why want to, Pavel not know. He not a man you should be in hurry to see. We should not be here, should go now.'

'He might know something about Sofia's abduction,' said Kaspar, his voice as icy as the snow that swirled around him. Pavel and Kurt Bremen exchanged wary glances, neither liking the lethal edge to the ambassador's voice.

'Ambassador von Velten,' said Bremen. 'If Chekatilo does indeed know something of Sofia's whereabouts then we must be delicate in our handling of him. You cannot afford to antagonise him.'

'Don't worry, Kurt. I can be diplomatic if I need to be,' assured Kaspar, pushing open the door to the brothel and stepping through into the semi-darkness. The stench of unwashed bodies and cheap perfume filled the air, the latter patently failing to mask the former.

Even in the light that filtered from the few hooded lanterns and low-burning fireplace, Kaspar could see the place was busy. It seemed that imminent war and death brought out the lust in Kislevite men and there were plenty filling the long hall willing to spend their last kopeks for the embrace of women who sold their flesh for coin.

A few heads turned at their entrance, but most were too deep into their labours or lost in the bliss of weirdroot dreams to pay them much mind. A fug of acrid smoke hugged the ceiling, its scent sweet and cloying, like musk from Araby, and Kaspar had a vivid recall of his campaigns fought in that bleak desert landscape.

He marched past the writhing bodies, ignoring the overly theatrical moans and cries of pleasure as he headed for a door at the back of the room, guarded by two cold-eyed men who made no effort to conceal the axes beneath their cloaks.

Kaspar halted before the men, who pointedly ignored him until he made to move past them. One spat a burst of muttered Kislevite at him, pushing his axe free of his cloak.

'Pavel,' said Kaspar, 'translate for me.'

'Very well,' grumbled Pavel, tearing his gaze from the copulation taking place all around him and moving to stand beside the ambassador.

'My name is Kaspar von Velten, and I am here to speak with your master, Vassily Chekatilo. I would be grateful if you were to convey my wishes to him.'

Pavel repeated Kaspar's words and he watched as the men exchanged an amused look before the man Pavel had addressed shook his head.

'Nya,' he said and the meaning was clear.

'Pavel, tell him that I have a detachment of Knights Panther at my disposal and that if Chekatilo doesn't consent to see me, then I will have them burn this filthy whorehouse down. With him in it if necessary.'

Again Pavel repeated Kaspar's words and this time the two men looked distinctly uneasy. A quiet, but heated discussion in rapid snatches of Kislevite ensued, followed by a raised palm and the man who had said no disappearing through the door. The remaining man gave a lopsided grin, exposing yellowed stumps of teeth.

The three men waited for several minutes, Pavel returning his attention to the libidinous activities going on around them and taking several swigs from his hipflask.

At last the door reopened and the messenger reappeared, beckoning with grubby fingers that they should follow him. Kaspar stepped after the man, making his way down a long, timber-floored corridor with velvet-curtained archways along both sides. Grunts and more groans of counterfeit pleasure came from behind them and Kaspar shut them out as they approached a heavy timber door banded with black iron. The man ahead of him drew out a long key and noisily unlocked the door before pushing it wide and indicating that they go through.

'Yha! You go, Yha?'

'Yha,' agreed Kaspar and stepped through into a well-appointed room of spacious dimensions and furnished with Empire-designed furniture and fixtures that Kaspar just knew had come from his embassy. Four women dressed in diaphanous silk gowns lounged around the room in various stages of weirdroot oblivion, their lips stained with narcotic juices. A naked woman danced clumsily before the enormous Chekatilo, who sat on a creaking wooden bench with his back to Kaspar. Standing at his side was a whip-thin man with the face of a fighter who stared at them with undisguised hostility.

Chekatilo clapped in time with the woman's gyrations and Kaspar could see from her stocky build and frightened, prosaic features that she was of peasant stock, no doubt here to earn a few copper coins to feed her through the winter.

'Herr Chekatilo,' said Kaspar.

The big Kislevite did not answer, holding his hand up to indicate that Kaspar must wait until the dance was over.

Kaspar bit his bottom lip and folded his arms across his chest. Bremen averted his eyes from the dancing girl and Pavel also had the decency to look away from her shame.

At last Chekatilo clapped and stood, ushering the girl away to retrieve her clothes.

'Rejak,' he said, turning to face the flint-eyed killer at his side. 'Put her to work in main hall, she won't do for the booths.'

Rejak nodded and led the girl to the door Kaspar and the others had entered through and pushed her into the corridor with a barked order to the guards at its end. He returned to his master's side, his hand clasped firmly around the hilt of his sword. Kaspar instantly recognised the man for what he was: an assassin and murderer.

At last Chekatilo deigned to face Kaspar and his entourage, his wide and intimidating features masked with a predatory smile. His beard was as huge as Kaspar remembered it and his leather and fur clothing was well cared for and expensive. He sat back down on the bench and said, 'You wanted to see me?'

'Yes, I'd like to ask you some questions.'

'I make it rule never to answer questions I do not have to,' said Chekatilo.

'You'll answer these ones,' said Kaspar.

'Really? What makes you so sure?'

'Because I'll kill you if you don't,' promised Kaspar.

Kurt Bremen flinched at Kaspar's threat and Chekatilo laughed, a booming peal that startled several of the stupefied women.

'I think you not know of your master's plan, knight?' asked Chekatilo.

Bremen did not answer as Chekatilo continued. 'Pavel Korovic! Is long time since I see you in here. Do you bring me another Empire ambassador to corrupt?'

Pavel shook his head hurriedly, casting his eyes to the floor when Kaspar glowered at him. Kaspar flushed as Chekatilo laughed once more. 'You come with questions, but you know nothing of the man you ask them of. And you threaten me in my own chambers? One word from me and you all die. There are dozen men in earshot I can call to kill you where you stand.'

'Maybe there are, and maybe there aren't,' said Kaspar, 'but could they get to us before I rammed a sword into your gut?'

'Perhaps not, but there are worse armours than many layers of fat, Empire man. I think you be dead if you try, and you not ready for that yet.'

'No?'

'No,' said Chekatilo. 'You got things to do before crows feed on you. I see this.'

Kaspar knew he had lost control of this conversation, if indeed he had ever had it in the first place, but he was desperate for something, anything, that might provide a clue as to where Sofia had been taken. And if Anastasia was right about Sofia's past, then there was every chance this bastard might know something of value.

Kaspar knew that he had come to this confrontation much less prepared than he ought to have been, now understanding that threats were not the way to get the answers he wanted, and so he switched tack.

'Herr Chekatilo, we are all men of the world here, are we not? We are behaving like animals in the wild, locking horns like stags trying to be the master of the herd. But this is your lair and I realise now that it is pointless to try and assert my authority here,' said Kaspar, spreading his arms wide in what he fervently hoped was a gesture of gracious magnanimity. 'I am in need of your help and come to you in desperate need. A good friend of mine has gone missing and I believe you may be in a position to help me find her.'

Chekatilo smiled, immediately reading Kaspar's gambit. 'Clever, Empire man, much cleverer than that fool, Teugenheim. He too thought he could be big man in this place. Sadly, he was wrong in all regards.'

'Then you'll help?'

'Perhaps. Who you lost?'

'My physician. Her name is Sofia Valencik and I am told she used to work for you.'

'Sofia!' barked Chekatilo. 'Ah, yes, I remember Sofia, but no, she never work for me, no matter how much money I offer her. I think she not like me.'

'I can't imagine why,' sneered Bremen.

Kaspar shot the knight a venomous glare as he saw Rejak stiffen, saying, 'Really? She never worked for you? Are you sure?'

Kaspar felt what little hope he had that this avenue of investigation might yield some result fade. Anastasia had convinced him that Sofia had worked for Chekatilo, and he would take her word over the fat Kislevite's every time, but his instinct told him that Chekatilo was not lying.

'You're sure?' repeated Kaspar.

Chekatilo scowled. 'I may be over forty, but memory not failing me yet. No, she never work for me. She came here a few times each year though.'

'What?' said Kaspar, horrified. 'Sofia came here, of her own free will?'

'Aye,' confirmed Chekatilo. 'Of her own free will. She looked after girls who worked the rooms here, gave them poultices for the pox and other such things. Sometimes she birthed or ended children as well. She tried to keep girls healthy.'

The fat crook grinned lasciviously. 'Not easy task in Kislev. But, no, she never work for me, though I was glad of her services. She was good woman.'

'Is,' insisted Kaspar. 'She *is* a good woman. And now she's missing, taken by the Butcherman.'

'Then she is dead. Cut up and eaten.'

'I don't believe that,' stated Kaspar.

'No? What make you so sure she alive?'

'I just am,' said Kaspar, his voice suddenly fatigued and drained of emotion. 'Until I see something that proves she's gone, I'll keep looking for her.'

'You in love with her?' laughed Chekatilo. 'I not blame you if you are. Sofia Valencik is handsome woman.'

'No,' said Kaspar, and Chekatilo smiled at the swiftness of his answer.

'I see, but why you think I can or will help you find her?'

'I don't know,' admitted Kaspar. 'I came here thinking that maybe you had taken her, but now I don't believe you have. I don't know if there is anything you can do to help me, but if there is anything at all, then I beg you to do it.'

Chekatilo considered Kaspar for long seconds before answering.

'I will help you, Empire man, though Ursun alone knows why. You and I would be enemies I think just now, if not for Sofia. What you offer me if I help you?'

'All I can offer you is my gratitude,' said Kaspar.

The giant Kislevite laughed before seeing that Kaspar was serious. 'Are you man of your word, Kaspar von Velten?'

'I am,' nodded Kaspar. 'My word is iron and once given is never broken.'

'Kaspar–' warned Bremen, but the ambassador waved him to silence.

Both men locked eyes before Chekatilo finally nodded and rose from the bench seat. 'I think that you are, Empire man, just be sure it not the end of you. Very well, I have many eyes and ears around Kislev and if there is anything to know, I will find it for you.'

Chekatilo leaned forwards. 'But if I do this thing for you…' he said, letting the sentence trail of meaningfully.

'I understand,' said Kaspar, wondering if he really did.

CHAPTER EIGHT

I

In the days following Kaspar's meeting with Chekatilo, the weather continued to worsen, the sagest of Kislev's older heads proclaiming that this could be the hardest winter since the time of the Great Tzar, Radii Bokha. Whether this was true or not, Kaspar did not know and didn't much care, so busy was he with the continued demands of maintaining an army of war during the interminable period when there was no fighting to be done.

As yet more days passed, thoughts of Sofia kept intruding on his dreams as well as his waking thoughts. In a rare show of compassion, Pashenko had personally informed him that his *Chekist* were now forced to abandon the search for her. As well as the four hearts that had been left outside the embassy, other mutilated bodies had since been discovered and demanded investigation that they might shed some light on the identity of the killer.

Despite Pashenko's admission of failure, Kaspar refused to give up hope that Sofia might, somehow, still be alive. Upon their return from Chekatilo's, he had told Anastasia what little they had learned and she had held him close, warning him not to trust the word of such a lowborn criminal. Kaspar wanted to let her convince him, but his earlier gut feeling that Chekatilo was telling the truth kept returning to him.

Anastasia had taken over the job of organising the distribution of supplies to the soldiers and refugees, throwing herself into the task with gusto and displaying a real aptitude for such work, though Kaspar had insisted that she do so from the embassy. He would not lose another to the Butcherman through carelessness.

She had taken the chambers adjacent to Kaspar's, and on the second night she had come to his bed, slipping easily into his embrace and they had comforted one another in the way of two lonely people needing to shut out the cruelties of the outside world for a time. Their lovemaking was gentle, tentative, each touch and caress a little afraid, and as he lay spent in her arms each night, Kaspar found himself uttering love's greatest lie: 'I'll never leave you.'

She came to him each night and he found himself more and more grateful for her attentions. They would lie together in the darkness, Kaspar telling her of Nuln and his life back in the Empire, and she in turn telling him fantastical tales of the ancient Khan Queens and the magical powers they were said to possess. The nights brought Kaspar closer to Anastasia, and they clung to one another tightly, taking reassurance from the simple act of holding another person near.

'It will be terrible when they come, won't it?' whispered Anastasia.

Kaspar wanted to lie to her, but could not force the words to come. Instead he simply nodded and said, 'Yes, the northern tribes are a terrible enemy. Hard, brutal men raised on war and bloodshed. They will not be easy to defeat.'

'But do you think you can defeat them?'

'Honestly? I do not know. A lot depends on what is happening in the Empire just now. I have heard that the great horde that destroyed Wolfenburg has retreated north for the winter and that Boyarin Kurkosk gathers a pulk in the skirts of the Kislev oblast.'

'Is that true?'

'It's hard to be sure, there are so few runners these days, but it sounds likely. If there are still Kurgan forces in the Empire, then Kurkosk could cut off their retreat and starve them to death.'

'What will happen if the Kurgans have already marched north?'

'Then they will meet the boyarin's army, blade to blade, and from what I have heard of Kurkosk, theirs will be the worst of *that* encounter.'

Anastasia pulled herself closer and ran her fingers through the silver hair on Kaspar's chest. 'Do other pulks gather in the oblast? Surely some of the other boyarins must be trying to amass their soldiers.'

'It's possible,' allowed Kaspar, 'but the bulk of the Kislevite soldiery are scattered throughout the oblast and steppe in their stanistas for the winter. It will be a devil of a task to gather them before the snows break.'

'Oh, I see,' said Anastasia, her voice fading as she drifted asleep.

Kaspar smiled indulgently and kissed her forehead before closing his eyes and eventually slipping into an uneasy sleep.

A COLD SLIVER of winter light awoke him hours later and he blinked in its unforgiving brightness. He yawned and smiled to himself as he felt the comfortable warmth of Anastasia's soft feminine body beside him.

Careful not to wake her, he slipped from the bed and pulled on his robe. Kaspar eased open the door to his study and softly closed it behind him. Once again, he missed the familiar smell of the harsh-brewed tea that Stefan always had prepared for him each morning.

He stood by the window, staring out at the snow-covered roofs of Kislev. At any other time, the scene would have been picturesque, even beautiful, but now all he could think of was the brutal killer out there that had taken Sofia.

Anastasia had tried to prepare him for the worst, gently pressing him to accept that she was gone, but Kaspar resisted the notion stubbornly.

Sofia was somewhere in this hard, northern city. He was sure of it.

* * *

II

THE WATER WAS gloriously cool and Sofia forced herself not to gulp huge quantities of the liquid. She knew well enough that her dehydrated body would rebel at too much water taken too quickly. Her eyes had long since grown accustomed to the gloomy attic and she no longer noticed the stench of rotted meat.

The mutilated body of Gerhard had gone, but his killer had not bothered to clean up the sticky pools that had collected beneath his hanging body and the vermin and carrion creatures had feasted well on the merchant's leavings.

Her body was a pain-filled mass, the hot agony from where her thumb had been severed then sealed with hot pitch merging with the ache of hunger in her belly and the rope burns on her arms and ankles. Rats had taken bites from her legs and the physician in her wondered about the likelihood of infection. Each time she found herself slipping into unconsciousness, a fiery bite on the flesh of her feet would hurl her back into her waking nightmare.

Her captor stood before her, his mask draped over his face as always, but his manner altogether different than before. Even through her pain, she had noticed that, for the last few days, he had been much less aggressive than usual, as though some better angel of his nature was slowly swimming its way to the surface of his madness.

The clay jug of water he held to her lips was just one indication of the change that had come over him. And before offering her the water he had, bizarrely, roughly brushed her hair with an antique brush of silver and inlaid pearl. It was an expensive item – obviously once the property of a woman of some means – perhaps a trophy taken from a previous victim.

'Please, some more,' she croaked as he withdrew the jug.

'No, I think you've had enough for now.'

'Just a little more…'

He shook his head and put down the jug.

'I don't understand, matka,' he said in a voice not unlike that of a little boy. 'Why do you want me to kill you? It's not fair.'

'Kill me? No, no, no, I don't want you to kill me,' begged Sofia.

'But I heard you,' he wailed. 'You said.'

'No, that wasn't me, that was something else.'

'Something else? What?'

'I... I don't know, but it wasn't your matka,' said Sofia, warming to her theme. 'I'm your mother. Me. And I want you to untie me.'

'I don't understand,' he said, rubbing the heels of his palms hard into his forehead. He let loose a plaintive moan and slid his knife from the flesh sheath on his stomach, dragging the edge across his forearms and leaving dripping blood trails. He wept as he cut himself.

'He used to do this to me, you remember?'

Understanding that her life hung by the most slender of threads, Sofia knew she had to play along with whatever internal fantasy was being enacted in his head.

'I remember,' she said.

'He used to burn me with hot embers from the fire,' he went on, tears running from beneath the stiffened flesh of his mask. 'He laughed as he did it as well, said I was a snivelling little brat and that he was cursed with me.'

'You weren't to blame, he was an evil man,' said Sofia, keeping her answers neutral and hoping that she would not step outside the boundaries of whatever history he was reliving.

'Yes, yes he was, so why did you stay with him? I watched him beat you unconscious with the flat of a sword once. He made me violate you time and time again and you did nothing. Why? Why did it take you so long to help me?'

Sofia struggled for an answer, eventually blurting, 'Because I was afraid of what he would do to us if I resisted.'

He dropped his knife and knelt before her, resting his head on her lap. 'I understand,' he said softly. 'You had to wait until I was strong enough to stand up to him. To kill him.'

'Yes, to kill him.'

'And I've killed him ever since. It was all for you,' he said proudly.

'Killed who?' said Sofia, and stifled a gasp as she realised the danger inherent in what she had just asked.

But he seemed oblivious to her slip from character and said, 'My father, the boyarin.'

He reached up and ran his fingers down the leathery mask, his words dripping with barely suppressed rage. 'That's why I wear his face; so that every time I see its reflection I see the man I must kill. I killed him once for you, and I'll keep killing him until we're safe, matka. Both of us.'

Sofia felt his chest heave with the effort of confession, but pressed onwards, knowing she would never get a better chance to perhaps direct his lunacy.

'But we are safe now, my brave son. I know you have suffered terribly, but we can be safe, you just have to help me do one thing.'

He lifted his head and stared, pleadingly into her eyes. 'What? Tell me what I have to do.'

'Untie me and let me go to Ambassador von Velten, he can help us,' said Sofia.

He shuddered and she felt him go rigid, as though in the opening throes of a seizure. His head snapped up and he pushed himself to his feet, snatching his knife up from the floor.

'Don't!' he roared, jabbing the knife against her belly. 'Don't try and trick me.'

Sofia cried as the tip of the blade drew blood. 'I'm not trying to trick you. I just want us to be safe, I just want us to live.'

'I... that's... I mean, so do...' he mumbled, dropping the knife again.

He gnashed his teeth and took great strides around the attic, punching the timber roof supports and bloodying his knuckles.

Eventually he stopped his pacing and stood before her, his chest heaving.

'I love you,' he snarled, 'but I might have to kill you now.'

'No, please...'

He bent to pick up the knife, his hand instead closing on the handle of the antique hairbrush. He raised it before him with difficulty, as though some inner part of him resisted, and held it close to his face. He gave a strangled laugh of release as he smelled the scent of her hairs that had caught on its bristles.

'Ambassador von Velten can help us?' he said in his little boy's voice.

'Yes,' nodded Sofia, through a mist of tears. 'The ambassador can help us.'

III

KASPAR DRAGGED THE wire brush through his horse's silver mane, smoothing it to a gleaming fringe that spilled over its powerful shoulders. The animal stamped the ground, its breath misting in the cold air and its tail whipping its rump for warmth.

'Steady there,' whispered Kaspar, rubbing his hand across the horse's flanks, feeling the thick muscles bunching beneath its skin. A bay gelding from Averland, its pedigree was clear and its bearing noble. His morning ritual of brushing the beast was cathartic and cleansing, and Kaspar enjoyed the simple, manual labour involved in maintaining a fine warhorse like this, despite Kurt Bremen's assertion that such work was for the squires.

Kaspar knew it was not a young beast, but it was strong and had spirit. He knew that its stubborn streak and silver mane had earned it the nickname 'Ambassador' amongst the embassy guards, men he could now be proud of thanks to Kurt Bremen's punishing regime.

The name did not trouble him, in truth he was flattered. As an infantryman by nature, Kaspar did not have the affinity with his mount that cavalrymen were supposed to have – often the subject of many a bawdy joke told in the ranks, remembered Kaspar – and he had never troubled himself to learn the horse's name before leaving Nuln.

But an animal as fine as this deserved a name chosen by its rider.

He had given the matter a great deal of thought, knowing that a name can carry great power and had finally settled on one that carried a weight of history to it, that Kaspar thought appropriate.

He would name his horse Magnus.

Finished with the brushing, Kaspar scooped a handful of grain from a feedbag hanging outside the beast's stall and offered it to the horse. The animal gratefully fed on the grain, good Empire feed that kept the beast's strength up and spurred its growth to the extent that, save for the majestic destrier ridden by the proud knights of Bretonnia, the warhorses of the Empire were the best in the world.

Kaspar turned as he heard a tentative knock on the stable door, seeing a sheepish-looking Pavel standing framed in the doorway, leaning against the gate of the horse's stall. Ever since the meeting with Chekatilo, Pavel had kept a low profile and this was the first Kaspar had seen of him since then.

'Is fine animal,' said Pavel at last.

'Aye,' replied Kaspar, tidying away the paraphernalia needed to care for a horse, 'he is indeed. What do you want, Pavel?'

'I wanted to explain about other night.'

'What's to explain? You let Chekatilo get his claws into Teugenheim and led him into disgrace. It all seems fairly clear to me.'

'No, that not what… well, is kind of what happened, yes, but Pavel was only doing what Teugenheim wanted to do. I not take him there myself.'

'Come on, Pavel. You're not a fool, you must have known what would happen.'

'Aye. Pavel thought he could look after him, but Pavel was wrong. I am sorry, Kaspar, I did not think it would get so bad.'

Kaspar pushed past Pavel, the sweat he had worked up cleaning Magnus chilling his skin as he came outside. He gathered up his leather pistol belt and strapped it on. Ever since discovering the hearts outside the embassy, he had made a point of never travelling unarmed. Pavel turned and trotted after the ambassador. 'Kaspar, I am sorry, I not know what else to say.'

'Then don't say anything,' snapped Kaspar. 'I thought you had changed, that you had found a sense of honour. But I suppose I was wrong, you're just the same selfish, self-obsessed man I knew all those years ago.'

Pavel flinched. 'Perhaps you right, Kaspar, but then you the same self-important Empire man with a stick up your arse.'

Kaspar bunched his fists and stared at his old friend for long seconds before taking a deep breath and shaking his head. 'Perhaps,' he allowed, 'but if there's anything else you've been up to in Kislev before I got here, then it ends now. Do you understand me? We have fought together for too many years to allow our friendship to be broken, but there is a war coming, and I can't afford to be looking two ways at once.'

Pavel smiled broadly, puffing out his chest and producing a leather canteen from his belt. He took a mighty swig and passed it to Kaspar, saying, 'Pavel will make priestess of Shallya look like gutter whore next to his saintliness.'

'Well, you don't need to go that far, but I appreciate the sentiment,' said Kaspar, taking the canteen and taking a more moderate mouthful of kvas. He handed back the wineskin and asked, 'Do you think we should contact Chekatilo again, see if he has managed to find out anything?'

'No,' said Pavel, shaking his head, 'he will contact you, but Ursun forgive me, part of me hopes he will find nothing. Chekatilo not a man you want to be indebted to.'

'I know what you mean, but I can't give up on Sofia. Anastasia keeps trying to prepare me for the fact that she may be dead, but...'

'Yes,' said Pavel, understanding. 'She is good woman is Sofia. Pavel like her.'

Kaspar did not reply, hearing a commotion that sounded as though it was coming from around the front of the embassy. He heard shouts and the sound of a horse's hooves stamping on cobbles.

Pavel heard it too and they shared a look, wondering what new mischief was afoot. Kaspar checked that his pistols were primed and they jogged around the side of the building to the grounds before the embassy.

Two Knights Panther stood behind the gates, their swords drawn, while on the other side, two of his liveried guards lay sprawled unconscious.

Circling the angel fountain in the small courtyard before the embassy was a single horseman clad in simple cavalry troos and a baggy white shirt. The fluid skill with the beast and the trailing topknot instantly identified the rider as Sasha Kajetan and Kaspar immediately drew his pistols and marched to stand with the two Knights Panther as more armed men hurried from the embassy.

Kajetan walked his horse towards the embassy gates and Kaspar raised both his pistols, pointing them at Kajetan's chest.

'Don't come any closer, or I swear I'll put bullets in you,' he warned.

Kajetan nodded, and Kaspar could see he was in tears, his face twisted in grief.

'I'm sorry,' he said, casting a plaintive gaze towards the embassy.

'What are you doing here, Sasha?' shouted Kaspar. 'Anastasia is not your woman, she never was. You have to accept that.'

'I need help,' answered Kajetan and Kaspar could see blood seeping through the sleeves of his linen shirt. 'I need to speak, now, before... before I can't do it any more.'

Kaspar had no idea what the swordsman was talking about and took a step forward, keeping his pistols trained on Kajetan's chest.

'Say what you've got to say and be gone,' he ordered.

'She said you would help!'

'Who?' asked Kaspar.

'Matka,' wailed Kajetan and hurled something gleaming at Kaspar.

Kaspar's instincts as a soldier took over and he ducked, squeezing the triggers of his pistols. Both weapons boomed, the bright muzzle flare and clouds of smoke blinding him temporarily. Men shouted and he heard a horse whinny in fear. The Knights Panther quickly moved to protect the ambassador and he was swept away from the gates in a bustle of armoured bodies.

'Stop!' he yelled, fighting his way free of the knights. 'I'm fine. Whatever it was, it missed.'

He looked over to the fountain, but Kajetan was gone, a drifting cloud of powder smoke the only indication that he had been there at all.

No, not the only one. Lying in the snow where it had fallen was the object Kajetan had thrown, and Kaspar saw it was not, as he had first thought, a knife.

It was a hairbrush. Silver and inlaid with pearls, Kaspar felt a surge of fear and hope flood his veins. Old and expensive, the brush's bristles were wound with auburn hair.

Sofia's hair.

IV

HE WAS GONE for now, but for how long? Sofia had bought herself some time; only a little perhaps, but time nonetheless. The fresh water and the embers of hope that she might yet live through this ordeal gave her new strength and determination, and she was not about to let either go to waste.

Her bindings were still as tight, but when he had rushed from the attic clutching the hairbrush, he had neglected to retrieve his knife, and it lay bloodied on the floor beside her. How she could pick it up she didn't know, but, inch by inch, she was able to slide the chair she was tied to towards it. At last she was in a position where her left hand was less than eight inches above the knife, but it might as well have been eight leagues for all that she could reach it.

Sofia gritted her teeth and strained uselessly against her bonds, moaning in pain as the ropes cut into her flesh. Blood ran down her fingers and she wept with frustration, knowing he would be back soon. As much as she hated the man who had done this to her, she also felt pity for him. He had not always been a monster, he had been made into one by the abuse of others. Physical abuse and emotional manipulation disguised as love had turned whoever he had once been into the deranged lunatic that was the Butcherman.

The thought that she had been taken by such a notorious killer terrified her, but Sofia Valencik was a woman of strength, and her determination not to end her days in this stinking death attic would not allow her to give up.

And then she knew how she might reach the knife. The chair was too heavy to tip over in her weakened state, but there was one way she could reach it…

She bit down hard on the rag in her mouth and began working the pitch-covered stump of her thumb up and down the rope. Shooting bolts of agony stabbed up her arm as the blackened scabbing came loose and the rope rubbed against the raw, ragged flesh of the stump. Blood streamed from the wound and tears rolled down her cheeks as her chest heaved with wracking sobs of agony.

Soon her entire hand was slippery with blood and she knew she was ready.

Sofia compressed the fingers of her left hand as tightly together as she could and pulled hard against her bindings, her screams of pain muffled by the rag.

Though the pain was incredible, she kept pulling, her blood-slick hand straining to come free. Without her thumb, there was fractionally more give in the rope. Her moistened hand slipped up a tiny amount and she redoubled her efforts, eyes screwed shut as the pain threatened to overwhelm her.

A flap of skin and muscle around the stump tore and as Sofia pulled harder, she felt the wound rip wider. Even more blood soaked her hands, pattering in a red rain to the wooden floor. But her hand slipped up a fraction more, and even though she felt the wound rip wider the harder she pulled, she kept going.

She gave one last muffled shriek of pain and it was done.

Bathed in fiery agony, her hand felt like it was immersed in hot lava.

But it was free, hanging limply at her side and no longer bound to the chair.

She fought to stay conscious, taking great sucking breaths as best she could through her gag. Sofia knew she was losing a lot of blood and could go into shock at any minute, so, as quickly as she was able, leaned over and gripped the knife handle with her numbing fingertips. It was heavy and she almost lost her grip on it several times, but at last she was able to lift it to her lap.

Freeing her left ankle proved difficult without her thumb to grip the knife's handle properly, but the Butcherman's blade was wickedly sharp and cut through the rope with ease. With her ankle free, she was able to twist her body around, though her movements were slow and painful. She could feel sores on the backs of her thighs and felt dizzy from the lack of food and water. She cut her other ankle and wrist free then stiffly pushed herself to her feet, using the chair for much-needed support.

Sofia ripped the gag free and felt hysterical laughter build within her.

She was free!

Though she wasn't out of danger, the thrill of imminent escape made her giddy. Knowing her legs would not properly support her, she crawled across the floor to the trapdoor that led from this place of horror.

Sofia pulled the bolt free and lifted the trapdoor open.

V

KASPAR BELLOWED AT the crowds before him to get out of his way as he charged along the Goromadny Prospekt on Magnus's back. He and every Knight Panther fit to ride had mounted up the instant Kaspar had realised what Kajetan had thrown him. He didn't know how the swordsman had come upon the brush with Sofia's hair, but knew that the bastard had some serious questions to answer.

Pavel had provided him with the location of the Gryphon Legion's billets and, while there was no guarantee that Kajetan would be there, it was as good a place to start looking as any.

Their helter-skelter ride through Kislev had passed as a blur, too many emotions fighting for supremacy in Kaspar's head for him to think clearly: anger, vengeance, fear and, most of all, hope. The chance that he might get Sofia back thundered in his head, pressing hard against his anger towards Kajetan. Had this all been some ploy born out of jealousy? The thought that a man could stoop so low for the sake of his twisted vision of love both disgusted and horrified Kaspar.

As he had swung into Magnus's saddle, Anastasia had run out to meet him, her expression of cold fury the equal of his own. She had taken his hand and looked deep into his eyes.

'If he has hurt Sofia, I want you to kill him,' she said.

'Don't worry,' promised Kaspar, 'If he's hurt her, then the gods themselves won't save him from me.'

CHAPTER NINE

I

Pain flared in his side like an angry sun, blood leaking from the hole blasted by von Velten's pistol ball. Sasha Kajetan kept his hand pressed against the injury, plugging the entry wound with his shirt-tail. He could feel that the ball had passed cleanly through him from the exit wound on his back, but knew that the real danger was the dirt and fibres that had been pushed into the wound by the ball. He had no wish to end his days convulsing in a fever in the Lubjanko, though he knew that was all he deserved.

His head hurt with the trueself screaming in anger at what he had done. It thrashed against the barriers he had erected, screaming at him that he was weak, a fool, a snivelling wretch who deserved nothing but the hangman's noose.

Kajetan knew that it spoke true and that he was damned, but he could try to make amends for the terrible things he had done. An impossible task, he knew, but that was no reason not to try. He had passed beyond the point where all mortal laws had any meaning for him and wept bitter tears as he rode through the gates of the Gryphon Legion's billet compound.

A trio of his shaven-headed warriors looked at him in puzzlement as he rode through the gates, vaulting from the saddle and slapping his horse on the rump. Kajetan drew one of his curved swords, keeping his free hand pressed to his wounded side. The warriors shouted to him, seeing the blood soaking his shirt, but he ignored them, limping across the courtyard to the unused tack stores, looking up at the dirty skylight where she awaited him.

One of the Gryphon Legion warriors took hold of his arm, but he shook it off, spinning and cutting the man down with one sweep of his sword and a cry of pain. The others drew back in horror, only too aware of his fearsome skill with a blade.

All he could do now was end everything. It was all he had left.

He would kill his mother and then he would kill himself. Their blood would mingle on the ground and they would spend eternity together.

They would die cradled in each other's arms and the thought of everything ending made him happier than he could ever remember being.

II

Sofia descended the ladder with exaggerated caution, every movement careful and precise, her rat-bitten feet tender and painful. Below the attic was what smelled like a rarely visited storeroom. The smell of animals was strong and she could see horse blankets, saddles and bridles piled around the long, dust-filled hall – no one had set foot in here for some time. The tack store ran the length of the building, forming a long mezzanine above a straw-floored stable with several horses in narrow stalls.

Dim light filtered in from a number of snow-covered windows and she could see another ladder leading down to the ground level of the stables. She had no idea where she was, but the glow of sunlight around the ill-fitting stable doors was like a beacon of wonderful, divine hope to her.

Sofia eased herself to the dusty floor and crawled towards the second ladder, as she heard shouting voices from nearby. She heard a cry of anguish and felt hot terror fill her.

The doors to the stables below were wrenched open and light flooded inside.

Sofia covered her eyes, unused to such brightness. She heard footsteps lurch through the straw and whimpered in fear, hesitantly opening her eyes as she heard someone climbing the ladder towards the mezzanine.

Did she hope or fear? Was this liberation or was this death?

She pulled herself towards the edge of the mezzanine, her eyes still watering in the bright sunlight. Sofia gripped the knife in her good hand as she saw a man climbing towards the mezzanine.

As he climbed higher, she saw the familiar form of Sasha Kajetan and let out a shuddering breath of relief. It wasn't Kaspar, but at least it was a face she knew. Then she saw the blood on his arms.

He looked up and she saw the madness within his piercing and terrifyingly familiar violet eyes.

'It was all for you...' he said.

She realised in that instant who the Butcherman had been all along and screamed.

III

THE KNIGHTS PANTHER rode towards the open gates of the Gryphon Legion's billets, charging through and drawing their swords as they saw the armed men milling in the central exercise yard. Kaspar reined in his horse and drew his own sword.

'Where is he?' thundered the ambassador, levelling his weapon at the nearest fur-clad warrior. 'Where's Kajetan?'

The Knights Panther spread out to surround the Gryphon Legion warriors. They held their swords threateningly and even the slowest of the Kislevite warriors could see that they were itching for a chance to use them. And though they were not men without courage, they knew that the armoured knights were more than a match for them.

Kaspar was about to shout his question again when he saw the dead warrior lying on the cobbles and the trail of scarlet that led to the sagging, open door of a long, high stable building at the far end of the yard.

He walked his horse forward and jabbed his blade towards the chest of the nearest Kislevite warrior and pointed at the stable.

'Kajetan?' he shouted.

The warrior nodded hurriedly, pointing to the stables. 'Yha, yha, Kajetan!'

Kaspar dragged on Magnus's reins and the horse galloped towards the building as he heard a piercing scream echo from inside the stables. He charged through the door on horseback, his eyes sweeping the interior for some sign of the swordsman. Kaspar heard a woman scream and his head snapped up to the top of a long ladder.

Kajetan was climbing the ladder, his curved cavalry sabre dripping with blood. Kaspar heard another scream, this time unmistakably that of Sofia.

'Kajetan! No!' he bellowed. Kaspar realised that there was no hope of climbing to Kajetan before the swordsman murdered Sofia. There was only one way to stop him. He raked back his spurs and roared in battle fury, charging his heavy horse towards the ladder.

At the last second he wrenched the reins to one side and the heavy horse hammered into the ladder side on, smashing its base to splinters. Above, Kaspar heard a wail of frustration and the thump of a body landing hard on the packed earthen floor of the stables. Horses whinnied in fear at the commotion, lashing with their iron-shod hooves at the gates of their stalls.

Kaspar wheeled his horse, fumbling for his pistol as Kajetan groggily picked himself up from the floor, his face a mask of fury and pain.

'She said you would help me!' he bellowed.

'I'll help you die, you murderous bastard!' yelled Kaspar, sliding from the saddle and advancing towards Kajetan with his pistol pointed at the swordsman's head. The shadows of the Knights Panther loomed black upon the ground as they blocked the exit from the stables.

Kajetan looked piteously at the upper level of the stables, tears coursing down his cheeks and cutting clear streaks through the dirt on his face. His breath came in quick, exhausted bursts. Though he was wounded, Kaspar had seen how deadly an opponent Kajetan could be and advanced cautiously.

The swordsman still held his blade before him and his eyes never left Kaspar's as Kurt Bremen shouted, 'Ambassador, get away from him, leave him to us!'

'No, Kurt, this is something I have to do. He killed Stefan.'

'I know, but he is *Droyaska*, a blademaster, you cannot best him in a duel!'

Kaspar smiled grimly. 'I don't intend to, Kurt,' he said and pulled the trigger.

The moment froze. Kajetan swayed aside and Kaspar was amazed to see his pistol ball blow out a chunk of the stable wall behind the swordsman. Kajetan's sword swept up, knocking the pistol from Kaspar's hand.

Kaspar leapt away, expecting a lethal reverse stroke, but was too slow.

Kajetan held the tip of his blade an inch from Kaspar's throat and sobbed, 'I am so sorry...'

The swordsman put up his weapon and spun away from the ambassador, vaulting into the stall of a rearing horse. He gripped its mane and swung smoothly onto its back. The beast's lashing hooves smashed down the stall door and with a feral cry of the steppe, Kajetan and his horse galloped out.

The Knights Panther charged, but Kajetan was a master of horse as well as blade and expertly controlled his mount with his knees while fighting with two swords. Even through his anger, Kaspar was amazed at the man's skill; not a single blade so much as grazed him as he fought his way clear of the knights. His own weapons slashed and cut with the ring of steel on steel and grunts of pain.

Kajetan forced a path through his opponents and his horse skidded out into the courtyard, its hooves throwing sparks from the cobbles. Kaspar sprinted after him, shouting, 'Close the gates for Sigmar's sake!'

But it was already too late.

Hunched low over his mount's neck, Kajetan shouted, 'Matka!', galloped through the gates and was gone.

* * *

IV

KASPAR APPLIED A damp cloth to Sofia's forehead, though the blood and filth that had accumulated from her many days in captivity had long since been cleaned off. When the surgeon had said she was out of immediate danger, Kaspar had prayed to Sigmar, Ulric, Shallya and any god that would listen to thank them for delivering her from the clutches of Kajetan, the Butcherman.

In the hours since her safe return, the *Chekist* and Pashenko had sealed off the stable block and were even now scouring the city for any sign of Kajetan, but not before a morbid fascination to understand a measure of what Sofia had suffered had led Kaspar to climb into the attic where she had been held. He had not known what to expect, but the ghastly sights he had witnessed there would haunt him for the rest of his days.

Blood covered virtually every surface and trophies of flesh hung on hooks nailed to the walls alongside cheap trinkets and items of clothing belonging to men, women and children. It seemed Kajetan exercised no discrimination in his killing sprees. A varied assortment of tools, knives, and pliers had been discovered, each encrusted with dried blood and matted with hair. How many people had died in that dark, horrible place was a mystery that perhaps even Kajetan did not know the answer to, but Kaspar vowed he would pay for what he had done.

Sofia had somehow survived her captivity in that dark place and Kaspar was filled with admiration at her strength and courage.

She lay asleep in his bed in the embassy, her wounds dressed by the finest physician Kaspar could afford. They could do no more for her just now and Kaspar knew that the rest was up to her.

He had seen many men, whom the surgeons had promised would live, slip away when their will to live simply gave out, but thankfully, he did not think Sofia Valencik lacked the will to live and he bent to kiss her forehead.

He whispered, 'I promise I'll find him for you,' as he heard someone enter the room.

Anastasia stood in the doorway, her arms folded across her chest.

'How is she?' she asked.

Kaspar smiled. 'I believe she will be alright, though Sigmar alone knows how an ordeal like hers will affect her in the days to come.'

'Has she said anything since you got her back?'

'Not much, no,' said Kaspar, rising to his feet and draping the damp cloth over the edge of a basin of water.

'But she said something, yes?' pressed Anastasia.

'In a manner of speaking,' replied Kaspar, puzzled by Anastasia's insistence. 'She said something about Kajetan not being born a monster, but being made into one. That someone wanted him no better than a beast.'

'That's ridiculous,' scoffed Anastasia. 'Sasha was simply jealous of you, albeit in a manner more intense than I would have thought possible.'

Kaspar shook his head. 'I think there's more to it than that, Ana, I really do. After all, if he really is the Butcherman, then he was killing before I even came to Kislev.'

'My point exactly. We don't even know for sure that Sasha really is the Butcherman. You said yourself that Pashenko thought that there were lunatics who murdered people in the same manner as the Butcherman to mask their own crimes. I think Sasha wanted us to think that he was the Butcherman.'

'But what about everything in the attic? Why would Kajetan do that?'

'I don't pretend to have any answers,' said Anastasia, leaning up to kiss his cheek, 'but it's more likely than what Sofia was saying, don't you think?'

Kaspar didn't reply, unconvinced by Anastasia's line of reasoning.

'But more to the point,' continued Anastasia, 'what is being done to catch Sasha? The thought of him still out there chills my blood, I don't mind telling you. I don't feel safe, Kaspar, tell me you'll keep me safe.'

'Don't worry, Ana,' said Kaspar, taking her in his arms. 'I said I wouldn't let anyone hurt you again and I meant that. They're hunting through the entire city for Kajetan right now.'

'Yes?'

'Yes, absolutely,' said Kaspar as a nagging memory tried to surface in the back of his mind. Something about family estates... but it slipped away as Anastasia said, 'You're going to have to kill Sasha, you know that don't you? He won't be taken alive.'

'If that's what it takes,' answered Kaspar.

'If that's what it takes...' repeated Anastasia, pushing free of his arms, sudden anger in her voice. 'He killed your oldest comrade and, from the looks of her, tortured your friend. What kind of man could let such insults to his honour go unanswered?'

Kaspar had not seen this side of Anastasia before and it unsettled him greatly, but he supposed that she had just found out a man she had counted as a friend and admirer had turned out to be a vicious killer.

'Don't worry, Ana,' said Kaspar. 'Kajetan will pay for his crimes. In any case, he may be dead already. When I saw him in the stables, he was wounded. I think I hit him with a pistol ball when he was outside the embassy.'

'Don't be so sure,' warned Anastasia. 'Sasha Kajetan is not a man who will die easily.'

'Perhaps not, but then I am not a man who gives up easily,' said Kaspar as the earlier, elusive memory rose to the surface with the suddenness of a bolt of lightning from a cloudless sky.

'Of course!' he shouted, snapping his fingers.

'Kaspar, what's the matter?' said Anastasia.

'I have to go!' said Kaspar, planting a hurried kiss on her cheek before running from the room and shouting for Pavel.

'Look after Sofia,' he called back. 'I think I may know where to find Kajetan.'

V

RASPOTITSA. ROADLESSNESS.

It was an apt term, thought Sasha Kajetan dreamily as he swayed on the back of his horse – coined with the prosaic practicality of the Kislevite peasant – and never more so than now. The sheer scale of the white, featureless steppe unfolding before him was an unending vista that would humble a lesser man and drive him to seek shelter within the walls of one of the many stanistas that dotted the oblast.

But Kajetan was denied any such succour. He could no longer show his face now that his trueself had been unmasked. He could feel it rage within his skull, but he kept it locked away, its restraint made easier the more distance he put between himself and Kislev.

The grey skies sprawled endlessly above him, vast and unforgiving. A man could lose himself in minutes in such conditions, but not him. He rode towards his destination as surely as though drawn by a sliver of lodestone metal. Though without any discernable landmarks in this icy desert wilderness anyone else would have been hopelessly lost by now.

Anyone else except him.

His side ached from where he had fallen from the ladder and he suspected that he had at least one broken rib. Below that, he had packed his gunshot wound with snow and bound it tight with his sword belt. He swayed unsteadily on the back of his horse, gripping its mane tight as it plodded north through the snow. He was confident that he could survive the trip, but would his mount? He had no grain, nor was there any forage to be had on the steppe that wasn't frozen beneath the snows.

None of that mattered though; he had his bow to hunt food and if his mount perished, then he would have fresh meat. There was snow enough to melt for drinking water and he knew that his wounds, while painful, were not mortal.

No, all that mattered was that he returned to where it had all began.

Then they could be together at last.

VI

'I DON'T CARE how busy he is,' snapped Kaspar, 'I need to see Minister Losov now.'

'I am sorry, Ambassador von Velten, but the minister has left strict instructions that he is not to be disturbed,' said the bronze-armoured knight, blocking their path towards Losov's chambers within the Winter Palace.

After leaving Anastasia and Sofia, he and Pavel had ridden to the grim, dark-stoned *Chekist* building as though the hounds of Chaos themselves were hot on their heels and Kaspar had explained to Pashenko his theory of where they might find the fugitive Kajetan. Remembering an offhand remark from Losov at the reception where he had been presented to the Tzarina and the last word Kajetan had shouted as he made his escape, Kaspar had been seized by a powerful intuition as to where Kajetan would flee.

The chief of the *Chekist* had been sceptical, claiming that if Kajetan had left Kislev to travel to where Kaspar suspected, then he was already as good as dead. But Kaspar had been stubbornly insistent and had convinced Pashenko to accompany him to the palace, understanding that his fearsome reputation might open doors that he himself could not.

One such door that was firmly shut before them was the door that led to the chambers of the Tzarina's chief advisor, Pjotr Ivanovich Losov, and was guarded by an armoured knight who carried a silver-bladed halberd.

'You don't understand,' explained Kaspar, his patience wearing thin. 'It is a matter of the gravest urgency that I speak to him.'

'I cannot allow that,' said the knight.

'Sigmar's blood,' snapped Kaspar and turned in exasperation to Pavel and Pashenko. He nodded imperceptibly to the *Chekist* and Pashenko took a brisk step forward to stand before the knight with his hands laced behind his back.

'Do you know who I am, knight?' asked Pashenko.

'Yes, sir, I do.'

'Then you will know that I am not a man to cross. Ambassador von Velten requires to see the Tzarina's advisor with information on a matter that may have grave ramifications for our great city. I am sure you, as one of our city's guardians, will understand that I, as a fellow guardian, must see that that information is delivered, yes?'

'I understand that, but–'

'It is a position of no small prestige to wear the armour of bronze is it not?' said Pashenko, abruptly changing tack and rapping his knuckles on the knight's breastplate.

'It is a position of great honour, sir,' answered the knight proudly.

'Hmm... yes, I imagine the shame of being discharged from the Palace Guard in disgrace would be equally great, would it not?'

Kaspar found Pashenko's methods distasteful, but told himself that they did not have the luxury of time to achieve their goal by honourable means. If they must threaten this no doubt courageous knight with disgrace then so be it. Every second they wasted in Kislev put Kajetan further beyond their justice.

'Sir–' began the knight, beginning to realise his predicament.

'And I should imagine the likelihood of securing a commission in another knightly order would be almost impossible with that kind of stain against your honour, would it not?'

Pashenko brushed a fragment of lint from the lapels of his long coat as he gave the knight time to sweat inside his armour and weigh up the alternatives.

At last the knight stood aside and said, 'The black door at the end of the hall is Minister Losov's private chamber, sir.'

Pashenko smiled and said, 'Kislev and I both thank you. Ambassador?'

Kaspar swept past the dejected-looking knight, pushing open the door and marching down a wide, stone walled corridor carpeted with emerald green rugs lined with gold and silver threads that traced an intricate pattern of cursive spirals. Gilt-framed portraits of the former holders of Losov's office lined the walls; grim-faced men with an air of pompous self-importance.

Kaspar paid them little heed as he grasped the gold handle of the black door at the end of the hallway. He turned to his companions and said, 'Whatever dirt or leverage either of you have on Losov, I need you to use it. Whatever it is, I don't care, we need to know what he knows.'

Pavel nodded, but said nothing, beads of sweat glistening on his forehead.

'If you think it will help us catch Kajetan, then I will do what I can,' said Pashenko.

Kaspar nodded in thanks and pushed open the door to Pjotr Losov's chambers without so much as a knock.

The Tzarina's advisor sat behind his desk, scratching at a long parchment with a grey goose feather quill and started in surprise as Kaspar, Pavel and Pashenko entered. Clothed in the ceremonial dress of the Tzarina's chief advisor, he cut a distinguished figure in his scarlet robes, threaded with gold trim and decorated with black bear fur and silver inlaid tassels, but neither Kaspar nor Pashenko were in the least bit intimidated by his rank or finery.

'What in Ursun's name are you doing in my private chambers?' snapped Losov, quickly opening a drawer and placing the parchment within.

'I need you to tell me something,' said Kaspar as Pashenko and Pavel spread out to either side of Losov.

'What? This is intolerable, Ambassador von Velten,' snapped Losov, 'an absolutely intolerable breach of diplomatic protocol. You know as well as everyone else that requests for an audience with the Tzarina must come to me in writing.'

'We not want to see Tzarina,' said Pavel hoarsely.

'No,' added Pashenko from Losov's other side, 'it is you we need to talk to.'

But Losov was an old hand at the diplomacy game and was not about to be put off balance by such obvious disorientation tactics. Instead, he sat back in his thickly cushioned chair and said, 'Very well, before I have you escorted from the palace and lodge a formal edict of breach of protocol I shall indulge you. What is it you want?'

'Kajetan,' said Kaspar simply.

'What about him?' replied Losov.

'He is the Butcherman,' said Kaspar. 'And I need to know where his family estates are. I am sure Kajetan will flee there now and at the reception where I met the Tzarina you said his family owned "wondrously picturesque estates on the Tobol". You know where they are, and you are going to tell me right now.'

Losov said nothing for long seconds as he digested this information. Eventually he said, 'You are trying to tell me that

Sasha Fjodorovich Kajetan, one of this city's greatest and most popular heroes, is the Butcherman?'

'Aye,' said Pavel. 'He is Butcherman, sure enough.'

Losov laughed and said, 'That is, quite possibly, the most ridiculous thing I have ever heard. Coming from you, Korovic, even more so.'

'You are snake, Losov,' said Pavel. 'You and I both know–'

'Know what?' sneered Losov. 'There is nothing you can say to me that matters any more, Korovic. My past is what I now decide to make it, is yours?'

Pavel bit his lip and said, 'Ursun damn you, Losov...'

'Quite,' said Losov, dismissing Pavel from his attentions and leaning forward to steeple his fingers on his expansive desk of imported Empire workmanship. 'Ambassador, that you could accuse one of Kislev's most noble warriors of such brutal crimes is an affront to my great nation, and I shall thank you not to repeat it.'

Kaspar leaned over the desk, planting his palms before Losov, 'Herr Losov, it has been proven beyond doubt that Sasha Kajetan is the Butcherman. We discovered his lair and have an eyewitness to his brutality, what more do you want?'

'And you have seen all this, Pashenko?' asked Losov.

'I have indeed, minister,' nodded the *Chekist*. 'The attic where Madame Valencik was help captive was a most... unpleasant place. I am fully aware of Sasha's reputation amongst the common folk, but have to confess that all the evidence seems to point to him being guilty. You should tell Ambassador von Velten what he needs to know and we will be on our way.'

'Ridiculous,' repeated Losov scornfully. 'I'll hear no more of these slanderous accusations.'

'Slanderous?' snarled Kaspar. 'Kajetan killed one of my oldest friends and tortured another. He brutalised her, starved her and beat her almost to death. He cut off her thumb, for Sigmar's sake! I'll not stand idly by while officious bastards like you let him get away. Now tell me where his damned estates are!'

Losov took a deep breath, calm in the face of Kaspar's outburst.

'I shall do no such thing, Ambassador von Velten, and if you would be so good as to leave now, I am a busy man and have much to do.'

Kaspar drew breath for another explosive outburst, but Pashenko gripped his arm and shook his head. Kaspar turned to see seven knights of the Palace Guard in bronze armour with their visors lowered and swords drawn gathering behind them. So furious was he that he had not even heard their approach.

Losov smiled, a loathsome reptilian smile, and said, 'These knights will escort you from the palace, Ambassador von Velten. Good day.'

VII

PAVEL TOOK ANOTHER long swallow of kvas and stared up at the moonlit silhouette of Chekatilo's brothel, his misery as all-enveloping as the cold that seeped into his bones with every passing second. The guilt that sat upon his shoulders, the guilt that had been growing each day for the last six years, had finally grown too heavy to bear and here he was, back where his fall into degradation and villainy had begun.

When they had confronted Losov earlier that day, his palms had been moist with sweat and his heart pounding in his chest. He had known exactly what he would say to Losov, had known exactly how to prise the information Kaspar so desperately needed from that corrupt sack of shit, but at the crucial instant where the courage of his convictions had been tested, he had crumbled and said nothing. The shame burned hot in his breast, but he could not have borne to disappoint Kaspar again, not after all he had done for him, now and in the past.

He raised the wineskin of kvas to his lips and as he smelled the sour, milky spirit, he tossed it away in disgust. Drink had led to his disgrace and he felt an immense wave of self-loathing wash over him.

Pavel knew that there was no point in delaying this any longer and pushed open the door to the brothel, taking a deep breath and inhaling the musky aroma of incense burners and sweat.

He nodded to a few familiar faces and worked his way through the libidinous crowd to take a seat at the simple trestle bar. He dropped a handful of copper kopeks on the stained wooden bar and accepted a wooden tankard of ale. It was stagnant and flat, but he drank it anyway and waited, shaking his head each time one of the whores attempted to part him from his money with clumsy, graceless attempts at seduction. He saw the girl they had watched dance for Chekatilo numbly ply her trade on a fat man who Pavel swore was insensibly drunk. The fool would wake up on the street without any memory of what had happened and an empty purse, knew Pavel. He had worked as a heavy on the floor of this place for too many years not to know that.

He didn't have to wait long before a callused, swordsman's hand tapped him on the shoulder.

'Hello, Rejak,' said Pavel without turning.

'Pavel,' answered Chekatilo's flint-eyed killer. 'He wants to see you.'

Rejak didn't have to say who 'he' was. Pavel nodded and climbed from his stool to face the assassin. 'Good, because I want to see him too.'

'Why are you here, Pavel?' growled Rejak.

'That's between me and Chekatilo.'

'Not if you want to see him, it isn't.'

'I want to ask him a favour,' said Pavel.

Rejak laughed, a thin nasal bray, and said, 'You always did have a good sense of humour, Pavel. I think that's the only reason he let you live.'

'Are you going to take me to him or not? Or are you just going to blow hot air up my arse all night?'

Rejak's scarred face twitched and Pavel saw the murderous hostility there. Then Rejak gave a thin-lipped smile.

'Like I said, a good sense of humour,' he chuckled and strode off to the same door Pavel, Kaspar and Bremen had passed through some days earlier.

Pavel followed him, only too aware of the dire consequences of what he was about to do. He had already failed one test of courage today, he would not fail at another.

He found Chekatilo eating a plate of steaming meat and potato stew. While Kislev went hungry, Chekatilo dined handsomely. He drank wine from a wooden goblet and did not look up as Rejak led Pavel into the room.

Rejak stood behind his master, crossing his hands before him and enjoying Pavel's obvious discomfort. Chekatilo waved Pavel to the seat opposite him without looking up and said, 'Wine?'

'No, thank you,' said Pavel, the smell of cooked meat making his mouth water.

'Pavel Korovic refusing a drink? Have the Chaos Wastes frozen over?'

'No,' said Pavel. 'I just don't want a drink. I've drunk too much already.'

'True,' nodded Chekatilo, mopping up the last of his dinner with a chunk of black bread and finishing his wine. He poured another and sat back as a girl appeared from behind Pavel to take away the plate.

'Now, what brings Pavel Korovic to me at this late hour?' asked Chekatilo.

'He says he wants a favour,' said Rejak.

'Does he now?' laughed Chekatilo. 'And why is he under the mistaken impression that I give out favours, Rejak?'

Rejak shrugged. 'I don't know. Perhaps he's gone soft in the head.'

'Is that it, Pavel?' asked Chekatilo. 'Have you gone soft in the head?'

'No,' said Pavel, growing tired of Chekatilo's theatrics.

'Very well, Pavel, tell me what you want before I say no.'

'We have Sofia Valencik back, we found her earlier today. She was being held by Sasha Kajetan. He is the Butcherman.'

'I know this already. The *Chekist* have been turning the city upside down looking for him ever since then. Tell me what this has to do with me?'

'Now that we have Sofia back, the ambassador owes you nothing,' said Pavel, hating himself for saying these words, but unable to stop. 'I can place him in your debt again.'

Though Chekatilo tried to mask it, Pavel saw a glimmer of interest in his eyes.

'Go on.'

'The ambassador is desperate to find Kajetan and make him pay for what he did, but he can't find him. He thinks that Kajetan will return to his family estates. Kaspar knows that Pjotr Losov knows where they are, but Losov isn't telling us anything. But you know things. You can put pressure on Losov that we cannot.'

'Ah, Losov, a despicable piece of human filth to be sure. I am surprised you did not use the intimate knowledge you possess to force him to tell the ambassador what he wanted to know.'

'I... I wanted to, but...'

Chekatilo laughed, 'But you could not say anything because you knew that Losov had more damning information concerning you.'

Pavel nodded mutely as Chekatilo continued. 'Tell me, Pavel, do you think your friend the ambassador would enjoy hearing how Minister Losov was the man who paid me to have Anastasia Vilkova's husband murdered, or that Minister Losov is said to enjoy the company of young children?'

'If it helps him find Kajetan, then, yes, he would,' answered Pavel neutrally.

'Yes, I'm sure he would,' grinned Chekatilo, 'but would the ambassador also enjoy hearing how his old friend Pavel Korovic was the very man who, six years ago, bashed Madame Vilkova's husband's brains out onto the cobbles not a hundred yards from this very building?'

Pavel said nothing, the guilt of what he had done while in the service of Chekatilo flooding back to haunt him once more. Chekatilo laughed at Pavel's silence and leaned forward.

'You know I only let you live because I was indebted to your uncle Drostya, don't you? You are a drunk, a thief, a murderer and a liar, Pavel Korovic; just because you swan about with an Empire ambassador now doesn't change that.'

Pavel nodded, tears of shame running down his cheeks. 'I know that.'

Chekatilo sat back and pulled a long cigar from beneath his furred cloak. Rejak lit it with a taper from the fire and the massive Kislevite exhaled an evil-smelling cloud of blue smoke.

'If I do this thing for you, the ambassador will be in my debt?'

'Yes.'

'Why?'

'You said it yourself, he is a man of honour and if you find out what he needs to know, he will not allow that debt to go unpaid,' said Pavel, twisting and knotting his fingers as he spoke.

Chekatilo considered this for a moment and took another puff on his cigar.

'Very well. I will see what I can do,' said Chekatilo eventually. 'But you know that it is not just the ambassador who is in my debt now.'

'Yes,' said Pavel wretchedly. 'I know that also.'

CHAPTER TEN

I

NIGHT AROUND THE Lubjanko was a time to be feared. The howls of the lunatics and dying within its fortress walls filled the air with cacophonous ravings and the fear that their madness or maladies could somehow be caught even by being nearby. As such it was a shunned place, the derelict buildings and empty streets around its spike-topped walls empty and deserted, even in a time when so many were desperate for shelter and warmth.

Even criminals, those to whom the scrutiny of others was unwelcome, did not often frequent the echoing prospekts around the death-house of the Lubjanko. Only those about some particularly dark business would dare the haunted shadows that gathered about it, and even then, they hurried to complete their business rather than linger too long.

But one such individual dared to venture here, working silently in a narrow alley that ran the length of the Lubjanko at its rear, beside an open gateway that led within. The hooded man lifted cloth-wrapped bundles onto the back of a high-sided wagon, sweating despite the cold as he hefted each one. He lifted six bundles onto the back of the wagon then stepped around its front, gripping the driver's bench and preparing to climb up.

'Still coming for the young pretty ones, Pjotr?' said a huge figure of a man as he stepped from the shadows. Vassily Chekatilo sauntered towards the wagon, looking for all the world like a man out for a leisurely stroll in his favourite park rather than in the shadow of one of the most dreadful buildings in all Kislev. His assassin and bodyguard, Rejak, followed him, his hand wrapped around the grip of his sword.

The man addressed turned and threw back his hood.

'What do you want, Chekatilo?' said Pjotr Losov.

Chekatilo rounded the wagon and lifted a flap of cloth from one of the bundles Losov had placed onto the wagon. A young girl, perhaps five years old, lay bound with cord, her eyes unfocussed. She was obviously drugged.

'She's pretty,' observed Chekatilo and Rejak sniggered.

Losov frowned and pushed past Chekatilo to pull an oiled canvas over the wagon's contents. Though dwarfed by the massive criminal, Losov showed no fear and repeated his question. 'I said, what do you want?'

'Well, since you're obviously in no mood to share a moment of friendly banter–'

'We are not friends, Chekatilo, I thought you understood that.'

'Now that hurts, Pjotr, after all I have done for you.'

'For which you have been adequately rewarded,' pointed out Losov.

'True,' said Chekatilo, 'but there is the matter of the man who worked for me that you shot in the head. What was his name, Rejak?'

'Sorka,' said Rejak.

'Yes, Sorka, not a particularly vital cog in my operation, but a cog nonetheless.'

'Never heard of him,' snapped Losov.

'Ah, well, he wasn't a particularly memorable man, but he had just delivered a rather expensive and dangerous item to you, a chunk of warpstone.'

Losov flinched as though slapped. 'Damn it, Chekatilo, you were paid not to look in the box.'

'Yes, but I could not resist having someone check for me. It would be remiss of me not to know what I was smuggling into the city for you, would it not?'

'Very well, what is it you want then?'

'I take it you know that Sasha Kajetan has fled the city, that he is the Butcherman?'

'Of course,' said Losov. 'I'm not an idiot.'

'You know where his family estates are, and I want to know where they are too.'

'What?' laughed Losov. 'Are you now the lapdog of von Velten? Did he send you here? Truly he must be desperate if he sends you to do his dirty work.'

'No, von Velten did not send me here, but that is irrelevant. You will tell me what I want to know or I shall make it known to your peers that you are a trafficker in forbidden magicks, that you are an abuser of children and a murderer to boot.'

'You can't scare me, Chekatilo,' scoffed Losov, though there was an edge of apprehension in his voice. 'Who in their right mind would believe a fat, lowborn bastard like you anyway?'

'You know as well as I do that belief doesn't matter, Losov. Mud sticks, does it not? Can a man in your position afford to have even the suggestion of such wrongdoings attached to his name?'

Losov chewed his bottom lip before saying, 'Very well, it matters little anyway, and the sooner he is dead the better. Expect to hear from me at first light; I shall send you what you want to know.'

'A wise choice, Minister Losov,' said Chekatilo, patting the side of the wagon. 'And have a pleasurable evening.'

II

THE DAWN BROUGHT fresh snows, but Kaspar was oblivious to the worsening weather as he sat on the edge of Sofia's bed and poured her a hot tisane. She sat up with a grimace of pain and accepted the delicate cup. She blew on the steaming liquid before taking a sip, wincing as it burned her cracked lips.

'Perhaps you should let it sit for a while,' suggested Kaspar.

'No, a tisane is most effective when hot,' said Sofia with a smile. 'First thing I learned from my father.'

'Was he a physician too?'

'No, he was a schoolmaster in Erengrad, and a good one too. It was my mother that was the physician in the family. I was apprenticed to her once I finished my schooling, then sent to Altdorf to finish my training at the Emperor's College of Physicians.'

Kaspar nodded, glad to have Sofia back and in, more or less, one piece. Even as he formed the thought, his eyes drifted to her bandaged hand. Sofia caught the glance and said, 'I know what you're thinking Kaspar, but I want you to promise me you won't kill Sasha out of hand.'

'I don't know if I can, Sofia. Not after what he did to you,' said Kaspar honestly.

'That's just it, he did it to *me*, not you. Killing him won't undo what he did, nothing can.'

'Then we should just let him get away with it?' asked Kaspar incredulously.

'No, of course not,' said Sofia, 'but I won't have murder done on my account, Kaspar. I'm a physician, a good one, and I save lives. I won't have any part in ending lives in that way. If Sasha is not already dead and you are able to catch him, then he must see justice at the hands of the proper authorities. And if that means he swings from the gallows pole, then so be it, I have no problem with that. At least it will be justice and not murder.'

Kaspar felt his admiration for Sofia soar at her ability to transcend hatred of a man who had so horrifically abused her. To show such restraint was something he knew he would not be able to exercise had someone wronged him so greatly.

'You know that you are a remarkable woman, Sofia?' said Kaspar, reaching up to stroke the side of her head. As his fingers touched her hair, she flinched and a shudder went through her entire body. The cup of tisane spilled from her hand and shattered on the floor as tears welled up in her eyes.

'I'm sorry,' said Kaspar hurriedly as she drew her knees up, her eyes wide and scared.

Sofia shook her head and sobbed, 'No, it's just...'

Kaspar leaned forward and Sofia threw herself into his arms, sobbing uncontrollably as the horror of her captivity, dammed for so long behind her reserves of determination to survive, finally broke through.

'It's alright,' whispered Kaspar, though he knew such a sentiment was wholly inadequate. He wished he knew the right thing to say to bring her out of the nightmare in her head, but he was only a simple man and did not know what else to do but hold her.

All he could do was say, 'It's alright, it's going to be alright, I promise.'

They sat that way for over an hour, Kaspar gently rocking Sofia and holding her tightly as her sobs gradually subsided. She gripped him tightly, until at last she pulled away and lay back on the bed, her head turned away from him.

'I never thanked you,' she said eventually.

'You don't need to, Sofia. I wouldn't give up on you. I knew you were out there.'

She turned her tear-streaked face towards him and smiled weakly, taking his hand.

'I know,' she said. 'I knew you wouldn't. I don't know why, but I just knew.'

'I'm just glad we've got you back.'

'It is good to *be* back. I didn't think I was ever going to get out of that place.'

Kaspar felt the rapid beat of Sofia's pulse through her hand and though he hated to press her on what had happened in the attic, he knew that any scrap of information she might be able to give him could prove vital in the hunt for Kajetan.

'You don't have to tell me,' he began, 'but why... why do you think Kajetan kept you in that place and didn't... you know...'

'Kill me?' said Sofia. 'I don't know, but for some reason I don't understand, he saw me as his mother. I think that's at the heart of what drives him. And I saw, or rather, I felt... something else there.'

'Felt what? Another person?'

'No, it felt like... like magic, I think,' said Sofia, becoming more animated as her thoughts crystallised. 'It felt like someone or something was using magic to talk to him, manipulate him. I knew there was another reason not to kill him out of hand, Kaspar! Someone made Sasha this way and you won't find out who if you spit him on a sword.'

'Very well,' said Kaspar, placing his hand over his heart. 'I swear I'll try not to let Kajetan get killed, but he may not allow himself to be taken alive.'

'I know, that, Kaspar, but try. Please try.'

'I will,' he promised as he saw a knight appear in the doorway and signal for his attention. He leaned down and kissed Sofia's cheek and said, 'Try to get some rest, I'll come and see you again soon.'

Sofia smiled and nodded, her eyes already drooping. 'I'd like that,' she said.

Kaspar straightened his tunic and followed the knight as he made his way down to the vestibule of the embassy.

'There is a man outside who claims to have information for you, ambassador,' said the knight as they descended the staircase.

'Who is he?'

'I don't know, sir, he has not given us his name and so we have not allowed him past the gates. He looks like a disreputable type though.'

'Don't they all?' muttered Kaspar and pushed open the front door. Snow swirled inside and the aching cold gripped him as he pulled on a cloak handed to him by the knight. He trudged through the slushy snow, the path having been cleared and salted earlier that morning.

A man dressed in thick furs paced around the icicle-wreathed fountain before the embassy, his face wrapped in a thick woollen scarf and shadowed in the depths of a hooded cloak.

Even before he pushed back his hood, Kaspar recognised the hostile stance of Chekatilo's assassin, Rejak. The man grinned and approached the gates, the knights and guards stationed there raising their weapons.

'It's alright,' said Kaspar. 'I know this man.'

'Ambassador,' nodded Rejak with a mocking bow.

'What do you want? We have Sofia back, and all without the help of your master,' growled Kaspar. 'If you are here to claim some kind of favour from me, you have made a wasted journey.'

'We know you have woman back, but Chekatilo still able to help you,' said Rejak, pulling a leather scroll case from within his cloak and holding it through the bars of the gate. Kaspar took it and untied the cap.

'What is this?' he asked.

'What you need,' answered Rejak as he stalked off through the snow. 'Just remember who got it for you.'

Kaspar upended the scroll case and pulled out a rolled up sheet of ragged canvas parchment. He handed the case to a guard and unrolled the parchment.

It was a map, a map of Kislev, and Kaspar wondered why Chekatilo had seen fit to deliver this to him. There was the city of Kislev itself, etched in copperplate lettering and there in the north was Praag, the city of lost souls, and in the west the port of Erengrad.

The map's significance was lost on Kaspar until he noticed that many locations were marked as the territories of various Kislevite boyarins and saw one particular marking, some hundred miles north of Kislev, where the two tributaries of the Tobol merged. Written in a small, precise script were three words that sent his pulse racing.

Boyarin Fjodor Kajetan.

He spun on his heel and shouted, 'Saddle the horses!'

III

'CHEKATILO KNOWS TOO much,' said Pjotr Losov, pacing the darkened interior of the derelict building. 'We should have had Kajetan kill him while we could.'

'What does he know, really?' said a figure dressed in long, iridescently dark robes that seemed to swallow what little light penetrated the boards nailed across the windows, its voice smoky and seductive. 'That he is party to smuggling warpstone into Kislev? Somehow I do not think that is knowledge he will be too keen to see brought into the light of day. And anyway, once the representative of the verminous clans reaches Kislev, it will be gone. We need not worry.'

'No,' agreed Losov, 'but it makes Chekatilo dangerous. He may tell the ambassador.'

'The ambassador is not a problem, Pjotr, my dear; he is already becoming a pawn of Tchar. And let me worry about Chekatilo. When the army of the High Zar has taken the stones at Urszebya and comes to raze Kislev, I will see that he inflicts the most painful of deaths upon Chekatilo.'

'I had to give Chekatilo the location of Sasha's family estates,' admitted Losov, 'and that he *will* tell the ambassador.'

'I know. The ambassador and his warriors set off earlier today to follow Sasha,' said the figure

'Damn,' swore Losov. 'They must not catch him.'

'Do not fret, Pjotr,' soothed the figure, drawing a long, thin bladed knife. 'Sasha had served his purpose and was of no more use to me anyway. He had become too deeply immersed in his madness to control effectively and that Valencik bitch had more cunning about her than I gave her credit for.'

'Then if Sasha is not dead, we must hope that von Velten kills him.'

'Have no fear of that, Pjotr, the ambassador is a man of fierce passions and even though Sasha is far from me, I can still exercise a measure of influence on my handsome prince. So either Kaspar will kill Sasha or Sasha will kill him. It is of no matter.'

Losov watched as the figure bent down to unwrap the bundles he had brought.

The children's pink flesh reflected from the polished steel of the knife.

'These are perfect, Pjotr,' said the figure. 'Pure and innocent. They will do nicely.'

IV

THE HORSE STUMBLED, its movements sluggish and uncoordinated. Sasha Kajetan knew that it would not live much longer, the cold and lack of fodder conspiring to kill it before it had borne him to his destination. But it had carried him further than he had expected and he admired its courage to have brought him this far.

Blinding snow flurried around him, but he guided the dying horse unerringly through the blizzard, his numb fingers entwined in its mane. Kajetan had ridden for perhaps three or four days, sheltering both himself and his horse in the lee of rocks and wrapping them both in the furs he had managed to steal before leaving Kislev. His bow provided him with food and he ate snow for water.

The more distance he put between himself and Kislev, the clearer his thoughts became, the painful hammering of his trueself on the inside of his skull diminishing until he found he could ignore its screaming altogether. The motion of the horse and the unending plateau of whiteness that stretched before him lulled him into a trance-like state where his mind emptied of conscious thought.

He lost track of time and distance, hypnotised by the numbing cold and bleak vista surrounding him, and felt his mind drift back over the years since he had killed his father.

The facts of what he had done to his father in the dark forest had been lost amid the scramble of the local boyarin who had fought to take over his lands. Men who had drunk kvas, hurled their glasses to the floor and filled the halls with their songs of war and sworn eternal brotherhood with his father soon fell to fighting as first one, then another would ride in with his men and take Boyarin Kajetan's halls for his own.

He and his mother would be swapped between the boyarin as they fought to claim the land. None wanted another man's wife and child, but knew that to harm them would invite a united retribution from the others. Such a state of affairs had continued for three years until the moment when his mother had sickened of a fever and, despite the most potent medicines of the local midwives, died one bright spring morning.

Sasha's entire world had collapsed around him, his beloved matka, the centre and extent of his existence was gone and as his father's halls fell into ruin he journeyed north to Praag and crossed the World's Edge Mountains over the high pass. He had travelled along what he later learned was known as the road of skulls and journeyed ever onwards to the fabled lands of the east, driven by a need to set eyes on things no man of Kislev could claim to have seen.

Here he had learned the skills of war from the hidden lords of the islands, channelling every aspect of his being into becoming a master of blades. In Kislev the word was *Droyaska*, blademaster, but on the islands, Sasha had transcended such a state and entered a realm of skill that went beyond such a poor description.

However, the call of his homeland was stronger than he would have believed possible and he had returned to Kislev, earning his passage as a guard on a merchant caravan travelling along the Silver Road to the land of his youth.

His horse stumbled again, breaking his reverie, and he felt himself slip from its back. His fingers slid from the animal's mane and he thumped onto his back in the snow, crying out in pain as the splintered ends of his cracked ribs ground together. He felt his furs soaking and rolled painfully onto his side. His horse was on its knees, its head buried in the snow and its back legs scrabbling weakly.

Sasha knew that the beast was finished and drew his sword, quickly slashing its throat to spare it from freezing to death. He bathed his hands in the animal's blood, feeling the pain race around his digits as the warm liquid spilled over them. Steam gusted from its ruined throat and Kajetan bade the animal's soul a good journey.

The heat of its blood and the hot, metallic scent brought unwelcome memories to him and he shook his head, unwilling to face them as he saw a pale, glowing nimbus of light form in the air before him. He moaned in fear as the shape resolved into a soft feminine face, smiling and ringed with auburn curls of hair.

He could hear laughter in his head and the scent of his horse's blood suddenly magnified until he could smell nothing but its vital fluid and the tantalising scent of its warm flesh. Sasha dropped to his knees and placed his mouth over the wound in the animal's neck and ripped a chunk of meat free. It was tough and stringy, the beast having lost much of its fat over the last few day, but as he chewed and felt the blood run down his chin, he felt stronger than he had in days, as though the essence of the beast's strength were passing to him.

Again his mother was watching over him and he roared as he felt new strength fill him, pulsing around his body with unnatural vigour. Once again she had kept him safe and he knew that he must be close to his destination.

He turned from the dead animal and set off once more, pausing only to gather up his swords and bow. His stride was long and sure and he made good time through the thick snow. As daylight faded, he did not stop, but pressed on throughout the night, the incredible vitality that had filled him upon eating the flesh of his mount still infusing his limbs with power.

DAWN BROKE, ACHINGLY bright and clear, and he gasped as he saw the familiar rocky outcrop he had known as the Dragon's Tooth as a child. The upthrust rock curled over like the tooth of a gigantic beast of legend and he remembered that his mother had once told him that it had belonged to a fiery dragon that had tried to eat the world only to be foiled by another dragon that continually chased it around the world.

Sasha remembered that the Dragon's Tooth was visible from the tallest room of his father's halls and set off again at a run, each stride fire in his lungs as the ground sloped upwards to a tree-lined ridge of evergreens. He scrambled for an hour through the snow, anticipation making him clumsy, until he reached the lip of the ridge and stared down into the hollow of his father's lands. For a moment all his cares vanished like morning mist and he felt an overwhelming sense of welcome and homecoming – as though from the very land itself.

A pair of foaming tributaries meandered down from the high country, looping across the valley floor before joining to form the River Tobol on the near side of a gently sloping hill. Atop the hill was a ruined keep of black stone, its walls cast down and layered in snow. His father's halls, abandoned and unwanted. Jagged timber roof beams speared from the walls and where there had once been a timber palisade there was now only a snow-filled ditch and a pair of splintered posts.

Home.

Further out, as the land rose in a gentle slope, was a thick forest of dark, densely packed evergreen trees and beyond even that was the distant shapes of the snow capped peaks of the World's Edge Mountains. The sky was gloriously clear and birds wheeled overhead, cawing loudly in their airborne kingdom and welcoming him home.

Sasha made his way into the hollow, pushing through the thick snow, a sudden sense of uneasiness building within him as he approached the place where everything had begun: his shame, his terror and finally, his liberation – or damnation – he wasn't sure which.

The earlier elation and strength that had fuelled his mad, all-night scramble through the wilderness evaporated and he sank to his knees, tears coursing down his cheeks as he stared up at the bleak hillside and the ruined hall at its summit.

'Why did you hate me so?' he shouted at the dark silhouette. 'Why?'

Birds took flight from their trees, startled by his yelling and the echoes that rippled back from the sides of the hollow. No answer was forthcoming, and nor did he expect one; his father was years in his grave and his mother had taken every step to ensure that no necromancer or fiend could raise him from it, burying him face down and nailing his burial vestments to the coffin with silver nails.

He felt the tears freezing on his cheek and scrambled to his feet, fording the tributary at its lowest point and beginning the climb to the mount's summit. His steps were halting and weaving, his strength and courage fading with every step he took.

Covered in sweat like a layer of frost on his body, he reached the blackened walls of the ruin and leaned against their reassuringly firm bulk. The stonework was black and glassy, worn smooth by hundreds of years of lashing winds, and he followed the walls around to the back of the building, supporting himself the entire way.

The ground here was uneven, two mounds of snow slightly raised from the uniform flatness of the rest of the summit. Each mound was topped with a simple carved headstone, the lettering faded and worn down by the elements.

He didn't need to see the lettering to know what they said; he had memorised the words long ago and found he could still remember every one.

He released his grip on the wall and staggered over to the grave on the right and dropped to the ground, hugging the cold granite of the headstone tightly. He cried onto the stone and slowly slipped down until he was lying in a foetal position before his mother's grave.

'I'm here,' he said softly. 'Your handsome prince is home, matka...'

Sasha felt the cold seep into his bones and knew that he was going to die here.

The thought did not trouble him overmuch, but the thought of dying alone roused him from his suicidal melancholy. Slowly and painfully he raised himself up and began clearing the snow away from her grave, smiling when he reached the cold, hard earth.

Sasha's hands were like blocks of ice themselves, and he could not feel the pain of digging in the frozen earth with his fingers. His nails tore off and his fingers were bloody in seconds, but he did not stop.

Nothing would stop them from being reunited. He would keep digging until his fingers were nothing more than bloody stumps of bone if he had to.

V

KASPAR STOOD ATOP a rocky crag overlooking the slow flowing Tobol and drained the last of his tea, shivering in the cold night air and staring northwards into the starlit darkness of the steppe. Behind him, the Knights Panther built up the fires that would keep their mounts warm through the night and prepared space to sleep for themselves. Kurt

Bremen sharpened his sword with a worn down whetstone, though Kaspar was sure it was as sharp as it was possible to be.

It was dangerous to be out on the steppe this far north, but Kaspar knew that so long as they were careful to only light their fires at night and in depressions in the landscape, the greatest danger was not roving bands of raiders or southerly riding tribesmen, but the cold emptiness of the steppe itself.

Unlike Kajetan, they had not simply ridden north into the depths of the snowy wasteland. They had instead been forced to ride west along the northern bank of the Urskoy, resting their horses at each stanista they encountered, until they reached the point where the slow flowing Tobol joined the Urskoy. Following the touchstone of the river would lead them straight to where Kaspar knew in his gut the murderous swordsman would be.

It had cost them valuable days to travel this way, but there was simply no other option. To ride into the steppe would be to die – a point Pavel and Pashenko had both made when they learned of the ambassador's plan to hunt Kajetan. But they had made swift progress and, by Bremen's reckoning, they should come upon the fork in the Tobol by mid-morning of the following day. Kaspar had forgotten how much he relished riding into the wilderness, the thrill of exploring unknown vistas and witnessing nature at its most savage and beautiful.

Though he told himself he was a pragmatist, Kaspar knew that he had a wild, quixotic core that lived for such experiences, even harsh and dangerous ones such as this – why else would he have become a soldier? The past week had been hard on him though, painfully reminding him that he was no longer a young man. His knee ached abominably and despite the thick gloves Pavel had given him, he could barely feel his fingers.

Pavel had been drunk when Kaspar and the knights had set off after Kajetan, a fact that caused the ambassador no small amount of concern. Far from the grim elation that had gripped Kaspar and the Knights Panther, Pavel's mood had been sullen and withdrawn ever since Rejak had brought them the map, and Kaspar had been disappointed that his old comrade had not even bothered to say farewell or wish them luck on their hunt.

How Chekatilo had known that Kaspar had needed such information was a mystery, but he was not one to look a gift horse in the mouth. Sofia had wished him success and Anastasia had kissed him fiercely, making him promise to come back safely. Gathering what supplies they would need for their journey, Kaspar and the Knights Panther had set off into the frozen steppe and he had felt a building finality to this journey, a sense that they were embarked upon the last steps of some momentous event whose consequences he could not even begin to fathom.

He trudged away from the rocky crag and descended into the lee of the tall boulders surrounding the place Kurt Bremen had selected as tonight's campsite. He rinsed his tin mug with snow and placed it inside Magnus's saddlebags before joining Bremen at the fireside. Valdhaas had walked the animal and brushed its flanks before throwing thick blankets and furs over it. As much as Kaspar enjoyed the splendour of the wilderness, he was grateful that the knight was relieving him of the time-consuming and tiring task of keeping his horse fit for travel. It was all very well grooming a horse in a well-appointed stable; quite another to look after it in the bleak steppe.

The fire crackled warmly, and Kaspar opened his cloak, allowing the heat to reach his body. On the other side of the fire, Bremen continued to sharpen his sword, careful to keep his eyes averted from the fire and preserve his night vision.

'Sharp enough?' asked Kaspar, nodding at the sword.

'A good blade can never be too sharp,' answered Bremen.

'I suppose not. You are expecting to use it?'

'Aye,' nodded the knight. 'If we do not encounter Kajetan or kyazak horsemen, then there are older, fouler things than men in this land.'

'There are indeed,' agreed Kaspar. 'There are indeed.'

'You know Kajetan's probably dead, don't you?' said Bremen at last, broaching the subject that none of them had talked about since they had left Kislev. The sheer numbing vastness of the steppe made virtually every subject of conversation seem meaningless and trite and each man had spent the journey alone with his thoughts. Only as darkness closed in and a man's surroundings became more comprehensible did it feel that words had reclaimed their meaning, and the knights spoke to one another as though they might never get another chance.

'Ambassador?' said Bremen when Kaspar didn't answer.

'It's possible,' allowed Kaspar eventually, unwilling to be drawn too heavily on the subject.

'Possible? If I may be blunt, Ambassador von Velten, you are not a stupid man, you must know that Kajetan is probably lying dead in a snowdrift right now. A death that's far too easy for someone as evil as him, if you ask me.'

'Evil, Kurt? You think Kajetan is evil?'

Bremen stopped his sharpening and looked quizzically at Kaspar. 'Of course I do. After what he did to Madame Valencik and my men, don't you?'

'I did, yes, but having heard Sofia talk about Kajetan, I'm not sure any more. She said that dismissing what he did just by saying he's evil doesn't really solve anything.'

'What do you think she meant?'

'I think she meant that it's easy to describe Kajetan as evil,' said Kaspar, 'because it's seductive and doesn't require any self-reflection or assessment of the context for his acts. Sofia said that Sasha Kajetan wasn't born a monster, but that he was made into one and I think she's right. She said that if we simply label him as evil and use that as a convenient explanation for his crimes, we're spared from asking why he acted as he did, what drove him to such vile, unthinkable acts.'

'Very well, so why do *you* think he committed these crimes if not for evil's sake?'

'I don't think we'll ever know that for sure, Kurt. Maybe if we take him alive we can find out.'

'Are you that sure you really want to know, Kaspar? It won't be easy taking a man like Kajetan prisoner. I won't allow any more of my men to be killed needlessly, and if I don't think we can capture him safely…'

'I understand, Kurt, and if it comes to it, I'll kill him myself. Have no fear of that.'

'Good. We understand each other then,' said the knight.

Kaspar nodded and said, 'We should try and get some sleep. I have a feeling we will need all our strength tomorrow.'

Kaspar did not know how right he was.

CHAPTER ELEVEN

I

THE MORNING SUN rose early, and it felt to Kaspar as though he had just put his head down to sleep when its brightness roused him from his dreams. He sat up, feeling the cold seep into his bones as he pulled away his furred blankets. The Knights Panther were already awake, rubbing down their horses and ensuring their mounts were fed and watered before seeing to their own needs.

The fires had smouldered down to glowing embers and a knight went round each one in turn, dumping handfuls of snow on them to extinguish them without smoke. Kaspar pushed himself to his feet, rubbing his knee and wincing as his aged frame protested at another night spent on the ground instead of a soft bed.

'Good morning, Kurt,' he said as Bremen climbed down from the craggy ridge above.

'Ambassador,' acknowledged the knight, pulling his panther pelt pelisse over his shoulder guard. Bremen chewed on a hunk of black bread and cheese and tore off a piece for Kaspar.

The ambassador took it gratefully, wolfing down the meagre breakfast as he shivered in the cold air. Quickly he pulled on his many layers of clothing and finally dragged on the thick, bearskin cloak that kept out the worst of the Kislevite weather.

'I think today we should reach our destination,' he said.

'Aye,' agreed Bremen, 'if the map is accurate enough then I think we'll be there before noon.'

Kaspar nodded and climbed to the top of the crags where he had stared out over the steppe the previous night. He stiffly walked away from the campsite to find some privacy and empty his full bladder, returning to find that Valdhaas had saddled his horse and was rubbing warmth into its forelegs. He smiled his thanks to the knight and lifted his pistol belt from where it hung on the saddle horn. Both pistols were primed and loaded, though the flintlocks were safely pushed forwards. His sword was tied behind the saddle and he drew it, enjoying the sensation of its finely balanced weight in his palm.

Beautifully crafted by Holberecht of Nuln, the blue-steel blade was smooth and double edged, narrowing to a fine tip that could penetrate the hardest mail shirts. The hilt was of black iron, wound with soft leather and finished with a rounded pommel of bronze. Simply but elegantly designed, it was a functional weapon, forged by a craftsman who understood exactly what a sword was for: killing.

'May I?' asked Kurt Bremen, admiring the blade after readying his own horse.

'Certainly,' said Kaspar, reversing the blade and handing it to the Knight Panther.

Kaspar was a competent swordsman, but he watched in awe as Kurt Bremen swung the sword about his body in a series of intricate manoeuvres. The blade glittered in the morning light, each cut, thrust and block flawlessly executed and designed to kill an opponent quickly and efficiently.

Bremen spun the blade and returned it to Kaspar.

'It is a fine, trustworthy blade,' said Bremen, 'well balanced and with a good weight, though perhaps centred a little too far from the tip for my liking.'

'It was commissioned specially for me,' explained Kaspar.

'Ah, then the weight is distributed to your preference.'

'Yes, Holberecht and I spent many weeks sparring together with different weapons so he could accurately gauge my strength and reach before he ever laid hammer on iron.'

'A craftsman worthy of the name then,' said Bremen.

'Aye, he is a man of rare skill,' agreed Kaspar, sheathing the blade.

Kaspar planted his foot in his horse's leather stirrup and hauled himself into the saddle, the knights swiftly following his example. Bremen swung onto his own mount and plucked his lance from the snow, resting its butt in the toughened leather cup buckled to his saddle.

The other knights followed suit and as the standard of the Knights Panther rose above the mounted warriors, they bowed their heads in prayer to Sigmar. They prayed a verse particular to their order and Kaspar silently whispered his own words of devotion to the Empire's warrior god, asking for the strength and courage to face whatever trials this new day might bring.

Their prayers complete, Kurt Bremen shouted, 'Knights Panther, ho!' and kicked back his spurs, leading them into the north.

II

ONCE AGAIN, THE unending emptiness of the steppe overwhelmed them, and they rode in silence for several hours, the sun climbing further and further into the cloudless sky. The Tobol flowed darkly alongside them, the soft white noise of its waters quietly comforting and hypnotic as the cold winds whipped along its length.

Noon came and went with no sign of the fork in the river and Kaspar hoped that the map had not been grossly inaccurate in its depiction of scale. They had, at best, another few days' worth of food and fodder before they would have to turn back, and the thought of failing so close to their goal would be galling indeed.

Soon after Bremen called a halt for a rest stop, Valdhaas, who had been riding ahead of the main body of knights, rode back with an excited cast to his features. He carried his lance aloft, its purple pennons snapping noisily with the speed of his gallop.

He reined in his horse in a flurry of snow. 'A mile ahead, perhaps a little more, there is a small valley where the river forks at the base of a hill. There is a ruined hall at its top and some smaller outbuildings strewn about the valley. I believe that is our destination.'

Kaspar leapt to his feet. 'Did you see Kajetan?'

'No, but I did not approach the hall, I rode back as soon as I laid eyes upon the place.'

'What is the best approach?' asked Kurt Bremen.

'As we are,' said Valdhaas. 'This route will take us through a copse of firs and bring us to the southern slopes of the valley. The hill upon which the hall sits commands the valley, and if anyone is there they will see us descending to the valley floor no matter which direction we approach from. There is a ford near the base of the hill and dense forest to the north as well, but I saw no one else around.'

'Then we proceed as planned,' said Bremen. 'Knights Panther, column of pairs.'

The knights mounted up and assumed the formation of fast march, setting off at the canter with Kaspar riding alongside Bremen. He thought of the promises he had made back in Kislev, one to kill Sasha, one to take him alive, and wondered which one he would be able to keep. Though his warrior's heart and sense of honour wanted to cut Sasha Kajetan down like a beast, his intellect and civilised soul knew that to do so would be to perpetuate the evil that had surrounded Sasha for Sigmar alone knew how long.

As he had said to Bremen the previous night, evil was a concept that he had, until recently, used without thought to describe the enemies of his nation. The greenskin tribes he had fought as a pikeman had always been described to him as evil, as had the beasts of the forests that preyed upon isolated settlements of the Empire. But were any of these threats truly evil? Or were they simply acting as whatever had created them had intended?

He remembered a similar conversation he had had many years ago with Stefan as the army of Grand Countess Ludmilla camped in the hills the night before the notorious massacre at Owsen's Ford.

'This battle reeks of ambition, nothing good can come of it,' Stefan had said, sipping a mug of hot-brewed tea.

'What do you mean?' asked Kaspar. He had been a young infantryman at the time and looked to the sergeants and officers of the regiment as fonts of all knowledge.

'I mean that the countess may think that she is doing the right thing here,' replied Stefan, 'but then evil often grows from doing good.'

'I don't understand. How can evil come from doing good?'

Stefan smiled grimly and said, 'Let's say a man stands above a child with a spear poised to kill him. What do you do?'

Kaspar's reply had been immediate. 'I would stop him.'

'How?'

'I would kill him.'

'Very well, let us say you kill this man and save the child. The child then grows up to become a tyrant and is responsible for the deaths of thousands. Have you not then caused great evil by doing good?'

'No, I mean, I don't think so. You're saying I should have let the child die? I could not do that.'

'Of course not, because most men have a code of honour that does not allow them to let evil go unopposed. Had you let the child die, part of you would have died too. Your honour would never let you forget that you had allowed an evil act to prosper.'

'But does that not meant that the killing of the child would be an evil act that would result in good?' asked Kaspar.

Stefan had winked. 'Aye, it is a dilemma is it not?'

It had confounded him then and confounded him still. How could any man know the consequences of his actions? What might be seen as the only true and noble course of action might, in hindsight, be the catalyst for some great evil. The future was unknown and unless a man believed in fate there was no way to judge the outcome of his actions.

All a man could do was uphold his own code of honour and oppose evil wherever he saw it and, after the shameful victory at Owsen's Ford, this had been the bedrock of Kaspar's beliefs.

Kaspar was shaken from his thoughts as they rode into the darkness of the copse Valdhaas had spoken of. Here, the knights were forced to slow their advance, walking their horses through the unnatural gloom of the forest for fear that their mounts might plunge a limb into a concealed hole in the forest floor and break a leg.

They made their way through the forest for perhaps another hour, before slivers of light from ahead announced their emergence from the oppressive trees. The daylight was uncomfortably bright after the forest, but Kaspar saw that everyone in the group was glad to be free of the dark evergreens.

As he trotted to the top of a snow-lined ridge, he saw what was left of the valley estates of Boyarin Fjodor Kajetan. Though Valdhaas had told him the hall was in ruins, he had not expected to feel such an air of abandonment.

The blackened stone of the ruined hall filled him with a sense of melancholy. From the little Sofia had been able to tell him, he knew that the young Kajetan had suffered terribly in this place, that great evil had been born here through repeated and systematic abuse.

The tributaries of the Tobol foamed through a crease in the snowy folds of the valley, tumbling down over sprays of shale and granite before meandering across the valley floor to join the lazily flowing main body of the river. As Valdhaas had said, there was a ford at the base of the hill and they rode quickly down into the valley, making good speed across the rolling landscape.

The horses plunged into the icy waters of the ford, whinnying in discomfort as the water reached up their legs to their knees.

Kaspar looked up at the ruined hall, and for a second he thought he saw a shadow of movement. Kajetan? He didn't know.

But for good or ill, their journey was almost over.

III

KAJETAN WATCHED THE knights ford the river through blurry, sleep-deprived eyes. At the head of the knights rode the ambassador and he choked back a sob. He burned with pain and fought to hold himself from slipping into darkness. His endurance, once so prodigious, was at its limit and all that was left was… nothing.

Nothing but the fervent desire to atone for what he knew he had done. His memory of what had happened while the true-self had been uppermost in his soul was still indistinct, like the ragged fragments of a half remembered nightmare, but he remembered enough to know that he must be punished.

He stumbled back towards the open grave, dropping to his knees before the bones he had exhumed. He lifted his mother's skull, still dotted with patches of faded auburn hair, and kissed it goodbye before slinging his bow over his shoulder and gathering up his twin swords.

Sasha Kajetan dug deep for the last reserves of his strength, whispering the Mantra of Inner Power.

Death might be hovering over his shoulder, ready to claim him, but he would spit in its eye one last time before going into the darkness.

Sasha had seen the cold determination in the ambassador's expression as he rode his horse through the river. He drew his swords, knowing that matka had been right.

The ambassador *could* help him.

IV

THE KNIGHTS PANTHER spread out into a long line as they approached the ruined hall, the wind howling mournfully around its shattered walls and empty windows. Kaspar drew his sword, scanning the high walls and broken rubble for any sign of Kajetan.

He and Bremen rode around the far corner of the ruin and there he was.

The swordsman stood before a dark gouge in the ground, browned bones arranged in the shape of a human body lying beside it. A tattered blue dress had been laid across the bones and a grinning skull topped the macabre ensemble.

Kajetan looked terrible, his hands dripping blood along the length of his swords to the snow, and the bottom half of his baggy white shirt stiffened with dried blood. His face was gaunt and drawn, his hair wild and bedraggled. Gone was the arrogant, confident warrior Kaspar had first seen, and in his place, a haunted, wretched man with the light of madness in his eyes.

But he had his swords drawn and Kaspar had seen enough of his sublime skill to know that even in this forlorn state, Kajetan was not a man to underestimate.

The swordsman looked up as Bremen shouted, 'Knights Panther, to me!'

Kajetan calmly watched as the knights converged on their leader's shout, surrounding him in an impenetrable ring of steel.

'It's over, Sasha,' said Kaspar, walking his horse forward. 'You don't have to die here, you know that?'

'No,' said Kajetan sadly. 'I do, I really do.'

'I know what you went through here, Sasha,' said Kaspar, keeping his tone even and measured. He heard Bremen's horse approach behind him and slowly waved him back.

'Don't think you do, ambassador. You can't. I did... things, terrible things, and now I have to pay price. I am tainted. Tainted with evil, with Chaos.'

Kaspar saw the agonised look in Kajetan's eyes and slowly dismounted from his horse. Remembering his promise to Sofia to try and take Kajetan alive, Kaspar unbuckled his pistol belt and hung it from Magnus's saddle horn.

'Ambassador von Velten,' said Kurt Bremen, urgently. 'What are you doing? Step back.'

'No, Kurt,' said Kaspar. 'Remember what we talked about last night? This is how it has to be.'

'Matka said you could help,' said Kajetan.

'I want to help,' replied Kaspar, lowering his sword.

'I know,' nodded Kajetan with a last look at the skeleton beside the grave. He turned back to Kaspar and said, 'I'm sorry...'

Before Kaspar had a chance to answer, Kajetan leapt forwards, his swords singing through the cold air towards him. Kaspar barely brought his own blade up in time to block the thrust and parried a blow aimed at his stomach from Kajetan's other sword. Instinct took over and he launched his own attack. Kajetan's blades deflected his blows and he took a step back as the Knights Panther closed in.

The two men traded blows, back and forth, for several seconds before Kaspar realised that Kajetan was not trying to kill him. A warrior of Kajetan's skill could have finished him with the first strike of any such contest and as Kaspar thrust his sword towards the swordsman's heart, he realised what it was that Kajetan truly wanted.

Kaspar's world narrowed to encompass only the tip of his sword as it travelled the short distance towards Kajetan's exposed chest. Time slowed and he saw the forlorn look in the swordsman's eyes replaced with one of gratitude.

Unable to halt his blow, Kaspar rolled his wrist and managed to alter the angle of his thrust. His blade descended and plunged into Kajetan's thigh, stabbing through the muscle, fat and bone and sliding effortlessly from the back of his leg.

Kajetan grunted in pain, collapsing as his leg gave out beneath him, tearing the sword from Kaspar's grip. Kaspar stumbled backwards as the Knights Panther closed in and kicked away Kajetan's swords. Kurt Bremen planted his foot on Kajetan's chest and raised his sword to strike the deathblow.

'Kurt, no!' shouted Kaspar.

The knight's sword hovered above the swordsman's neck and Kajetan screamed, 'Do it! I deserve to die! Kill me!'

Kaspar gripped Bremen's arm and said, 'Don't, Kurt. If we kill him like this we only perpetuate the evil that caused this and we will have learnt nothing.'

The knight reluctantly nodded and lowered his blade as other knights moved in to drag Kajetan to his knees and bind his wrists with rope. Valdhaas braced his armoured boot against Kajetan's side and dragged the ambassador's sword free in a wash of blood.

'No, no, no...' wept Kajetan. 'Please... why won't you kill me?'

Kaspar knelt beside the weeping swordsman and said, 'I won't lie to you, Kajetan, you are going to die, though it will be at the end of a hangman's rope, not like this. But I swear to you that I will see that those who made you this way are punished as well.'

Kajetan did not reply, too lost in his own misery, and Kaspar pushed himself to his feet, suddenly drained of energy. As the knights bound the wound in Kajetan's leg, he collected his sword from Valdhaas and gathered up the swordsman's weapons, slinging them across his saddle.

Kurt Bremen joined him and the two men shared a moment of quiet reflection.

'I think I understand now,' said Bremen at last. 'What you were saying around the fire.'

'Yes?'

Bremen nodded. 'Kajetan will die for his crimes, I have no doubt about that, but at least this way, people who hear of what made him such a monster may learn from it.'

'Perhaps,' said Kaspar. 'We can but hope, eh?'

Before Bremen could reply, a shout arose from the edge of the hill.

''Ware cavalry!' bellowed one of the knights, pointing to the far side of the valley. Bremen cursed and ran to gather his warriors as Kaspar rushed to the edge of the hillside.

Across the valley, emerging from the shadowed treeline on the northern slopes of the valley were scores of dark horsemen on snorting steeds.

Kurgans! The northern tribesmen. Warriors of the Dark Gods.

Armoured in black chainmail and lacquered leather plates, their painted bodies and wild coxcombs of hair were bestial and ferocious. They carried a terrible array of broad bladed war-axes and huge two-handed broadswords.

Packs of fanged warhounds, their fur stiffened and matted with blood, snapped and howled around the legs of the stamping horses.

Kaspar ran back to his horse, clambering into the saddle as a Kurgan horseman blew a long, braying note on a curled horn and the warhounds were set loose.

'Knights Panther!' bellowed Bremen. 'We ride!'

* * *

V

KASPAR RAKED BACK his spurs and Magnus set off at the gallop down the hillside towards the river. The Knights Panther unholstered their lances from the leather cups and even amid the desperate flight from the ruined hall, Kaspar was struck by their magnificence. Armour blazing silver in the sun, their standard raised high and iron lance tips gleaming, they were the very image of courage and nobility.

The baying warhounds sprinted downhill to intercept the knights before they could make their escape, leaping in great bounds through the snow and closing the gap between them rapidly, with the Kurgan horsemen following. Kaspar saw the dark armoured warriors were splitting into two groups, one following the warhounds, the other riding in a wider circle to cut off their escape should the knights make it past the first group.

Kaspar drew his sword, wrapping the reins around his left wrist as their mad ride carried them closer to the river. The wind whipped past him and he leaned forward into the saddle, bracing his weight on the stirrups and holding his sword in front of him as Bremen had taught him. Valdhaas, the knight with Kajetan tied across his horse's saddle, rode on the flank furthest from the Kurgan horsemen and Kaspar could see how much it chafed him not to be riding with his lance at the ready.

The horses thundered into the ford, glittering spumes of water thrashed into mist by their swift gallop. But it was already too late to escape. Baying for blood, the warhounds were upon them, leaping into the water with their fanged jaws snapping at their prey.

The knights roared and lowered their lances and the first beasts were spitted upon their iron tips. Wood splintered as lances snapped, the water foaming red with the warhounds' blood and the dying animals thrashed in their death throes. Swords flashed and more yelps of pain sounded as warhounds died. Horses whinnied and reared up as more beasts surrounded them, darting forward to snap at their flanks.

A knight was unhorsed as his mount's legs were bitten from under him. He splashed into the river and was immediately set upon by a trio of snarling beasts. All was noise, yelling, howling and confusion as the knights circled in the middle of the river, fighting to drive off the blood-maddened warhounds.

Kaspar wheeled his mount to aid the fallen knight, stabbing with his sword and drawing yelps of pain from the warhounds. He slashed his blade through a hound's back, leaning back into the saddle as another leapt for him.

Its fangs snapped inches away from his thigh, it claws raking bloody furrows in Magnus's side. The horse reared and lashed out with its iron-shod hooves, stoving in the warhound's skull. Kaspar fought to stay in the saddle as the unhorsed knight rose from the water, his left arm hanging uselessly at his side and blood pouring from a deep wound in his shoulder.

The knight nodded his thanks then fell back into the water as a black-fletched arrow punched through his breastplate, the shaft fully as thick as Kaspar's thumb. Kaspar turned his mount as more arrows slashed into the combat. The riders who had followed the warhounds to the ford galloped towards them, shooting powerful recurved bows from the saddle. He saw a hound plucked from the air in mid leap by an arrow meant for a knight and leaned low over his horse's neck. A flurry of arrows slashed through the air, most ringing from the fine dwarf-crafted armour and shields of the knights. Grunts of pain told Kaspar that not every arrow was thus defeated, that some had found homes in the flesh of the knights.

Kurt Bremen hacked his sword through the last warhound's neck and wheeled his mount to face the oncoming horsemen. With perfect martial discipline, the remaining knights rallied around their leader, the standard of the templars of Sigmar raised high.

Kaspar rode alongside Bremen, breathing hard and streaked with blood.

'Charge!' bellowed the leader of the Knights Panther. 'For Sigmar and the Emperor!'

With their leader's battle cry echoing in their warriors' souls, the knights rode out to meet the Kurgan horsemen. Kaspar felt himself carried along with the knights, caught up in the desperate heroism of Bremen's warriors. More arrows clanged from armour and shields, but Kaspar saw there were fewer than before as the horsemen swapped their bows for long handled flails with barbed iron balls whirling on the ends of chains. As he rode his horse from the river, he realised that these horsemen had made a dangerous mistake.

Sure that the hounds and arrows would defeat their enemies, the Kurgan horsemen had ridden too close to their foe, and were unprepared for the swiftness of the knights' charge.

They desperately readied themselves for the attack, but in a contest of arms between armoured knights and lightly armoured horse archers, there could be only one outcome. The charge of the Knights Panther hit the Kurgans like a hammer blow, lances and swords plucking the ferocious northmen from their saddles in a few heartbeats of brutal, close quarter fighting.

Steel rang on iron and men roared in pain. Kaspar saw a Kurgan punched screaming from his saddle on the end of a knight's lance, scarlet blood spraying from around the shaft. Horses fell and men knocked from their mounts were crushed beneath the stamping hooves of the swirling melee.

Kaspar fired his pistol into the face of a screaming northman, the ball ricocheting within the man's skull and blasting a hole through the side of his helmet. He shoved the smoking weapon through his belt and drew his second pistol as another tattooed warrior charged him, swinging his flail above his head. Kaspar blew out his shoulder with his shot, but the man kept coming, roaring in his feral northern tongue.

Kaspar rode at him and hammered his sword through the Kurgan's chest, dragging the blade clear before it could be caught in the dead man's armour. He fought for breath, exhausted despite the desperate energy that pounded through his veins.

But before the knights could press their advantage, the Kurgans wheeled their mounts, expertly disengaging from the fight and galloping away. Kaspar felt a surge of elation as he watched them ride away and shouted in triumph.

He made to rake back his spurs and give chase, but heard a soaring trumpet blast that he knew was the signal for Imperial cavalry to hold pursuit. Heart pounding in his chest, he dragged on the reins and turned away from the fleeing Kurgans.

Then saw that this small victory had been part of the Kurgans' plan all along.

Further south, blocking their escape along the river were over thirty riders – the second group of Kurgan horsemen. While the hounds and the first group of horsemen had kept the Imperial knights occupied, these horsemen had cut off their escape and now advanced towards them. No lightly armoured fighters, these hulking warriors were protected by armour of dark iron plate, with horned helms and wooden, bronze-bossed shields. They carried long broadswords and double-bladed axes and Kaspar knew that these men would be the most deadly of foes.

The armoured Kurgan warriors slowly walked their horses towards the knights, their manner arrogant and disdainful, though Kaspar knew that thirty warriors of Chaos could afford to be.

The Knights Panther gathered around Kurt Bremen, tense, but unafraid. The horse of their fallen brother cantered alongside them, but even with his loss, the knights were still twelve strong. And twelve of the best and bravest Knights Panther was still a force to be reckoned with. Their confidence and bravery was a physical thing and Kaspar felt a grim pride that if he were to die in this bleak valley, then he would at least die in the finest company possible.

'There's only one way we can do this, Kurt,' said Kaspar, hurriedly reloading his pistols.

'Aye,' nodded Bremen, raising his visor and offering his hand to Kaspar. 'Straight through them with courage and steel.'

'Courage and steel,' agreed Kaspar, shaking the knight's hand.

'Ambassador!' said a voice behind Kaspar. He turned to see Kajetan holding his bound hands out towards him.

'Untie me,' said Kajetan. 'I can help you.'

'What?' scoffed Bremen. 'You truly are mad if you think we're going to release you, Kajetan.'

'What do you have to lose?' pleaded Kajetan. 'They kill me just as happily as you. You and I both know you cannot win here. You will kill many men, but you will fail. Is of no matter if I die, but I can help you live. Let me do this last thing for you.'

Realising that Kajetan was right, Kaspar rode up to Valdhaas and said, 'Let him down.'

The knight pushed Kajetan off his horse, the swordsman stumbling as he landed on his injured leg. He lifted his hands to Kaspar who held out his sword and allowed Kajetan to cut his bonds on the blade.

'Kaspar!' said Bremen.

'He's right, Kurt. They're going to kill us all and I believe he wants to help.'

'Quickly, my weapons,' said Kajetan. 'The enemy is almost upon us.'

Kaspar unhooked Kajetan's weapons and tossed them to the swordsman, who slung his swords from his saddle horn and notched an arrow to his bowstring.

'Damn you, Kaspar, I hope you know what you're doing!' swore Bremen, raising his sword as Kajetan vaulted into the vacant saddle of the fallen knight. There was no time to worry about Kajetan now, and he turned his horse to face the approaching Kurgans.

Kaspar fervently hoped the same as he turned his own horse to face the enemy. Less than a hundred yards separated the two forces, and with a roar of bestial fury, the Kurgans kicked their mounts to the gallop.

The Knights Panther, Kaspar and Kajetan answered with their own bellowed challenge and charged towards the armoured Kurgans. Snow churned as the two groups of horsemen hurtled towards one another.

An arrow flashed through the air and the lead Kurgan horseman toppled from the saddle, a grey fletched shaft protruding from his helmet. Another closely followed it, and another, and another. Each arrow punched a Kurgan from his horse and Kaspar watched, amazed, as Kajetan shot warrior after warrior with swift, methodical precision at the gallop.

The swordsman accounted for eight warriors before hurling aside his bow and shouting a Kislevite war cry. Without the weight of a heavily armoured warrior on its back, Kajetan was able to coax extra speed from his mount, and pulled ahead of the knights.

He drew both his swords and struck the Kurgan line in a whirlwind of blades. His weapons were twin blurs of silver steel, swirling and slicing through flesh and armour with every cut. Three warriors fell from their horses in as many strokes and the momentum of their charge was lost as Kurgan warriors fought to defeat this insane swordsman in their midst.

Axes and broadswords slashed all around Kajetan, but none could strike him. Guiding his horse expertly with his knees, he dodged and parried every attack, his every riposte tearing open a throat or stabbing through a gap in armour to open an artery.

The Knights Panther struck the milling Kurgans and battle was well and truly joined, though Kaspar knew that they would be lucky to live through it.

He saw a Kurgan warrior ride up behind Kajetan and shot the northman in the back of the head. The valley echoed to the ring of Empire forged steel on heavy iron breastplates and the screams of wounded men. Heavy axes punched through plate armour and another Knight Panther fell, cleft from collarbone to pelvis.

The battle degenerated into a confused mass of barging men and horses, blades, blood and screams. Denied the momentum of their charge, the Kurgans had lost the initiative of the fight. The shouts and bellows of battling men filled the valley, and Kaspar could see that the battle hung on a knife-edge. The old instincts of a general returned to him and he saw that the pivotal point of the battle had been reached.

The Kurgans had been shocked by Kajetan's wild charge and had been unprepared for the fury of the knights' attack, but they would soon recover and use the full weight of their numbers to destroy them.

It would take only the smallest spark of courage or panic to win or lose this day.

He chopped his sword through the arm of a bellowing Kurgan warrior, leaning back to kick him from the saddle as he saw a bearded giant with a scarred face cut a knight from horseback with one blow of his huge war-axe. The Kurgan warrior wore crimson stained armour with a breastplate etched with looping spirals, his bare arms beringed with beaten iron trophy rings and Kaspar knew he looked upon one of the mighty champions of Chaos, a ferocious killer said to be favoured by the dark gods.

Warriors surrounded him, each bearing their champion's mark upon their breastplates. Kaspar fired his last pistol at the giant, but his shot went wide, tearing open the throat of a horseman beside the armoured giant. The brutish champion dragged his horse around, raising his huge war-axe and riding straight at Kaspar.

Kaspar swayed in the saddle and the axe whistled past his head, striking his shoulder and tearing free his pauldron. He yelled in pain as the axe blade bit into his flesh, the force of the blow almost wrenching him from the saddle. He regained his balance and struck out at the warrior as he passed, his sword clanging from his foe's thick armour.

Both men circled to face one another again, and Kaspar saw that this was a fight he could not win. The Kurgan saw the same thing and shouted something in his coarse tongue as he charged towards Kaspar.

Kaspar saw a sudden flash of silver and a fountain of red. The bearded giant fell from his horse, his head spinning through the air. Kajetan rode past, bleeding from a score of cuts, his swords flashing as he killed and killed and killed.

Kaspar watched in utter disbelief as Kajetan fought with such grace and skill that it defied all reason. He had heard it said that the true genius of a warrior was to find space in which to manoeuvre, to see the opportunity for the killing blow, while simultaneously denying the same to an opponent. He watched as Kajetan flowed like liquid through the battle, axes and swords seeming to float past him as he spun and dodged with preternatural skill. His blades sang out and wherever they struck, a foeman died.

Kaspar turned his horse, ready to rejoin the fight, though his sword arm burned with fatigue and each breath seared his lungs.

But the Kurgan horsemen were already scattering. The sudden death of their war leader had broken their courage and they galloped their horses northwards, back towards the treeline they had first come from.

Kaspar lowered his sword and let the exhaustion of the battle claim him. He patted Magnus's heaving flanks and ran a hand across his sweat-streaked scalp, groaning as he felt the pain in his shoulder flare where the Kurgan war leader's axe had struck him. His arm felt numb and he flexed his fingers experimentally.

He forced himself to remain in the saddle and turned as he heard someone call his name. Sasha Kajetan rode up alongside Kaspar, his bloodstained swords still gripped in his fists.

Kaspar glanced at the weapons and wondered if he was to survive the battle only to die at the hands of the swordsman.

But Kajetan did not have murder on his mind and spun the swords, offering them to Kaspar hilt first. Kaspar took the blades and only then did he notice the many wounds Kajetan bore, each bleeding steadily and strongly.

Kurt Bremen rode up to Kaspar, his silver armour dented and torn, its surfaces slathered in blood. He saw the wounded Kajetan lower himself across his horse's neck and shook his head.

'I have never seen his like,' said the knight.

'Nor I,' wheezed Kaspar, amazed they still drew breath. To have fought against such numbers and prevailed was staggering. 'He was incredible.'

Bremen circled his horse, watching as the surviving Kurgan warriors regrouped at the ford.

'We should go now,' said the knight. 'Most likely that was a scouting party seeking a route southwards for the High Zar's army. There will be more behind them.'

Kajetan groaned in pain as Bremen rallied his warriors. Kaspar did not know what to say to the swordsman. The man had killed his oldest friend, tortured another and had now saved their lives.

He remembered the look in Kajetan's eyes as they had fought at the top of the hill and Kaspar smiled, finally understanding the dilemma Stefan had posed before the battle at Owsen's Ford.

'Ambassador,' said Bremen. 'We need to go now.'

'Aye,' said Kaspar, helping Kajetan to sit up in his saddle. 'Let's get out of here.'

Epilogue

I

KASPAR KNEW HE had never seen a more welcome sight than the towers and buildings of Kislev, ringed by the high wall and sprawling camps of refugees and soldiers. He remembered his first sight of the walls, nearly four months ago, and the sense of anticipation he had felt.

The ride south towards Kislev had been exhausting, Kurt Bremen unwilling to tarry any longer in the north than he had to. There was every possibility that more Kurgan riders would come after them, but they had seen no signs of pursuit and their travels had been without incident. Despite the incredible feat of defeating so many foes, the knights were subdued, partly due to the emptiness of the steppe, and partly due to the loss of three of their brethren to the Kurgans. The standard of the Knights Panther had been kept lowered and Kaspar knew it pained Kurt Bremen to have to leave their bodies behind, but there had simply been no time to recover them.

Their riderless horses were tethered to the saddles of the surviving knights and followed sadly behind the group, as though they knew that their masters were never to ride them into battle again. Kajetan had said nothing the entire journey, save to thank the knight who had stitched his wounds. Since the battle at the ford, he had retreated into a catatonic state, ignoring every question and keeping his head bowed whenever he was addressed. Though he had made no attempt to escape, Bremen was taking no chances and had ordered his wrists bound and that Valdhaas lead his horse.

Understanding a measure of Kajetan's madness, Kaspar did not believe such precautions were necessary, but was in no mind to argue with the knight.

'I never thought I would be glad to see this place again,' said Bremen, riding alongside Kaspar.

Kaspar nodded, too weary to reply. His injured shoulder still hurt like hell, but he smiled to himself, looking forward to seeing Sofia, Anastasia and Pavel again. He twisted in the saddle, seeing Kajetan looking up at the city with an expression of fear and loathing. He supposed that was understandable, given that the *Chekist* would in all likelihood want to hang him as soon as he was within the walls.

That was something Kaspar was determined to prevent. There were powers at work behind Kajetan, and Kaspar was unwilling to let the swordsman go to the gallows without first trying to discover who they were. He could already anticipate the confrontation with Pashenko.

Kaspar sighed. He had hoped that with the capture of the Butcherman, the coming days would be somewhat less chaotic than he had seen so far.

But he had a feeling that that was not going to be the case.

II

SNOW SWIRLED ALONG the night-shrouded length of the valley as the nine riders climbed their way to the top of its rocky sides. Swathed in thick furs, they resembled wild beasts more than humans.

Nothing lived here; nothing could, the rocky ground and howling winds ensured that nothing could survive and kept this part of Kislev uninhabited.

The riders forced their weary mounts to the top of the valley, a deep gouge in the earth that looked for all the world as though the land had split apart and pulled itself a long, snaking wound. Fighting against the worsening weather, the riders pushed onwards and upwards, though it seemed as though the very elements fought to prevent their progress.

Through the blizzard, a vast upthrust crag emerged from the night. A tall menhir, some forty or fifty feet high and formed of a hard, smooth stone, its top was lost in the snow and darkness. Wedged deep in the earth and spearing into the moonlit sky, the huge stone was etched with angular carvings that might once have been crude pictograms before the wind had rendered them illegible.

The riders halted at the base of the huge standing stone, dismounting and pacing around its bulk as though inspecting it. One of the riders, a broad shouldered giant with a horned helm and visor carved in the form of a snarling wolf stepped forward and placed his gauntleted palm against the stone.

'Be careful, my lord,' said a rider hung with bones and charms. 'The stones sing with power.'

'Good,' said the helmeted warrior, turning to face his shaman. 'Bring forth the offering to Tchar.'

High Zar Aelfric Cyenwulf placed his other palm against the stone and smiled. The Dolgans called this place Urszebya – Ursun's Teeth – believing them to be fragments of the bear god's fangs left behind after he took a bite from the world. He smiled at the ridiculousness of such a notion.

Though he knew it was reckless of him to come this far south without his army, he had needed to see the stones for himself, and as he removed a mailed gauntlet and placed his callused hand against the cold stone, he knew that the dangerous journey had not been made in vain. Though no sorcerer, he could feel the power that suffused the stone and gave praise to Tchar that he had been led to this place.

'My lord,' said his shaman, pushing a bound man to his knees before the High Zar.

Aelfric Cyenwulf stepped away from the stone and opened his furs, letting the cloak fall to the ground. Beneath his furs he wore iridescent plates of heavy steel armour that rippled and threw back the moonlight as though a sheen of oil slithered across its surfaces. Edged with fluted spirals of gold and silver, the breastplate was moulded to resemble powerful pectoral and abdominal muscles. The flesh of his arms was all but obscured by the many beaten iron trophy rings and painted tattoos that writhed with the bulging of his corded muscles. A huge pallasz, its blade fully six feet in length, was sheathed over his shoulder, its pommel worked in the shape of a snarling daemon.

He removed his helmet and handed it to one of his warriors. A wild mane of silver hair, with a streak of black at either temple spilled around his shoulders, framing a face ritually scarred – six cuts on the left cheek, four on the right – that radiated a ruthless intelligence.

The High Zar loomed above his warriors, a powerful champion in the service of the mighty gods of the north, the true gods of man, Masters of the End Times and soon-to-be inheritors of this world.

Before him, the captive shivered and wept, now naked but for a soiled loincloth.

The High Zar smiled, exposing teeth filed down to sharpened points and bent down to lift the captive by the neck in one meaty hand.

The man struggled in the High Zar's grip, but there could be no escape. The towering champion of Chaos pulled the captive close and bit out his throat with a roar of praise to Tchar, holding the shuddering corpse towards the stone and allowing the jetting blood to spatter the giant menhir.

His shaman leaned forward, examining the patterns formed by the blood as it flowed down the stone, tracing his own designs in the sticky liquid as it reached the faded pictograms. The High Zar tossed aside the dead body, spitting a mouthful of flesh at the base of the stone and said, 'Well? What do the omens say?'

The shaman turned and said, 'I can feel the pulse of the world beneath us.'

'And?'

'It is afraid.'

The High Zar laughed. 'It has reason to be.'

BOOK TWO
URSUN'S TEETH

Prologue

KAR ODACEN KNEW that the lightning bolt he had waited his entire life for would strike the mountain long before it split the sky. A mighty peal of thunder rolled across the heavens, the rain falling in an unending torrent, as though the seas of the world had been carried into the sky by the gods and now flooded forth in an attempt to drown all the lands of men.

He could feel the power of the lightning seething above him, summoned to the land below by the magicks he and every shaman of the Iron Wolves before him had drawn to these mountains since time before memory.

The jagged peak above him was a dark spike against the flickering sky, the gods battling in the clouds casting their ghostly lights across the highlands of the World's Edge Mountains. He felt the hairs on his scarred and becharmed arms stand erect as he passed a column of bleached skulls, fully as tall as the greatest warrior of the Wolves, the tip of the copper pole they were impaled upon protruding a span above the topmost skull. Ripples of blue fire danced along the length of the column of bone, flickering within the empty eye sockets of the grinning skulls, imparting them with a malicious anime. Hundreds of such tribute poles ringed the peak of the mountain, a sign to the Old One who slept beneath the world that he was remembered; that the warriors and shamans of the Iron Wolves had not forgotten him. These mountains were old when the world was young and the Iron Wolves had never dared forget their duty to them.

The High Zars of the Iron Wolves had laid a thousand times a thousand skulls from a hundred lifetimes of war at their shamans' feet and, as the centuries passed, each generation would add more skulls on their copper poles to the mountain. In preparation for his attack into Kislev, the High Zar of the Iron Wolves, Aelfric Cyenwulf himself, had bade his shaman raise countless skulls in honour of the Dark Gods.

Kar Odacen passed one such tribute pole, a sense of fearful anticipation growing within his breast. He had awoken from a dream in which packs of the ravenous, black-furred wolves of the north chased a solitary white wolf across the heavens. Upon the shimmering white wolf's back was a mighty-thewed warrior clad in furs who wielded a great warhammer, and though this wolf was powerful, it could not outpace its hunters. The white wolf turned at bay atop a tall peak of ice-slick rock and together it and the rider fought the snapping packs of northern wolves. Man and wolf fought hard and well, spilling the blood of hundreds of their foes, but even as they took heart in their slaughter, the dark wolves changed to become a roiling storm cloud of impenetrable darkness, pierced only by lava-hot spears of lightning that opened great gashes in the flesh of both man and wolf.

Though he could not see within the cloud, Kar Odacen's dream-self knew that something unimaginably ancient and monstrously evil lay at its heart. And even he, who had sent his spirit into the realm of the daemonkin, knew to dread its power.

Without warning the dark storm suddenly swelled to swallow the man and his wolf whole and Kar Odacen had woken knowing that the night his distant predecessors had prophesied had finally come. He had set off into the darkness, climbing breathlessly for hours as the rain pounded like hammer blows on his shaven, tattooed head and his feet were torn bloody by razor-sharp rocks.

Another boom of thunder, like the gods' footsteps on the world, rolled across the sky, but Kar Odacen did not bother to look up, knowing in his bones that it was not yet time.

He reached a plateau of sheared rock, two hundred yards or more below the peak, his breath like hot smoke in his lungs, and dropped to his knees with arms raised above him in praise of this most holy night. Even over the unceasing roar of the rain he could hear the crackling from the skull columns below him grow louder, feeling the heat of the fire that danced between them as it reached deep into the heart of the mountain.

The skies rumbled and the mountain shook, as though bracing itself for what must happen next and Kar Odacen felt a swelling of dark and terrible power. He looked up as the heavens split apart with a vast, incandescent sheet of lightning that struck the highest peak of the mountain, its brightness searing the sight from his eyes.

The mountaintop exploded, disappearing in a gigantic cloud of rubble and smoke. Rocks were hurled hundreds of yards into the air, tumbling down in an avalanche of blasted shale. Kar Odacen screamed the name of his Dark Gods as the rubble smashed down all around him, pulverising the slopes of the mountain, but, impossibly, leaving him unscathed. Blood dripped from his ears and he blinked the searing after-image of the lightning from his eyes as he felt the hard rain cease and the deafening echoes of the thunder and explosion fade to nothing, leaving him swaying and alone on the smashed mountaintop.

Kar Odacen lowered his arms, feeling a tremor of dread run through the rock of the mountain. A similar feeling of fear and awe took him in its grip. The sudden silence of the mountains after the violence of the storm was more terrifying than anything he had known before.

A creeping horror slowly overtook him, rising languidly through his bones as the throat of something that had seen the birth of the world took its first breath in uncounted ages. Blinking away tears of rapture and terror, Kar Odacen saw a writhing column of impossibly black, lightning-hearted smoke rise from the smashed caldera of the mountaintop, its sapphire innards crackling with a horrifying, fiery urgency. Though no breath of wind disturbed the night, the smoke gathered itself together, and slid down the mountainside like a dark slick upon the air.

The mountain shuddered with the tread of something magnificent and terrible, rocks crushed to powder beneath its weight and power. The baleful glow from the smoke's innards grew fiercer as it approached the paralysed shaman, the horror concealed there pausing to regard him with as much interest as a man might pay an ant before continuing on its thunderous journey towards the new world below.

Kar Odacen shivered and let out a juddering breath, shaking like a newborn foal.

'The End Times are upon this world...' he whispered through trembling lips.

CHAPTER ONE

I

Built atop the *Gora Geroyev*, the city of Kislev was an impressive sight. High walls of smooth black stone were topped with saw-toothed ramparts and constructed with the practicality common to its northern inhabitants. Tall towers jutted from either side of the thick timber gate and enfilading cannon positions covered the road leading towards the city with their bronze muzzles.

The tops of tall buildings reared above the walls, as if daring an attacker to try and sack them, and the tips of the spears carried by the fur-clad soldiers who walked the ramparts glittered in the low, evening sun. Surrounding the base of the walls were thousands of refugees, people driven from their homes in the north of the country by the warriors of High Zar Aelfric Cyenwulf, a blood-thirsty war leader of the Kurgan tribes.

A sprawling canvas city housing thousands – tens of thousands – gathered around the city, clinging to the walls as though seeking safety by virtue of their proximity.

'Precious little protection to be had here,' whispered Kaspar von Velten, ambassador of the Emperor Karl-Franz, pulling his cloak tighter about himself as a blast of freezing air whipped across the packed hillside. The Tzarina had been forced to bar the gates to prevent further refugees from entering the already overcrowded city. When the High Zar's army came south, as soon it must, the city would quickly starve should the entirety of the fleeing populace be given sanctuary within its walls.

'No,' agreed Kurt Bremen, leader of the group of Knights Panther who rode with Kaspar. 'It will be a slaughter.'

'Perhaps,' said Kaspar. 'Unless Boyarin Kurkosk can stop the Kurgans north of here.'

'Do you think he can?'

'It's possible,' allowed Kaspar. 'I'm told the boyarin is a great warrior and he gathers nearly fifty thousand men to his banner.'

'For these people's sake, let us hope he is a great leader of men as well as a great warrior. The two are not always the same thing.'

Kaspar nodded, guiding his horse along the frozen, rutted roadway between twin rows of makeshift campsites and riding towards the gates of the city. Cold, frightened people glanced up as he and his knights passed, but their misery was too complete for them to pay much attention to them. He felt his heart go out to them, brutalised as they were by months of war and hardship, and wished he could do more to help them.

The gates of the city groaned open as his weary group approached, crowds of desperate people gathering what meagre belongings they had managed to carry from their stanistas and hurrying towards the gates, pleas for entry pouring from every mouth.

Kossars in long, padded coats and green tabards emerged from within and blocked the gateway with long-hafted axes and shouted oaths. Fierce-looking men with helms of bronze and long, drooping moustaches, they pushed the wailing refugees back without mercy and Kaspar had to fight the urge to shout at them. These were their own people they were condemning to the freezing temperatures, but the part of Kaspar that had once been a general in the Emperor's armies knew that they were only obeying orders that he himself would have given were he in charge of the city's defences.

He eased his silver-maned steed, Magnus, through the yelling crowds, turning as a weeping woman pulled at his snow-limned cloak. She wore a threadbare pashmina over a coarse black dress and thrust a swaddled babe towards him, pleading with him in snatches of rapid Kislevite.

Kaspar shook his head, 'Nya Kislevarin, Nya.'

The woman fought off the kossars' attempts to pull her away from Kaspar, screaming and fighting to place the baby in his arms. Even as she was finally dragged away, Kaspar could see that her efforts had been in vain: the child was long-dead, blue and frozen.

Fighting back his sadness, he rode through the cold darkness of the gateway, pathetically grateful to emerge into the cold, miserable confines of the winter-gripped city. The scene inside the walls was little better, the streets lined with gaunt, fur-wrapped people, huddled together and shuffling aimlessly and fearfully along the city streets.

Though he knew his actions in Kislev over the last few months had already saved many lives, having stopped a corrupt Empire merchant from profiteering from stolen supplies destined for the people of Kislev, Kaspar felt fresh resolve to do more.

His personal guard of Knights Panther, mighty armoured knights atop enormous Averland destriers, were weary after nearly two weeks spent out in the frozen wilderness of Kislev. They followed him inside, all visibly struggling with the idea of leaving these people outside the walls.

In the centre of the Knights Panther rode Sasha Kajetan, once the most beloved and heroic figure in Kislev, a swordsman beyond compare and leader of one of the Tzarina's most glorious cavalry regiments. Kajetan was now a broken man, virtually catatonic and skeletally thin after his flight into the oblast.

Kajetan's hands were bound before him, his true nature as a brutal murderer having only recently come to light when he had killed Kaspar's oldest friend, before abducting and torturing his physician.

But Kajetan was now captured and though the feared *Chekist* would surely want him hung, Kaspar was determined to delay the swordsman's fate for as long as possible to try and fathom what had driven the man to such murderous extremes.

Kajetan caught Kaspar's look and nodded weakly in acknowledgement. Kaspar was surprised; it was the first human gesture the swordsman had made since they had fought their way through the Kurgan scouting party in the oblast nearly a week ago.

Kaspar watched as the gates closed, pushed shut by nearly a score of kossars and barred with thick spars of hardened timber.

'Sigmar forgive us...' he whispered, turning his horse and riding along the Goromadny Prospekt towards Geroyev Square in the centre of the city.

During the summer and spring months, the square was traditionally the site of a thriving market, thronged with trappers selling their wares, horse traders and all manner of merchants. When Kaspar had first come to Kislev, enthusiastic crowds had gathered, yelling and cursing around a corral of plains ponies, the bidding spirited and lively, but now the square was packed to capacity with innumerable campsites, clusters of tents and sputtering cookfires covering every inch of ground.

It was a sight typical around Kislev, a city in which there were many wide boulevards lined with hardy evergreens – most of which had long since been cut down for firewood. The hulking iron statues of long-dead tzars watched over their people's misery impassively, powerless to aid them in their time of need.

The Winter Palace of the Ice Queen dominated the far side of the square, its white towers and gleaming marble walls of ice glittering like glass in the low evening sunlight.

'The Ice Queen left the gates open too long,' observed Kurt Bremen. 'There are too many people within the walls. Many of them will starve to death when Kislev comes under siege.'

'I know, Kurt, but these are her people, she could not leave them all to die. She would save her city, but lose her people,' replied Kaspar, riding along the edge of the square towards the Temple of Ulric and the Empire embassy that lay behind it.

'Unless there is some better news from the Empire, she may lose it anyway. With Wolfenburg gone, it is doubtful the Emperor will send his armies north when there are enemies within our own lands.'

'They will come, Kurt,' promised Kaspar.

'I hope you are right, ambassador.'

'Have you ever met the Emperor?' asked Kaspar, turning in the saddle to face the knight.

'No, I have not had that honour.'

'I have, and Karl-Franz is a man of courage and honour,' said Kaspar. 'He is a warrior king and I have fought alongside him on more than one occasion. Against orcs, Norse raiders and the beasts of the forests. He has sworn to aid Kislev and I do not believe he will forsake that oath.'

Kurt Bremen smiled. 'Then I too will believe it.'

II

BOTH RATCATCHERS WERE so inured to the reek of shit that neither now paid it any mind. Hundreds of tonnes of human and animal waste flowed through the sewers below the streets of Kislev, carried through the oval tunnels dug through the rock and earth of the *Gora Geroyev* to empty far downriver into the Urskoy.

Commissioned by Tzar Alexis and designed by the ingenious Empire engineer, Josef Bazalgette, the tunnels below Kislev were amongst the greatest engineering marvels of the north, effectively eliminating the scourge of cholera from the Kislevite capital. Mile upon mile of twisting tunnels extended in a labyrinthine maze beneath the streets like the tunnels beneath the Fauschlag of Middenheim; though these tunnels were formed of bricks and mortar rather than from the natural rock.

A pair of small dogs padded before the two ratcatchers along the ledge that ran alongside the foaming river of effluent, their tails erect and ears pressed flat against their skulls. The rushing of the sewage echoed from the glistening brick walls, keeping conversation to a minimum.

Both men were clad in stiffened leathers, crusted with age and filth, and high, hobnailed boots. They wore thin metal helmets, padded with matted fur and scarves around their mouths and noses. Though they barely noticed the smell any more, they wore the protective scarves through force of habit. Each man carried a long pole over one shoulder, a single rat dangling by its tail from each of them.

'A poor day, Nikolai, a poor day,' said the shorter of the two ratcatchers with a weary shrug that made the rat on his pole dance in an imitation of life.

'Aye, Marska, few vermin to catch today,' agreed his apprentice, Nikolai, casting an irritated glance at the two dogs. 'What shall we eat tonight?'

'I think we shan't be presenting these sorry specimens to the city authorities for a copper kopek,' sighed Marska. 'I fear we may be dining on rat again, my friend.'

'Perhaps tomorrow will be better. We could sell some to the refugees?'

'Aye, maybe we can,' said Nikolai doubtfully.

Winter's icy grip and the bloodthirsty ravages of a Kurgan barbarian war leader, whose armies were even now closing on the city, had displaced thousands of people from their homes on the steppe and many now huddled, cold and frightened, around the walls of the northern capital. It was true that the refugees who flocked to the camps outside the city walls were willing to eat pretty much anything and there had been some nice money in selling rat meat to them. But that had been before the cold had killed most of the rats and the few emaciated creatures they had managed to trap were the only food that they themselves could expect to see for some time.

The two men trudged on in silence for some time until Nikolai nudged Marska as he saw the two dogs suddenly stiffen and draw their jowls back over sharp teeth. Neither dog made a sound, their vocal chords having long since been cut, but their bowstring-taut posture told both ratcatchers that they had sensed something they didn't like. Ahead, Marska knew the passage widened into a high-domed chamber where a number of divergent effluent tunnels converged before heading out to the Urskoy.

Marska unhooked a small hand crossbow from his belt and eased back the string, wincing when the mechanism clicked as it caught. But to keep the weapon cocked would lose the tension in the string and reduce the power in the bolt. The weapon was an indulgence; most ratcatchers could only ever afford a sling and pebbles for shot, but one glorious summer, Marska had discovered a body floating in the sewers with a purse bulging with gold coins. He had hidden the coins about his person for many months before daring to spend them. Nikolai slipped a rounded pebble into his sling and eased himself past the two dogs, his footsteps silent for such a big man.

Ahead, Marska could hear voices, muffled and obscured, but years of working below the streets of Kislev had given him a good ear for picking out sounds that wouldn't normally be expected here.

Nikolai turned and gestured quizzically along the length of the tunnel to a sprawling pile of debris, bricks and mud that lay on the ledge that ran alongside the effluent. The rubble looked for all the world as though it had been pushed from the wall and Marska wondered who in their right mind would want to tunnel *into* a sewer. The dogs padded along silently, stopping as they reached the tumble of debris, dipping their heads to sniff at something on the ledge.

Marska ghosted forwards and crouched beside the mud that had spilled from the hole in the wall. Tracks, but tracks that didn't make any sense. They were smudged and deep, as though whoever or whatever had made them had been carrying something heavy, but that wasn't the first thing Marska noticed that was odd. It was hard to be sure, but the prints looked as though they only had four toes on each foot, and from the conical depression a little beyond each toe, it appeared as though they were clawed...

It was obvious that whatever had made the tracks walked on two legs, but what manner of man had only four toes and claws? An altered perhaps, or one of the beasts of the dark forests come down from the north? Marska felt a flutter of fear race up his spine at the thought of one of these hideous creatures loose down in his sewers. As a child, he had seen such a beast when a band of Ungol horsemen had ridden through his stanista with the corpse of one of these monstrous, horned creatures and Marska remembered the terror he had felt at the size of the beast.

The voices came again, thrown from far away by the curve of the tunnel. Only fragments of conversation echoed back towards the ratcatchers, but Marska knew that they must be talking about something important. After all, people did not meet in the sewers to discuss the latest harvest or the weather.

As a member of the Guild of Ratcatchers, Marska was also part of the network of informers who worked for Vassily Chekatilo, the ruthless killer who controlled everything illegal in Kislev, a dangerous man who traded in stolen goods, narcotics and flesh. Part of his power came from knowing things that he should not know and the ratcatchers were an important part of that, for who paid any attention to the filthy peasant covered in shit who cleared your house of vermin?

Taking great care to tread silently, the two ratcatchers crept forward, at last reaching the edge of the fallen pile of brickwork. Now that they were closer, Marska could see that the hole in the wall disappeared into the darkness for some way.

Moving slowly so as not to draw the eye of any observers, Marska and Nikolai eased their heads above the level of the rubble.

The domed chamber echoed with the lapping sewage, ripples of reflected light dancing on the vaulted ceiling. A circular ledge, some six feet wide, ran around the circumference of the chamber and eight, half submerged, pipes disgorged their filthy cargo into the central reservoir that drained downriver. On the far side of the chamber stood four figures beside a ramshackle cart, like that used by the collectors of the dead. An apt choice of conveyance, thought Marska, seeing a bronze coffin sealed with a number of rusted padlocks atop the cart. Two figures dressed in rippling robes that appeared to change colour stood closer to the wall of the chamber, while another pair stood beside the cart.

These last two figures were smaller than the others, hunched over, and even over the reek of the sewers the stench emanating from the nearest was overpowering. Dressed in excrement-smeared rags and bound around the arms and chest with weeping bandages, it was bent almost double by a collection of thick, brass edged books tied to its back. A cracked bell hung from a rope belt around its waist and its face was, thankfully, obscured by its patchwork hood. Its companion was hidden in the shadow; so well that Marska had very nearly missed him. Swathed from head to foot in black robes the figure clutched what appeared to be a long-barrelled musket of some kind, though it was festooned with brass fittings, coils and pipes whose purpose escaped Marska.

The tallest of the figures in the multi-coloured robes took a hesitant step forward, holding a metal box, some six inches square. The filth-smeared figure beside the bronze coffin raised its head, as though scenting the air, its head darting quickly from side to side. Marska watched as the lid of the box was opened and a soft, pulsating emerald-green light radiated from inside it, bathing the chamber in a fearful, sickly glow.

'Your payment,' said the figure holding the box, its voice smoky and seductive.

The filthy hunchback snatched the box with a squeal of pleasure, almost quicker than the eye could follow, and stared deep into the glowing depths, as though inhaling the scent of whatever lay within.

'And this is what you bring me?' asked the former owner of the box, reaching out a delicate hand to touch the coffin.

A blur of motion, black on black, and a clawed hand snatched out and grabbed the hand reaching for the coffin. Marska was amazed; without seeming to move, the black robed figure with the musket had darted from the shadows to intercept the hand reaching for the coffin. No man could move that fast; it was inhuman.

The filthy book-carrier shook its head slowly and the hand was withdrawn.

Marska turned and cupped his hands around Nikolai's ear, whispering, 'Nikolai, get back to the surface. Chekatilo will want to hear of what's happening down here.'

'What about you?' hissed Nikolai.

'I want to see if I can hear anything else, now go!'

Nikolai nodded, and Marska could see that his young apprentice was glad to be leaving. He didn't blame him, but he had to stay. If Chekatilo found out – and he would – that he had seen these events and not learned all he could, he might as well slit his throat now.

As Nikolai slipped away, Marska turned his attention back to the drama unfolding before him in time to hear the rotten, bandaged figure reply to an unheard question, hissing a single word that sounded as though it came from a mouth never meant to speak the tongues of men.

'Eshhhiiiiin...' it said, bobbing its head, pointing to the figure dressed in black. As it did so, Marska saw what looked like a long, fat worm waving in the air behind it. His lip curled in distaste before he realised that he was not looking at some serpent as people were often wont to claim dwelled in the sewers, but a tail. A pink tail, hairless save for a few mange-ridden patches of coarse, wiry fur.

Revolted, he drew in a sharp breath, and in that moment knew he had doomed himself as the figure in black's head snapped in his direction.

'No...' he hissed, pushing himself to his feet to sprint away.

He had barely risen when a flurry of silver flashed through the air and struck him in his chest. He grunted in pain, turning to run, but his legs wouldn't obey him, and the ground rushed up to slam into his face as his limbs spasmed violently. Marska rolled onto his back, seeing a trio of jagged discs of metal with dripping blades protruding from his chest. Where had they come from, he wondered, as he felt his muscles jerk and his lungs fill with froth?

He tried to move, but was helpless, dying.

With the last ounce of his strength he yelled, 'Run, Nikolai, run! They're coming!' as a dark shadow enveloped him, darker even than that pressing in on his eyes.

Marska looked into the face of his killer and realised that Death had a sense of irony after all.

III

THE GOROMADNY PROSPEKT was busy despite the late hour. People with no homes to call their own wandered the streets, rightly fearing that to lie down in the cold snow would be to die. Snow drifted up the sides of buildings, the central thoroughfare of the city trodden to brown slush. Those few taverns with any wares left to sell burned what fuel they had to keep the worst of the cold at bay, but it was a futile gesture against the aching, marrow-deep cold of Kislev.

Families huddled together for shared warmth in doorways, fur blankets pulled tight around them, yet still shivering in cold and fear.

Harsh times had come to Kislev, but worse was yet to come.

The scrape of metal on stone was the first hint that something out of the ordinary was happening, but most folk ignored it, too cold and hungry to pay any mind to matters beyond their concern.

A rusted iron manhole slid through the snow, grating on the cobbles, bloodied hands reaching up from below the street. A man, covered in muck and screaming in terror hauled himself from the sewers, jerking like a marionette as he rolled in the slush.

Something fell from his dirty clothing, a short-bladed dagger with a curved blade; a blade that had caught in the folds of his leather tabard and nicked the surface of his skin.

The man thrashed upon the ground, desperately trying to put as much distance between himself and the entrance to the sewers. His back arched as he convulsed and his screams of agony moved even the hardest hearts to pity.

As curious onlookers cautiously approached, the man screamed, 'The rats! The rats! They're here, they've come to kill us all!'

People shook their heads in weary understanding, now seeing the man's ratcatching apparel, guessing that he had simply spent too long below ground and thus fallen prey to lunacy. It was sad, but it happened, and there was nothing they could do. They had troubles of their own.

As the onlookers dispersed, no one noticed the venomous yellow eyes that stared out from the blackness below, or the clawed hand that reached up to slide the manhole back in place.

IV

IF KASPAR HAD been grateful to see the spires of Kislev as they rode from the oblast, it was nothing compared to his relief at returning to the Imperial embassy. Snow clung to its walls and long daggers of ice drooped from the high eaves, but a warm homely glow spilled into the night from the shuttered windows and smoke spiralled lazily from the chimneys. He and his knights rode up to the iron, spike-topped gates, blue and red liveried guards eagerly opening them and welcoming their fellow countrymen back.

A tutting farrier took the bridle of Kaspar's horse and he dismounted, wincing as the stiffness of two weeks in the saddle pulled at his aged muscles. The wound he had received from the leader of a Kurgan scouting party pulled tight, the stitches Valdhaas had pierced his flesh with still raw beneath a fresh bandage.

The door to the embassy opened and Kaspar smiled as Sofia Valencik strode along the path towards him, a heartfelt smile of relief creasing her handsome features. The physician's long, auburn hair was pulled in a tight ponytail and she wore a green dress with a red, woollen pashmina wrapped around her shoulders.

'Kaspar,' she said, throwing her arms around him, 'it's so good to see you.'

'And you, Sofia,' replied Kaspar, returning the embrace and holding her tight. He was pleased Sofia was on her feet again; the last time he had seen her, she had been confined to bed, recovering from her brutal kidnapping by Sasha Kajetan. Her left hand was still bound with bandages where he had severed her thumb.

Thinking of the captured swordsman, Kaspar opened his mouth to speak.

'Sofia–' he began, but she had already seen her former captor being pulled from the saddle by one of the Knights Panther. He felt her go rigid in his arms.

'We were able to capture him, Sofia, as you wanted,' said Kaspar softly. 'I've sent word to Pashenko that we'll bring him to the *Chekist* building tomorrow and–'

But Sofia appeared not to be listening, pulling free of Kaspar's arms and marching stiffly towards Sasha. Kaspar made to follow her, but Kurt Bremen gripped his arm and shook his head slowly.

Sofia hugged her arms tightly about herself as she neared Kajetan, the swordsman's emaciated frame held aloft by two knights. Kaspar could see how much courage it took her to face her abuser and felt his admiration for Sofia soar once more. Hearing her steps, Kajetan turned and Kaspar saw the swordsman shudder in... what? Fear, guilt, pity?

Kajetan met the woman's eyes for as long as he could before dropping his head, unable to endure the cold heat of her accusing gaze any longer.

'Sasha,' she said softly, 'look at me.'

'I can't...' whispered Kajetan. 'Not after what I did to you.'

'Look at me,' said Sofia again, this time with steel in her voice.

Slowly Sasha's head rose until once again their eyes met. Tears streamed down Kajetan's cheeks and his eyes were violet pools of sorrow.

'I'm sorry,' he choked.

'I know you are,' nodded Sofia. And slapped him hard across the face.

Kajetan didn't flinch, the red imprint of her hand bright and vivid against the ashen pallor of his face. He nodded and said, 'Thank you.'

Sofia said nothing, wrapping her arms around herself once more as the knights led Kajetan to the cell beneath the embassy. Kaspar moved to stand behind Sofia as the Knights

Panther attended to their mounts and the embassy guards closed the gates once more.

'Why did you bring him here?' asked Sofia without turning.

'I wasn't about to hand Sasha over to Pashenko before getting some assurances that he wouldn't hang him the minute my back was turned,' explained Kaspar.

Sofia nodded and turned to face him once more. 'I am glad you are home safely, Kaspar, I really am, and I'm happy that you managed to bring Sasha back alive. It was just a shock to see him there like that.'

'I understand, and I'm sorry. I should have sent word ahead.'

'It brought it all back, the terrible things he did to me. I almost couldn't move, but...'

'But?' asked Kasper when Sofia's words trailed off.

'But when I saw what had become of him, I knew that I wasn't about to let what he'd done beat me. I'm stronger than that and I had to show him that, even if it was just for my own sake.'

'You are stronger than you know, Sofia,' said Kaspar.

Sofia smiled at the compliment and linked her arm with Kaspar's, turning him around and walking back to the embassy with him.

'Come on, let's get you into a hot bath, you must be frozen to the marrow,' said Sofia playfully. 'I don't know, a man of your age gallivanting outside in the middle of winter like you're some kind of young buck.'

'You're starting to sound like Pavel,' chuckled Kaspar, his grin fading as he saw Sofia's face darken at the mention of his old comrade in arms.

'What's the matter?'

Sofia shook her head as they entered the embassy and shut the door behind them. Kaspar immediately felt the warmth of the building envelop him as one of the embassy guards helped him off with his frosted cloak and muddy boots.

'It is not my place to say,' said Sofia archly.

'But I can see you're going to anyway.'

'Your friend is *nekulturny*,' she said. 'He spends all his time drinking cheap kvas, and falling into the blackest of moods. He hasn't been sober since you left to go after Sasha.'

'He's that bad?'

'I don't know what he was like before, but he seems intent on drinking himself into the Temple of Morr as soon as he can.'

'Damn it,' swore Kaspar. 'I knew something was wrong before I left.'

'I don't know what's the matter,' confessed Sofia, 'but whatever it is, he needs to sort it out soon. I don't want to have to stitch a shroud for him.'

'Don't worry,' growled Kaspar. 'I'll get to the bottom of it, that's for damn sure.'

V

VASSILY CHEKATILO THREW a handful of thin branches onto the crackling fireplace and took a drink of kvas from a half-drained bottle, enjoying the comfortable warmth filling his chambers at the rear of the brothel. His establishment was busy tonight – as it had been for the last few months since the refugees had begun streaming south – and several whores sprawled on chaise-longues in various states of undress and narcotic oblivion, waiting to be called back to the main chambers.

Most of them had once been pretty. Chekatilo only employed pretty ones, but they were now shadows of their former selves, the rigours of their profession and the escape of weirdroot soon robbing them of whatever beauty they might have possessed. Once, he had thought that having such nubile creatures around his chamber gave it an air of exotica, but now they merely depressed him.

Though sumptuously furnished with many fittings and furniture he had extorted from the previous ambassador from the Empire, Andreas Teugenheim, his chambers were nevertheless assembled with the taste of a peasant. His criminal enterprises had garnered him great wealth and many fine things, but there was no escaping his humble origins.

'A piece of shit in a palace is still a piece of shit,' he said with a smile, watching a pair of black-furred rats gnaw on something unidentifiable in the corner of the room.

'Something funny?' asked Rejak, his flint-eyed assassin and bodyguard, who had entered the room without knocking.

'No,' said Chekatilo, masking his annoyance by turning and drinking some more kvas. He offered the bottle to Rejak, but the assassin shook his head, circling the room and unashamedly ogling the naked women sprawled around the room. As he reached the chamber's corner, his sword flashed from its scabbard and stabbed downwards. A pair of squeals told Chekatilo that the two feasting rats were dead. Trust Rejak to find something to kill.

'Did you see the size of those creatures?' asked Rejak. 'I swear the damn things are getting bigger every day.'

'Wars are always good for vermin,' said Chekatilo.

'Aye,' agreed Rejak. 'And ratcatchers, well, except for the poor bastard they pulled from below the Goromadny Prospekt today.'

'What are you talking about?'

'Oh, just something that happened earlier tonight. One of the guild ratcatchers who sometimes feeds me information was hauled off to the Lubjanko screaming that the rats were coming to kill us all. They say he climbed from the sewers like all the daemons of Chaos were after him and started acting like a lunatic. I think he hit some people before the watch came and dragged him away.'

Chekatilo nodded, filing the information away as Rejak wiped his sword on a dark rag before sheathing it and slumping into a chair before the fire. Chekatilo sat opposite his assassin and stared into the fireplace, enjoying the simple act of watching the flames dance and listening to them devour the new wood in the grate. He sipped the kvas, waiting for Rejak to speak.

'Damn, but it's cold out there,' said Rejak, shifting his sword belt and holding his hands out to the fire.

Chekatilo bit back a retort and said, 'What news from the north? What are people saying?'

Rejak shrugged. 'The same as they've been saying for weeks now.'

'Which is?' said Chekatilo darkly.

Finally catching his master's mood, Rejak said, 'More people are coming south every day. They say that the armies of the High Zar are getting bigger with every passing week, that each of the northern tribes he defeats he swears to his banner. And that his warriors leave nothing alive behind them.'

Chekatilo nodded. 'I feared as much.'

'What?' said Rejak. 'That the Kurgans are coming south? They've done that before and they'll do it again. Some peasants will get killed and once the fighting season is done, the tribes will return to the north with fat bellies, slaves and some plunder.'

'Not this time, Rejak,' said Chekatilo. 'I can feel it in my bones, and I've not lived this long without trusting them. This time it will be different.'

'What makes you say that?'

'Can't you feel it?' asked Chekatilo. 'I can see it in every desperate face that comes here. They know it too. No, Rejak, the High Zar and his warriors do not come for the plunder or rape, they come for destruction. They mean to wipe us from the face of the world.'

'Sounds like the kind of talk I hear in the gutter grog shops,' said Rejak. 'Old men telling anyone who'll listen that these are the End Times, that the world is a more wicked place than when they were younglings and that there is no strength here any more.'

'Perhaps they are right, Rejak, did you ever think of that?'

'No,' confessed Rejak, placing his hand over his sword's pommel. 'There is still strength in me and no bastard is going to kill me without a fight.'

Chekatilo laughed. 'Ah, the arrogance of youth. Well, perhaps you are right and I am wrong. It is a moot point now anyway.'

'You are still set upon leaving Kislev then?'

'Aye,' nodded Chekatilo, looking around his drab chamber, his eyes fastening upon another mangy rodent feasting upon the bodies of the dead rats in the corner. Rejak was right; these damned rodents *were* getting bigger.

He put the rats from his mind and said, 'This place will be no more soon, of that I am sure, and I have no desire to end my days spitted on a Kurgan blade. Besides, Kislev bores me now and I feel the need for a change of scenery.'

'Did you have anywhere in particular in mind?'

'I thought Marienburg would be an ideal destination for a man of my talents.'

'A long journey,' pointed out Rejak. 'Dangerous too. A man travelling with wealth would find it hard to reach his destination intact without protection.'

'Yes,' agreed Chekatilo, 'a hundred soldiers or more.'

'So where are you going to get a hundred soldiers? It's not as though the Tzarina is going to let you have a regiment of kossars or her precious Gryphon Legion.'

'I thought I might ask Ambassador von Velten.'

Rejak laughed. 'And you think he'll help you? He hates you.'

Chekatilo smiled, but there was no warmth to it. 'If he knows what's good for him, he will. Thanks to Pavel Korovic, the ambassador owes me a favour, and I am not a man to allow a debt like that to go unanswered.'

CHAPTER TWO

I

Despite the biting chill of the morning and the stiffness in his muscles from two weeks in the saddle and sleeping on the cold ground, Kaspar's spirits were high as he rode through the busy streets of the city. Last night he had enjoyed a long, hot bath to wash off the grime of his adventures in the desolate wilderness of the Kislev oblast, before retiring to bed and falling asleep almost before his head hit the pillow.

Awaking much refreshed, he had dressed and sent word to Anastasia that he would call upon her for an early breakfast. He looked forward to seeing her again, not least because it had been many years since he had been sharing his bed with an attractive woman, but also because she was a tonic for his soul. He found her playfulness and unpredictability fascinating; keeping him forever guessing as to her true thoughts. She was at once familiar and a mystery to him.

He wore his freshly cleaned and dried fur cloak over a long black frock coat with silver thread woven into the wide lapels, and a plain cotton undershirt. A tricorned hat with a silver eagle pinned to it sat atop his head, its design old fashioned, but pleasing to him. Four Knights Panther rode alongside him, clearing a path for the ambassador with their wide-chested steeds.

Word had spread to the people of the city that Kaspar had been instrumental in the apprehension of the Butcherman, and there was much doffing of hats and tugging of forelocks as he passed.

The streets widened as his journey took him into the wealthier parts of the city in the north-eastern quarter, though even here, there was no escaping the depredations of war. Families and scattered groups of Kislevite peasants huddled close to the walls, utilising their meagre possessions to fashion rough lean-tos and shelters from the worst of the cold winds that whistled through the city. He rode past cold and hungry groups of refugees towards the Magnustrasse and Anastasia's house, turning into the wide, cobbled boulevard to find it similarly inhabited.

The stand of poplars opposite Anastasia's house was gone, hacked stumps all that remained of them, and as Kaspar rode through the open gateway in the dressed ashlar walls of her home, he saw several hundred people camped within. Anastasia's home was tastefully constructed of a deep red stone, situated at the end of a long paved avenue that was lined with evergreen bushes – though Kaspar noticed that many of these were afflicted with a sickly discolouration of their greenery. Perhaps the cold was too severe even for these normally hardy plants, though the low temperatures did not seem to bother the darting rats that scurried through the undergrowth.

Dressed in a white cloak edged with snow leopard fur and with her long, jet-black hair spilling around her shoulders, Anastasia Vilkova was an unmistakable sight. Kaspar watched as she distributed blankets to those most in need.

She looked up at the sound of horses' hooves and as he drew nearer, Kaspar saw her face flicker before breaking into a smile of welcome.

'Kaspar, you're back,' she said.

'Aye,' nodded Kaspar. 'I promised you I'd come back safely, didn't I?'

'That you did,' agreed Anastasia.

He swung his leg over the saddle and dismounted, saying, 'Though two weeks in the oblast is more than enough for any man.'

Anastasia, still carrying an armful of blankets leaned up to kiss him as he handed Magnus's reins to a green-liveried stable boy.

He returned her kiss fiercely, revelling in the softness of her lips against his own until she pulled back with a wicked sparkle in her eyes.

'You *have* missed me, haven't you?' she laughed, turning away and handing out the last of the blankets to the people camped within her walls.

'You wouldn't believe how much,' nodded Kaspar, walking alongside Anastasia as they made their way towards her home. 'You seem to have a great many guests just now.'

'Yes, I have space within the grounds here, and it seemed to make sense to allow these poor people to make use of it.'

'Always trying to help others,' said Kaspar, impressed.

'Where I can.'

'Regrettably, people like you are rare.'

'I remember saying something similar to you once.'

Kaspar laughed, 'Yes, I remember, the first time I called upon you. Perhaps we are two of a kind then?'

Anastasia nodded, her jade eyes flashing with secret mirth, and said. 'I think you might be more right than you know, Kaspar.'

They reached the black, lacquered door to Anastasia's home and she pushed it open, saying, 'Come inside, it's cold out here, and I want to hear all about your adventures in the north. Was it hard? How silly of me, I suppose it must have been. To catch and kill a monster like Kajetan can't have been easy.'

Kaspar shook his head. 'It was hard, yes, but I didn't kill him.'

'Of course not, I suppose it was one of those brave knights who killed him.'

'No, I mean Sasha is not dead, we were able to take him alive.'

'What?' said Anastasia, her jaw dropping open and her skin turning the colour of a winter sky. 'Sasha Kajetan is still alive?'

'Yes,' said Kaspar, surprised at the sudden chill in Anastasia's tone. 'He's in a cell below the embassy and once our meal is over I shall be taking him to Vladimir Pashenko of the *Chekist*.'

'You didn't kill him? Kaspar, you promised! You promised you'd keep me safe!'

'I know, and I will,' said Kaspar, confused at the passion of her reaction. 'Sasha Kajetan is a shell of the man he once was, Ana, he won't be hurting anyone. I promised you I wouldn't let anyone hurt you again and I meant that.'

'Kaspar, you promised,' snapped Anastasia, her eyes filling with tears. 'You said you would kill him.'

'No,' said Kaspar firmly. 'I did not. I never said I would kill him. I wouldn't say such a thing.'

'You did, I swear you did,' cried Anastasia. 'I know you did. Oh, Kaspar, how could you fail me?'

'I don't understand,' said Kaspar reaching out to put his arms around her.

Anastasia took a step backwards, folding her arms and said, 'Kaspar, I think you should go, I don't think I can talk to you just now.'

Kaspar started to say that he would still keep her safe, but his words trailed off when he saw the frosty hostility in Anastasia's eyes and felt a flash of anger. What did she want of him? Had he not ridden into the depths of the harshest country imaginable for this woman?

'Very well,' he said, rather more sharply than he had intended. 'I will bid you good day then. Should you wish to see me, you know where to find me.'

Anastasia nodded and Kaspar turned on his heel, snapping his fingers at the stable boy to bring his horse. He would hand Kajetan over to the *Chekist* and that would be the end of the matter.

II

HIS BREATH MISTED before him, the thin blanket his gaolers had given him doing little to prevent the cold of the cell penetrating him to the marrow. Sasha Kajetan sat on the thin mattress that, save for the night-soil bucket, was the only furnishing within the small cell beneath the embassy. He shivered, the pain of his many wounds dulled by the numbing cold.

His upper body was crisscrossed by freshly stitched scars – wounds taken in battle with Kurgan tribesmen – though his greatest wound was to his thigh, where the ambassador had driven his sword after denying him the death he knew he deserved.

Sasha wished that Ambassador von Velten *had* killed him. The woman who had slapped him – the woman he had once believed was his beloved matka – had promised him that the ambassador would help him, but she had lied. The ambassador had not helped him to die, but had spared him, prolonging the agony of his existence and he wept bitter tears of frustration, knowing that he was too weak to end his life himself and hearing the mocking laughter of the trueself as a hollow echo in the depths of his mind.

The trueself was still there, lurking like a sickness, though instead of swallowing him whole as it had done for so long, it gnawed and worried at the frayed ends of his sanity. He held his shaking hands out before him, the blackened tips of his fingers raw where exhuming his mother's corpse from the frozen ground and frostbite had claimed them.

There was nothing he could do to atone for what he had done, though he had hoped that the ambassador's blade would grant him the absolution he craved. He knew that the *Chekist* would hang him for his crimes and, while he welcomed the oblivion the hangman's rope promised, he was tormented by the suspicion that death would not be enough of a punishment. Why the ambassador had not killed him, he did not know. Surely someone he had wronged so terribly should have cut him down like the animal he was?

But he had not and Sasha was consumed with the need to know why.

With a clarity borne of the acceptance of death, Sasha understood that his and the ambassador's fates were still intertwined, that there were dramas yet to unfold between them.

Von Velten had not killed him and as he felt the trueself continue to erode his reason, Sasha Kajetan just hoped that the ambassador did not live to regret that clemency.

III

Pavel Korovic opened his eyes and let out a huge belch, his mouth gummed with dried saliva. Bright spears of light streamed through the high window, stabbing through his eyes, and he groaned as the hammer blows of a crushing headache began to build.

'By Tor, my head...' he mumbled, rubbing the heel of his hand against his forehead. Gingerly, he rose from his bed, grimacing as the headache worsened and he felt his stomach lurch in sympathy.

Pavel smelled the stench of himself, stale sweat and cheap kvas, and saw that he had fallen asleep in his clothes again. He didn't know when he had last bathed and felt the familiar sense of shame and self-loathing wash over him as his memories swam to the surface of his mind through the haze of alcoholic fog. He needed to eat something, though he doubted if he could keep anything down.

He swung his legs from the bed, knocking over a trio of empty bottles of kvas, which shattered on the stone floor. The fire in the grate had long since burned to ash and the cold knifed through his clothing as he pushed himself upright, careful to avoid the pile of broken glass.

Where had he gone last night? He couldn't remember. Some darkened, backstreet drinking den no doubt, where he could lose himself once more in the oblivion of kvas.

The guilt was easier to deal with that way; the guilt of what Vassily Chekatilo had forced him to do – many years ago and recently – did not eat away at him when he could barely remember his own name.

Though it had been six years ago, Pavel could still remember the murder he had committed for Chekatilo. He could still hear the sickening crack as he had brought the iron bar down on Anastasia Vilkova's husband's skull; see the brains that had spilled onto the cobbles and smell the blood that gathered like a red lake around his head.

The killing had shamed him then, and it shamed him still.

But to Pavel, the worst betrayal had been at his own accord when he had knowingly placed Kaspar, his oldest and truest friend, in debt to Chekatilo. He told himself it was to help the ambassador find Sasha Kajetan, but that was only partly true...

By trying to erase one mistake, he had made a greater one and now it wasn't just him who would pay for it.

How could he have let himself sink so low?

The answer came easily enough. He was weak; he lacked the moral fibre that made men such as Kaspar and Bremen such honourable figures. Pavel put his head in his hands, wishing he could undo the pathetic waste of his life.

Despite the vile taste in his mouth, the headache and the roiling sensation in his belly, he wanted a drink more than anything. It was a familiar sensation, one that had seized him every day since he had gone to Chekatilo's brothel and sold what shreds of his dignity and self-respect remained to a man he hated.

He pushed his giant frame from the bed, swaying unsteadily and feeling his legs wobble under him. His grey beard was matted with crumbs and he brushed it clear of the detritus of long ago meals, stumbling over to a polished wooden chest sitting in the corner of the room.

Pavel dropped to his knees before the chest and lifted the lid, hunting through his possessions for the bottle of *kvas* he knew lay within.

'Looking for this?' said a voice behind him.

Pavel groaned, recognising the icy tones of Sofia Valencik. He turned his head to see her standing beside his open door, an upturned and very empty bottle of *kvas* held in her hands.

'Damn you, woman, that was my last bottle.'

'No it wasn't, but don't bother looking for the others, I emptied them too.'

Pavel's shoulders slumped and he slammed the lid of the chest down before standing and turning to face the ambassador's physician.

'Now why would you go and do that, you damned harpy?' snapped Pavel.

'Because you are too stupid to see what it is doing to you, Pavel Korovic,' retorted Sofia. 'Have you seen yourself recently? You look worse than the beggars on the Urskoy Prospekt and smell worse than a ratcatcher who's fallen in the sewer.'

Pavel angrily waved her words away and returned to his bed, reaching down to lift his boots from the floor. He sat on the edge of the bed, dragging them on and fighting down the urge to vomit.

'Where are you going now?' asked Sofia.

'What business is it of yours?'

'It is my business because I am a physician, Pavel, and it is not in my nature to stand by while another human being attempts to destroy himself with alcohol, no matter how stubborn and pig-headed he may be.'

'I am not trying to destroy myself,' said Pavel, though he could see that Sofia didn't believe him.

'No? Then go back to bed and let me get you something to eat. You need sleep, some food and a wash.'

Pavel shook his head. 'I can't sleep and I don't think I could eat anything anyway.'

'You have to, Pavel,' said Sofia. 'Let me help you, because you'll die if you carry on like this. Is that what you want?'

'Pah! You are exaggerating. I am a son of Kislev, I live for kvas.'

'No,' said Sofia, sadly, 'you will die for kvas. Trust me, I know what I'm talking about.'

'I don't doubt it,' said Pavel, rising from the bed and pushing past Sofia, 'but before you try and save someone, make sure that they want to be saved.'

IV

A FOG HAD descended upon Kislev by the time Kaspar returned to the embassy, wrapping the city in a muffling blanket of icy mist. The cold was worse than Kaspar could ever remember, even in the far north when they had pursued Kajetan into the wilderness.

The Knights Panther had prepared Kajetan for his journey to the *Chekist* gaol, wrapping him in furs and a hooded cloak to obscure his features. It had now become common knowledge around the city that the Butcherman murders had been committed by Sasha Kajetan, and Kaspar was taking no chances that a lynch mob would take the law into their own hands to administer vigilante justice on the swordsman.

The fog would help also, and as he tightened the saddle on Magnus, he watched Valdhaas help Kajetan onto the back of a horse, since, with his wrists and ankles bound, the swordsman was forced to ride sidesaddle. Kajetan looked up, as though sensing Kaspar's gaze and gave him a vacant look, utterly devoid of human emotion that chilled Kaspar worse than the cloying scraps of fog.

Kaspar shuddered, sensing the hollow emptiness of Kajetan's soul. The man was a void now, drained of emotion and humanity. The swordsman had been unresponsive and lethargic when they had taken him from his cell, and Kaspar feared that he would learn little of whatever twisted fantasies had driven him to murder so many people.

'We're ready to go, ambassador,' said Kurt Bremen, startling Kaspar from his reverie.

'Good,' nodded Kaspar. 'The sooner he's gone from here the happier I'll be.'

'Aye,' agreed Bremen. 'I have lost good men thanks to him.'

'Very well then, let's get this over with, I'm sure Vladimir Pashenko is eager to get his hands on the Butcherman.'

'Do you think he will keep his word and not hang Kajetan the first chance he gets?'

'I don't know,' admitted Kaspar. 'I do not like Pashenko, but I believe he is a man of his word.'

Bremen gave him a sceptical look, but nodded and turned to accept the reins of his horse from his squire. 'What is it you hope to gain by keeping Kajetan alive anyway?'

Kaspar planted a foot in his stirrup cup and hauled himself onto the back of his horse, adjusting his cloak over the animal's rump and tightening his pistol belt.

'I want to know why he killed all those people, and what could make a man do such vile, unthinkable things. Something made him the way he is and I want to know what.'

'I remember asking you on the oblast if you were sure you really wanted to know the answer to that. The question still stands.'

Kaspar nodded, guiding his horse to the embassy gates.

'More than ever, Kurt. I don't know why, but I feel that much depends on knowing those answers.'

Bremen raised his mailed fist and the knights set off, with Kajetan riding in their midst, a ring of steel preventing the swordsman's escape or his murder by a vengeful mob.

Kaspar and Bremen led the way, walking their horses along the street that led to Geroyev Square, the fog so thick that they could barely see the walls to either side of them.

The solemn procession emerged into the square, the fog deadening sounds and forcing them to keep to the edges of the square for fear of losing their bearings. The jingle of the horses' harnesses and their muffled steps through the snow the only sounds that disturbed the eerie silence that had descended upon the city.

They passed shadowy outlines of small encampments of refugees and saw the occasional glow of cooking fires, but even with these touchstones, the silence and sense of isolation were unnerving, especially in a city so thronged with people. People moved like ghosts in the fog, drifting in and out of sight as they moved from the horsemen's path.

Eventually Kaspar and Bremen reached the Urskoy Prospekt, the great triumphal road that led to the Tzarina's Winter Palace and housed the *Chekist* building. Named for the great reliquary at its end that housed the remains of Kislev's greatest heroes, the wide boulevard was also strangely quiet as they rode along its length, though, looking up, Kaspar could see the weak rays of the sun finally beginning to penetrate the fog.

Ahead, Kaspar could see the grim outer walls of the *Chekist* building emerge from the mist, a pair of armed men in black armour standing before the imposing black gates. He twisted in the saddle, pulling on the reins and drawing level with Sasha Kajetan. The swordsman glanced up as Kaspar rode alongside him, but said nothing, returning his gaze to the snow.

'Sasha?' said Kaspar.

The swordsman did not reply, lost in whatever thoughts were echoing within his tormented soul.

'Sasha,' repeated Kaspar. 'Do you know where we're going? I am taking you to Vladimir Pashenko of the *Chekist*. Do you understand?'

Kaspar thought he was going to have to repeat himself again, but almost imperceptibly, Kajetan nodded.

'They will hang me...' whispered the swordsman.

'Eventually, yes, they will,' said Kaspar.

'I am not ready to die. Not yet.'

'It is too late for that, Sasha. You killed a great many people and justice must be done.'

'No,' said Kajetan, 'that's not what I mean. I know I deserve to die for things I have done. I meant that there are things I have yet to do.'

'What do you mean? What kind of things?'

'I know not yet,' admitted Kajetan, raising his head and fixing Kaspar with his dead-eyed stare. 'But know that it involves you.'

Kaspar felt a thrill of fear slick across his skin. Was the swordsman threatening him with violence? Unconsciously, his hand slipped towards his pistol, his thumb hovering over the flint, as he realised just how far away the Knights Panther were from him. It was a few feet at best, but it might as well have been a mile, for Kaspar knew how quick and deadly Kajetan could be. Had Kajetan simply feigned docility so that he might now escape and continue his grisly work?

But it seemed that Kajetan did not have violence in mind, his head drooped again and Kaspar let out a long breath, his eyes narrowing and his brow knitting in puzzlement as he saw something peculiar.

A flickering glow of green light wavered on Kajetan's stomach. Kaspar watched as it slowly eased up his body until it settled in the centre of his chest.

Mystified, Kaspar could see a pencil-thin line of green light, a light that would surely have been invisible but for the fog, tracing an arrow-straight course from Kajetan's chest upwards into the mist.

He waved his hand through the light, feeling a tingling warmth through his thick gloves as he broke its beam. He tried to follow the line of the green light. He soon lost it in the fog. As a breath of wind parted the murk for an instant, he saw a dark, hooded shape atop one of the redbrick buildings of the prospekt silhouetted against the low sun, holding what looked like one of the long rifles made famous by the sharpshooters of Hochland.

Kaspar's heart raced and he reached for one of his flintlocks as he realised what he was seeing.

'Knights Panther!' he yelled, reaching out and dragging Kajetan from his saddle as he heard a sharp crack from above. Instinctively, Kajetan twisted free of Kaspar's grip and the two men tumbled to the snow as something slashed past Kaspar's head and exploded against the wall behind them, blasting bricks and mortar to powder.

Kaspar rolled, the wound in his shoulder flaring as the stitches tore open. He flailed against Kajetan as the swordsman sprang to his feet.

'Kurt! On the roof! Across the street!' shouted Kaspar as the Knights Panther hurriedly wheeled their horses and closed on the struggling pair. Another bang echoed along the prospekt and Kaspar watched horrified as the closest knight was spun from his feet, his shoulder blown out in a shower of red. The knight fell screaming and, behind him, Kaspar could see a smudge of greenish smoke from where the shots had been fired.

He clambered to his feet and took hold of Kajetan as the knights formed a protective cordon of armoured warriors around them. Valdhaas lifted the downed knight to his feet as Kaspar drew his pistol and hurriedly aimed at the rooftop across the prospekt. The chances of hitting anything were negligible, but he fired anyway, the pistol bucking in his hand and further obscuring his view.

'Ambassador!' shouted Kurt Bremen. 'Are you hurt?'

'No, I'm fine, but we need to get off the street! Now!'

Bremen nodded, shouting orders to his knights and the group made its halting, stumbling way towards the *Chekist* building. Kaspar half carried, half dragged Kajetan onwards, the bindings on his ankles limiting the speed at which he could move considerably.

'Pashenko! Vladimir Pashenko!' bellowed Kaspar. 'Open the gates! This is Ambassador von Velten! For the love of Sigmar, open the gates!'

The black armoured soldiers Kaspar had seen standing before the gates emerged from the mist, cudgels at the ready, and, as they saw the desperate group of Imperial knights hurrying towards them, turned to open the gates behind them.

Kaspar knew a disciplined handgunner could load and fire between three and four aimed shots a minute, but a long rifle took somewhat longer, with its finer powder and more exacting preparations. Exactly how much longer, he didn't know and as each second passed, he kept waiting for another shot to pitch one of their number to the snow.

But no shots came and they gratefully hurried through the thick gates of the *Chekist* building, emerging into a wide, cobbled courtyard before the fortress-like headquarters of Kislev's feared enforcers. Two *Chekist* hurriedly shut the heavy gate behind them as Kaspar pushed Kajetan to the ground. He took out his other pistol and pointed it at the swordsman, lest he use the confusion of the attack to make his escape. But the prisoner merely knelt in the snow with his head bowed.

Valdhaas lowered the screaming knight to the ground, hurriedly unbuckling his breastplate and shoulder guards to get to the wound. Blood steamed in the cold air as it sheeted down the man's armour. *Chekist* were running from the building's main door and Kaspar could see Vladimir Pashenko amongst them.

'Is anyone else hurt?' shouted Bremen.

No one else was, and Kaspar felt himself relax a fraction when another crack echoed and a portion of the gateway was blown to splinters as something smashed through. A man screamed and Kaspar saw a *Chekist* in front of him drop, a bloody hole blasted through his chest. Knights and *Chekist* alike threw themselves to the ground, horrified that anything could have penetrated the thick timbers of the gateway.

'Everyone inside!' yelled Kaspar, rolling aside and finding himself face to face with Pashenko.

The head of the *Chekist* nodded and helped Kaspar drag Kajetan towards the doors of the building. The knights and *Chekist* soldiers backed towards the entrance, anxiously scanning the tallest rooflines for the would-be assassin.

Pashenko kicked open the door and Kaspar fell through it, collapsing in a heap with his back to a corridor wall. Kajetan rolled onto his back, moving out of the way of the open door.

Kaspar did likewise as the last of the knights entered the safety of the building and Pashenko slammed the door shut. He threw heavy iron bolts across before sliding down the wall to rest on his haunches.

'Ursun's blood, what just happened here?' said Pashenko, his face a mask of fury.

'I don't know exactly,' said Kaspar. 'We were riding along the Urskoy Prospekt when someone started shooting at us.'

'Who?' asked Pashenko.

'I didn't see him clearly, just a dark shape, maybe with a hood, on the rooftop.'

'What in Ursun's name was he firing? It penetrated nearly a span of seasoned timber with enough power left to kill one of my men. Save a cannon, what manner of weapon could do such a thing?'

'No blackpowder weapon capable of being carried by a man, that's for sure,' said Kaspar. 'Even the contraptions designed by the College of Engineers in Altdorf are not that powerful.'

'Trouble has a habit of following you,' observed Pashenko.

'Aye, don't I know it,' agreed Kaspar, as two *Chekist* soldiers lifted Kajetan and led him towards the cells below.

'I would suggest you remain here for a while, ambassador,' said Pashenko, picking himself up and straightening his uniform. 'At least until my men ensure that whoever attacked you is not still lurking and waiting for you to emerge.'

Kaspar rose to his feet and nodded, though as he watched Kajetan's disappearing back, he had the strong impression that whatever the purpose of this attack had been, he had not been the intended target.

V

NIGHTS IN THE brothel were always busy, filled with men afraid to die affirming that they were alive in the most primal way possible. Chekatilo did not usually trouble himself to visit the main floor, but for reasons he could not fathom, he had decided to drink and smoke amongst the common herd tonight. Most people here had come from the north and would not even know his name, let alone be fearful of him, though the imposing figure of Rejak, standing behind his chair, left no one in any doubt that he was a man not to trifle with.

Chekatilo watched the crowd, seeing the same sick desperation in every face. He saw a young boy, probably barely old enough to need a razor, enthusiastically coupling with a woman draped in red silks and furs. He was watched by a similarly-featured man, old enough to be his father. Chekatilo guessed that this was a father's last gift to his son: that if he were to die, it would be as a man and not a boy.

Such pathetic scenes were played out throughout the brothel: old men, perhaps desiring one last memory to take to the next life, young men for whom their existence was one long indulgence and those who had already resigned themselves to the fact that life had nothing more to offer them.

'This places reeks of defeat,' muttered Chekatilo to himself. 'The sooner the Kurgan burn it to the ground the better.'

Watching the parade of human misery before him made him all the more sure that he was making the right decision to leave Kislev. He had no great love for his country, and its dour, provincial nature was suffocating for a man of his ambition. Marienburg, with its bustling docks and cosmopolitan nature, was the place for him. He had made a great deal of money in Kislev, but no matter how much he possessed, he would never escape his birth. Respect and esteem were for those of high birth, not for a filthy peasant who had managed to haul himself out of the gutters and fields.

In Marienburg, he would never have to worry about freezing winters and raiding northmen. In Marienburg, he could live like a king, respected and feared.

The thought made him smile, though as Rejak had pointed out, it was a long way to Marienburg – through Talabheim, on to Altdorf and finally westwards to the coast. He would need help to get there safely, but knew exactly how to get it.

The door to the brothel opened and Rejak said, 'Well, well, look who's back again.'

Chekatilo looked up and smiled as he saw Pavel Korovic enter, shivering and stamping his heavy boots free of snow.

'Pavel Korovic, as I live and breathe,' laughed Chekatilo. 'I would have thought he'd had enough of this place to last a lifetime.'

'Korovic?' said Rejak. 'No, ever since he came begging for you to help the ambassador, he's been coming here, swilling bottle after bottle of kvas till dawn before somehow managing to stumble out the door.'

Chekatilo saw Korovic notice him, and blew a smoke ring as the big man nodded curtly before making his way to the bar and tossing a handful of coins to its surface. Korovic snatched the bottle of kvas the barman brought and retreated to an unoccupied table to drown his sorrows. Chekatilo toyed with the idea of going over and speaking to him, but dismissed the thought. What did he have to say to him? Korovic knew his place and Chekatilo had no wish to bandy words with a drunkard.

He caught a flash of swift movement in the corner of the hall and jumped as something bristly rubbed against his leg. Startled, he looked down and saw a sleek, black-furred shape dart beneath his chair.

'Dazh's oath!' he swore disgustedly as another rat, this one the size of a small dog, joined the first. 'Rejak!'

Even as he shouted the name he saw more rats, dozens, scores, hundreds of them, boiling out from unseen lairs to invade his brothel. The screams started seconds later as the tide of vermin attacked, a swarming, squealing mass of furry bodies, pointed snouts and razor-sharp incisors that bit and clawed at exposed flesh.

Chekatilo surged from his chair, toppling it as Rejak stamped down on a rat and broke its spine. He stumbled backwards, horrified as he saw the young boy dragged down by the sheer weight of rats, his face a mask of blood as they ripped off long strips of his flesh. Men and women crawled across the blood-slick floor, unable to believe that this was happening to them as frenziedly biting rats clung to their bodies.

A naked man struggled with a pair of rats while yet more bit and clawed his lower body to the bone. He smashed one rat's skull to splinters against the wall, but another leaped from the stairs and fastened its teeth around his neck, biting out his throat with its powerful jaws. Bright arterial spray spattered the walls as the man collapsed and the scent of so much blood drove the swarming rats into an even greater frenzy.

'Come on!' yelled Rejak, pushing Chekatilo towards the door that led to the chambers at the back of the brothel. Screams and sobs of pain filled the air, mixed with the sounds of breaking glass, smashing furniture and squealing rats. Hundreds of darting black shapes sped through the rooms and corridors of the brothel, as if directed by a malign intelligence, snapping and squealing in a frenzied mass as they attacked with teeth that cut like knives.

A frantic woman, flailing at a rat caught in her hair and biting her neck and shoulders, knocked a lamp from its mounting on the wall. It fell and smashed on her head, spraying blazing oil across her and the floor. She screamed as the flames hungrily seized her clothing, blundering blindly through the brothel and igniting furnishings, spilled alcohol and other patrons as she went. Fire roared through the place with horrifying speed in her wake.

As Rejak pushed him towards safety, Chekatilo saw Pavel Korovic under attack from a dozen or more rats that were biting his legs and arms and raking his chest with their sharp claws. He slashed at them with a broken bottle and stamped on others as he backed towards a shuttered window. A pair of rats leapt towards the giant Kislevite, but he dropped the bottle and caught them in mid-air, slamming them together and dropping the limp corpses as he tore the window shutters from their hinges and leapt through the glass to the street.

Chekatilo yelled as he felt a sharp pain and forgot Pavel Korovic as a rat took a bite from his ankle. He reached down, grabbing the rat by its neck and tearing it from his flesh, ignoring the pain as blood poured from the wound.

The rat twisted and bit his hands, claws like razors drawing blood with every slash. Chekatilo wrung its neck as he saw Rejak sheath his sword and draw a short-bladed dagger, the longer weapon too large to wield effectively against such small, nimble opponents. He stabbed and slashed at any rats that approached, stamping and kicking at those he couldn't kill with his blade.

Rats were closing in around them and Chekatilo barged open the door to the back as another huge rat launched itself at him. He ducked and the rat slammed into the wall behind him. Before it could recover, he turned and hammered his boot down on its chest, hearing a satisfying crack as its ribs shattered.

Smoke, heat and flames filled the brothel as Rejak pushed him through the door, hauling it shut behind him as several heavy thumps slammed into it from the other side. The door shuddered in its frame as the rats hurled themselves at it. Chekatilo could hear splintering, scratching noises as they began gnawing their way through.

'Come on!' shouted Rejak, setting off up the corridor. 'The door won't hold them for long!'

Rejak ushered him into his chambers as he heard wood splinter and saw a pointed snout, wet with blood, push its way through the closed door. Giant teeth ripped the hole wider and Chekatilo watched in disbelief as an enormous rat pushed its wriggling body through. The creature landed on the floor and fixed him with its beady black eyes. It squealed in a high, child-like manner, spraying pink-flecked saliva, and the pounding and scratching noises from the other side of the door doubled in their intensity.

Chekatilo followed Rejak numbly, unable to believe the single-minded intelligence of the rats, and shut the door behind him. Who could believe that vermin would attack in such numbers and with such ferocity? He had never heard the like and could only shake his head at such madness.

He could hear the roaring flames crackling through the door, over the diminishing screams from the main hall, and knew that this place was finished. It was of no matter, he had other places and its loss would barely affect him.

But as he and Rejak made their escape from the burning brothel, he felt a chill in his blood over and above the horrors he had just witnessed. He thought back to the rat that had gnawed its way through the door and locked eyes with him. He had seen its feral intelligence and had been seized by a sudden unshakeable intuition.

He was sure the rat had looked at him with something other than hunger in its eyes.

It had been seeking him.

CHAPTER THREE

I

IN THE CLOSING days of Uriczeit, word reached Kislev that Norscan raiders had sacked Erengrad. Hundreds of longships with sails bearing the marks of the old, northern gods had sailed into the port and disgorged thousands of berserk warriors who had swept through the city and killed thousands in their bloody rampage.

The Kislevite priesthood, never the most optimistic fraternity, took to the streets of Kislev and proclaimed that the doom of a wicked mankind was at hand, that these were the End Times as prophesied in the Saga of Ursun the Bear and that everyone should prepare their souls for death. Some of the more eloquent fanatics attracted quite a following and on some days the wide boulevards of Kislev were filled with marching columns of flagellating priests and crowds of zealots who mortified their flesh with scarifying belts, hooks and whips.

Such displays of fanatical piety inevitably led to the zealots taking it upon themselves to root out those they perceived as the cause of the city's woes. Lynchings and beatings became a daily occurrence and over two-dozen people were killed – for no more a crime than hailing from the blighted city of Praag – until Vladimir Pashenko rounded up the most vocal of these doomsayers and locked them away. But the sense of fear they had fostered within the city was harder to dispel. Stories of battles fought between armies in the west and north were told around every campfire and in every tavern.

Sorting fact from fiction proved more difficult than anyone could have guessed. Riders from various parts of the country provided many contradictory tales which were often embellished beyond recognition by the time they reached those who desperately needed accurate information.

To add to Kislev's woes, it soon became apparent that a pestilence had taken hold in the poorest quarters of the city. At first, the outbreak was not recognised for what it truly was, as physicians denied that plague could take hold in such cold conditions and many of the initial deaths were thought to have been caused by the freezing temperatures. But as Uriczeit turned to Vorhexen, it could no longer be ignored and soldiers with scarves soaked in camphorated vinegar wrapped around their mouths and noses were drafted in to quarantine several districts.

Riverboats from the Empire continued to arrive, carrying much needed supplies, but none lingered longer than they had to and their frequency was growing less and less as famine began to take hold in the land of Karl-Franz and the Emperor was forced to husband his resources for his own people. Anastasia Vilkova continued to lead caravans of wagons into the refugee camps as well as those of the Kislevite and Empire regiments to distribute food and water to the soldiers there. With her distinctive, snow-leopard cloak, she soon became known to the soldiers as the White Lady of Kislev.

But such symbols of hope were rare and the coming days would require them like never before.

II

KASPAR SAT ATOP his horse at the base of the *Gora Geroyev*, watching as his embassy guards sparred with the Knights Panther, enjoying the simple spectacle of good soldiers learning quickly. Kurt Bremen's punishing training regime had worked wonders with the embassy guards, transforming them from the slovenly layabouts he had inherited from Andreas Teugenheim into soldiers he could be proud of. Leopold Dietz, a young soldier from Talabecland, had assumed the leadership of the guards – a role Kaspar was happy for him to have. The lad was confident, skilled and understood how to motivate his men; qualities Kaspar knew were essential in a leader of warriors.

The cold was still numbing, but Kaspar could tell that the worst of the winter was over and that these warriors would be called upon to fight when the snows broke. The fighting season was a month away at most and soon an army that had driven thousands of people from their homes would be coming this way. It was now not a matter of if, but when.

Kaspar was pleased to see that the officers of the Kislevite and Empire regiments realised this also and had begun a program of marching and drilling to prepare their men for the coming conflict.

He returned his attention to his own soldiers, walking his horse forward as he saw that Kurt Bremen had called a halt to their training for today. The knights' squires and lance carriers distributed fresh water and food to the soldiers while the knights gathered in a circle for prayer.

Kaspar rode up to Leopold Dietz, who sat on a bare rock and chewed his meal of bread and cheese with gusto.

'My compliments, Herr Dietz. Your men are looking good.'

Dietz looked up, shielding his eyes from the low sun and stood, straightening his uniform and running a hand through his unruly dark hair.

'Thank you, sir. I told you they was good lads, didn't I?'

'Yes, you did,' agreed Kaspar. 'It does the heart proud to see.'

Dietz beamed at the compliment and Kaspar rode on, allowing the men to eat their food. He did not interrupt the knights at their prayer and wheeled his horse as he heard the sound of iron-rimmed wagon wheels clattering along the roadway.

Anastasia sat on the buckboard of an empty wagon, expertly guiding it towards him with a shy smile. He had not seen her since they had argued at her house. A wilfully stubborn streak had prevented him from visiting her, and, despite wishing to appear calm, he couldn't help but smile as she drew nearer.

'Hello, Kaspar,' she said as she drew level with him.

'Hello. It's good to see you, Ana,' he said, dismounting from his horse as she climbed down from the padded seat of the wagon.

They faced each other in awkward silence, neither quite knowing what to say, until Anastasia finally said, 'Kaspar, I am sorry, I shouldn't have been so hard on you. I just–'

'No,' interrupted Kaspar, 'It's alright, you don't need to apologise.'

'How I've missed you, Kaspar,' said Anastasia, opening her arms and hugging him tightly. He was surprised, but held her close, smelling the perfume of her black hair and the scent of her skin. He wanted to say that he too had missed her, but settled for simply holding her and enjoying her nearness.

He stroked her hair and she lifted her head, allowing him to lean down and kiss her on the mouth. The taste of her full lips and tongue was like the forgotten taste of a fine wine suddenly and forcefully recalled. He felt a thrill of arousal and broke the kiss, taken aback by the force of the sensation. A man of passion, but outward reserve, Kaspar was not normally given to such public displays of affection and as he heard the good-humoured wolf-whistles drift from his guards, he felt his skin redden.

Anastasia laughed. 'You are blushing, Ambassador von Velten.'

Kaspar smiled, and it felt good. After the violence of taking Kajetan to the *Chekist* and the recent turmoil in the city streets it felt good to smile again.

'Come on,' he said, 'let's go back to the embassy.'

III

KASPAR AWOKE HEARING people moving downstairs and yawned, shifting his position in the bed to slip his arm from around Anastasia's shoulders. She gave a little moan, but did not wake and Kaspar watched her sleep for a few moments, enjoying the softness of her features and the heat of her pale skin.

They had returned to the embassy the previous evening and made a pretence of having a light supper, but there was little doubt in either Kaspar or Anastasia's mind that they had an urgent physical need to be with one another.

Unlike their previous lovemaking, which had been gentle and tentative, this was fierce and passionate, surprising them both with its intensity. They had tired one another out, satisfying their pent up needs before falling into a contented and dreamless sleep.

Kaspar leaned down and kissed Anastasia's cheek before sliding towards his side of the bed. As he moved, she turned onto her side and said, 'Kaspar?'

'I'm here, Ana, it's morning.'

'Are you getting out of bed?' she said sleepily, sliding towards him and draping her arm across his chest.

'I should, I arranged to speak with Sofia, she has been working with the apothecaries and city officials to try and halt the spread of the plague. I think she wants to make sure I'm not coming down with anything.'

'No…' whispered Anastasia, 'stay here with me. Given your performance last night, I think I can safely say that you are in rude health.'

Kaspar laughed. 'Thank you, but I do need to get up. There are ambassadorial duties I have to attend to as well.'

'More important duties than staying in bed with me for the day?' grinned Anastasia, playfully reaching below the bedclothes.

'Well, if you put it like that,' said Kaspar rolling towards her.

SEVERAL HOURS LATER they lay back, pleasantly exhausted and covered in a light sheen of perspiration. Kaspar propped up his pillows in order to sit upright and allow Anastasia to lie with her head on his stomach. He reached over and poured himself a glass of water from a pewter jug. It was a day old, but refreshing nonetheless.

He offered the cup to Anastasia, but she shook her head.

'So what ambassadorial duties *did* you plan to do today?' she asked sleepily.

Kaspar stroked her sculpted shoulder and said, 'I had planned to visit the officers commanding the Empire forces outside the walls and keep them informed of what news there is from the field.'

'From what I hear, there's not much to tell. No one seems to know for sure exactly what's happening. There are all kinds of wild stories going around.'

'Aye, there are, but I have it on good authority that Boyarin Kurkosk has inflicted considerable damage on a large army of Kurgans massing in the north-west.'

'Really? That's wonderful news. Where is Kurkosk now? Does he march to Kislev?'

'No, his army divided for the winter, ready to gather when the fighting season begins again.'

'Oh, so he's not coming here?'

'I don't think so. Kurkosk gathered the pulk at a place called Zoishenk, so I think he will muster his warriors there in the spring when the Imperial armies march out.'

'Your Emperor is sending his armies north, how wonderful.'

'Yes, I received word that the counts of Stirland and Talabecland muster their men in readiness to march north. An army of the Empire is a fine thing to see, Ana, rank after rank of disciplined regiments, trains of cannon and hundreds of armoured horsemen, their banners and guidons like a rainbow of colour across the landscape. If any army can defeat the Kurgans it will be an Imperial one.'

Kaspar spoke with the fierce pride of a man who had led such fine soldiers in battle and the regret that came of knowing he had passed on the responsibility and honour of such duties to other, younger men.

They lay in silence for a little longer before Kaspar finally extricated himself from the bedclothes and dressed in a simple doublet and riding britches. As he picked up his boots, Anastasia propped herself up on her elbow and hesitantly said, 'Kaspar?'

He turned, hearing the tremor in her voice, and said, 'Yes?'

She asked, 'Kaspar... have... have you seen Sasha since you handed him over to the *Chekist*?'

'Sasha?' he said warily, remembering her reaction the last time they had spoken of the murderous swordsman, but unwilling to make himself a liar. 'Yes, I have. I saw him the previous week.'

'And what was he like?'

Kaspar considered the question for a moment. 'He's not the man he once was, Ana, and he won't be hurting anyone ever again. He's gone; there's nothing left of Sasha Kajetan as far as I can see. I think whatever made him human died out in the wilderness.'

'Were you able to learn why he did all those terrible things?'

'Not really,' said Kaspar, pulling on his boots. 'I could barely get him to speak at all, in fact.'

'That doesn't surprise me, Kaspar. It's plain now that Sasha was evil, simply evil, so you shouldn't waste any more time with him. Are they not planning to hang him soon anyway?'

'Eventually they will, but I've persuaded Pashenko to give me some more time to try and get through to the man before they send him to the gallows.'

'I think you're wasting your time, Kaspar.'

'Perhaps, but I have to try.'

Anastasia did not reply, drawing the sheets up to her neck and rolling over so that she had her back to him.

Kaspar knew when not to push a point and opened the door to his study, leaving Anastasia in bed. He strolled over to his desk to see if any correspondence had been delivered while he had tarried in bed, but there was nothing that demanded his immediate attention and he walked over to the frosted window that looked out over the snow-capped roofs of Kislev.

If not for the fact that he knew the city was full of desperate, cold and hungry people and that soon there would be an army coming to destroy it, the serene view would have calmed him. He cast a glance over his shoulder at the door to his bedroom, seeing a sliver of pale flesh as Anastasia shifted in the bed.

Her dismissal of his attempts to understand Kajetan disturbed him, but he had no real reason he could put his finger on to feel that way. After all, he was not the one who had been close to Sasha Kajetan before it came to light that he was a killer. Indeed, Anastasia had been the object of Kajetan's obsessive infatuation for some time and perhaps she felt that that was a convenient enough explanation for his crimes. But Kaspar could not so easily believe this, and Anastasia's refusal to countenance any other motive sat ill with him.

He scratched his chin, unsure as to what to think, when there came an urgent knocking at his door.

'Come in,' he said, turning from the window as Sofia Valencik entered, not bothering to close the door behind her. He could see from her face that something terrible had happened.

'Sofia, what is it?'

'You need to come downstairs now,' she said.

'Why, what's the matter?'

'It's Pavel.'

IV

AT FIRST KASPAR did not recognise his old friend, so bloody and covered in filth was he. The sleeves and trouser legs of his long coat were shredded and bloody, stinking of the filth of the street and his normally robust frame was a shadow of its normal size. His skin was the pallor of a corpse and his forearms and face were lined with deep cuts that had healed badly and, in some cases, were clearly infected. Kaspar could see thin splinters of glass still embedded in his face.

The giant Kislevite lay unconscious on the floor of the embassy vestibule, his breathing ragged and his eyes glazed. Two guards stood beside the open door, and Kaspar saw that both of them had angry bruises flowering on the sides of their faces. Kaspar knelt beside his comrade in arms and clenched his fist as he felt his anger build towards whatever brute had done this.

'What happened?' he demanded. 'And close that bloody door. Do you want him to freeze to death?'

The shorter of the two guards answered, his words coming out in a rush as the other closed the embassy door. 'We was on gate duty as normal and we saw Herr Korovic staggering towards us, except we didn't know it was him at first. He tried to get in the gate, but we weren't having any of that. We thought he was some mad beggar or something.'

The other guard picked up the tale as Sofia bent to examine Pavel's wounds.

'Aye, then he comes up and tries to barge through the gate. Course, we weren't having none of that and showed him the business end of a halberd, but he weren't taking no for an answer.'

'Then what?' snapped Kaspar as the guards shuffled embarrassed from foot to foot.

Sofia waved over a group of Knights Panther, who had emerged from their quarters at the rear of the building upon hearing the commotion, and ordered them to carry Pavel to his room.

Kaspar straightened as the knights struggled to lift Pavel's weighty body upstairs, following close behind and indicating that the guards should follow him.

'Well, sir...' said the first guard, hurrying to keep up. 'We tries to stop him, but he just shouts something in Kislevite and starts laying about with his fists. He knocked Markus flat on his arse, then put me down next to him sharpish. Then he pushes open the gate and marches right through to the door, raving something about rats before collapsing in a heap. That's when we recognised who he was and called for Madame Valencik.'

Kaspar turned to face the guards as the knights carried Pavel into his room. 'You did the right thing. Now get someone else to man the gate and have someone take a look at your faces. Dismissed.'

The guards saluted and returned to the vestibule. Kaspar strode along the corridor to Pavel's room to find Sofia barking quick-fire orders at the knights.

'Prepare a warm bath as fast as you can! A warm bath, mind, not hot, you understand? And get me some clean, warm water in a basin and some cloths to wash these cuts with. Heat as many blankets as you can find as well, we need to get him warmed up quickly. Someone get my satchel as well, the one with my needles and poultices. And prepare some sweet tisane, it'll help his body fight off the cold from within.'

As the knights hurried to obey her commands, Kaspar said, 'What can I do?'

'Help me get his clothes off. It looks and smells like he's been outside on the streets for a week or more. These cuts have festered with dirt and it looks like some of them have gone septic.'

'Sigmar's blood, how could this have happened?'

'Knowing Pavel, anything's possible,' said Sofia, cutting away Pavel's trousers using a long, thin bladed knife with a serrated edge and Kaspar winced as he saw the hurt done to his friend's body.

Kaspar began pulling off Pavel's shirt, tearing it where necessary and tossing the bloody scraps of linen to one side. The ashen skin of his friend's shoulders, face and upper body were scored with deep gashes, many of which still glittered with glass fragments and were crusted over with dried blood. He saw that his fingers and arms were similarly crusted with blood, though the wounds there were much smaller.

As Sofia finally cut away Pavel's trousers and undergarments, Kaspar saw that his ankles and lower legs were covered with similar wounds to those on his arms and wondered again what had happened. These smaller wounds looked like bites, but what could have caused them?

'Holy Sigmar,' whispered Kaspar when he saw the full extent of the damage done to Pavel. 'What the hell trouble has he gotten himself into now?'

'We can worry about that later, Kaspar,' snapped Sofia. 'We need to get him clean and warmed up. He's almost frozen to death and if we don't raise his body temperature he may die anyway.'

News of Pavel's condition spread quickly throughout the building and the embassy staff hurried to procure everything Sofia had asked for. Anastasia had joined the effort to help

Pavel also, cutting linen bedsheets into swathes of bandages and helping to warm water for a bath. The fire in the grate was lit and warmed blankets were wrapped around Pavel's shivering body while Sofia used thin forceps to remove the jagged splinters of glass from his cuts.

As each wound was cleaned, Kaspar gently doused a cloth in warm water and washed it as gently as he could. Pavel moaned, but did not regain consciousness as they carefully cleansed him of dried blood.

Kaspar heard the door open behind him and a group of knights, Kurt Bremen among them, dragged a heavy iron bath into the room. Water splashed over the side and Sofia said, 'Put it in front of the fire and lift him in. Carefully now.'

The knights lifted the naked form of Pavel and gently lowered him into the warm bath. More water splashed onto the floor, as the bath was too small for someone of Pavel's size, and under any other circumstances, the sight of such a big man in the bath would have been comical.

'Is there anything else we can do?' said Kaspar, suddenly very afraid for his friend.

Sofia shook her head and put her hand on Kaspar's arm. 'No, all we can do now is hope that his body temperature has not dropped too far. We'll need to leave him in the warm water for a while then get him dried off and just keep him warm. Then we need to worry about those bites. I'm pretty sure they are rat bites.'

'Rat bites? Is that what they are?'

'Yes, and I am worried that they might be infected. It's possible Pavel's been wandering the streets delirious and in a fever for days. It's a wonder he found his way back here at all.'

'But so many bites? I've never heard of so many rats attacking a grown man.'

'And there is something else,' said Sofia.

'What?'

'Some of the city doctors think the contagion that's broken out in the city is spread by rats, so we're going to have to keep everyone out of here from now on in case Pavel is infected.'

'Oh no, Pavel...' whispered Kaspar as a wave of sadness threatened to engulf him. He had lost one great friend in Kislev already and fervently hoped he would not lose another.

'I'm sorry, Kaspar,' said Sofia as Pavel stirred, muttering something under his breath.

Kaspar knelt beside the bath and said, 'I'm here, old friend.'

Pavel's eyes flickered open, though Kaspar saw no recognition there, and he tried to speak, but only succeeded in making a series of barely audible groans.

'What is it Pavel?' said Kaspar, though he was unsure if Pavel could even understand him. 'Who did this to you?'

He placed his head next to Pavel's as his deathly ill friend tried to speak once more, uttering a string of slurred Kislevite. Kaspar listened intently, his expression hardening into one of cold, lethal anger as he made out a single word amongst Pavel's delirium.

He stood and marched swiftly to the door, saying, 'Look after him, Sofia.'

'Wait, what is it, Kaspar? What did he say? Did he say who did this to him?' asked Sofia, hearing the murderous edge to Kaspar's voice.

Kaspar gripped the door, his knuckles white and face flushed.

'He said "Chekatilo".'

V

'Ambassador, think of what you're doing,' said Kurt Bremen.

'I don't want to hear it, Kurt,' snapped Kaspar, buckling on his pistols and looping his sword belt around his waist. 'You saw what he did to Pavel.'

'We don't know that for sure,' pointed out the knight. 'This is Pavel we're talking about, anything could have happened to him.'

'He said Chekatilo's name, damn it, what am I supposed to think?'

'That's just it, ambassador, you are not thinking. You are allowing your hatred of Chekatilo to blind you to reason.'

Kaspar pulled on his long cloak and turned to face the leader of the Knights Panther, who stood between him and the door.

'This is something I need to do, Kurt.'

Bremen folded his arms and said, 'I told you once before that we could not perform our duties to you if you behaved in a manner that forced us to violate our order's code of honour. I am telling you that again.'

'So be it,' snarled Kaspar, moving towards the door.

Kurt Bremen's hand shot out and gripped the ambassador's shoulder, holding him fast. Kaspar's eyes flashed with sudden anger and his fists bunched.

As clearly and evenly as he could, Bremen said, 'If you murder Chekatilo then neither my knights or I will remain oath-bound to you.'

Kaspar locked eyes with the knight, knowing that he was right, but too consumed with anger to countenance any other course of action. He reached up and slowly lifted Bremen's hand from his shoulder.

He looked straight at the grim-faced knight and said, 'Either come with me or get out of my way. Because one way or another, I am going through that door.'

'Don't do this, Kaspar. Think about what you are about to do.'

'It's too late for that, Kurt. Much too late.'

Kaspar pushed past the knight and hurriedly descended the stairs to the vestibule. He paused at the bottom as he heard Kurt Bremen coming down after him, and looked up to see him buckling on his own sword belt.

'What are you doing, Kurt?'

'Sigmar save me, but I'm coming with you.'

'Why?'

'I told you, I won't help you murder Chekatilo, but someone has to try and keep you from getting yourself killed, you damn fool.'

Kaspar smiled grimly. 'Thank you.'

'Don't thank me too soon,' snapped Bremen, 'I may have to put you on your arse to do it.'

THE COLD OF the early evening could not cool the heat of Kaspar's rage, but he was wholly unprepared for the sight that greeted him when he and Kurt Bremen rode up to the brothel where they had last met with Chekatilo.

Instead of the nondescript building of sagging black timbers and random blocks of rough-hewn stone, there was only a swathe of fire-blackened timbers and rubble. Soot-coated fragments of coloured glass and the burned remains of a crimson sash flapping from the melted finial protruding limply from the ruins were all that remained of Chekatilo's brothel. The buildings to either side of the brothel had escaped the fire's worst attentions, saved from destruction by the snows that had doused the blaze and allowed the fire watch to extinguish the conflagration before the entire quarter went up in flames.

Not that Kaspar imagined there would have been much of a public-spirited attempt to save Chekatilo's establishment. The people huddled in the lee of the buildings were a pathetic sight, wrapped in furs and covered with a fresh dusting of snow, and Kaspar could not picture them helping Chekatilo. If anything, he imagined they had simply gathered to enjoy the fleeting warmth offered by the burning structure.

'What the hell happened here?' wondered Kaspar as he dismounted. He kicked a scorched piece of timber in frustration.

'Perhaps someone with a grudge against Chekatilo?' suggested Bremen.

'Well that only leaves an entire city full of suspects,' replied Kaspar, crunching through the snow towards the remains of the brothel. Even in the chill air he could smell a sickeningly cloying aroma he knew to be burnt human flesh. He had lit enough funeral pyres in his time to recognise the familiar smell.

Kaspar pointed to the people gathered in their shelters against nearby buildings and said, 'Kurt, you speak more Kislevite than I, ask these people if they know what happened here.'

Bremen nodded as Kaspar hitched Magnus to a protruding spar of timber and clambered over the rubble of the destroyed building to begin sifting through what little wreckage remained of the brothel. It had been thoroughly scavenged by the people of Kislev, those timbers not completely burned to ash taken for firewood and any trinkets that had survived stolen that they might be traded for a little food. As he was about to give up, Kaspar noticed the corpses of several rats, their bodies burned and twisted into unnatural angles by the heat of the flames. As he studied them, he was amazed at their size – fully eighteen inches or more from tip to rump.

He knelt beside the charred corpse of a rat and used a broken piece of furniture to turn its stiff body over. Its black fur had been crisped from its body, but the flesh of its back still remained and Kaspar could see three crossed red welts on its skin that formed an uneven triangle.

'What is it? Have you found something?' called Bremen from the edge of the ruins.

'A rat, and a big one at that,' said Kaspar, 'but it looks for all the world like it's been branded with a mark.'

'Branded? Who in their right mind would bother to brand a rat?'

'I have no idea,' said Kaspar, 'but…'

'But what?'

'I was just thinking of something Sofia said about the plague. She said that the city's doctors feared that it was being spread by rats. I'm seeing this brand and wondering if it is possible that such a thing could be somehow directed by someone?'

'You're saying that the plague is deliberate?'

'I don't know, maybe,' said Kaspar, standing and brushing ash from his britches. 'Did you find anything out from these people?'

'Not much,' admitted Bremen. 'Their Reikspiel is as almost as bad as my Kislevite. The few that were here when it happened say they heard screaming from inside just before it went up in flames.'

'That's it?'

'That's it,' nodded Bremen with a shrug. 'I couldn't understand much more than that.'

'Damn, there's something important here, I can feel it, but can't see it.'

'Maybe the *Chekist* or the city watch know something. They are bound to have been here already.'

Kaspar nodded. 'True, I can't imagine Pashenko won't have taken an interest in one of Vassily Chekatilo's haunts being burned to the ground.'

'Even if he does, do you think he will tell you anything?'

'It has to be worth a try,' said Kaspar, emerging from the brothel and climbing back onto his horse. 'The worst he can do is say no.'

Bremen took a last look into the ruined brothel and said, 'I wonder if Chekatilo was inside when it burned down?'

Kaspar shook his head. 'No, I don't think we could be that lucky. I'll wager that bastard is too slippery to be killed that easily.'

KASPAR FELT A flutter of nervousness as he and Bremen turned their horses into the Urskoy Prospekt, remembering the last time they had come this way and the carnage that had followed. The Knight Panther who had been shot had lost his arm and shortly after succumbed to a malignant sickness that Sofia could do nothing to halt.

They kept to one side of the thronged prospekt, Kaspar noticing that Bremen too was scanning the rooflines and dark windows that overlooked the street and taking comfort in the fact that he was not alone in his caution.

A group of armoured kossars marched down the centre of the street, resplendent in scarlet and green and armoured in a mix of iron and bronze breastplates. They carried wide-bladed axes and had short, recurved bows slung at their sides. All wore furred colbacks and had thick scarves tied around the lower portion of their faces. The black armbands they wore told Kaspar that they had been detailed to those areas of the city closed off because of the plague and he saw that the people camped in the prospekt shrank back in fear from the soldiers.

Kaspar nodded to the leader of the kossars, but the man ignored him and he and his men passed, barely registering their presence.

Eventually they reached the *Chekist* compound and announced themselves to the two guards at the gate. Both men seemed taken aback by Kaspar's request for entry, more used to people begging *not* to be taken within. But, recognising the Empire ambassador, they opened the gate with some difficulty and allowed Kaspar and Bremen to ride through into the cobbled courtyard beyond.

As the gate closed behind them, Kaspar saw it had been heavily reinforced with thick spars of timber, the hole blasted by the marksman's weapon patched with a sheet of iron. Pashenko was obviously taking no chances that a skilled marksman might use the same hole to put another bullet through.

The black door in the grim façade of the *Chekist* building opened and the leader of the *Chekist* emerged into the evening's twilight, his dark armour reflecting the light from the torches either side of the entrance.

'Ambassador von Velten,' said Pashenko in his clipped tones. 'This is a coincidence. I do hope you are not bringing trouble to my door once more.'

'No, not this time,' said Kaspar. 'And why is it a coincidence?'

'Never mind, why are you here?'

'I have just come from where a brothel belonging to Vassily Chekatilo once stood. Do you know anything about what happened?'

'It burned down.'

Kaspar bit back an angry retort and said, 'I wondered if you might have had any idea who might have done it.'

'I might, but it would take from now until this time next year to arrest all the possible suspects. Chekatilo was not a well-liked man, ambassador.'

'A friend of mine is badly hurt and may die. I think he might have been there the night the brothel burned down. I just want to find out what happened.'

Pashenko waved a pair of stable boys forward to take Kaspar and Bremen's horses and said, 'Come inside, there is little I can tell you about the fire you probably do not already know, but as I said, it is a coincidence that you have come here tonight.'

Kaspar and Bremen handed their reins to the stable boys and followed Pashenko into the *Chekist* building, removing their heavy winter cloaks as they entered.

'So you have said, Pashenko. Why?' said Kaspar, his patience wearing thin.

'Because less than an hour ago, Sasha Kajetan began begging to be allowed to see you.'

VI

FLICKERING LAMPLIGHT ILLUMINATED the brickwork passageway that led to the cells beneath the *Chekist* building and Kaspar felt his skin crawl as a low moaning drifted from below. The echoes of their footsteps on the stone steps rang from the walls and, though he had never been particularly susceptible to claustrophobia, Kaspar had an instinctive dread of this place, as though the walls themselves had seen too many miseries and could contain them no longer, bleeding its horror into the air like a curse.

Flaking paint coated the walls and old stains the colour of rust were splashed across the brickwork. Pashenko led the way, carrying a hooded lantern that swayed with his every step and cast monstrous shadows around them.

How many men had been dragged screaming down these steps, never to return to the world above, wondered Kaspar? What was the word Pavel had used? Disappeared. How many people had been disappeared in the cold darkness below this feared place? Probably more than he dared think about and he felt his loathing for Vladimir Pashenko grow stronger.

He saw the leader of the *Chekist* reach a solid iron door with a mesh grille set at eye level and bang his fist against it, the sound booming and somehow dreadful. A light grew behind the grille and Kaspar heard the rattle of keys and the sound of several iron bolts being pulled back. The door squealed open and Pashenko led them through into the cells.

They descended into a wide, straw covered gallery that stretched off into darkness, the brick walls pierced at regular intervals with narrow doors of rusted iron. The stench of stale sweat, human waste and fear made Kaspar and Bremen gag, but Pashenko appeared not to notice it.

'Welcome to our gaol,' smiled Pashenko, his underlit face looking daemonic in the lamplight. 'This is where we keep the enemies of Kislev, and this is our gaoler.'

The gaoler was a heavyset man with thickly muscled arms who carried a hooded lantern and a spike-tipped cudgel. His face was obscured by a black hood with brass-rimmed eye-pieces fitted with clear glass and a thick canvas mouth filter. He wore an iron breastplate, leather gauntlets studded with bronze spikes and heavy, hobnail boots, putting Kaspar in mind of the handlers of the lethally exotic beasts kept by the Emperor in his menagerie at Altdorf. Were the captives kept here as dangerous? The thought gave him pause and Kaspar shared an uneasy glance with Kurt Bremen.

'Where is Kajetan?' asked Kaspar, wanting to leave this cursed hellhole as quickly as he could. Pashenko chuckled and pointed along the ink-black corridor.

'On the left, the cell at the end,' he replied, leading the way. 'He is securely chained to the wall, but I would not recommend approaching him too closely.'

'Has he become violent again?' asked Bremen.

'No, he is just covered in his own filth.'

Kaspar and Bremen followed the *Chekist* along the corridor, the gaoler bringing up the rear. Kaspar could hear desperate shuffling and muffled pleas for help or mercy from behind each cell door as they passed.

'Truly, this place is hell,' whispered Kaspar, unconscionably grateful when they reached the end of the bleak, soulless passage.

'If it is hell,' said Pashenko, 'then everyone here is a devil.'

The gaoler stepped up to the cell door, searching on his belt for the correct key; his actions slowed by the thick gauntlets and cumbersome hood he wore. At last he found the correct key and spun the tumblers of the lock, opening the door for them.

Pashenko stepped inside the cell and Kaspar followed, the stench of human excrement almost overpowering him. The lamplight threw its flickering illumination around a square cell of crumbling brickwork, the floor dank and glistening with patches of moisture. Kaspar covered his mouth with his hand to ward off the stench and felt his skin crawl as he saw the naked form of Sasha Kajetan curled in a foetal ball in the corner.

The swordsman had been a shell of his former self when Kaspar had last seen him, but he was now little more than a beaten wretch, his body covered in a patchwork of bruises and cuts. The lamplight threw the shadows where his ribs poked from his emaciated frame into stark relief and his cheeks had the sunken hollowness of a famine victim.

He whimpered as they entered, covering his eyes against the light, the thick chains securing him to the wall rattling as he moved. Despite the horror of his crimes, Kaspar could not help but feel pity for any man subjected to such brutal conditions.

'Kajetan,' said Pashenko. 'Ambassador von Velten is here.'

The swordsman's head snapped up and he tried to stand, but the gaoler stepped forward and slammed his cudgel into the side of his thigh. Kajetan grunted in pain and collapsed into a groaning heap, streamers of blood running down his leg.

'Ambassador…' he hissed, his voice hoarse and cracked. 'It was all for her…'

'I'm here, Sasha,' said Kaspar. 'What did you want to tell me?'

Kajetan's chest heaved, as though every breath was an effort, and said, 'The rats. They everywhere here. Just when you think you all alone, I see them. They keep watch on me for her. Tried to kill me once already, but happy now just to watch me suffer.'

'Rats, Sasha? I don't understand.'

'Filthy rats! I see them, I feel them!' wailed Kajetan and Kaspar feared the swordsman's mind had finally snapped in this intolerable place. 'Above in the city, I hear their little feet as they plot and plan with her.'

'With who, Sasha? I don't understand,' said Kaspar approaching Kajetan.

'Ambassador,' warned Bremen, 'be careful.'

Kaspar nodded as he listened to more of Kajetan's ramblings. 'The pestilent clans of the Lords of Vermin are here. Evil in me can feel them, brothers of corruption we are. Told you once I was tainted with Chaos and so are they, but they glad of it. I feel them in my blood, hear their chittering voices in my head. They bring their best sickness and death here for her, but it won't take me. It won't take me!'

'Sasha, slow down, you are not making any sense,' said Kaspar, reaching out to touch Kajetan's shoulder.

With a speed that belied his pitiful form, the swordsman's hand snapped forward and seized Kaspar's wrist.

'Their sickness won't take me because I am like them, creature of Chaos! You not understand?'

Kaspar pulled away as Kajetan released him and he tumbled onto his backside as the gaoler leaned in and hammered his gauntleted fist into Kajetan's face. Blood exploded from the swordsman's nose and he gave a wild, animalistic howl, but rolled with the punch, lunging forward to wrap his hands around the gaoler's neck.

But Kajetan's strength was not what it once was and the gaoler was no apprentice when it came to dealing with violent prisoners. He slammed his spiked gauntlet hard into Kajetan's solar plexus, driving him to his knees, but the swordsman refused to let go, his chest heaving with violent spasms.

The gaoler raised his spiked cudgel, but before he could land a blow, Kajetan vomited a froth of gristly black blood over the man's breastplate. Kaspar watched horrified as the viscous liquid spilled down the armour, melting it with a noise like fat on a skillet. Stinking smoke hissed from the dissolving metal and the gaoler howled in pain as his armour was eaten away. He dropped his weapon and struggled to undo the straps that held the liquefying breastplate to his body.

Bremen rushed to help him and, between them, they were able to strip the armour off and hurl it to the ground where it crackled and hissed as Kajetan's tainted vomit completed its destruction.

Kajetan slid down the wall of his cell, weeping and rubbing the heels of his palms against his forehead. Bloody vomit dripped from his chin, displaying none of the corrosive properties towards him as it had to the armour.

'Sigmar save us!' cried Bremen, dragging Kaspar to his feet and hauling him from the acrid reek of the cell. 'He is an altered!'

The gaoler stumbled from the cell, his padded undershirt burned away and his chest raw and bleeding. Pashenko, who looked more terrified than Kaspar could ever remember seeing a man, closely followed him. The head of the *Chekist* shouted at the stumbling figure of the gaoler. 'Lock the door! Shut that monster in now!'

Kurt Bremen kicked the cell door shut and the gaoler eventually managed to find the key to lock Kajetan away once more.

'Ursun's blood,' breathed Pashenko, coughing at the foul stink still emanating from Kajetan's cell. 'I have never seen the like.'

Kaspar's senses still reeled from the horror of what he had just seen, his skin crawling at his proximity to a creature surely touched by the power of the Dark Gods. He had thought that Kajetan's claim to be a creature of Chaos on that lonely hilltop in the oblast was the delusion of a madman.

Now he knew better.

Without another word, he and Bremen fled the cells of the *Chekist*.

VII

KASPAR AND BREMEN returned to the embassy in silence and darkness, still in shock at what they had witnessed. The moon was high by the time they reached it and upon entering the warmth of the building, one of the embassy guards gestured towards the receiving room where guests would await the ambassador's pleasure.

'Someone to see you, Ambassador von Velten,' said the man.

Kaspar was in no mood for visitors at this hour and said, 'Tell them I am–'

But the words died in his throat and his pulse raced as he saw the three men within the receiving room.

The first was a man he knew to be a cold-eyed killer; the second a dishevelled man he did not recognise, but the third…

'Good evening, ambassador,' said Vassily Chekatilo.

CHAPTER FOUR

I

KASPAR COULD NOT believe that Chekatilo dared set foot in his embassy and for a moment he was stunned rigid, shocked that this piece of filth had actually sought *him* out after the events of the past few days. Chekatilo's killer, Rejak, stood beside him, taut like a stretched wire, with one hand resting on the pommel of his sword, the other gripping the filthy collar of a man smeared with dirt and of wild, unkempt appearance.

Before another word could be said, Kaspar whipped his pistol from his belt, pulling back the flintlock with his thumb and raising it to aim at Chekatilo's head.

'Kaspar, no!' shouted Bremen as Rejak released the man he held and moved with blinding speed, his sword slashing from its scabbard like a striking snake.

Bremen drew his own sword, but Rejak's blade was at the ambassador's neck before the weapon had cleared its scabbard.

'I'd lower that pistol if I were you,' said the assassin.

Bremen raised his sword, ready to strike at Rejak's heart. 'If you so much as draw a single drop of the ambassador's blood, I will kill you where you stand.'

Rejak smiled, predatory, like a viper. 'Better men than you have tried, knight.'

Kaspar felt the steel point press into his flesh and calculated his chances of pulling the trigger and evading a killing stroke of the blade at his neck. He felt Rejak's icy resolve and knew he wouldn't even manage to fire the pistol before the assassin opened his throat.

He saw Chekatilo disdainfully turn away from the unfolding drama and Kaspar felt his finger tighten on the trigger. How easy it would be to shoot this bastard, who had caused so much misery to the city of Kislev. He pictured the path the bullet would take, the terrible, lethal damage it would do to Chekatilo's head and was shocked to find that he *wanted* to pull the trigger. When commanding men in battle he had killed his foes because he had been ordered to, because that was what his Emperor had commanded. And when he had fought the kurgan horsemen in the snowbound landscape around the Kajetan family estates, he killed those men because they were trying to kill him.

But now he wanted to shoot someone who was not actively trying to kill him and whom he had not been ordered to put to death.

'You cannot do it, can you?' said Chekatilo without turning. 'You are not able to murder me in cold blood. It is not in your nature.'

'No,' said, Kaspar releasing a shuddering breath and lowering his arm. 'Because I am better than you, Chekatilo. I despise you and I will not become like you.'

'Sensible,' said Rejak.

'Take your sword away from his neck, you bastard,' hissed Bremen.

Rejak smiled and put up his sword, sheathing it with a flourish and stepping away from the ambassador. Kurt Bremen quickly stepped forward and, keeping his sword drawn, put himself between Kaspar and Rejak. He reached for Kaspar's pistol and carefully eased the flint down.

Hearing the click, Chekatilo turned and smiled at Kaspar. 'Now we have necessary show of bravado out of way, maybe we can get to talking, yha?'

Kaspar walked over to a long sideboard and carefully put his pistol down, gently – as though it were a piece of delicate crockery – feeling the tension slowly drain from his body. His heart was pounding fit to crack his chest and he gave thanks to Sigmar that he had not become the very thing he hated: a cold-blooded murderer.

'Why are you here, Chekatilo?' asked Kaspar.

'Same reason you wanted to kill me tonight,' said Chekatilo, sitting in one of the receiving room's large, leather chairs. The filthy man he and Rejak had brought whimpered as the giant Kislevite passed him, and curled into a foetal ball.

Chekatilo tugged at the drooping ends of his moustache as he continued, 'Someone has attacked me and now I want to hurt them back.'

'And what has that to do with me?' asked Kaspar.

'Because I think ones who tried to kill me are same as attacked you in Urskoy Prospekt and hurt your friend. More happening in Kislev than you or I know. Perhaps we can help each other, you and I?'

'What makes you think I would help you with anything?' laughed Kaspar. 'I loathe you and your kind.'

'That not important, Empire man,' said Chekatilo, with a dismissive wave of his hand.

'It's not?'

'No, what important is that we have common enemy. Like I said, those who try and kill you try to kill me too. There is old Kislev saying, "Enemy of my enemy is friend".'

'I will never be your friend, Chekatilo.'

'I know this, but we can at least not be enemies for now, yha?'

Kaspar considered Chekatilo's words, fighting not to let his loathing for the fat crook cloud his judgement. If what Chekatilo was saying was true, then he would only be putting himself and others in harm's way by ignoring this offer of co-operation. And after the terror of what had happened to Sofia and now Pavel, he was unwilling to run that risk again. He nodded warily and said, 'So what would this help cost me?' asked Kaspar.

'Nothing,' said Chekatilo. 'You help me, I help you.'

'Kaspar, no, you cannot trust this man,' protested Kurt Bremen.

'Your knight speaks true, you should not trust me, but I not lie.'

'Very well, suppose I believe that you are sincere,' said Kaspar, ignoring Bremen for the moment, 'who do you think orchestrated these attacks?'

'I not know, but think on this: on same day my brothel overrun by every rat in Kislev, you shot at by killer with gun that can see through walls and kill a man through thick timber. Same day. I not believe in coincidences, Empire man,' said Chekatilo, reaching down to haul the dishevelled man that Rejak had been holding to his knees. He stood and pulled the whimpering man to his feet. In all the excitement, Kaspar had quite forgotten that this sorry specimen of humanity was still in the room.

The man was tall, but Kaspar could see his spine was hunched, as though he had spent long years stooped over. He wore little more than a filthy smock of stiffened linen, and Kaspar could see he was absolutely terrified, his face alive with tics and twitches. His hair and beard were long and unkempt, his eyes darting to the skirting and corners of the room as though afraid of something that might be lurking there.

'Who is this?' asked Kaspar.

'This sorry specimen is Nikolai Pysanka,' said Chekatilo, 'and I just fished him from the Lubjanko.'

Kaspar knew of the feared Lubjanko, the dark-stoned building on the eastern wall of Kislev that had once been a hospital, but was now a dumping ground for the dying, the crippled, the sick and the insane. Its dark, windowless walls carried a terrible weight of horror and Kaspar had felt a nameless dread of the place when he had seen it.

'Nikolai was once a ratcatcher who worked in sewers and homes of rich and powerful people. I pay ratcatchers for the nuggets of information they bring me. It is great profit to know the thing they tell me.'

The wretched man flinched at the sound of his name, his eyes filling with tears. He squirmed in Chekatilo's grip, but had no strength left and eventually ceased his struggles.

'What happened to him?' asked Bremen.

'That I not so sure of,' admitted Chekatilo, 'he raves much of time, screams about rats coming to kill everyone. Now, I see many ratcatchers go mad from time in sewers and most hate rats, but Nikolai screams fit to burst lungs if he see one now.'

Kaspar felt a shiver up his spine, remembering similar thoughts spoken by another madman that very night. Kajetan had spoken of rats too and the similarity in these lunatics' words was chilling.

'I pay no mind to this at first, but then my brothel is attacked by rats so large I think they are dogs. Giants they were, with fangs to bite a man's hands off.'

Chekatilo lifted his arm, exposing several deep cuts and bites, and Kaspar recognised them as identical to the bite marks on Pavel's body.

'The rats kill everyone in brothel – ate them up, snap-snap!'

'I saw them, their bodies I mean,' said Kaspar, 'when I went there tonight.'

'Rats that big not natural, eh?'

'No,' agreed Kaspar.

'So, Rejak here has told me of Nikolai earlier and now I think maybe he not as mad as people think, so we go and speak to him. He not do so good now, no one does in Lubjanko, and he even madder than when they put him in. People they put in there not good people, do terrible things to each other, but who cares, eh? I speak to Nikolai and not get much sense out of him, but he says some things that make me interested.'

'Like what?' said Kaspar, thinking of the triangular brand on the burnt rat's corpse.

'He say he saw things in sewer,' whispered Chekatilo. 'A box that glow with green light. A coffin. And rats that walk like men.'

Kaspar laughed, feeling the tension in his limbs evaporate. He had heard the tales of the ratmen who supposedly lurked beneath the cities of the Old World and plotted the destruction of man, but did not believe them – what civilised man would?

'I too have heard of the ratmen,' scoffed Kaspar, 'but they are nothing more than stories to frighten children. You are a fool if you believe that, Chekatilo.'

Chekatilo pushed the ratcatcher to the ground and snarled, 'You are the fool, Empire man. You think you cleverer than Vassily? You know nothing.'

He knelt beside the quivering ratcatcher and pulled up his smock, exposing his scrawny naked flesh. Chekatilo held the struggling man down and said, 'Look at this and tell me I am fool!'

Kaspar sighed and knelt beside the convulsing Nikolai, his eyes widening as he saw what Chekatilo was pointing at. On the ratcatcher's side there was a small wound, little more than a scratch.

But the wound suppurated, weeping a thin gruel of pus, and the flesh around the wound was a peculiar shade of green, a spiderweb of necrotic jade veins radiating outwards from the cut. Kaspar had seen many wounds that had become infected, but had only ever seen something like this once before...

In the shoulder of the Knight Panther who had been shot by the mysterious sharpshooter on the Urskoy Prospekt just before he died from the rampaging infection that Sofia had been unable to halt.

'Show me where this happened,' said Kaspar.

II

Pjotr Ivanovich Losov, chief advisor to the Tzarina of Kislev, scratched nervously at the parchments before him, signing orders, authorising promotions and dating proclamations. But his mind was unfocussed and eventually he stood the quill in the inkwell before him and leaned back in his chair.

He knew now that the attack on Chekatilo's brothel had failed to kill the crook and that Kajetan had somehow survived the assassin's attempt to prevent his handover to the

Chekist. Losov felt a sheen of perspiration across his body, despite the chill of his private chambers, and rubbed a hand across his thin, ascetic features. His robes of office were scarlet, wound at the collar and trims with gold thread and decorated with black fur and silver tassels. Normally it gave him a sense of security to be so dressed, but he felt acutely vulnerable just now.

What if Chekatilo and the ambassador were to join forces? She said they would not, that the ambassador's hatred for the Kislevite would blind him to the idea of co-operation, but Losov was not so sure. She also believed she had him wrapped around her little finger, that he danced to her tune, but Losov did not think that von Velten was a man who could be so easily manipulated.

Who could have predicted that he would not kill Kajetan? After the violation of his physician, they had felt confident that either Kajetan would kill the ambassador and then be cut down by the Knights Panther, or that von Velten would be forced to kill the swordsman. Either way, it was a problem solved. But when the ambassador had returned with Kajetan alive, it had thrown them into a panic.

It did now appear their alarm had been unfounded, however, Kajetan now little more than a catatonic wretch awaiting death. She was content to simply have Kajetan watched now, saying that his continued descent into madness might yet prove useful to the Dark Gods.

If only Teugenheim had not been such a bloody libertine and got himself sent back to the Empire in disgrace. The man had been a weak-willed fool and easy to control, but von Velten was a different kettle of fish, disrupting plans that had been years in the making with his unthinking blunderings.

Well, at least Pavel Korovic was probably out of the picture. That thought alone gave him comfort; that the fat bastard he had had kill Andrej Vilkova would, if not already dead, be dying an extremely painful death. He wondered if von Velten knew of Korovic's murky past and briefly pondered how he might allow it to reach the ambassador's ears without incriminating himself.

He smiled, feeling sure the ambassador would enjoy hearing that particular nugget of information.

III

SOFIA SAT ON the edge of Pavel's bed, gripping his wrist and feeling the weak, thready beat of his pulse. She had managed to prevent the cold from killing him, but shook her head, knowing that the big man was not out of danger yet.

Colour had returned to his face, but he was still desperately fevered, needing rest and nourishment if he were to regain his strength. She had stitched the cuts and bites across his flesh, sitting up all night to drain the infected wounds of pus and evil humours, and applying ointments that she hoped would kill whatever filth had got into his blood. She had seen too much death recently and was damned if she would lose Pavel. The ambassador had asked her to look after this man and she would not let him down, not for anything.

She felt her eyelids drooping, more tired than she could ever remember. The last few weeks had passed in a blur, the nightmare streets of the city where the plague had taken hold haunting her dreams when she was able to snatch a few fitful hours of rest.

Hundreds had already died and the contagion was spreading. The other physicians did not want to believe that their quarantine and so-called cures were failing to halt the spread of the disease. Starting in the poorer quarters of the city adjacent to the Goromadny Prospekt, the plague had, at first, spread in a highly unusual manner, appearing in areas of the city nowhere near the initial outbreak. Worse, the epidemic seemed to change with each passing day, manifesting symptoms amongst its victims of a dozen different contagions.

While studying in Altdorf, she had read the journals of those physicians who had attempted to fight off the great plague that had swept the Empire in the twelfth century, learning the patterns in which such epidemics typically spread. At first the outbreak in Kislev had defied all that she had learned, appearing to move like a wayward traveller through the city and alter its effects before settling on a final epicentre. If only they could find the source and nature of the contagion they might stand a chance of defeating it.

But she was tired, so very tired, and could think of nothing but how good it would be to fall asleep curled up beneath soft, warm bedsheets.

Sofia cried out as she felt a hand on her shoulder, realising she had fallen asleep for a moment. She shook herself awake and smiled weakly as she saw Kaspar standing over her.

'You startled me,' she said.

'Sorry, I didn't mean to.'

'What time is it?' asked Sofia, rubbing her eyes.

'It's morning,' said Kaspar. 'How is he?'

Sofia brushed a strand of lank, auburn hair from her forehead and said, 'He is better, but is far from well, Kaspar.'

'Will he live? Honestly?'

'Honestly, I do not know,' admitted Sofia. 'I am trying all I can, but there is only so much I can do for him.'

'You should get some sleep,' said Kaspar. 'You look dead on your feet.'

'I cannot sleep,' said Sofia, rather more sharply than she intended, 'there is too much to do. I have to go out, there are more cases of the plague every day and we can't seem to stop it.'

'You need sleep,' pressed Kaspar. 'You will be of no use to anyone if you make a mistake through tiredness.'

'And how many more will die because I am sleeping and unable to care for them?' demanded Sofia, immediately regretting the words. Kaspar seemed not to notice and put his hand back on her shoulder. Without thinking, she reached up and took his hand.

'You can't save them all, Sofia. No matter how hard you try.'

'I know,' she said, 'but it hurts. Every one you lose hurts.'

'Aye, I understand,' agreed Kaspar. 'I felt the same every time I walked the field before a battle. Knowing that no matter what I did, many of my soldiers would die. There is nothing so much like a god on earth as a general on a battlefield, Sofia. With a word I was condemning men to death and nothing I could do would prevent that.'

Sofia nodded, finally noticing the utilitarian clothes Kaspar was clothed in: plain riding britches and a several layers of quilted jerkins. He carried a small pot helmet under one arm and instead of his usual rapier, wore a short, stabbing sword buckled at his waist next to his ubiquitous pistols.

'Where are you going dressed like that?' she asked.

'Below the city, into the sewers.'

'Whatever for?'

'Because I think that we might find something that will explain what the hell is happening to this city. Too much is going on that doesn't make sense, and I think we might get some answers down there.'

'Are you going with Chekatilo? I heard what happened last night.'

'Aye,' nodded Kaspar.

'Do you trust him? Because you shouldn't.'

'No, I don't, but I think he's right, there are forces working against us and I need to know more.'

Seeing that Kaspar would not be dissuaded from this course of action, Sofia simply nodded and said, 'Please be careful, Kaspar.'

'I will,' he promised and leaned down to kiss her cheek.

Neither of them saw Anastasia watching from the hallway.

IV

REJAK WEDGED THE tapered end of the iron bar beneath the rim of the sewer cover and pushed down, levering it from the cobbles of the Goromadny Prospekt. As the heavy bronze cover rose, Kurt Bremen reached down and wedged his fingers beneath it, dragging it away from the opening. A foul stench wafted up from below and Kaspar was glad of the camphor-doused scarf Sofia had given him before leaving the embassy.

He pulled the scarf over his mouth and nose as Bremen finally lifted the sewer cover clear and stared down into the darkness.

'Sigmar's oath, it smells worse than an orc down there.'

'What you expect? It's a sewer,' sneered Rejak, getting down on his haunches and swinging his leg onto the rusted ladder. He wore faded leather riding clothes with a pair of long-bladed daggers sheathed at his waist. In addition to his weapons, he carried a clinking canvas satchel slung over one shoulder and a pair of hooded lanterns over the other. Bremen ignored him and followed the assassin into the sewers with a grimace of distaste. The knight had relinquished his normal plate armour and instead wore a plain iron breastplate over a padded leather jerkin. Kaspar could see how much it irked the Knight Panther to be out of his armour.

As Bremen disappeared below the level of the street, Kaspar and Chekatilo shared an uneasy glance. There was no love lost between them and the idea of descending into the labyrinthine darkness below Kislev with someone who would quite happily see him dead was clearly not an appealing prospect for either man.

'After you,' said Kaspar.

'The ambassador is too kind,' grumbled Chekatilo, lowering himself to the sewer entrance. He clambered onto the ladder and Kaspar feared for a moment that the giant Kislevite crook's girth would be too great to fit through the hole in the ground. Taking a deep breath and sucking in his prodigious gut, Chekatilo was able to squeeze through and, as his head vanished into the darkness, Kaspar followed him down.

THE INKY BLACKNESS was utterly impenetrable beyond the diffuse cone of light that descended from the world above. A glistening tunnel stretched off into the darkness, its continuing course lost to sight. Once Kaspar stepped from the ladder, Rejak knelt at its base and removed a tinderbox, striking sparks with the flint and blowing the tinder to life to light the oil-soaked wicks of the two lanterns.

He handed one lamp to Bremen, keeping the other for himself, and the yellow light cast its warm glow around the dripping echoes of the sewer tunnel. The wet brickwork threw back glittering reflections of light, pinpoints of brightness that rippled on the surface of the sluggish river of effluent that ran down the centre of the sewer tunnel.

'Now what?' asked Kurt Bremen, panning the light from his lantern around the tunnel.

Rejak examined the mud around the base of the ladder, saying, 'Is good. Ground has frozen, so tracks still here.'

'What can you tell?' asked Kaspar.

'Tracks of a man come from that way,' said Rejak, pointing northwards along the length of the tunnel. 'Lot of space between each track, so man was running to ladder.'

'Like a man running from rats that walk like men,' pointed out Chekatilo.

'Running from something, perhaps, but let's wait and see what we find before leaping to wild conclusions,' said Kaspar.

Chekatilo shrugged and set off after Rejak, who started up the tunnel, keeping his eyes locked to the frozen muddy ground. Kaspar followed Chekatilo, with Kurt Bremen bringing up the rear.

The curved roof of the tunnel was just low enough to force him to stoop and Kaspar knew that he would suffer for this expedition on the morrow. The ground was hard and rutted, the imprint of the ratcatcher's tracks clearly visible, and Kaspar wondered what exactly had happened down here to drive the man Chekatilo had brought him to such a state of lunacy.

The tunnel echoed with the steady drip of moisture, the noise of their footsteps and the sound of their breathing. Kaspar's breath misted before him and he shivered in the oppressive gloom that the lamps did little to dispel. Even with the scarf he wore wrapped around his mouth and nose, the stench from the dark water that ran beside them was horrendous.

The four men made slow progress along the curving brickwork tunnel, Rejak stopping every now and then to more carefully examine a track in the frozen mud. Kaspar began to regret his decision to come down here; there was nothing here in the sewers except the stench and the cold.

He pulled the scarf from his face, grimacing as the full force of the sewer stench hit him, ready to call a halt to this foolhardy expedition, when Rejak spoke, his voice magnified in the dim light of the tunnel. 'Something strange.'

'What is it?' asked Kaspar.

'Look,' said Rejak, pointing to where a sprawling pile of debris, bricks and mud lay on the ledge that ran alongside the effluent, leaving a gaping black hole in the wall.

'Some bricks and stone, what of it?' said Kaspar.

'You not see?' said Rejak. 'Bricks been knocked *into* tunnel. Someone broke down wall and tunnelled in here.'

'Why would someone need to tunnel into the sewers?' asked Kurt Bremen.

'Perhaps because they could not travel on the streets above,' suggested Chekatilo.

Kaspar knelt beside the rubble as Rejak shone the light of his lantern into the hole in the wall. The tunnel was wide and high, several yards in diameter, and disappeared into darkness. Kaspar had the sudden sensation that the passage led to a place of terrible nightmares.

Rejak joined him and said, 'More tracks. Two sets, smaller, not human.'

'Not human?'

'No, see. These tracks barefoot and only four toes. Clawed too. Two sets come out, but only one goes back.'

'What do you think made them?'

Rejak shrugged, running his fingers around the edges of the tracks. 'I do not know, but whatever they were, they carried something heavy with them. Tracks coming into tunnel very deep, but one that goes back not so deep.'

Kaspar could see no difference between the tracks, but trusted that Rejak knew what he was talking about. The assassin moved off to continue following the tracks and Kaspar's knee began to ache from crouching, but as he made to stand up, he saw the frozen corpse of a huge rat lying partially buried in the rubble.

'Wait a moment,' said Kaspar, lifting broken bricks from the dead rat and pulling its stiff and frozen body free of the debris. Its spine had been broken, presumably by the tunnel wall when it had collapsed, and a thin line of blood had frozen around its jaws.

'You find something?' asked Chekatilo.

'Maybe,' said Kaspar. 'Kurt, bring the lamp closer.'

Bremen stood behind Kaspar and held his lantern close to the dead rat. Kaspar turned its furry body over, unsurprised to see a triangular brand mark imprinted on its back.

'What is that?' asked Chekatilo. 'A scar?'

Kaspar shook his head. 'No, I don't think so. I saw this same mark on a rat I found in the remains of your brothel. I think it is some kind of brand or something.'

Chekatilo nodded as Kaspar dropped the rat. 'Still think this a fool's errand?'

'I'm not sure what to think just now,' admitted Kaspar, standing and brushing his gloves against his britches; touching the rat had made him feel unclean.

They set off once more, the tunnel curving and soon widening into a domed chamber with a vaulted ceiling and a wide pool of lapping sewage at its centre. The smooth enamelled tiles of the ceiling threw the light from their lamps around the echoing space and Kaspar could see submerged sewage pipes just below the surface of the water. A circular ledge some six feet wide ran around the circumference of the chamber and Kaspar admired the scale of engineering skill that had built these tunnels, proud that it had been one of his countrymen who had designed them.

The group made its way around the edge of the chamber, Rejak following the tracks to a point on its far side. Here, he stopped, kneeling to better examine a patch of ground where a number of differing tracks converged.

'We need some more light,' said Kurt Bremen, squinting at the tracks.

'Not a problem,' said Rejak, opening the clinking canvas satchel he carried and removing thin lengths of timber with their ends tightly wrapped in cloth. Kaspar could smell the acrid reek of lamp oil on the cloth as he took the torch from Rejak and lit it from the flame of Bremen's lamp.

Flickering flames illuminated the chamber and Kaspar took some reassurance from the simple act of having a flame in the darkness. Rejak returned his attention to the tracks as the last of the torches were lit.

'They met someone. Two people,' he said. 'A man and a woman.'

'How can you tell?' asked Kaspar. To him, the tracks were little more than a jumble of impressions in the mud that could mean anything.

'Woman's feet much smaller, not as deep as man's and she wears woman's shoe,' explained Rejak. 'They brought cart or dray with them, see?'

That at least Kaspar could read from the tracks: parallel grooves in the frozen filth running towards an arched opening in the chamber's wall. A brickwork tunnel curved away into the darkness beyond the archway, but even with his burning torch, Kaspar could not see more than a few yards along its length.

'Why would someone in a sewer need a cart?' he wondered.

'Whatever the ones who broke into tunnel were carrying must have been taken away on the cart. Perhaps coffin Nikolai spoke of,' said Chekatilo. 'That explain why tracks that went back into tunnel not as deep. They brought it here, but not leave with it.'

'But who did they bring it for?' wondered Kaspar.

Bremen walked over to the archway, shining the light from his lantern into the tunnel beyond. He bent to examine the cart tracks and said, 'The cart they used has a cracked rim on one of the wheels on its left side, look. See, every revolution it leaves a "v" shaped impression in the mud.'

Rejak nodded. 'Yha, true enough.'

Kaspar shivered, the cold, dark and dampness of the sewers beginning to unnerve him. He held the warmth of his torch close to his body and cast his gaze around the chamber as Rejak and Bremen sought to unlock more secrets from the tracks.

'See, Empire man. Vassily told you more going on than we know,' said Chekatilo, joining him at the edge of the rippling pool that filled the chamber. Dark shapes bobbed in the water and Kaspar looked away, confident that he did not want to see anything that might be drifting in a sewer.

'Just because you may have been right about finding something down here, does not make us friends, Chekatilo. There is still to be a reckoning between us.'

'I know that, Empire man,' promised Chekatilo, the flames from his torch making his features dance. 'Debts to be honoured.'

'What are you talking about?'

'Who do you think got you the map of the boyarins' territories that allowed you to hunt Sasha Kajetan?' asked Chekatilo. 'You think Rejak just found it on street and thought to give it to you? I did this favour for you and will soon ask you to repay that debt.'

'I knew that it had come from you,' said Kaspar. 'But one thing I never understood was how you knew I needed it.'

Chekatilo laughed. 'Thank your fool of a friend, Korovic, for that.'

'Pavel? Why?'

'He came to me and told me you had been to see that snake, Losov. Said you needed to find Boyarin Kajetan's lands quickly, but that he had thrown you out of his office.'

'He wouldn't believe that Sasha was the Butcherman,' said Kaspar.

'Pavel begged me to help you, said you would be in my debt if I did.'

Kaspar's jaw tightened and he shook his head at Pavel's foolishness. It was typical behaviour for him, doing what he thought was for the best, but leaving someone else to pay the price for his good deeds. And to be indebted to a man like Chekatilo...

Who knew what he would demand in return for the aid he had given.

But misguided though Pavel may have been, Kaspar knew that without the map Chekatilo had provided, they would not have been able to bring Sasha Kajetan to justice.

Before Kaspar could ask what price Chekatilo would demand of him he heard a faint scratching noise, barely audible above the noise of the sewer and just at the edge of hearing. He glanced over his shoulder to Rejak and Bremen, who had ventured down the passageway through the archway to examine the cart tracks, but they seemed oblivious to the noise.

A prickling sensation worked its way up his spine as he turned back and saw the dark shapes he had noticed earlier in the water drifting towards them at the edge of the pool. Almost immediately Kaspar saw that the water's current was flowing out of the chamber and that the dark shapes were moving against it.

The scratching noise was getting louder too; he was sure of it.

'We need to get out of here,' he said. 'Right now.'

Chekatilo gave him a puzzled glance then followed the direction of his stare, his eyes widening as he saw what the ambassador was looking at.

'Ursun's blood,' he hissed, backing away from the edge and shouting. 'Rejak!'

Kaspar backed away with him and drew his sword as the scratching noise suddenly swelled in volume and hundreds of enormous black-furred rats swarmed into the chamber, pouring from almost every passageway and climbing from the water with lethally sharp fangs bared for attack.

V

SASHA KAJETAN THRASHED at his bindings, screaming himself hoarse. He could feel their scratching, clawing presence in his mind, their Chaos-tainted blood calling to his own polluted vital fluid. He could sense their hunger and their malice as a physical thing that echoed in his trueself and filled him with dark thoughts of murder and mayhem.

He knew he would not be able to resist the trueself's embrace for much longer and all that was once human of him would be swallowed by its lethal madness.

The door to his cell opened and the hooded gaoler came in, his cudgel raised.

'Time you shut your mouth, you murderous bastard.'

'You don't understand,' yelled Kajetan. 'Death is abroad this night, I cannot stay here!'

'I said be quiet!' shouted the gaoler, hammering the sole of his hobnail boot into Kajetan's face. The swordsman's head slammed into the wall and he felt blood and teeth fly from his jaw.

'Please!' wailed Kajetan, spitting a phlegmy wad of bloody spittle.

He pulled himself upright and had a last fleeting image of the gaoler's cudgel before it slammed into his skull and sent him spinning into unconsciousness.

VI

KASPAR DREW HIS sword as the rats poured into the chamber, fear dumping a hot jolt of adrenaline into his system. The surface of the pool thrashed with swimming rats, their bristle-haired fur black and shining in the lamplight as they sped through the water towards their prey.

'Sigmar's hammer,' hissed Kurt Bremen, drawing his sword and rushing to Kaspar's side. Chekatilo and Rejak hurriedly backed away from the passageway the cart tracks disappeared into as they heard the frantic scratching of hundreds of claws and the shrill squealing of yet more rats from its darkened depths.

Kaspar held his sword and burning torch before him, ready to defend himself, but the rats seemed content simply to watch them, gathering their numbers before closing for the kill.

'Why don't they attack?' whispered Kaspar, as though volume alone might trigger an assault.

'I not know,' said Chekatilo, as something pale and bloated moved sluggishly through the undulating mass of vermin. They parted before the passage of this creature and as it emerged from the mass of rats, Kaspar saw with disgust that it was a large, albino-haired rat with long, distended fangs and bloated belly. The rat looked up at them and hissed, the lamplight reflecting as tiny red pinpricks from its slitted eyes.

As the rat stared at them, Kaspar was struck by the dreadful intelligence he saw there, realising that it was somehow appraising them. Its pointed snout twitched, sniffing the air. Kaspar heard a clink of glass behind him and risked a hurried glance over his shoulder. Rejak rummaged through the canvas satchel once more, removing a handful of glass vials filled with a translucent liquid.

'What are you doing?' hissed Kaspar.

Rejak looked up and grinned. 'After rats attack brothel, I decide I will be prepared if I see many rats again.'

Kaspar nervously licked his lips, unsure as to what Rejak meant, but said nothing, watching the monstrous white rat as it cocked its head to one side as though listening to a sound only it could hear.

'When I shout "run", you run like all the daemons of Chaos were after you. Back the way we came, you understand?' said Rejak.

The white rat hissed again and the rats surged forwards in a heaving, snapping mass, Rejak threw the vials of liquid at the nearest rodents. Chekatilo hurled his torch as the vials shattered and a sheet of flame erupted in the midst of the rats. They squealed and dashed away from the blazing oil, burning rats screeching and rolling in agony as they died.

'Run!' shouted Rejak, sprinting through the gap that had opened in the mass of rats and leaping over the flames. Kaspar bolted after the assassin, swinging his sword at a rodent that leapt towards him with its fangs bared. The blade chopped into its body and sent it tumbling as Kaspar hurdled the flames unleashed by Rejak's vials of oil.

He landed badly, his knee twisting under him, but managed to keep his footing as Chekatilo and Bremen ran along behind him, the rats swarming after them.

Kaspar heard another vial of oil shatter ahead.

Chekatilo shouted, 'Ambassador! Hurry!'

Kaspar turned into the tunnel they had come from, jolts of pain shooting up his leg as his twisted knee flared painfully with each stride. He passed Rejak, who had lit another torch as a boiling mass of rats surged into the tunnel after them. Kaspar heard a whoosh of flames and the tunnel was suddenly illuminated with dancing flames. More rats were dying, but uncounted others were bypassing the flames by leaping into the effluent and swimming past the flaming barrier.

'Hurry!' shouted Rejak. 'Fire will give us time, but not much.'

Chekatilo moved fast for such a big man and overtook Kaspar, whose knee was now an agonised knot of fire. His pace slowed and he knew he could not carry on for much longer. He heard the click, click, click of clawed feet racing towards him and forced himself onwards, fighting to ignore the pain from his knee.

Kurt Bremen helped Kaspar as the rats swarmed forwards, their speed and tenacity incredible. Their squeals were deafening, magnified by the water and close confines of the tunnel. Kaspar heard a loud squeal, far too close, and felt a heavy weight land on his back. He stumbled, pitching forward and was only saved from falling flat out by Bremen's hand.

He twisted wildly, slamming his back against the wall of the tunnel in an attempt to dislodge the rat. He heard it squeal in pain then screamed as he felt its razor-sharp teeth bite into his neck. Its powerful jaws bit again before Kurt Bremen spun him around and hacked the rat in two with one stroke of his long blade.

Even in the midst of this horror, Kaspar was amazed at Kurt Bremen's precise swordsmanship, and pressed onwards, pressing his hand to his bleeding neck. The Knight Panther followed the ambassador, jogging backwards and watching for any other rats that might have managed to get past the flames. Blood spilled around Kaspar's fingers and he knew he was lucky the rat hadn't bitten through the main artery in his neck.

Kaspar ran on blindly, following the bobbing light of Rejak's lamp that glowed like a beacon ahead. He didn't know how far they had to go before reaching safety, but prayed that it would be soon.

He heard Kurt Bremen yell in pain and turned to see the knight struggling with a horde of biting and clawing rats. Three clawed at his legs, while another dragged its long incisors down the metal of the knight's breastplate. He swung the lantern and stabbed with his sword, but the rats were too quick, darting away from the deadly point of the weapon.

Kaspar drew his pistols and leaned against the tunnel wall for support, taking careful aim at the struggling knight. His first shot blew the rat clawing at Bremen's chest apart, his second hurling another into the sewage. The rats paused in their attack, frightened by the sudden noise, and the knight gave them no chance to recover, stamping down on one and skewering the other with his sword.

'Good shooting,' he panted, limping as fast as he could along the tunnel. Beyond the lantern's glow, Kaspar could see a writhing mass of black-furred bodies as they swarmed along the tunnel towards them and realised Rejak's fiery barrier must have finally gone out.

He jammed his pistols into his belt, struggling onwards with Bremen and hearing the scrabble of claws and snap of sharpened teeth growing louder and louder as they ran. They rounded a bend in the tunnel and Kaspar shouted, 'There!' as he saw the cone of daylight that descended from the sewer opening on the Goromadny Prospekt. Chekatilo was nowhere in sight, but Rejak remained at the bottom of the ladder.

'Must hurry!' shouted Rejak and Kaspar had never more wanted to punch him.

He reached the ladder, his chest heaving and his knee throbbing in pain, but began climbing as quickly as he could towards the light and safety. He gritted his teeth against the pain, feeling more blood pulse from the wound in his neck.

As he reached the top, Chekatilo's thick hands reached down and pulled him through the sewer opening. He took a great gulp of fresh air, like a drowning man breaking the surface of the ocean, and rolled away from the opening. Snow soaked through his clothes in seconds and he felt icy chill seep into his bones, but he was too glad to be out of the sewers to care.

Rejak quickly followed, vaulting through the opening in the ground and grabbing hold of the bronze sewer cover. Kurt Bremen came next, the knight bleeding from a score of bites.

'Hurry!' he cried. 'Sigmar help me, but they're climbing the ladder!'

He stumbled over to Rejak and helped him drag the cover over.

Between them, they manhandled the heavy plate over the sewer entrance and dropped it in place with a loud clang, falling back in fear-induced exhaustion.

The four men backed away from the sewer cover, weapons poised, but whatever nightmarish intelligence the rats possessed, it did not stretch to passing through heavy bronze. Long seconds passed in silence before all four men let out a collective breath and gradually lowered their weapons.

'I hate rats,' said Kaspar finally, sagging against Kurt Bremen as the pain in his knee and neck returned with renewed ferocity.

Kurt Bremen took the weight of Kaspar's injured knee, though he too was badly hurt.

'We need to get back to the embassy,' said the knight. 'Get Madame Valencik to look at that bite and get some ice on your knee.'

Kaspar nodded and said, 'Chekatilo, where is that ratcatcher you brought to the embassy?'

'Back in the Lubjanko,' said Chekatilo. 'Best place for him.'

'Meet us there in two hours, I need to speak to him.'

'What for?'

'I want to know if he saw who was in that sewer,' said Kaspar. 'He might be our only chance of finding out what the hell is going on here and I need you to translate for me.'

CHAPTER FIVE

I

WITH KURT BREMEN'S help, Kaspar made it back to the embassy, though his knee was an agonised mass of pain by the time they passed through the iron gates of its courtyard. The embassy guards helped the knight carry the ambassador inside, calling for Madame Valencik as they lifted him into the receiving room.

Sofia hurried into the receiving room as the guards laid him on a long couch, tying her long hair into a ponytail and rubbing her red-rimmed eyes. Even through the pain of his knee and the bite on his neck, Kaspar was struck by how tired Sofia looked.

She knelt by his side as Kurt Bremen carefully removed his boot and gently rolled up the leg of his britches. A basin of water and cloths were brought and Sofia began cleaning the wound at his neck.

'You stupid old fool,' said Sofia, dabbing water on the cut. 'This is no way for a man of your age to behave.'

'I am beginning to agree with you…' he hissed as she moved on to prod at the swollen bruising on his kneecap.

'And a man of your standing, running around in sewers,' she said, shaking her head. She beckoned one of the embassy guards over and despatched him to get some ice and wrap it in a towel.

'Turn your head,' she said, returning her attention to Kaspar. 'What happened anyway?'

'I jumped and landed awkwardly.'

'No, I mean to your neck.'

'A rat bit me. A big one.'

Sofia nodded and removed a jar of a white, oily cream from her satchel and scooped a handful onto her fingers. Kaspar smelled its strong odour and winced at Sofia spread it liberally over the bite on his neck.

'What it that? It stings like hell.'

'Camphor mixed with white wax and castor oil,' explained Sofia. 'It should help fight any infection the rat's bite might have carried and will numb the area a little.'

With the bite cleaned, she applied a folded bandage and bound it in place with another, which she wrapped around him and tied off behind his neck.

Kaspar grunted in pain as she began massaging his knee, working her fingers deep into his flesh and kneading the ligaments beneath. The guard she had commanded to retrieve ice returned and she placed the freezing bundle of cloth atop Kaspar's knee.

'Let us hope that the cold will bring down the swelling,' said Sofia, turning from the ambassador to begin seeing to the wounds suffered by Kurt Bremen.

'By Sigmar, I hope so,' said Kaspar.

'And did you find anything?' asked Sofia without turning. 'Was it worth all the trouble to go down there after all?'

'Yes, Kaspar, did you find anything?' said Anastasia, appearing at the entrance to the receiving room, her arms folded across her chest and dark hair bound up in a severe bun.

Kaspar nodded, wary at the mocking tone he heard in Anastasia's question.

'I think so, yes,' he answered. 'Tracks and rats. Lots of rats.'

'Tracks of what?'

'People and a cart by the look of them. I think someone had tunnelled into the sewers to deliver something to someone. The ratcatcher Chekatilo found in the Lubjanko said he saw people and a coffin, but I don't know how reliable a witness he is.'

'If he came from Chekatilo, then I would say highly unreliable,' snapped Anastasia.

'I'm not so sure,' said Kaspar, angry that Anastasia was once again dismissing his theories so quickly. 'I don't think he would make such things up.'

'Last night you said the man was a lunatic,' said Anastasia. 'You said he spoke of rats that walked like men? Seriously, have you ever heard of anything so ridiculous?'

'There are beasts that walk on two legs in the depths of the forests and in the far north,' pointed out Sofia. 'Perhaps it was one of those monsters he saw?'

'Oh, you would take his side, wouldn't you?' sneered Anastasia.

'What is that supposed to mean?' demanded Sofia.

'You know fine well. Don't think I haven't seen the way you fawn all over him. I know what you want.'

Kaspar could feel this confrontation spinning out of control and said, 'I agree that it does sound far-fetched, but I think he did see something down there. And as soon as the swelling on my knee goes down, I shall go to the Lubjanko and find out what.'

'It is a fool's errand,' said Anastasia.

'Perhaps,' snapped Kaspar, 'but I will go anyway.'

'I cannot believe you are trusting Chekatilo,' said Anastasia, shaking her head incredulously. 'After all that's happened, you'd take his side over mine.'

'Sides? What are you talking about, woman? This is not a matter of sides, it is a matter of getting to the bottom of what has been happening in this damned city for the past few months.'

'Then I think you are a gullible fool, Kaspar,' cried Anastasia. 'I think you are being taken in by a fat crook who wants nothing more than to take advantage of your stupidity!'

Kaspar's lips pursed in anger. He was unused to being spoken to in this manner and felt his temper fraying rapidly.

'Damn it, Ana, why must you always ridicule what I think?' shouted Kaspar. 'I have many faults, but I flatter myself that I do not count stupidity among them. Chekatilo is involved in this, yes, but I do not believe he is behind what is happening. There is conspiracy afoot in Kislev and I mean to get to the bottom of it.'

'Then you will do it alone,' said Anastasia, spinning on her heel and storming from the room. A heavy silence fell and Kaspar felt every eye in the room upon him.

'Nobody say a word,' he cautioned, simmering in anger.

II

THE LUBJANKO WAS just as grim and foreboding as Kaspar remembered it, the high, spike-topped walls and windowless façade warning away those who would dare to approach. Pillars of smoke billowed into the sky from behind the building, but even the warmth generated from the death pyres was not enough to entice the refugee population of Kislev to draw near this dreaded building.

The Lubjanko was now home to many of those struck down with the plague, the lower halls of the former hospital now given over to the business of death, the wails of the dying and afflicted echoing within its dark walls as though the building itself were screaming.

Kaspar and Bremen rode towards the Lubjanko, their horses plodding through the deep snow that lay thick and undisturbed – further proof that no one came this way. Since leaving the embassy, Kaspar had said nothing, still angry at the confrontation in the embassy's receiving room. Anastasia had infuriated him and, despite the many things he enjoyed about her, he knew that there would be no reconciliation this time. His instincts told him that events in Kislev were rapidly approaching a critical point, and he could not be distracted by those who would continually pour scorn on his thoughts.

After Anastasia had left he had endured another hour of ice on his knee until the swelling had gone down to a level where he could put his weight upon it again. Then he had changed into fresh, dry clothing and gathered up his weapons once more.

Sofia had advised him to rest some more before heading to the Lubjanko, but upon seeing Kaspar's resolve, settled for applying a cold compress to his knee and making him swear to be careful. In deference to Sofia's advice, he travelled on his horse, though he could still feel the ache in his joint even as he rode.

Kossars with black armbands and gauze facemasks stood at the gateway of the Lubjanko, an entrance with no gates that symbolised its initial purpose of caring for all who came within its walls. They allowed the ambassador past without comment, resting on the hafts of their long axes and gathered around burning braziers.

'This is a terrible place,' said Kurt Bremen, staring up at the featureless walls.

Kaspar nodded, turning in the saddle as he heard footsteps crunching through the snow behind them. Chekatilo and Rejak approached them, wrapped in furs and struggling through the deep snow with difficulty.

'Well met, ambassador,' said Chekatilo. 'You have recovered enough?'

'Enough,' agreed Kaspar. 'Let us get inside. I have no wish to tarry in this awful place longer than necessary.'

Chekatilo nodded and approached the heavy doors that led within. Twin statues of Shallya flanked the doors, with a Kislevite translation of one of her prayers carved above. Kaspar and Bremen dismounted, tying their horses to the hitching rail beside the door.

'Should I see if one of those soldiers will watch our horses?' said Bremen.

Kaspar shook his head. 'No, I do not think that will be necessary. Even though food is scarce, I have the feeling that few horse thieves would risk coming near this dreadful place.'

Bremen shrugged as Chekatilo hammered on the door and the four men gathered on the icy steps. Kaspar's knee hurt, but it was bearable, though he felt the cold seep into his body as they waited for someone to respond to the knocking.

'Damn this,' he said finally, pushing open the door without waiting for an answer. Kaspar stepped into the gloomy halls of the Lubjanko, the stone flagged hall he found himself within, cold and empty. A set of wide stairs led up to his left and a set of double doors marked with a painted white cross led deeper inside.

'Where will we find this ratcatcher, Chekatilo?' he asked.

'Upstairs. White cross means lower chambers are kept for those who will soon be dead from plague. Not so much work to carry them to the pyres if they kept here.'

Kaspar nodded and set off up the stairs, feeling his knee twinge with each step. Bremen, Chekatilo and Rejak followed him quickly, each sensing his dark mood. The stairwell was lit by the occasional lamp, doglegging several times before emerging onto a landing. Screams, hacking coughs and weeping could be heard from behind a nearby doorway and Kaspar pushed it open as Chekatilo nodded.

The long hall appeared to run the width of the building, the walls lined with wooden cots upon which desperate unfortunates rested in various stages of madness or catatonia. What little space was not filled with beds was occupied by sorry specimens of humanity curled up on blankets as they waited to die or go mad with cold and hunger.

Hundreds of people filled the hall, their demented wailings echoing from the high ceiling like a chorus of the damned. Black robed priests of Morr made their way up and down the aisles between the people who had been dumped here, speaking words of comfort to those who would listen or signalling the ragged orderlies to bring a shroud to wrap another body in.

The babble of lunatic voices was disorienting, hundreds of human beings reduced to such wretched misery by war, suffering and poverty. Kaspar felt his anger turn to sorrow as he took in the scale of human anguish he saw around him.

This was the result of wars, he knew. Men might tell grand tales of the glory of battle and the eternal struggle for freedom, indeed he himself was guilty of such sentiments, having spoken of these things before battle was joined to rouse the courage of his soldiers. But Kaspar knew that such talk was easy when the battle was long over, when the terror, bloodshed and suffering was nothing but a half-remembered nightmare, and he felt a deep wave of loathing wash through him.

Amidst such thoughts, he saw a hugely fat man standing beside a bed containing a supine young man. The man snapped his fingers to summon the orderlies before drawing his finger across his throat. The meaning was clear and Kaspar found this callous display of inhumanity utterly unforgivable.

As he moved onto the next bed, the fat man noticed Kaspar and his companions and limped towards them, his ruddy features clouded with anger. He unleashed a torrent of Kislevite, and Kaspar fought the urge to smash his fist into the man's ugly features.

Seeing Kaspar did not understand, he switched to heavily accented Reikspiel.

'Who you and what you be doing here?' he demanded.

'Dimitrji...' said Chekatilo. 'It is good to see you too.'

The man appeared to notice the fat crook for the first time and sneered. 'Vassily? What you here for?'

'I want to see Nikolai again,' said Chekatilo.

'Pah! That madman!' snapped Dimitrji. 'I have priest of Morr give him much laudanum to keep him quiet. His ravings set others off and place become madhouse.'

'I thought it already was.'

'You know what I mean,' growled Dimitrji, his flushed features red with a lifetime's abuse of kvas.

'Where can I find him?' pressed Chekatilo.

'In storeroom at end of hall,' said Dimitrji, waving his hand vaguely towards the far end of the scream-filled hall. 'I keep him apart from others.'

'Your compassion does you credit,' chuckled Chekatilo.

Dimitrji sneered and limped off, leaving them to make their way through the hall. They stood aside respectfully for the shaven-headed priests of Morr, stately and dignified in their long black robes and silver amulets bearing the symbol of their god, the gateway that separated the kingdoms of the living and the dead.

The Lubjanko was truly a place of horror. Kaspar saw all manner of disfigurements, both physical and mental in the forms of the inmates sequestered here. Those cursed by deformities from birth, mutilated by war, ravaged by sickness or left with broken minds following some nightmarish trauma; all were equal within the walls of the Lubjanko.

So touched by the scale of suffering he saw, Kaspar didn't notice the hooded priest of Morr coming the other way until he ran into him.

'I'm sorry–' began Kaspar, but the stoop-shouldered figure ignored him, walking quickly in the opposite direction, his plain black robes swathing him from head to toe. Kaspar shrugged, his nose wrinkling at the rank smell that came from the priest, but supposed that working in such a terrible place did not leave much time for personal hygiene. Something about the priest seemed out of place, but Kaspar could not say what and put the encounter from his mind as they reached the door to the storeroom Dimitrji had indicated.

He pushed open the door and immediately saw that they had made a wasted journey.

Nikolai Pysanka lay on a simple cot-bed with his throat pumping a jet of blood onto the floor. His slack, dead features were twisted in an expression of pure terror, as though his last sight had been of his greatest fear made flesh. There was no need to check if he was still alive; no man could live with his throat opened like that.

'By Sigmar!' swore Bremen, rushing to the corpse. 'How could anyone have known?'

Rejak stepped over the spreading pool of blood and said, 'This done not long ago. Blood still flowing from him.'

'Whatever Nikolai knew, he takes to Morr's kingdom with him,' said Chekatilo.

'That's it!' exclaimed Kaspar and bolted from the storeroom. He ran back to the wide hall full of human detritus and quickly scanned the room. There! Bremen, Chekatilo and Rejak joined him, looking quizzically at the ambassador as he shouted, 'You! In the black robes, stop!'

Kaspar set off in the direction of the stairs

Various priests of Morr looked up from their labours at the sound of Kaspar's shout, but he ignored them, running as fast as his injured knee allowed towards the man he had bumped into; the man who did not wear a pendant with the gateway symbol of Morr.

The figure ignored him and Kaspar drew his pistol, pulling back the flint with a loud click. He aimed just above the figure's head and shouted again. 'Stop! Stop now or I fire!'

The black robed figure was almost at the door that led to the stairs and Kaspar had no choice but to pull the trigger. The pistol boomed, the noise deafening, and the din in the hall rose as the inmates, frightened by the gunshot, erupted in a heightened cacophony of shrieks and wails. Madmen surged from their beds, cripples diving to the floor as nightmare memories of battle returned to haunt them.

The figure at the end of the hall spun, inhumanly quick, and Kaspar saw its hands dart beneath its robes. He jammed his pistol into his belt and ducked towards the cover of a stone column as he drew his second pistol and a blur of silver steel flashed through the air towards him.

He heard a series of clangs and risked a glance around the column, seeing three razor-edged triangular throwing stars embedded in the stone. He felt hands upon him and turned to see a filthy man dressed in a soiled smock pawing at his shoulders.

'Yha, novesya matka, tovarich!' yelled the man, spittle flying from his cracked lips.

Kaspar pushed the man away as Rejak and Bremen pounded past him, heading after the figure in black as it dashed through the door to the stairs.

Kaspar ran after them, fighting his way through the mad press of bodies that filled the hall. Screaming lunatics surrounded him, yelling insensible babble. Madness shone from every face as he fought to break free and pursue the ratcatcher's murderer. Hands tore at him, broken nails drawing blood from his cheeks as they clawed at his eyes. He felt himself being borne to the ground and lashed out with his fist and elbows as they began tearing at his clothes.

'Get off me!' he yelled, but either they did not understand him or paid him no mind if they did. A bare foot hammered his groin and the breath was driven from him, his body jack-knifing in pain.

Then suddenly it was over as Kurt Bremen returned and fought his way through the crowd of attacking madmen. His fists and feet cleared a path and the others fell back, terrified at this fearsome warrior in their midst.

'Ambassador! Grab my hand!' shouted Bremen. Kaspar reached up and Bremen hauled him to his feet, dragging him towards the stairs.

'Did you catch him?' managed Kaspar at last.

'Rejak is going after him.'

Kaspar and Bremen barged through the door and hurried downstairs in time to find Chekatilo's assassin lying at the foot of the stairs, his left arm hanging uselessly at his side. The man's face was deathly pale and blood matted the furs he wore.

'Rejak!' shouted Kaspar. 'Where is he?'

'Outside,' said Rejak slowly. 'Ursun save me, but he was quick. Fastest bladesman I ever see. He make me look like child. A heartbeat slower and my guts be all over floor.'

Kaspar had seen Rejak's speed with a blade and felt a chill race up his spine at the thought of an opponent faster than him. The only man faster with a blade that Kaspar knew of was securely locked away.

Bremen pulled open the Lubjanko's main door and raced outside into the snow.

Kaspar knelt by the wounded swordsman and tried to assess the damage. He was no surgeon, but knew that Rejak was lucky to be alive. Blood soaked his stomach and britches where a blade had cut him across the belly. A fingerbreadth deeper and Rejak would have died, not that Kaspar would have shed any tears for him.

'You are lucky to be alive,' said Kaspar as Chekatilo finally reached the bottom of the stairs. Chekatilo glanced at Rejak's injury and said, 'Will he die?'

'I'm not sure. I don't think so,' said Kaspar, 'but he needs a physician or he will.'

Chekatilo nodded, his breathing ragged and uneven. 'I not built for running.'

'You are not built for anything, Chekatilo,' said Kaspar bitterly.

'No sign of him,' said Bremen, returning to the entrance hall, frustrated at their failure to capture the killer.

'Damn,' swore Kaspar. 'Now we are back to square one.'

His heart sank as he knew that their best chance to unravel the truth had just been snatched from beneath their very noses.

III

THERE SEEMED LITTLE point in any further action that day so Kaspar and Bremen left the Lubjanko to return to the embassy, leaving Chekatilo to requisition a genuine priest of Morr to tend to Rejak's wounds until a priestess of Shallya could be brought.

Rejak's survival was a matter of supreme indifference to Kaspar, but the thought of how easily the man had been bested by the black-robed killer unsettled him greatly. Were their unknown foes so highly skilled? The only man of such skill Kaspar had seen was Sasha Kajetan, and he wondered if the swordsman would know of anyone else in Kislev with similar gifts. He wondered if there was enough of Kajetan's mind left to ask.

Kislev was quiet as the afternoon drew on, the low sun bright in a sky of azure blue, the day seeming so much brighter than it had earlier on. Kaspar wondered if this were really were true or whether it was simply the joy of leaving such a dark hellhole that made it seem so.

They rode back to the embassy in silence. He dismounted and handed the reins of his horse to one of the Knights Panthers' lance carriers, feeling a real sense of hopelessness.

He was not equipped to deal with such matters. Understanding the nature of warfare and how best to motivate his troops; those things he understood, but intrigue and mysteries were matters he felt were beyond him. The thought depressed him, but as he limped into the embassy and saw Sofia smiling at him, he felt his spirits lift.

He saw her notice the weariness in his face and said, 'What happened?'

Kaspar shook his head. 'I'll tell you later, but right now I need a drink.'

She stepped close and took his arm. 'Are you alright? Are you hurt?'

'No, I am fine, I am just... tired,' said Kaspar. 'Very tired.'

Sofia saw the exhaustion in his eyes and knew not to press the point. 'Very well. I have some news that might cheer you.'

'That would be a nice change. What is it?'

'It looks as though Pavel's fever has broken,' said Sofia. 'I think he is over the worst of his ordeal. If he can stay off the kvas, he may actually live to see the new year.'

Kaspar looked up. 'Is he awake?'

Sofia nodded and Kaspar set off upstairs to Pavel's room, where he found his old comrade sitting up in bed blowing on a bowl of hot soup. Pavel was still a terrible sight, covered in stitches and bandages and Kaspar forced himself to smile as he entered the room.

Pavel looked up and grimaced. 'I look that bad?'

'You've looked better,' answered Kaspar. 'But I'll wager the other man looks worse.'

'Ha! If by other man you mean rats and a broken window, then yha, they look worse.'

'What happened?' asked Kaspar, pulling up a chair and sitting beside the bed. 'How much do you remember?'

'Pavel not remember much after the rats. By Olric that was bad. Hundreds of rats, they came from everywhere at once. Biting, clawing and killing. I never see anything like it in all my days. They kill everyone...'

'What happened to you after that?'

'I... I am not sure. I was very drunk already when I get there and had begun to drink more when it all happen. To get away from the rats, I jump through window and cut myself badly.'

'You will have some fine scars, it's true,' said Kaspar.

'Perhaps they make Pavel more handsome,' laughed Pavel, grimacing as the stitches in his face pulled tight.

'Maybe,' said Kaspar, doubtfully, 'you never know what some people find attractive.'

'Yha, Pavel will be dangerously handsome with scars, but to

be honest, I not know what happened after the rats. I wandered through streets and collapsed. All I remember is terrible dream about falling and then thinking that I had to get back here. I not know how long I was away or how I find my way back. Next thing I knew I was back here with Madame Valencik cleaning my wounds.'

'Well, I'm glad you are on the mend, Pavel.'

Pavel nodded and took a mouthful of soup. 'Sofia tell me that you and Chekatilo working together now. He is dangerous man, you sure that is wise?'

The question was asked lightly, but Kaspar could sense the tension behind it.

'He told me you went to see him, Pavel,' said the ambassador. 'That you asked him to help me find Kajetan.'

'Kaspar, I–' began Pavel, but Kaspar cut him off.

'I know you went to him for all the right reasons, but you once said that Chekatilo was not a man to be indebted to, and that's just where you have put me. Haven't you?'

Pavel hung his head and did not reply.

'Haven't you?' barked Kaspar.

'Yha,' said Pavel at last.

'I told you before that I cannot afford to be looking two ways at once and, now more than ever, that still holds true. I have excused your foolishness in the past because I know you acted with good intentions, but no more, Pavel. If I find that you have done anything else stupid, then, by Sigmar, you and I are finished as friends. I will throw you out on your arse and you can drink yourself to death for all I care. Do we understand each other?'

Pavel nodded, and Kaspar could see the remorse etched across his features. He did not enjoy saying these things, but knew he had no choice. If Pavel were to remain here, then he would need to learn that he could not continue to behave in such a manner.

He turned and left the room without another word, leaving Pavel to his misery.

* * *

IV

THE DAYS DRAGGED on with no end in sight to the winter, though some who claimed a sense for such things, spoke of a coming thaw with the break of the new year. The days passed slowly and painfully, with Kaspar enduring agonising days of Sofia massaging his injured knee and exercise to reduce the swelling. He was past the age when such injuries could be shrugged off so easily and Sofia predicted that his knee would be weak for the remainder of his days.

Pavel also recovered his strength slowly, though he kept a remarkably low profile around the embassy. Sofia ensured that he kept off the kvas and as the weeks passed, the big Kislevite's strength gradually returned.

The year turned from 2521 to 2522 with little fanfare, the city too beaten down to celebrate Verena's sacred day. Though plague continued to kill scores every day, it appeared that the outbreak had at last been contained. Scant comfort to those quarantined within the affected areas, but a source of great relief to everyone else.

A number of Kislevite boyarin gave rousing speeches to the soldiers on the first day of Nachexen, promising them a year of battle and victories. Kaspar himself was called upon to make a number of speeches to the Empire regiments camped beyond the walls of the city when riders from Talabheim delivered missives that informed him that the armies of Talabecland and Stirland were on the march to Kislev.

Perhaps it was the hope of reinforcements, or perhaps it was the lengthening days and the breath of the new year, but a tangible sense of optimism began to permeate the Kislevite capital.

V

HE HAD NEARLY forty thousand warriors, and more were arriving every day. High Zar Aelfric Cyenwulf of the Iron Wolves watched with satisfaction as yet more riders rode in from the cold steppe of the north to join his army, their ragged skull totems raised as high as their ululating war cries. Victory bred victory and the tribes of the north – the Kul, the Hung and the Vargs, as well as Kyazak raiders – were flocking to his banner, eager to share in his future successes. Individual warbands of fearsome champions came too, and his army grew.

The warriors he had assembled to fight for him were the fiercest he could have wished for. No other army of the north had won so many battles or conquered so many tribes. No other army had provoked such fear and loathing in its victims, or slaughtered so many of its vanquished.

Hundreds of horsemen and thousands of warriors on foot gathered on the snow-covered landscape below him, too many to be seen at once. Whole wings of his army were scattered, a day's ride or more from here, spread out across the steppe until the order was given to march south. Men and monsters fought for the High Zar, malformed trolls from the high mountains, bestial monstrosities gifted by the touch of the Dark Gods and mindless things so twisted and mutated that they defied any easy description.

It was an army raised not for conquest, but destruction.

The people of the southern lands knew a terror of him and his armies, and the High Zar knew that such tales would do more to defeat his foes than axe or sword.

The High Zar was a giant of a warrior, broad shouldered and powerful, carrying his horned, wolf-faced helm in the crook of his arm as he stood atop the craggy foothills of the mountains and allowed his army to see him. His cloak billowed behind him in the wind, the iridescent plates of his heavy armour gleaming in the late winter sun.

He raised his tattooed arms, the many trophy rings wrapping his muscles glinting as they caught the light. He held his mighty pallasz above his head, hefting the fearsomely heavy weapon as though it weighed nothing at all. He towered above the eight handpicked warriors who accompanied him, a mighty champion of Chaos, favoured son of Tchar and soon to be destroyer of nations.

Silver hair, with a streak of pure black at either temple, rippled in the wind and framed a scarred face that had known only victory. He smiled, exposing teeth that had been filed to sharp points.

The spring thaw was upon the land and his shaman, Kar Odacen, had promised him that the snows were already receding. Come the morning, they would march south, following the line of the World's Edge Mountains and skirting Praag before turning westwards towards the great scar on the landscape known as Urszebya.

Ursun's Teeth.

'Many warriors,' said a voice that sounded like glaciers colliding, and the smile fell from the High Zar's face.

He felt his skin crawl and the hairs on his arms crackle with the arrival of the Old One as it climbed the rocks behind him. The ground shook with its weight and sapphire sparks began dancing around the gold-fluted edges of Cyenwulf's armour at its presence. He licked his suddenly dry lips before replying.

'Aye, many warriors. We take war to the south on the morrow.'

Wisps of dark, flickering smoke curled around his body as the beast that had awoken from beneath the mountains stepped forwards, its heavy tread shaking the mountain. The High Zar dared not look too closely at it; he had seen the fate of those who had done so, and had no wish to end his days a burned out husk of dead flesh.

'I do not remember this world,' it said. 'I remember the destruction of the Great Gateway and the world in turmoil, but all this... all this was young then. I have slept for so long that I do not remember it any more.'

'It is ours for the taking,' promised Cyenwulf.

'Yes...' rumbled the creature, the smoke that concealed its dark majesty pulsing with cerulean lightning, and the High Zar breathed a sigh of relief as it turned and climbed back down the mountainside.

VI

WHEN KASPAR HAD been told that Vassily Chekatilo was downstairs, he had assumed that the Kislevite had come with further news of the unseen enemy who had thus far eluded them. But now, sitting in his study with Chekatilo lounging beside the fire, he wished he had never allowed the smug bastard within the walls of the embassy. Many days had passed since the events at the Lubjanko and Kaspar had put off speaking to Chekatilo for as long as he could.

'You cannot possibly expect me to do this,' said Kaspar, his lips pursed in a thin line.

Chekatilo simply nodded. 'I do indeed, ambassador.'

'I won't.'

'I think you will, it is in your interests to do so,' said Chekatilo ominously. 'Remember, you were only too willing to put yourself in my debt when your precious Sofia was missing, when Sasha Kajetan was torturing her in his death attic. You begged me to help.'

'But we got Sofia back without your help,' pointed out Kaspar.

'Aye, that you did, but without my help you not have caught Kajetan, eh?'

'No,' admitted Kaspar, 'but I never asked you to do that. It was Pavel who came to you. I owe you nothing.'

Chekatilo laughed. 'You think that matter, Empire man? If a man owes me money and he dies, do I not demand the money from his woman? And if she dies, do I not then demand it from his son? It the same thing, the debt passes. You owe me and I remember you giving me your word on this. Said it was iron, once given, never broken.'

Kaspar got up from behind his desk and turned his back on Chekatilo, staring through the window over the rooftops of Kislev. The snows were retreating and the first rains had turned the streets into slushy quagmires, dampening the optimism the new year had brought to the city.

Armies were on the march, he knew. Forward riders from the vanguard of the army of Talabecland had already arrived, bringing news of the arrival of nearly seven thousand fighting men under General Clemenz Spitzaner, a man Kaspar knew well and did not particularly relish meeting once more. He wondered briefly if the years had dimmed the man's bitterness, but supposed he would find out soon enough.

'Ambassador?' said Chekatilo, startling him from his reverie.

'What you are asking me to do violates every duty and oath I took when I accepted this posting to your miserable country,' said Kaspar, facing Chekatilo once more.

'So? Such things not a problem for your predecessor.'

'I don't suppose they were, but Teugenheim was a coward and I will not be blackmailed in the way he was.'

'I am not blackmailing you, Empire man,' said Chekatilo. 'I only ask you to honour your debt to me. I am leaving Kislev for Marienburg and need to travel very far. Through your land – and land at war is a dangerous, suspicious place. As Empire ambassador, you can sign documents that will allow me to pass... what is the phrase? Ah, yha, "without let or hindrance" through Empire. Teugenheim also tell me that as ambassador you entitled to soldiers from Empire regiments to protect you on journeys.'

'I know all this,' snapped Kaspar.

'I know,' smiled Chekatilo. 'You will authorise men from your soldiers to see me safely to Marienburg. After all, they sit outside of walls of Kislev and do nothing anyway, it not like they do anything useful.'

'But they will be called upon soon,' said Kaspar. 'It may have escaped your selfish notice, but war is coming to your land and these men will soon risk their lives defending it.'

'Pah, is of no matter, I not ask them to come here. I think many of them would be glad of chance to get out of Kislev before war.'

'You may have no sense of honour, running from your country like a cowardly rat, Chekatilo, but I do and I will be damned if I will sign any travel documents or assign you any of my nation's soldiers to do so.'

'You refusing your debt to me?' said Chekatilo darkly.

'You're damn right I am.'

'I not ask politely again, Empire man. You *will* give me what I ask for.'

'Over my dead body,' growled Kaspar.

'If not yours, then someone else's perhaps,' promised Chekatilo, rising from the chair and taking his leave.

VII

PAVEL TRUDGED THROUGH the slush of the Goromadny Prospekt, keeping his head bowed against the drizzling rain that greyed the sky and washed the colour from the world. He knew he should not be out in this kind of weather – Sofia had warned him as much – but he could not stay in the embassy. Not with the constant reminders of his shame at having let the ambassador down all around him in the accusing stares of his knights and guards.

He wished that he had a bottle of kvas, but was also glad that he did not. The past weeks had been a constant battle between his craving for the powerful spirit and a desire to not let his oldest friend down again. If he was honest, he knew he was probably too weak to win that battle, but hoped to eke out what little remained of their friendship before he inevitably failed once more.

'You are a stupid old fool,' he said to himself.

'You'll get no argument from me on that score,' said a cold voice from the street corner ahead of him. His heart sank as he recognised the voice and looked up into the flinty eyes of Chekatilo's killer, Rejak.

Rejak lounged on the corner of a redbrick building, his left arm held in a sling that was bound tightly to his body. Pavel could also see a thickness at the man's waist where the cut across his stomach had been heavily bandaged.

'Rejak,' said Pavel guardedly. 'I heard you were dead. What do you want?'

'No greeting for an old friend? And no, I'm not dead, sorry to disappoint you.'

'We were never friends, Rejak, even then. You are a cold blooded killer.'

Rejak laughed. 'And you are not? I seem to remember it was you who cracked open Andrej Vilkova's skull. I only held him down for you.'

Pavel closed his eyes, feeling the familiar guilt as he thought back to that dark night of murder. He took a deep breath to clear his head and said, 'I see someone taught you a lesson in swordplay. Almost emptied your belly to the floor, I heard.'

Rejak's eyes flared. 'It won't happen a second time,' he snarled. 'When I see that tricksy bastard again, I'll take his damned head off.'

Pavel laughed, tapping Rejak's injured arm. 'Best hope not to meet him too soon, eh?'

'I could still best you right now,' snapped Rejak.

'I don't doubt it, but that's not what you're here for is it?'

Rejak smiled, regaining his composure, and said, 'No, you're right, it's not.'

'Then what is it? Hurry up and tell me so I can get out of this bloody rain.'

'Chekatilo wants to see you.'

'Why?'

'He needs you to do something for him.'

'What?'

'Ask him yourself. I'm taking you to him.'

'What if I don't want to see him?' said Pavel, though he knew it was pointless.

'That doesn't matter. He wants to see you and I won't ask you again,' grinned Rejak, lifting aside his cloak with his good arm to show the hilt of his sword.

Pavel sighed in resignation, knowing that to follow Rejak was to damn himself completely, but knowing he was too pathetic to refuse and suffer the consequences.

Rejak smiled, seeing the defeat in Pavel's eyes, and turned to walk up the street.

Pavel followed him.

CHAPTER SIX

I

WITH ITS GOLDEN, eagle-topped banner poles shining in the sun, brightly patterned standards flapping in the stiff breeze and gaudily caparisoned knights, the army of Talabecland was a vibrant sight as nearly seven thousand men marched in good order along the rutted roadway towards Kislev. Kaspar's heart swelled with admiration to watch such an overt display of martial might, proud to see such fine men of his nation coming to the aid of their ally.

He and Kurt Bremen sat atop their steeds to one side of the main road at the foot of the *Gora Geroyev*, wrapped in thick fur cloaks. Officially, he was here in his capacity as Imperial ambassador to greet the army's general and welcome him to Kislev, but Kaspar knew Clemenz Spitzaner from the days he had carried his own general's baton and was in no hurry to renew that acquaintance.

No, Kaspar had come for the spectacle.

Densely packed blocks of pikemen in long tabards of red and gold marched behind halberdiers in padded, cross-coloured surcoats who carried their long-hafted weapons proudly, the blades gleaming like a forest of mirrors. Kaspar watched the different regiments as they passed in a riot of colours, golds, reds, whites and blues; swordsmen in feather-peaked sallets bearing iron-rimmed shields on their back: arquebusiers wrapped in long tunics and bristling with silver cartridge cases; archers in cockaded tricorne hats with bows wrapped in oilcloth; warriors in gleaming hauberks and scarlet puff-breeches who carried heavy greatswords over their shoulders.

Regiment after regiment of the state infantry of Talabecland marched to the beat of the drummer boys, who played rousing martial tunes accompanied by the horns of the following regiments.

Cavalry riding fine, grain-fed Empire steeds rode alongside the infantry, their mounts of obvious quality and a sure sign of wealth. The young riders wore light, flexible breastplates of toughened leather and plumed helmets, their long barrelled carbines holstered from looped thongs fastened to the saddle horn. Fast, deadly and brave to the point of recklessness, many an enemy had cause to regret underestimating these lightly armoured cavalrymen.

But the glory of the army was the knights in gleaming plate armour riding monstrous horses, fully seventeen hands or more. Great, northern-bred warhorses, these snorting, stamping beasts carried the Knights of the White Wolf: fearsome, bearded warriors, who matched their mounts' wild appearance. Wrapped in shaggy wolf pelts and disdaining to carry a shield, they carried heavy cavalry hammers and shared raucous jokes with one another as they rode.

'That is no way for a Templar to behave,' said Kurt Bremen, shaking his head.

Kaspar chuckled, well aware of the rivalry that existed between the Templars of Ulric and Sigmar. He smiled, finally catching sight of the black and gold banner tops of the Nuln artillery train. Straining oxen and shouting teamsters with whips guided the massive cannons and bombards along the road, sweating teams of muscled men pushing the monstrously heavy bronze guns when their carriage wheels became stuck in the mud. Wagon after wagon followed the artillery, laden with shot, shell, black powder, handspikes and rammers.

'Ah, it does the heart proud to see the guns here, Kurt. The Imperial Gunnery school still produces the best guns in the world, no matter what the dwarfs might say.'

'You can keep your guns, Kaspar,' said Bremen with a smile. 'Give me an Averland steed and a sturdy lance any day.'

'Warfare is moving on, Kurt,' said Kaspar. 'The things the School of Engineers are producing now are frightening in their potential. Pistols that do not need to be loaded again until a revolving mechanism is expended, black powder rockets that can reach further than the heaviest cannon, though they can't hit anything worth a damn, and armoured machines that can carry a cannon across the battlefield.'

'Aye, soon a soldier himself will be incidental.'

'I fear you might be right, Kurt,' said Kaspar sadly. 'Sigmar save us from such times. I fear for what wars we might make when we no longer have to fight the foe face-to-face. How much easier will it be to kill when we can do it from leagues away and don't have to feel the enemy's blood on our hands or look into his eyes as he dies?'

'All too easy I suspect,' replied Bremen.

Such melancholy thoughts soured Kaspar's enjoyment of watching the spectacle of his countrymen's arrival in Kislev and he felt his mood worsen as he saw the unmistakable banner of its general approaching: a scarlet griffon rampant on a golden background, surrounded by a laurel wreath and decorated with numerous scrolls and trailing prayer pennants.

'Damn, here comes the man himself,' sighed Kaspar.

'You know the general?' asked Bremen.

Kaspar nodded. 'He was an officer on my staff that I could never quite shake loose. Unfortunately, his family had money and I was obliged to keep him around. A competent enough soldier, but there is no humility to the man, no sense that he owes it to his soldiers to try and bring as many of them back alive as he can. Show him a battle and he will hurl men at it until it is won, regardless of the cost.'

'From that, I take it there is no love lost between you?'

'Not much,' Kaspar chuckled. 'When I retired from the army, Spitzaner assumed that, as ranking officer, he would take over, but there was no way I was going to let him have it. Instead I promoted an officer named Hoffman, a good man with a brave heart and uncanny sense for good ground.'

'That can't have been easy to bear, a more junior officer being promoted over him.'

'No, but I was damned if I was going to let "Killer Clemenz" have my regiment. Thank Sigmar, the countess-elector's father, who was the Count of Nuln back then, agreed with me and Spitzaner left, purchasing a commission in a Talabecland regiment.'

'Where he has obviously prospered if he is now a general,' pointed out Bremen.

'Or, more likely, his money has greased his ascent up the promotions ladder.'

Further discussion was prevented by the arrival of Spitzaner and his coterie of horsemen: his officers, his priests, his book-keepers, his historical recorders, his personal valets, a pair of men in long frock coats with the Imperial seal of Karl-Franz pinned to their lapels and a group of fork-bearded men with long swords who looked like they knew how to use them. As well as his banner bearer, General Clemenz Spitzaner travelled with his own trumpeter, who blew a series of rising notes on his brass bugle as the group of horsemen approached Kaspar and Bremen.

Spitzaner was a man in his early forties, but appeared much younger, thanks to a life free of the vice and loose living that so typified much of the Empire's nobility. His thin face was sallow and angular, as though his bones pressed too tightly against his skin and his eyes were a pale shade of green. The general wore a scarlet greatcoat with gold braid looped across one shoulder and a golden-fringed pelisse of emerald green velvet draped across the other. His riding britches were a spotless cream and his knee-length boots a brilliant, lustrous black.

Kaspar could tell that Spitzaner had known who he was going to meet at Kislev by the general's attire. Any other man would have ridden in practical furs and quilted jerkin, but not Spitzaner; he had a point to make. Kaspar wondered how long he had forced the army to wait, just outside of view of Kislev, while he changed into this ridiculous finery.

The general's group halted in a jingle of trace and bridle and Kaspar put on his best smile of welcome.

'My compliments to you, General Spitzaner. As ambassador to Kislev I bid you welcome to the north,' said Kaspar, turning to indicate the knight by his side. 'Allow me to introduce Kurt Bremen, leader of my detachment of Knights Panther.'

Spitzaner bowed to Bremen before nodding curtly to Kaspar and saying, 'It has been a long time, von Velten.'

'Aye, it has that,' said Kaspar. 'I believe it was the countess-elector's ball of 2512 we last spoke.'

He saw Spitzaner's jaw clench and could not resist twisting the knife a little further.

'And how is Marshal Hoffman? Do you keep in touch?' he said.

'No,' snapped Spitzaner. 'Marshal Hoffman and I do not correspond.'

'Ah, so often that is the way when brother officers are promoted over one another. I, on the other hand, still receive letters from him every now and then. One of my most gifted protégés, I always thought. No doubt you will be pleased to know he prospers.'

'Indeed, but be that as it may,' said Spitzaner, a little too loudly. 'He is not here and I am. I am general of this regiment and you would do well to accord me the respect that my rank demands.'

'Of course, general, no disrespect was intended,' said Kaspar.

Spitzaner looked unconvinced, but did not press the point, casting his gaze out over the unkempt soldiers camped around the city walls and seeing scattered Empire standards planted in the hard ground.

'There are Imperial soldiers here already?'

'Aye,' said Kaspar. 'Remnants of the regiments scattered after the massacre at Zhedevka. Perhaps three thousand men.'

'Are they quality?' asked Spitzaner.

Kaspar bit back an angry retort and said, 'They are men of the Empire, general.'

'And who commands them?'

'A captain named Goscik, a good man. He has kept the soldiers together and in readiness for the fighting season.'

'A captain commands three thousand men?' said Spitzaner, outraged.

'He is the highest ranking and most competent officer who survived the battle.'

'Intolerable! I shall assign a more senior officer from my staff once we have established ourselves in this dreadful country. I would be grateful if you could show us to out billets, it has been a long and arduous ride from the Empire.'

'So I see,' said Kaspar, admiring Spitzaner's gleaming uniform.

Spitzaner ignored Kaspar's barb and turned in his saddle to wave forward the two men who bore the Emperor's seal in their lapels.

'This is Johan Michlenstadt and Claus Bautner, emissaries from the Emperor,' said Spitzaner by way of introduction. 'Their safe passage to Kislev was entrusted to me by the Reiksmarshall himself.'

Kaspar nodded a greeting to the two men, wondering how desperate Kurt Helborg must have been to trust Spitzaner with keeping these men alive. 'A pleasure to make your acquaintance, gentlemen.'

'Likewise, Ambassador von Velten,' said Michlenstadt.

'Yes, General Spitzaner has told us a great deal about you, though I am sure he exaggerates sometimes,' said Bautner.

Kaspar caught the man's ironic tone and warmed to Bautner immediately. He could well imagine the poison Spitzaner would have been spreading about his former general, and was pleased to meet someone who could see through it.

'I am sure the general does me proud with his tales,' said Kaspar graciously, 'but I am intrigued as to what manner of mission you would be upon that the Reiksmarshall himself would take such interest in it.'

'A matter of gravest urgency,' said Michlenstadt. 'It is imperative that we see the Ice Queen at the earliest opportunity.'

'Yes,' continued Bautner. 'We bring missives from the Emperor himself and must deliver them to the Tzarina's own hand.'

'That might not be so easy,' said Kaspar, faintly amused by the two emissaries' habit of finishing each other's sentences. 'The Tzarina is not an easy woman to see.'

'It is vitally important,' said Michlenstadt.

'Yes,' nodded Bautner. 'The fate of the world depends upon it.'

II

ICICLES DROOPED FROM the cellar's roof, the steady drip, drip of moisture on the top of the bronze coffin echoing loudly in the icy room. The pale blue of the ice that covered the walls and floor was shot through with black and green veins, poisonous corruption that had spread quickly from the miasma that surrounded the coffin and infected everything around it with deadly, mutating sickness.

The plague that stalked the streets above and killed scores daily was ample demonstration of the power of what lay within the coffin, its pestilent makers having excelled themselves in its creation. Perhaps too much so, she thought as she idly paced in a circle around the coffin, her breath feathering before her in the chill air. The force within was a living thing now – its power to corrupt growing with every passing day – and it had taken potent wards to keep its malice in check lest its eagerness to writhe and mutate unmask her before she was ready to unleash it.

The tiny corpses lying frozen in the corner of the cellar gave testimony to the amount of innocent blood it had taken to subdue its malice, but fortunately Losov could obtain an almost limitless supply of such nameless, faceless victims from the Lubjanko.

When it came time to break those wards and allow that malice its full, unchecked rein, she would relish the spectacle of painful death and mutation that would swiftly follow. The arrival of the Empire force, two days ago, had filled her with elation then disappointment. She had been told that the armies of both Talabecland and Stirland would be coming to Kislev, but now it seemed as though the Stirland force was marching west to link with the forces of Boyarin Kurkosk.

With so many men camped outside the city wall, she could feel the pulsing, deathly desire of the corruption locked within the coffin to be released, to wreak its misery upon so many living things, to reduce them to foetid piles of mutated flesh and bone. She suspected that the Stirland army would come to Kislev eventually, and knew that she could inflict much greater suffering were she to bide her time.

She ran her delicate fingers along the rusted top of the coffin, feeling its power and its desire to inflict horrific change. But she was touched by the Dark Gods' favour and was resistant to its evil.

'Soon,' she whispered. 'Curb your wrath for but a little longer and you shall be the unmaking of more life than you know.'

She turned on her heel, more pressing business now occupying her thoughts.

Sasha Kajetan.

She knew that the swordsman had now descended to the point where his madness was complete and his obsession with the ambassador had consumed him utterly.

It was time to set her handsome prince on the hunt once more.

III

'DAMN IT, HOW much longer must we wait?' snapped Clemenz Spitzaner, pacing up and down before the great portrait of the Khan Queen Miska in the Hall of Heroes. The interior of the Tzarina's Winter Palace was just as impressive as Kaspar remembered, the walls of solid ice glittering in the light of a thousand candles hung from shimmering chandeliers. Columns of black ice, veined with subtle golden threads rose to the great, vaulted ceiling with its mosaic depicting the coronation of Igor the Terrible.

'You'll wear a rut in that rug, general,' said Kaspar, standing with his hands laced behind his back. Though he hated its ostentation, he wore his formal attire for the audience the Tzarina had finally deigned to give them: a cockaded hat with a long blue feather, a long embroidered coat with a waistcoat held shut by engraved silver buttons and elegant britches tucked into polished black riding boots. Spitzaner and his staff officers wore their colourful and ridiculously impractical dress uniforms, laden with gold braid, lace trims and bronze epaulettes.

Both emissaries of the Emperor wore sober dark dress, their only concession to decoration the gold and scarlet sashes they wore bound about their waists and the Imperial seals pinned to their lapels. Bautner stared in wonder at his surroundings, while Michlenstadt picked small pieces of lint from his coat.

'You are the ambassador,' said Spitzaner angrily. 'Shouldn't you be able to procure us an audience with Tzarina quicker than this? My army has been camped beyond the walls of her damned city for five days now. Does she not want our help?'

'The Tzarina makes her own decisions as to who she sees and when,' explained Kaspar. 'Her advisor, Pjotr Losov is... shall we say, not the most cooperative of men when it comes to facilitating audiences.'

'Sigmar damn her, but this tries my patience,' grumbled Spitzaner.

'I do not believe we have any choice but to wait,' said Michlenstadt amiably.

'Yes,' said Bautner. 'None of us can force a monarch to move to the beat of any drum but their own. We must await her pleasure, for we have strict instructions to deliver our missives to her hand and her hand alone.'

Kaspar forced himself to ignore the impatient pacing of Spitzaner – the man had been nothing but an arrogant ass and pain in the backside the last few days – and moved further down the length of the hall, halting before the portrait of the other infamous Khan Queen, Anastasia. The woman in the picture was depicted riding her war-chariot, arms aloft as the heavens raged above her. Tall and beautiful, this Anastasia had a fierceness to her features that the Anastasia he knew did not, a ferocity that echoed the harshness of the land that had borne her. She was a living, breathing representation of all that made the Kislevites such a hardy race of passionate warriors.

Thinking of Anastasia brought a familiar melancholy to him as he thought of how they had become estranged. Part of him wanted to reach out to her and make amends for the harsh words that had passed between them, but he knew that too much time had passed for him to know how to make such an approach. Sadness touched him at his limitations, but he knew himself well enough to know that it was too late for him to change and that the easiest way to bear that sadness was to lock it away in the deepest corner of his being.

The chiming of the clock above the beaten golden double doors shook Kaspar from his thoughts and he turned back to the main hall as Spitzaner and his gaudily dressed officers arranged themselves before the doors, a strict hierarchy observed in their positioning.

Bautner and Michlenstadt stood slightly behind and to the left of Spitzaner, who, naturally, took centre stage for the promised audience. As the ninth chime struck, the doors to the inner apartments swung open and the Tzarina Katarin, Ice Queen of Kislev entered the Hall of Heroes.

Once again Kaspar was struck by the sheer primal force of her beauty. The Ice Queen's sculpted features were regal and piercing, as though carved from the coldest glacier with eyes like chips of blue diamond. She inspired awe and Kaspar remembered the fear and wonder that had passed through her subjects when he had last seen her move amongst them. A long, glittering gown of ivory trailed behind her, layered with ice-flecked silk and strings of pearls. Her hair was a fierce white, the colour of a winter's morning, threaded with rippling ice-blue streaks and braided with strings of emeralds beneath her glittering crown of ice. Kaspar saw she was armed with the mighty war-blade of the khan queens, Fearfrost, and could feel the bow-wave of chill that preceded her.

Unusually, she came without her normal array of flunkies, hangers-on and family members. Instead, four bare-chested warriors with shaven heads and long topknots and drooping moustaches followed her, bearing a heavy golden throne between them. Each carried a pair of curved sabres across his back and had a long, thin bladed knife sheathed in a fold of flesh on their flat stomachs.

Warriors from Sasha Kajetan's former regiment, thought Kaspar, recognising their skin-crawling habit of scabbarding blades within their flesh. A show of bravado, a rite of passage or a tradition? Kaspar didn't know which and had no desire to ask.

The temperature continued to drop as the Ice Queen approached, and a ghostly mist rose around their ankles. Kaspar heard a soft tinkling, as of ice forming, and the scent of cold, hard, northern forests swelled to fill the air. He heard muffled gasps of unease from the men of the Empire as they bowed to her, a chill wind carrying the bitter cold of the oblast snaking around them. Every one of them would have heard the Tzarina's reputation as a powerful sorceress, but none of them had expected to feel such power so closely.

Kaspar smiled to himself as he bowed. For all her intelligence, the Ice Queen was not subtle in the demonstrations of her power, and Kaspar was struck by how much he actually liked her. Her guards placed the throne behind the Tzarina and she arranged herself artfully upon it, the warriors taking up position either side of her, their arms folded and their posture aggressive.

'Ambassador von Velten,' said the Ice Queen, her voice unexpectedly warm. 'It is good to see you again. We have missed you at the palace.'

Kaspar bowed again graciously. 'It is an honour to be here again, your majesty.'

'And how is that temper of yours?' she asked playfully.

'As bad as ever,' smiled Kaspar.

'Good,' nodded the Ice Queen, inclining her head. 'And who is this you have brought to see me? Other men of ill-temper?'

'I fear not,' said Kaspar, turning to introduce his companions. 'This is General Clemenz Spitzaner of Nuln, your majesty. He commands the army camped beyond your walls.'

'An honour, your majesty,' said Spitzaner, bowing elaborately and sweeping his feathered hat in an overblown gesture of greeting.

'Quite,' said the Ice Queen, her eyes sliding from the colourful martinet.

Kaspar continued his introductions, saying, 'And these are the envoys from your brother monarch to the south, the most noble Emperor Karl-Franz. Emissaries, Michlenstadt and Bautner.'

Kaspar saw a flash of anger cross Spitzaner's face at being so easily dismissed from the Ice Queen's notice, but wisely the general said nothing.

Emissary Michlenstadt stepped forward as the Ice Queen said, 'I am told you come with news of great import for me?'

'Indeed we do, your majesty,' said Michlenstadt, striding forward and reaching within his coat's inside pocket. He had taken only a few steps when the warriors behind the Tzarina had their blades drawn and were holding them at the emissary's throat.

'What?' gasped Michlenstadt, his face ashen as he pulled a wax-sealed letter from his coat. The nearest warrior grunted and snatched the letter from his hand, turning and passing it to the Tzarina.

'Sigmar protect us,' whispered Bautner as the shaking Michlenstadt backed away from the fierce warriors.

'Forgive their ardour,' said the Ice Queen. 'Protecting my life is a duty these men take very seriously, and they take a dim view of folk they do not know approaching me.'

'Quite alright,' gasped Michlenstadt, though Kaspar could see the man was visibly shaken. 'Their devotion does you credit.'

The warriors returned their blades to their sheaths and stepped back behind the throne, though Kaspar was in no doubt that the Ice Queen was fully capable of protecting herself should the need arise. She broke the seal on the letter and unfolded the parchment, quickly scanning the words written there.

'Emissary Michlenstadt,' said the Ice Queen without looking up.

'Your majesty?'

'Explain this to me, if you would.'

'I am not sure I understand, your majesty,' said Michlenstadt, sharing a confused glance with Bautner. 'I helped draft the Emperor's letter myself and strove for clarity in every word.'

'Indulge me,' said the Tzarina, and Kaspar could sense the cold undercurrent to her words. 'Pretend I am some simple girl-queen you wish to impress with your fine words. Tell me what this letter asks of me.'

'It is an invitation to journey to Altdorf and join with those who would stand against the forces of darkness that threaten to destroy us all,' said Michlenstadt. 'The Emperor has decreed that on the Spring Equinox there shall be a great Conclave of Light, a gathering of the great and mighty where the fate of the world shall be decided.'

'You think its fate is yours to decide?' laughed the Tzarina. 'Then you are a fool. So like men to believe that the world is theirs to save or destroy as they choose.'

Both emissaries stared at each other in confusion, unable to have anticipated this reaction.

'This world will turn regardless of what you and your Conclave of Light decides. What matters now is not talk, but action. Armies pillage my land, kill my people and sack my cities. My warriors fight and die, and your Emperor would have me leave my land in its hour of greatest need?'

'He seeks only to defeat the greater menace that threatens us all,' protested Michlenstadt.

'Yes,' agreed Bautner. 'As free peoples we must all stand together or we shall surely perish separately.'

'A convenient sentiment now that there are armies despoiling your own land,' said the Tzarina, turning towards Kaspar, and he felt the chill of her gaze upon him, his skin prickling to goosebumps beneath his clothes.

'Ambassador von Velten,' began the Ice Queen, 'you say nothing here?'

Kaspar knew he would need to choose his next words with great care, seeing the emissaries' desperate eyes upon him.

'I leave such games of state for those best suited to them, your majesty.'

The Tzarina scowled, 'You are the Emperor's ambassador to Kislev are you not?'

'I am,' agreed Kaspar.

'And as his ambassador, you speak here with his voice do you not?'

'I do, yes,' said Kaspar, seeing the trap she had laid for him, but unable now to remove his head from the snare.

'So tell me, ambassador, what would your Emperor do were the situations reversed, if the Empire were ravaged by war and he was called to abandon his land while enemies killed his people and burned their homes?'

Kaspar hesitated before speaking, though he knew the answer to the Tzarina's question clearly enough.

'He would refuse to go, your majesty,' said Kaspar, hearing outraged intakes of breath from Spitzaner and the Emperor's emissaries. 'Karl-Franz is a man of honour, a warrior king, and he would never abandon his people while his heart still beat.'

The Tzarina nodded, smiling as though she had known exactly what answer Kaspar would give. She rose from her throne and addressed the two Imperial emissaries directly.

'You may take word to your Emperor that I thank him for his invitation, but that, regretfully, I must decline. I have a land to save and I cannot leave it while the tribes of the north make war upon us. I shall send my most trusted envoys with you on your return to Altdorf and they shall speak with my voice at this conclave.'

The Tzarina bowed gracefully to the men of the Empire before turning away and gracefully departing the hall through the golden doors from whence she had come, her warriors following closely behind her. As the doors shut, a detachment of bronze armoured knights threw open the entrance that led to the vestibule of the Winter Palace, standing guard to either side.

Thus dismissed, Kaspar and his fellow countrymen marched dejectedly from the Hall of Heroes under the unchanging gaze of the Tzars and Khan Queens of Kislev.

IV

KASPAR SHOOK HIS head as the squire came forward to take Magnus's reins, dismounting and leading the horse around the side of the embassy to stable the horse himself. He could see the guards who had accompanied him to the palace groan at the thought of not getting inside the warmth of the embassy and said, 'You men go on. I won't be long.'

The guards gratefully retreated into the embassy, leaving Kaspar to open the frost-limned stable door and lead his horse inside. He was cold and tired, but his nerves were wound too tightly for him to think of sleep just yet. He bent down, wincing as his knee cracked, and undid the girth around Magnus's belly, removing the heavy leather saddle and slinging it across a nearby rail.

He fed the horse a few handfuls of grain then took out a stiffened wire brush and began giving the horse's coat a thorough rub down, combing his mane and working out the stresses of the day with every stroke.

Though he knew he could not have given the Tzarina any other answer, he wondered if the Emperor would see it that way when Michlenstadt and Bautner returned to the capital and informed him of her refusal to attend his conclave. Spitzaner and the emissaries had been furious with him upon leaving the Winter Palace.

'Sigmar damn you, von Velten!' Spitzaner had shouted, his normally pale features ruddy with outrage. 'Do you know what you have done?'

'I said nothing the Tzarina did not already know,' pointed out Kaspar.

'That's not the point,' said Michlenstadt, trying to keep his voice even.

'No,' agreed Bautner, shaking his head. 'An ambassador is not simply the Emperor's voice at another court, but a means of enacting his will. You should not have said what you did, ambassador, it was highly inappropriate.'

'You mean I should have lied?'

Bautner sighed, as though being forced to explain something straightforward to a simpleton. 'These are dark times we live in, ambassador, and sometimes the values we cherish in peacetime must, shall we say, bend in times of strife. If the idea of lying is offensive to you, perhaps you could simply have omitted to mention certain truths that might have influenced the Tzarina's decision.'

'Omission of the truth? Since when is that not lying?' asked Kaspar.

'In the affairs of courtly politics it can be an important distinction sometimes,' said Michlenstadt.

'She would not have gone to Altdorf regardless of what I said.'

'We do not know that for sure, von Velten,' snapped Spitzaner. 'Make no mistake, the Emperor will hear of what happened here tonight.'

'Of that I have no doubt,' said Kaspar, already weary of Spitzaner's voice.

The general and the emissaries had ridden back to their billets in the city without another word, escorted by their halberd-wielding soldiers, leaving Kaspar and his guards to ride through Geroyev Square towards the embassy.

The night had been cold, but without the sharpness that had characterised it throughout the winter and it was plain to see that, while winter had not yet released its grip on Kislev, it was definitely in retreat.

Kaspar had worked up a sweat while grooming Magnus and felt its chill on his skin as he finished the task of stabling his mount for the night. He threw a thick, brightly patterned blanket over the horse's back to keep him warm overnight and left the stables, careful to drop the latch as he left.

He trudged across the slushy ground towards the servants' door at the rear of the embassy, deciding that he could use some food and a drink of kvas. Kaspar pushed open the door, surprising the few servants gathered there playing cards with his arrival. They hurried to make themselves look busy, but Kaspar bade them return to their game, removing his boots and cloak and handing them to his manservant.

Wanting a light supper to take to bed, he cursed softly as he remembered that there was no kvas in the embassy; Sofia having made sure that every drop of the spirit had been poured into the gutters to keep Pavel from temptation.

Kaspar shrugged. Probably for the best anyway; the last thing he needed at the moment was alcohol. He might have put the final nail in his ambassadorial career tonight, but he was damned if he was going to face any repercussions of what had happened with a hangover. He cut some slices of bread, cheese and ham and prepared a sweet tisane before picking up a candle and climbing the back stairs to the upper floor of the embassy and his bedroom.

The servants' corridors were dimly lit by tallow candles that flickered in the draft from below, but they were quiet and, for that, Kaspar was grateful. He had no wish for conversation tonight and just hoped he would be able to snatch a few hours of sleep before first light.

He pushed open the servants' door to his bedroom and set his supper down on the table beside his bed. He could see a bulge in its centre where a bronze bedwarmer filled with heated coals had been placed and angled the candle he'd taken from the kitchen to light the lamps at the side of his bed.

Something registered at the corner of his vision and he paused, cocking his head to one side as he heard a rustle of papers and a soft thump from his study next door. He lifted the candle away from the lamp, leaving it unlit and gripped the butt of his pistol with his free hand. There should be no one in his study at this time of night and his mind filled with dark possibilities as to who might be within.

Treading carefully so as not to alert the intruder, Kaspar approached the door to the study, his anger building with each soft step. He knew he should go back downstairs and alert his guards to this trespasser, but his already dark mood was filling him with the desire to hurt the bastard himself. He eased the flint back on his pistol, seeing a flicker of light and shadow beneath the bottom of the door.

He held his pistol before him, took a deep breath and kicked open the study door.

'Don't move!' he shouted, quickly entering the room. 'I am armed.'

He saw a bulky figure standing behind his desk and was about to repeat his warning when he recognised the man rifling through the contents of his desk.

Pavel. It was bloody Pavel.

V

SASHA KAJETAN GROANED as he shifted his weight, the chains around his wrist digging into the raw flesh of his wrists. His world had shrunk to the point where all he knew now was pain and hunger and he welcomed it. The trueself had eroded all but the last remnants of his sanity and all that remained in his mind were thoughts of violence and death.

He knew his longing for atonement would never come now and silently prayed for death from whatever deities might not yet have abandoned him. But death would not take him. It seemed even the kingdom of Morr was to be denied him. He could not blame the guardian of the kingdom of the dead; after all, who would want such a wretched soul as his?

He had accepted now that this was his lot – an eternity of suffering and starvation in this gaol with nothing but the steady drip of water and mange-ridden rats for company.

One such specimen sat on its haunches at the doorway, where it had pushed itself through a gap between the rusted iron door and the crumbling brickwork. It scrabbled at the hole it had come through with its claws, digging away the sodden brickwork for some unguessable purpose.

He watched the rat for a while, losing track of time as he became transfixed by its diligent labours. Eventually, it completed its task and turned to face him, squealing at him as if trying to impart some message. He gave the appearance of ignoring it and the animal drew closer, squealing with greater urgency.

His foot lashed out. The rat darted aside, but not fast enough as the heel of the swordsman's foot caught it in the centre of its spine and broke its back. He grinned crookedly as the rat twitched and died. He might now be a broken, shell of a human being, but he was still quick. He dragged the dead rat towards him with his feet, leaning down to sink his teeth into its furry belly.

Sasha felt thin bones snap under his rotten teeth and tasted the rodent's warm blood fill his mouth like a tonic. He swallowed a gristly lump of meat, biting off another chunk as he suddenly became aware of being watched, turning his head to see a bloated white rat squeeze its bulk through the widened hole in the brickwork. Its fangs were long and curved, like the daggers of the steppe nomads, and its small, slitted eyes glittered an unhealthy red.

He watched the rat for several seconds, blood dripping from his chin, as it looked him up and down as though appraising him. Its lips curled back from its fangs and it gave a long, squealing bray, unlike any sound Sasha would have expected a rat to make.

Was this some kind of sign? He had felt the rats above him before, plotting and planning, but until now they had been content to merely watch him. Did they now have greater designs in mind for him?

Dimly, he heard the clang of an iron door and, seconds later, saw a soft glow from beneath his cell door. Fear fluttered in his breast as he heard the rattle of keys and the cell door was flung open. The white rat scurried from the cell, but it was forgotten in an instant as Sasha saw the glowing shape that filled the doorway.

She stood before him in all her remembered glory, beautiful, auburn haired and full of love for him. She wore a long green gown, the shimmering fabric and pale nimbus of light haloing her head hurting his eyes.

'Matka...' he whispered, weeping tears of shame, love and happiness as his matka opened her arms to him. Sasha sobbed like a child, the trueself surging to the forefront of his consciousness at the sight of her. He reached for her, but was prevented from touching her by the shackles that bound him to the wall.

As if in answer to that thought, the gaoler stumbled into the cell, blubbering uncontrollably as he was hurled to the floor by a stooped figure swathed in black robes and carrying a short, curved sword.

'Free him,' said his matka.

The gaoler nodded hurriedly, fumbling for the key in terror. At last he found the correct key and unlocked the fetters that bound Sasha. The swordsman slumped to the ground, his wrists raw and bleeding and skin covered with festering sores.

His matka knelt beside him, cupping his head in her wonderfully soft hands. He couldn't see her face properly, her features blurred and indistinct as the light swum around her head.

'It's me, my handsome prince,' she said.

'Matka…' he hissed, his throat parched and constricted.

'Yes. I've come for you.'

'So sorry,' he managed, pushing himself upright.

His matka wiped a finger across his jaw, flicking the rat's blood at the brickwork walls of the cell. She shook her head. 'Wouldn't you rather have something else? Something better than the blood of vermin?'

The robed figure with the sword darted forward, grabbing the gaoler by the neck and, tearing his glass-lensed hood off, slashed his sword across the man's throat. Blood fountained from the wound, arterial spray gushing like a hose over Sasha's face.

Hot blood, straight from a beating heart filled the swordsman's mouth and he drank it greedily, feeling his matka's hands upon him as he swallowed and swallowed. He felt her hands warm him, a pleasant heat and arousal radiating outwards from where she touched him.

Fresh vigour seeped into his body and he felt forgotten strength flow through his atrophied muscles as he drank and his matka somehow restored his life. He snarled, feeling the trueself's lust for death grow. He reached out and took hold of the twitching gaoler, biting and tearing in a frenzy at the flesh of the man's neck.

'Yes,' said his matka. 'Feed, grow strong. Tchar has need of you.'

Sasha hurled aside the mutilated corpse and pushed himself to his feet, hot, angry energy coursing around his body.

'Not too fast, my love,' cautioned his matka, as he steadied himself against the wall of his cell. 'It will take time for your strength to return in full.'

He nodded, watching as the gaoler's killer wiped his sword on his victim's undershirt. The hands clasping the sword's hilt were furred and clawed and, as though sensing his scrutiny, it turned towards him, hissing in challenge.

Sasha stared into the beady black eyes beneath the hood and wondered if this – thing – was also a minion of the bloated albino-furred rat.

He turned his back on the verminous killer, following his matka from the cell and along the corridor towards an open iron door that led to some stairs. A body lay at the foot of the stairs, a triangular piece of metal embedded in its neck.

'Come, Sasha,' said his matka. 'I have such things for you to do...'

The trueself nodded, hearing the little boy that had once been Sasha Kajetan screaming from the depths of his tortured soul.

CHAPTER SEVEN

I

KASPAR LOWERED THE pistol as the two men faced one another over the top of his desk. A lamp sat on its corner, casting a fitful illumination around them, but leaving the rest of the room in shadow. Pavel said nothing, clutching a sheaf of papers in one hand and a wooden handled seal-stamp in the other.

'What the hell do you think you're doing, Pavel?' asked Kaspar, lowering the flint and jamming his pistol through his belt.

'Please,' begged Pavel. 'Let me do this and go. You never see me again.'

'I asked you a question, damn it.'

Pavel circled the desk and said, 'I can explain this.'

'You bloody well better,' snapped Kaspar. He closed with Pavel and snatched the papers and stamp from his old comrade's hands. Pavel bit his bottom lip as Kaspar moved towards the lamp, examining what had been taken from his desk. The seal was his personal crest, ringed by the spread wings of the Imperial eagle, while the documents were letters of transit, letters that would allow the bearer to traverse the length and breadth of the Empire without let or hindrance.

He recognised the documents for what they were and his heart sank as he realised who Pavel must have been stealing them for.

He sat down heavily in his chair, dropping the items and rubbing the heels of his palms across his scalp.

'Damn it all to hell,' he whispered to himself.

'Kaspar, please–' began Pavel.

'Shut up!' roared Kaspar. 'I do not want to hear it, Pavel. Everything that comes out of your mouth now is nothing but dung! It has been so long since I heard you speak the truth I have forgotten what it sounds like.'

'I know,' said Pavel. 'I stupid fool. But I sorry.'

'Don't tell me you are sorry, you miserable piece of shit, don't you dare tell me you're sorry! You were stealing these for Chekatilo, weren't you? Answer me! Weren't you?'

Pavel slumped into one of the chairs beside the fireplace, his face wreathed in dark shadows as he moved away from the lantern.

'Yha, I was stealing them for Chekatilo.'

Kaspar felt his anger at Pavel reach new heights, heights he did not believe it was possible to reach. Was there no limit to Pavel's betrayal?

'Why, Pavel, why? Help me understand why you did this, because I cannot fathom it. What would make you turn your back on your friend to do this for such a loathsome piece of scum like Chekatilo?'

'It because I am your friend that I do this,' said Pavel.

'What? You steal from me because you're my friend?' snapped Kaspar. 'Well I suppose I should count myself lucky I am not one of your enemies, for I would hate to see what you do to them.'

'I mean it,' barked Pavel.

'Talk sense, man.'

'Chekatilo sends Rejak for me, tells me I am to steal these things from you.'

'And you said yes?' asked Kaspar. 'Why?'

Pavel shook his head. 'I cannot say.'

'You bloody well will say,' promised Kaspar. 'I want to know what that bastard said to make you betray me.'

Pavel surged from the chair and planted his hands on Kaspar's desk and shouted, 'I cannot tell you!'

Kaspar rose from his chair and faced Pavel, his anger hot and raw. 'Either tell me or get out of here now. I warned you what would happen the next time you did anything stupid, did I not?'

'Aye, but, please, Kaspar. I cannot tell you, it was before you came here. Chekatilo knows things of me, bad things, secret things. Trust me, I cannot tell you.'

'Trust you?' laughed Kaspar coming from behind the desk and jabbing his finger against Pavel's chest. 'Trust you? Am I hearing you right? You are asking me to trust you?'

'Yha,' nodded Pavel.

'Oh well, then I suppose I should, eh? Now that you have led one ambassador astray, put me in debt to Chekatilo and then tried to steal from me, I suppose I should. What could I possibly have to lose?'

Pavel's face darkened and he said, 'You always so perfect, Empire man? You never make mistakes?'

'Mistakes?' snapped Kaspar. 'Mistakes, yes, but betray my friends? Never. What kind of mistake would make you betray me, Pavel? Tell me. We fought together for years, saved each other's lives more times than I can count. Tell me the truth, damn you!'

Pavel shook his head. 'You not want the truth.'

'Yes,' shouted Kaspar, getting right in Pavel's face. 'I do, so damn well tell me!'

Pavel pushed the ambassador away and turned his back on him. A great sob burst from the burly Kislevite and he said, 'I murdered Andrej Vilkova, Anastasia's husband. Rejak and me killed him. We caught him outside Chekatilo's brothel and beat him to death. There! You happy now?'

Kaspar felt his senses go numb and a sick feeling spread from the pit of his stomach to his furthest extremities. He put a hand out to lean on the desk, his mind a whirlwind of confused thoughts.

'Oh, no, Pavel, no...' hissed Kaspar, the breath tight in his chest. 'You didn't, please tell me you didn't.'

Pavel returned to his seat and hung his head in his hands. 'I so sorry, Kaspar. Chekatilo has held this over my head since that night. He said he would tell you if I not do this for him and I not want you to find out about what I did, what a pathetic, snivelling piece of scum Pavel Korovic is.'

Kaspar could not answer Pavel, still reeling from the shock of discovering that one of his oldest friends was revealed as a murderer, no better than Sasha Kajetan. He felt tears of betrayal course down his face, horrified that a man he had trusted his life to on so many occasions was nothing but a common killer.

Pavel stood and put his hand on Kaspar's shoulder.

'Don't touch me,' roared Kaspar, throwing off Pavel's hand and backing away from him. He could barely stand to look at him.

Anastasia...

By Sigmar, all these years thinking that some street thug had murdered her husband, and all the time the killer was sitting in the Empire embassy, friend to her new lover. As he attempted to comprehend the scale of Pavel's crime, a soft knock came at the main door of the study and one of the embassy guards entered.

'Sorry to disturb you, sir. Heard shouting and wondered if everything was alright?'

Kaspar did not trust his voice yet, so simply nodded and raised his hand. The guard, sensing the mood within the room, said, 'Very good, sir,' and withdrew.

Silence descended on the study, uncomfortably stretching until Kaspar felt like his heart would burst. He wiped his face with his sleeve and managed to say, 'Why?'

'Why what?' asked Pavel.

'Why was he killed, damn it?'

Pavel shrugged, defeated, and said, 'I not know. All I know is Losov came to Chekatilo and paid him to have Andrej Vilkova killed.'

Kaspar rubbed a hand across his jaw, his brow furrowing as he realised he recognised the name Pavel had mentioned.

'Losov? Pjotr Losov? The Tzarina's advisor? Are you telling me that he paid Chekatilo to have Anastasia's husband murdered?'

'Yha, I heard him. I think that why Chekatilo have me do it.'

'That son of a bitch,' swore Kaspar, now realising the source of the enmity between Pavel and Losov. 'Why the hell would he do that?'

'I not know,' said Pavel.

'I wasn't talking to you,' said Kaspar, his jaw clenched and his fingers beating a nervous tattoo on his desktop. 'Damn you, but I should hand you over to the *Chekist*.'

'Yha, probably you should,' agreed Pavel.

'No,' said Kaspar, shaking his head. 'I won't. You have saved my life too many times for me to send you to those bastards, but...'

'But what?'

'But you and I are finished,' said Kaspar. 'Get the hell out of my embassy. Now.'

Pavel rose from the seat and said, 'For what it worth–'

'Stop,' said Kaspar, his voice little more than a whisper. 'Just go. Please, just go.'

Pavel nodded sadly and walked to the door. He turned as though about to say something, but thought the better of it and left without another word.

As the door shut, Kaspar put his head in his hands and wept openly for the first time since he had buried his wife.

II

Morning brought a cold rain from the east. Kaspar sat behind his desk as weak sunlight spilled in through the window behind him. He had not slept since Pavel had left, his emotions too raw, too near the surface for him to close his eyes. Each time he tried, he would picture Anastasia's face and the pain would surface again. Part of him wanted to tell her of her husband's murder, to lay to rest the ghost of his death, but to renew a friendship on such news was not a possibility.

He missed her, but felt powerless to do anything about it. She had made her feelings plain and there was nothing he could do to alter them. He was too set in his ways and she in hers for either of them to change and though he craved her company, he knew that they would soon go through the same dance again should they renew their relationship. He would always care for her, but could not allow himself to do more than that.

And Pavel...

He cursed Kislev, cursed its people, its language, its customs, its... everything. He felt an intense wave of bitterness rise in him, wishing he had never set foot in this godforsaken country again. It had brought him nothing but pain and misadventure.

He rubbed his tired eyes, knowing he was reacting with his heart and not his head, but unable to curb the bile he felt. He knew his eyes must be swollen and bloodshot from tears and lack of sleep, so he stood and ran a hand across his scalp, making his way towards his bedroom.

As he rose from behind his desk, he glanced through the window, seeing a lone horseman ride hard for the embassy, jerking his horse to a sliding halt at the gates. The man wore black armour and an all-enclosing helm of dark iron, but Kaspar immediately recognised him as Vladimir Pashenko, head of the *Chekist*. He swore silently to himself. Today of all days, he could do without this. But he had a duty to his position here and reluctantly straightened his clothing, still the formal regalia he had worn to the Winter Palace the previous evening.

He watched Pashenko push through the gate and march purposefully towards the embassy door. His haste and obvious anger told Kaspar that something serious had happened and he wondered what calamity would drive the normally emotionless Pashenko to such heights of agitation.

The door below slammed shut and he heard heavy footfalls ascend the main stairs, hurried steps following them along with blustering protests. Kaspar seated himself behind his desk again and waited for Pashenko to enter, which he did seconds later, hurling the door open and striding straight towards Kaspar. His helmet was held under the crook of his arm, but he threw it on a chair as he approached.

'Ursun damn you, von Velten!' shouted Pashenko, his face purple with rage.

Of all the things Kaspar might have expected Pashenko to say, this was not one of them. He raised his hands and said, 'What is going on? Why are you here?'

'I'll tell you why,' snapped Pashenko, his accent slipping towards his native Kislevite. 'Because thirteen of my men are dead, that's why!'

'What? How?'

'That *Svolich*.'

Kaspar felt a chill seize him and raised a hand to his temple, feeling the onset of a pounding headache. He shook his head free of his tiredness and faced the angry Pashenko once more.

'Kajetan?' he said. 'I don't understand. How could he kill thirteen of your men?'

'No,' said Pashenko, shaking his head and pacing the room like a caged animal. 'Not Sasha, someone else. Someone else.'

'Pashenko, slow down, you're not making any sense. Tell me what has happened.'

The head of the *Chekist* took a deep breath, forcing himself to be calm. Kaspar could see that Pashenko had not slept for some time either by the look of him. His normally clean-shaven cheeks were stubbled and hollow, his long hair wild and unkempt.

'This does not happen to the *Chekist*,' he said. 'We are feared and that is how we are able to do our job. People fear us and they do not violate our laws because of that. That is the way it is supposed to be anyway. But now…'

Kaspar could not bring himself to feel sorry for Pashenko, knowing the brutal methods his *Chekist* employed and having seen the horror of the gaol beneath their grim building on the Urskoy Prospekt. But the pain of losing men under your command was something he was all too familiar with, so in that at least they had a common bond.

'I am still not sure what happened,' continued Pashenko, 'but it looks as though two people walked into our building and slaughtered their way towards the cells.'

'Two people killed thirteen of your men? Who were they?'

'I do not know, but it was only one.'

'One what?'

'Only one person killed my men, a man who wore black robes and a hood. And who was quicker than a snake by all accounts.'

'I think I know of this man,' said Kaspar. 'He attacked us in the Lubjanko.'

'The Lubjanko? What took you to that wretched place?'

'It is a long story,' said Kaspar, not wanting to go into the details of his earlier co-operation with Vassily Chekatilo in front of the *Chekist*. 'But I have seen his speed, it is incredible, inhuman almost. Who was the other person?'

'A woman, but no one I've spoken to can give me a good description of her.'

'Why not?'

Pashenko shrugged and Kaspar could see the deaths of his men and the apparent ease with which they had been killed had hit Pashenko hard.

'It is strange,' said Pashenko. 'I have spoken to the survivors of the attack and every one of them gives me a different description of her. And not just little things that I could put down to simple errors, but major differences. Some saw a young woman, others an older woman. To some she was blonde, to others dark haired and yet others saw her as auburn haired. Some saw a thin woman, while others say she was heavyset. But all of them agree that she was beautiful, that they could no more raise a blade against her than stop their own hearts from beating.'

'How do you think she was able to confuse so many people?'

'I do not know, but all of them said she had a... a radiance to her, as though her skin had a light burning beneath it. It reeks of sorcery to me.'

Kaspar felt his skin crawl, remembering Sofia describing something similar while she had been held within Sasha Kajetan's death attic, a magical light that had spoken with a woman's voice. She had not been able to see the face of the speaker, but taken together with the hooded assassin, it was surely too great a coincidence that these events could not be linked. How far back did everything go? The Butcherman, Sasha, the black robed killer, the rats? Was it all connected?

Something in Pashenko's words tugged at a faint memory, but it was not until Sofia appeared in the doorway of his study, her hair worn down around her neck, that it hit him.

'Is it true?' asked Sofia, her arms wrapped about herself. 'Has Sasha escaped from your gaol?'

Pashenko nodded. 'Yha, last night.'

'Did he kill anyone?'

'Probably. The gaoler had his throat torn out, most likely by someone's teeth, and it looks like some of his flesh was eaten. It is the same as the Butcherman killings. It could only have been Kajetan.'

Kaspar leaned forwards. 'You said that some of the people who saw this woman saw her as auburn haired?'

'Yes, but lots of other colours too.'

Kaspar moved from behind his desk towards Sofia, reaching up to lift a handful of her long, auburn hair.

'I think this is partly what stayed Kajetan's hand when he held Sofia prisoner,' he said. 'His madness saw her as his matka, his mother reborn. And when I saw the skeleton he had dug up on the grounds of his family's land, the skull had scraps of auburn hair still attached to it. Whatever magicks this woman was able to conjure, it was for one purpose and one purpose alone – to make Sasha Kajetan believe his mother had come back to him.'

'Everything he did, he did for her,' said Sofia. 'Every murder was for her.'

'And now he is free, ambassador,' hissed Pashenko, 'and it will be your fault when he kills again.'

'Mine?'

'Yha, Kajetan *should* have been hanged weeks ago, but no, the ambassador wants to keep him alive to learn what made him a monster. And like a fool I agree, I think that this new Empire man is clever and may be right. Now look where your curiosity had led us.'

Kaspar wanted to argue, but knew that Pashenko was right: Kajetan should have been executed long ago.

'Well, what is being done to find him?' asked Kaspar. 'And what can I do to help?'

'Nothing. On both counts.'

'Nothing? You are not making any effort to catch him?'

'I have no men to spare, and the city is so crowded I could search for years and never find him. And I think that whoever has him now will be keeping him well hidden, don't you? No, I will not waste more of my men's lives in hunting Kajetan down. If he is truly mad then he will surface again when he kills, and sooner or later we will catch him.'

Pashenko turned to retrieve his helmet and turned, bowing stiffly to Kaspar and Sofia.

'But there will be more deaths, of that I am sure. I just wanted you to know that,' he said and marched from the study.

Sofia shivered and Kaspar put his arm around her. 'You shouldn't worry, Sofia. I don't think Kajetan will come for you again. He has his matka now.'

She shook her head.

'I'm not worried about him coming after me,' she said at last. 'I'm worried about him coming after you.'

III

As THE NEW moon rose on the thirteenth night of Nachexen, riders entered the city from the west. Ungol horsemen of wild appearance, they had ridden hard from the western oblast to bring great news, news they shouted from their horses as they galloped through the city streets towards the Winter Palace.

Cheers followed the riders, all of whom looked on the verge of collapse, who were kept in the saddle by sheer joy. The news soon spread through the city, Boyarin Kurkosk's Sanyza pulk and the army of Stirland had fought and destroyed a great mass of northmen led by a chieftain named Okkodai Tarsus at Krasicyno, putting it to flight and killing thousands of the tribesmen.

It was the first tangible victory for the allied armies and when he woke to the news, Kaspar had a real sense of history unfolding before him. This was a time of great moment and heroes were being forged daily on the fields of battle. Another horde of tribesmen, many times the number of the allied armies, was said to be marching back from the Empire to destroy Kurkosk's army and both the army of Talabecland and the Kislev pulk were being called to battle at a place called Mazhorod.

In the days that followed the news, the city had seethed with activity as warriors were mustered and the Kislevite pulks, camped along the Urskoy within a day's march of the city, were finally drawn together to head westwards.

Kaspar watched the preparations for march from the snow-capped ramparts of the city wall with thousands of the city's populace who had turned out in the icy chill to cheer their brave warriors. It did Kaspar's heart a world of good to see such an ebullient display of optimism shining from every face around him.

He watched the preparations below with a mixture of pride and regret. The greater part of him wanted to ride alongside these brave men of Talabecland, but without a field rank – something he knew Spitzaner would never grant him – he would simply be an observer. The thought of being powerless to intervene in whatever battles these men would soon have to fight was an intolerable prospect.

Spitzaner had made it perfectly clear that he did not want Kaspar to accompany his army and Kaspar could not blame him. It would undermine Spitzaner's authority were Kaspar, his former commanding officer who many knew had passed him over for promotion, to be there, and Kaspar had reluctantly accepted that he must remain in Kislev. The Emperor's emissaries, Michlenstadt and Bautner, travelled with the general, accompanied by the envoys of the Tzarina who would journey to Altdorf in her stead.

For all his faults, Clemenz Spitzaner knew how to get an army ready to move with commendable speed. The general had been angry to have missed the great battle at Krasicyno and was determined not to miss this chance for glory. His soldiers were drawn up in their regiments along the roadway, thousands of men formed in column of march, with their weapons high and their colours flapping in the cold wind.

The general himself rode up and down the line of men, inspecting his soldiers with the eye of a man who knows people are watching.

Soldiers shivered and stamped their feet in the snow to ward off the cold as they awaited the order to march, fife and drum keeping the men entertained with martial tunes as black-robed Kislevite priests pronounced blessings upon them. But Kaspar's attention was not for the army of his countrymen, but the magnificent spectacle of the Kislev pulk.

The Kislev pulk was a wondrous thing to behold. Kaspar had thought the army of Talabecland had been a colourful sight when it had arrived, but it was as nothing compared to the glory of a Kislevite army bedecked in all its finery.

Glorious red horsemen with eagle-feathered back banners and shining, fur-edged helmets gathered at the foot of the *Gora Geroyev*, their scarlet and gold banners streaming behind them as they galloped westwards. He felt a stab of sadness as he remembered going into battle alongside such warriors and the memory of Pavel leading them in a magnificent charge. He missed his comrade, and had not seen him since throwing him from the embassy, but he could not undo what had been done.

The lighter cavalry was followed by their more heavily armoured brethren, colourfully caparisoned knights in bronze armour who carried long lances and an enormous banner embroidered with a bear rampant. Swirling hordes of ragged but magnificent-looking archers on horseback whooped and hollered, the long scalp-locks whipping around them as they rode marking them as Ungols.

Singing blocks of Kossars marched down the frozen roadway from the city gates, their strong voices easily carrying to the people on the walls. Each block wore a riot of colourful shirts and cloaks, baggy troos held at the waist by scarlet sashes and pointed iron helmets fringed with mail. Each man carried a long, heavy-bladed axe and Kaspar saw a great many carried powerful bows slung across their backs. Some carried shields, but it seemed that carrying something that could kill northmen was more important than a shield to most.

Every single group of men carried either a wolf-headed standard, colourful banner or trophy rack bedecked with wolf tails, skulls and captured weapons and the barbaric splendour of the army was a truly breathtaking sight.

But greatest of all was the Tzarina herself.

Positioned at the head of her army, she was ready to take the fight to these northern barbarians who dared invade her land. Riding atop a tall, high-sided sled of shimmering icy brilliance, she watched her warriors prepare for march with an aloof gaze. A team of silver horses whose flanks shimmered with hoarfrost and whose breath was the winter wind were hitched to the front of the sled. The Tzarina's crown of ice glittered at her brow and her azure gown sparkled in the afternoon sun. Fearfrost was sheathed at her side and she wore a cloak woven from swirling crystals of ice and snow.

A team of bare-chested warriors carried her banner, a monstrous, rippling thing of sapphire and crimson, and her soldiers cheered with their love for her as they gathered.

The shouts of the soldiers and spectators died away at some unseen signal, the drummer boys and pipers quieting their instruments as a series of mournful peals were rung from the bells of the Reliquary of Saint Alexei. The pulk dropped to one knee, each man whispering a prayer to the gods that they would be victorious as the bells tolled across the silence of the steppe.

As the last echoes of the bells faded, the Ice Queen drew her mighty war-blade and the armies of the Empire and Kislev marched westwards to war.

Kaspar watched them go and prayed that Sigmar would watch over them.

IV

THE FROZEN EYES of the children stared unblinkingly at him, refusing to avert their dead, accusing gaze from him. Sasha Kajetan sat on a cold, damp floor of earth with his back to an icy cellar wall, hugging his knees tightly to his chest. The dead children with the slashed throats in the corner of the room were his only company and all they did was accuse him.

Had he killed them? He could not remember having slaughtered them, but memory meant nothing when it came to his murderous nature.

His breath misted before him and he wondered when his matka would return. She had led him to this icy cellar and commanded him to wait. And as he had done since he was old enough to walk, he had obeyed her.

But this was a terrible place, even the trueself retreating from the uppermost reaches of his consciousness at the pure, undiluted malice that seeped from the thing held within the locked bronze coffin that sat in the centre of the room.

The scale of its desire to do harm exceeded even that of the trueself and he knew it was an unnatural creation that, but for the darkness within his own soul, would have killed him the instant he had set foot in this room.

Sasha could feel his strength growing with each passing day he spent in the gloom of the cellar, the fragments of his rational mind that remained realising that it returned with unnatural speed, but grateful for whatever his matka was doing to hasten his recovery.

He would need all his strength if he were to fulfil the purpose of his continued existence, and he allowed himself a tight smile as he thought once more of Ambassador von Velten.

CHAPTER EIGHT

I

THE DRUMS OF war beat out the pace of march, vast kettledrums mounted on brazen war-altars and struck by grossly swollen men covered in writhing tattoos and little else. Skulled totems raised on the backs of the war-altars were branded with the marks of the Dark Gods, shaggy, bestial creatures capering behind them braying their praise to their infernal masters.

High Zar Aelfric Cyenwulf rode at the head of forty thousand warriors, an army of northern tribesmen that had never known defeat, and watched the lightening sky to the east as the first signs of the sunrise spilled over the snow-capped peaks of the World's Edge Mountains. The new year was barely weeks old and foaming rivers spilled down the flanks of the dark mountains, cold and hard with melted ice water as the breathlessly young spring took hold.

He and his dark knights, giant warriors mounted on midnight black steeds barded with blooded mail, halted on the crown of an upthrust crag of black rock. Their giant horses had coal-red eyes, wide chests and huge, rippling muscles, each beast at least twenty hands high, the only mounts in the world capable of carrying the High Zar's armoured knights of Chaos.

The High Zar scanned the ground before him, spotting the route his army must take through the foothills of the mountains without difficulty; his forward scouts having travelled this way earlier the previous year to find the best route for his army to travel. Soon their course would lead them westwards towards the southernmost tributary of the Tobol and the valley of Urszebya.

They had bypassed Praag over a week ago without incident, his Kyazak outriders capturing and skinning itinerant rotas of Ungol scouts that approached too incautiously. Cyenwulf knew it was inevitable that word of his army's route would soon reach the south, but the longer he could delay it the better.

He twisted in the saddle of his huge black mare, watching his horde of dark armoured warriors, beasts, monsters and heavy chariots as it emerged from a deep cut in the foothills. What force in the world could stand against such an army? He longed for battle again, the enforced preparations over the winter chafing at his warrior's soul that hungered for the screams of his enemies, the lamentations of their womenfolk and the glory of Chaos that would be his when they swept aside the armies of the southlanders.

A hoarse cheer went up from the army as the concealing darkness of the Old One came into sight through the cut in the ground. Cyenwulf saw that the lightning sheathed darkness surrounding it seemed somehow thinner, less substantial, as though the further it travelled from its mountain lair, the less concealment it could summon. Massive-thewed reptilian limbs, with claws as large as a man's arm, and a wild mane of shaggy black fur were all he could make out through the thinning smoke, but he now knew that the stories of the Old One's strength and power were not misplaced.

The bestial ones of his army abased themselves before the creature, howling in praise of its terrible majesty and waving their crude iron axes as it passed. Cyenwulf had seen that his own warriors were now worshipping this creature as a sign of the dark gods' favour, offering the skinned, still-living bodies of prisoners for it to devour.

The Old One was a blessing, but, as was typical for the blessings of Tchar, it came with a price. With the Old One's presence they could not lose, but as its worship spread throughout his army, he could feel its fighting discipline diminish.

Some groups of fierce norsemen had already descended into blood madness and slaughtered one another that it might glance their way. Other tribes were turning to cannibalism, which, in itself, was not that unusual, but these killers were preying on warriors from other tribes and such slaughter could only lead to devastating blood-feuds.

Such bloody displays of devotion were growing daily and Cyenwulf knew that he had to bring his army to battle soon or risk it becoming a thrashing, mindless mob.

II

CHEKATILO DRAINED THE last of his kvas, hurling the glass into the roaring fire, where the residue of the spirit flared briefly with a bright flame. His temper had deteriorated as the weeks had passed and spring took hold of Kislev, even the great victory of the allies at Mazhorod not quelling his desire to leave the city.

Yesterday, forward riders of the Tzarina's personal guard had brought news that the combined armies of Kislev and the Empire had met the army of a Kurgan war leader named Surtha Lenk at the river crossing of Mazhorod and destroyed it utterly. Boyarin Kurkosk remained in the west to hunt down the last elements of Lenk's army, but the armies of Stirland and Talabecland had buried their dead before marching east towards Kislev with the Tzarina to fight a host of northmen rumoured to be following the course of the World's Edge Mountains. It was said the allied armies were a day from Kislev's walls.

Chekatilo needed to be away from Kislev, a growing sense of being suffocated in this doomed city growing with each day. But without the ambassador's travel documents and Imperial seal, it would be a risky venture at best to travel through Kislev and the Empire towards Marienburg. The odds were against him arriving as anything other than a pauper, and that was *not* going to happen.

Rejak poured him another kvas in a fresh glass and said, 'You'd best not break this one, it's the last of them.'

Chekatilo grunted in acknowledgement. Rejak took a swig from the bottle as he paced the room, the fire casting a flickering glow on the bare timber walls. Chekatilo's valuables were packed into a train of covered wagons ready to be driven to the Empire once he had what he needed from the ambassador.

It still galled him that von Velten had refused to honour his debt. Such things simply did not happen. Not to him.

'You're sure there's still no word from Korovic? It's been weeks,' said Chekatilo.

'None at all,' confirmed Rejak. 'I don't expect any either, I think he's probably fled the city already. And even if he hasn't, he's not going to do it. He won't betray the ambassador.'

'You underestimate Korovic's weakness, Rejak,' said Chekatilo.

'You should have let me kill him long ago.'

'Perhaps,' agreed Chekatilo, 'but I owed Drostya and could not do that, but the time has passed for observing such niceties.'

Rejak grinned. 'I can kill Korovic then?'

Chekatilo nodded. 'Of course, but I think von Velten needs to learn the meaning of pain first. I think then he will begin to regret his decision to throw his debt back at me.'

'What do you have in mind?' asked Rejak eagerly.

'I have been too forgiving with the ambassador,' mused Chekatilo. 'I think that I quite liked him, but it is of no matter. I have killed men I liked before.'

'You want me to kill von Velten?'

'No,' said Chekatilo, shaking his head and sipping his kvas. 'I want him to suffer, Rejak. A foolish sense of honour has kept me from treating him the way I would anyone else, but that ends now. Tomorrow night I will speak to Ambassador von Velten again and tell him to give me what I want.'

'What makes you think he will agree this time?'

'Because before I go, I want you to go to the home of that woman he cares for, Anastasia Vilkova, the one the soldiers call the White Lady of Kislev.'

'And do what?'

Chekatilo shrugged. 'Rape her, torture her, kill her; it is of no matter to me. You saw how desperate von Velten was to get his physician back, so imagine how much more terror he will feel when I tell him that you have Anastasia Vilkova prisoner. He will have no choice but to give me what I want. By the time he discovers she is already dead, it will make no difference.'

Rejak nodded, already anticipating the terrible things he was going to do to Anastasia Vilkova.

III

THE BANQUETING HALL of the Winter Palace was the centre of the formal ensemble of parade halls in the Tzarina's fastness. Like the Gallery of Heroes, the walls were fashioned from smooth ice with central doors that led onto a terrace overlooking the gardens below. From where he sat, Kaspar guessed that the room was set for about four hundred diners with service stations along the wall, one for each table. The table settings included all the glassware required for the meal, flawlessly etched and enamelled with the Tzarina's monogram and Kislevite bear. The excited buzz of conversation filled the hall, officers and soldiers animatedly telling tales of the battles won and battles yet to be fought.

The allied army had arrived at Kislev that morning, amid celebrations so riotous that Kaspar had thought the war already won. Cheering crowds lined the road to the city to welcome home their victorious Tzarina, hanging garlands of spring flowers around the necks of the returning soldiers. The men were weary and hungry, having marched almost non-stop to reach Kislev as quickly as they could. Kaspar just hoped they had enough time to rest, because if the rumours of Aelfric Cyenwulf's horde were to be believed, then the chieftain of the Iron Wolves came with a force much larger than anyone had expected.

With a speed Kaspar found incredible, the Tzarina had announced a victory banquet at the Winter Palace and, as ambassador, he had received his gilt-edged invitation that very afternoon. It seemed inappropriate to feast while so many people went hungry in the streets of the city, but as Pavel had pointed out many months ago, etiquette demanded that the Ice Queen's invitations take precedence over all other previous engagements, even duty to the dead.

As Kaspar and Sofia had made their way to their table, he had stepped from the path of a red uniformed lancer, whose faded tunic strained to contain his prodigious gut, before realising with a start that the man was Pavel.

'Pavel? Why are you here?' Kaspar had asked.

His old friend had shuffled nervously from foot to foot before saying. 'I rejoin old regiment now that war has come. Many die at Mazhorod and they need every man who can fight. Because I fight for them before they make me *towarzysz*.'

Kaspar nodded, saying, 'Good, good.'

'It means "comrade",' explained Sofia, seeing Kaspar's confusion. 'It is a leader of a cavalry troop.'

'I see,' said Kaspar. The thought of his old comrade going into battle without him gave him a dark feeling of premonition and they moved on.

'One day you will need to tell me what happened between the two of you,' said Sofia.

'Perhaps one day,' agreed Kaspar as they finally arrived at their designated table and sat in time for a short prayer of thanks from a priest at the top table.

Set with huge, solid silver candelabras, he and Sofia had been seated with several junior officers of the Stirland army and as the evening progressed, the conversation was lively and interesting. Whoever had decided upon the seating plan for this victory banquet obviously knew of his antipathy towards Spitzaner, who, along with the boyarins of the Kislev pulk and General Arnulf Pavian, commander of the army of Stirland, sat at the top table with the Ice Queen herself. Standing behind the Tzarina was Pjotr Losov, and Kaspar had to fight the urge to do something he knew he would regret.

He had brought Sofia because he hated to attend such occasions alone, knowing that while the commanders of the army might celebrate victory, the men who had won it were usually not enjoying the rewards of their courage. She looked stunning in a velvet gown of deep crimson, her auburn hair worn high on her head, exposing her long neck and shoulders. A smooth blue stone wrapped in a web of silver wire hung around her neck on a thin chain and Kaspar smiled, glad to have her with him.

Sensing his scrutiny, she looked up from a conversation she was having with a dark haired man wearing an ostentatious uniform of puffed blue silk and silver, with a white sash worn diagonally across his medal-strewn chest. His skin was swarthy and his moustache waxed in an elaborate upward curl. Sofia smiled back at him and said, 'Have you met General Albertalli, Kaspar? He leads the Tilean mercenary regiments that fought with General Pavian at Krasicyno and led a charge that broke the Kurgan line at Mazhorod.'

'No, I have not,' said Kaspar graciously, extending his hand for the Tilean to shake. 'A pleasure, sir.'

The man shook Kaspar's hand enthusiastically, saying, 'I am knowing you, sir. I read all about you. You never lost a battle.'

Kaspar tried to hide his pleasure at meeting someone who knew of his career in the army, but blushed as he caught Sofia smiling at his obvious pride.

'That is correct, sir. Thank you for mentioning it. My compliments on the victories at Krasicyno and Mazhorod.'

The Tilean bowed and said, 'Hard days, much blood shed to win them.'

'I do not doubt it,' agreed Kaspar. 'What were they like, the Kurgans I mean?'

Albertalli sucked in a great breath and shook his head. 'Bastards to a man. Big, tough men that fight like daemons, with swords as long as a tall man. Packs of wild hounds, and warriors on the biggest horses I ever see. No one want to say it, but we were damn lucky at Mazhorod. Fought on a river, should have been easy, yes? But the river freeze solid in an instant and Kurgans were all over us. Hard, bloody fighting that day, but we killed many men and it is they who run from us, yes?'

Kaspar and Albertalli fell deep into conversation concerning the Kurgans, their tactics and how the various generals had led their men on the day. Kaspar was surprised to learn that Spitzaner had actually done well, leading his soldiers competently and solidly.

The two men only paused in their discussion when a gong sounded and the victory dinner itself was served. It proved to be a lavish affair, consisting of seven courses of the finest quality accompanied by an equally impressive array of wines from the Morceaux Valley in Bretonnia and the hills around Luccini – a subject Kaspar saw was close to Albertalli's heart as he expounded on how the Tilean wines were clearly the superior.

As the evening progressed, Kaspar was quick to discover that there were unwritten rules to a Kislevite dinner, as his plate of roast veal was whisked away virtually untouched.

Before he could protest, Sofia explained that should a diner set down their knife and fork, it was the signal to the attending servants to remove his plate. It appeared that each course was rigidly timed, and an hour later, as the last plates were being cleared away, Kaspar found himself amazed at the sheer logistics of serving, feeding and clearing a seven course meal for four hundred people in under an hour.

With the dinner over, the speeches began and, despite himself, Kaspar felt himself getting caught up in the spirit of the evening. First the Empire generals spoke and Kaspar recalled similar speeches he himself had given. The boyarins spoke next and the difference was incredible. Where the men of the Empire spoke of duty and honour, the Kislevites filled the hall with hot-blooded passion, shouting and gesticulating wildly as they spoke.

Sofia translated parts, but Kaspar understood enough from the fierce zeal of the boyarins to know that they filled the assembled soldiers' souls with piss and vinegar. Rousing cheers and toasts were made and glasses smashed on the floor amid much yelling and punching of the air.

The soldiers filled the hall with their glorious cheering and Kaspar laughed as Sofia took his hand, utterly convinced that they would win this war.

* * *

IV

THE CRESCENT MOON slid behind a low cloud, wreathing the walls of the palace in momentary darkness. But it was long enough for the dark robed figure to nimbly slip over the spike topped wall and drop lightly into the palace grounds.

Hugging the shadows, the figure stealthily made its way through the Winter Gardens towards the palace.

Moonlight spilled around glittering, diamond-like flowers and trees of this winter forest of frosted grass. A gravel pathway wound its way between a host of exquisite sculptures of ice – carved trees, exotic birds and legendary beasts. The moonlight bathed everything in a monochrome brilliance, the silence and sense of isolation a physical thing within this icy wilderness of dragons, eagles and bone chilling cold.

The black robed figure halted suddenly, blending so completely with a pool of shadow that even the most dedicated of observers would have had trouble spotting its existence.

A pair of patrolling knights in bronze armour crunched along the pathway, their hands on their sword pommels. The silver bears on their helmets caught the moonlight and, without knowing it, the knights passed within yards of the intruder.

But lives can often hang on the slightest turn of fate and it was at that moment that the moon chose to emerge from behind another cloud, dispelling the shadows along this section of the pathway and bathing the robed figure in light.

One knight managed to shape words of warning before a silver steel slash opened his throat, the killer's blade expertly finding the gap between his helmet and gorget. The other guard had his sword partially drawn when the intruder's sword flashed again and the knight's head fell to the path and rolled into the glittering undergrowth.

Pausing only to clean his blade, the figure moved off again into the shadows.

The lights of the palace were just ahead.

* * *

V

KASPAR EXCHANGED PLEASANTRIES with Albertalli as they filed into the timber-panelled West Hall, where great oak beams ran the width of the hall and a vast fire set below a great stone mantle filled the room with warmth and the aroma of fresh-cut wood. Hundreds of candles lined the walls between the tall windows, together with innumerable shields and suits of bronze armour. Faded battle flags hung from the beams and the hardwood floors echoed to the jangle of sabres and spurs as the senior officers retired to plan their strategy against Aelfric Cyenwulf's horde with the Ice Queen.

The womenfolk and junior officers remained within the Banqueting Hall, finishing off the wine from dinner and speculating upon what was going on in the other hall. Under normal circumstances, Kaspar should have remained in the Banqueting Hall as well, but the Tzarina herself had sent a functionary to instruct him to attend upon her with the other commanders.

Sofia had remained behind, chatting with some dashingly attired lancers and Kaspar had been surprised to feel a pang of jealousy. There was no doubt he liked Sofia immensely, and he wondered whether their relationship had become something more than mere friendship after her abduction by Sasha Kajetan. He didn't know, but looked forward to the prospect of finding out.

The assembled officers and boyarin gradually fell to silence as the Ice Queen entered the hall together with her fierce, shaven headed guards and Pjotr Losov, who closed the doors to the Banqueting Hall behind him before vanishing into the background.

The Ice Queen marched to the centre of the hall as the boyarin formed a circle around her, kept at a respectful distance from their queen by her guards.

Without preamble, the Ice Queen said, 'The horde of Aelfric Cyenwulf draws near and it is time to take the war to him.'

The boyarins cheered loudly and the Empire officers clapped courteously. Now that he was closer, Kaspar could see the commander of the Stirland army more clearly, curious as to what kind of man he was. General Pavia was a slighter figure than Kaspar had first expected, not tall, but with a commanding presence to him that he immediately liked.

'He is cunning, this Cyenwulf,' continued the Tzarina when the cheering had died down. 'He comes with greater ambition than simple pillage.'

'Is of no matter, my Queen!' shouted a red uniformed boyarin of lancers. 'For we shall still send him back north without his balls, won't we, comrades?' Roars of affirmation and laughter followed the man's boast and Kaspar saw the Ice Queen fight to hold back a scowl. He remembered the Tzarina once talking of her father's boyarin, calling them an insufferable band of brutes, but men who had been the most loyal, steadfast warriors anyone could wish for. In that respect, the boyarin surrounding her seemed no different from those of her father, but he could see their raucousness did not sit well with her icy demeanour.

'I am sure we will, Boyarin Wrodzik,' said the Tzarina over the laughter, 'but this barbarian strikes for a place at the very heart of Kislev, he makes for Urszebya.'

The laughter faded quickly, replaced with a deadly earnestness and Kaspar was suddenly confused. What was Urszebya? After a moment's thought he hazarded a guess that it translated as Ursun's Teeth, but what was that but an earthy soldier's curse?

Satisfied that her words had had the desired effect, the Tzarina continued. 'This Cyenwulf knows what makes us who we are. Kislev is land and land is Kislev.'

'Kislev is land and land is Kislev,' repeated the boyarin in unison.

'The valley of Urszebya, the wound where Great Ursun took a bite from our land and left us his stone fangs is under threat and our enemies plan its desecration. Their cursed shamans would use dark magicks to pervert the spirit of the land, to corrupt the primal, elemental power of Kislev with Chaos and blight our great land forever.'

The boyarin roared a denial and Kaspar could see they were horrified by the notion of this valley's desecration.

'There is power there, my boyarin, power that must not be taken by the forces of the Dark Gods. It falls to us to stop him.'

The Ice Queen's eyes swept the assembled boyarin with a fierce pride and Kaspar shivered as her gaze fell upon him. She nodded slowly and said, 'The land has called every one of you to this place, to this time, and cries out for all those with the soul of Kislevite to rally to her defence. Will you answer her call?'

The hall rang to the sound of a hundred throats shouting that they would.

VI

It did not take long for the corpses of the two knights to be discovered. The security of the Tzarina was a duty taken very seriously by her protectors and within minutes of the killings, a second pair of knights found them lying in wide pools of rapidly cooling blood and raised the alarm.

But by then it was already too late.

VII

Standing near the windows of the West Hall, Kaspar heard the sound of hand bells over the cheering and wondered briefly what they signified. But as the urgent ringing continued, a growing sense of unease crept over him. Few of the boyarins had heard the bells and, surrounded by roaring warriors, none of the Tzarina's guards had heard it either.

His suspicion that something was amiss grew to a certainty as he looked through the window into the darkness and saw knights bearing lit torches and drawn swords running through the grounds of the Winter Gardens.

Kaspar turned from the window and began pushing his way through the cheering boyarin, many of whom were already three sheets to the wind and mistook his efforts to be drunken enthusiasm for the coming war. Ruddy-faced Kislevites gripped him by the shoulders and kissed both his cheeks with shouted northern oaths as he struggled to get through them to the Tzarina.

'Get off me, you oaf!' he yelled as a heavyset man gripped him in a tight embrace and shouted something at a nearby boyarin. The man released him and Kaspar pushed his way forwards once more. The Ice Queen's guards saw him coming and the frantic look in his eyes, the ringing of the alarm finally penetrating the slowly diminishing cheering.

'Your majesty–' shouted Kaspar as a window smashed inwards, glass shards falling to the floor as a spinning brass sphere bounced on the wooden floor and rolled across the rugs towards the assembled soldiers. Smaller than a cannon-ball, it wobbled slightly as it came to a halt before Arnulf Pavia.

'What the hell?' said the Stirland general.

'No!' shouted Kaspar, trying to force his way towards Pavia. He didn't know exactly what the sphere was, but knew enough to recognise trouble when he saw it. The general looked up in puzzlement and that was the last Kaspar ever saw of him as a shrieking darkness exploded outwards from the sphere.

Fell winds howled around the West Hall, extinguishing every candle in a single bellow, and the wails of the accursed filled the room with cacophonous screaming. Gibbering voices, plucked straight from the abode of the damned, rang within every skull and a terrifying, aching dread filled the soul as the lingering echoes of some vile otherworld seeped from the evil corona of energy that burned darkly in the centre of the hall.

Kaspar felt the innards of his soul ravaged by unseen claws of ice and cried out in pain as an aching cold of the spirit, far deeper than anything natural could ever be, stabbed through him. The fire below the stone mantelpiece dimmed as swirling shadows writhed around him, exposing him to the sheer vastness of the universe and his own insignificance within it. He tried to crawl away, but his limbs were leaden, powerless and he knew that this was his death, a meaningless speck in an uncaring universe.

Hands gripped him and he felt himself being dragged away from the nightmare vortex. He opened his eyes, the aching dark sliding from his soul, and he gasped at the dreadfulness of what he had felt. He rolled onto his side, heaving for breath as the swirling blackness in the centre of the room began shrinking away to nothing, closing the window to the horrifying realm beyond. The fire roared back to life as he pushed himself to his knees with a grimace and turned to thank his rescuer.

He recognised the flushed, firelit features of Pavel Korovic and gripped his old friend's shoulder tightly. 'Thank you,' he said.

'Is of no matter,' said Pavel, his face ashen and Kaspar could tell he too had felt the awful madness that lay within the darkness. He turned back to the centre of the room, seeing nothing but a shallow crater of splintered floorboards and fragmented foundations where the brass sphere had exploded. Of General Pavia and his senior officers, there was no sign.

Screams filled the room where men lay in pieces, entire limbs shorn from their bodies where the deadly energy of Chaos had touched them: boyarin with half their heads gone or missing the front of their ribcages lay around the circumference of the crater, blood spattered around their hewn corpses.

Kaspar looked for the Tzarina and saw her and her guards backing towards the main doors to the hall. Blood streamed from a deep cut on her temple and she was supported by one of her boyarin. An Empire captain of arquebusiers lay screaming before Kaspar, his legs severed from his body just below the pelvis by the lethal explosion.

Shouts of outrage and confusion began, but before anyone could do more than pick themselves up off the floor, Kaspar saw a dark shape ghost through the window, a solid darkness against the moonlit sky beyond.

'Watch out!' he yelled to the Tzarina's guards, pointing at the window.

Two of the bare chested warriors leapt towards the figure, the third remaining with their queen. Their swords were golden blurs as they attacked, sparks flying from the blindingly swift impacts. The figure in black swayed aside from a blow Kaspar felt sure would cleave him in two, rolling beneath his opponent's guard and with his sword flicking out. The first guard collapsed, his guts looping around his knees as he was expertly disembowelled and the second desperately parried, edging backwards from the terrifying speed of his opponent and employing every shred of his skill just to survive.

Kaspar desperately wished to help the man, but knew he would be dead in a heartbeat were he to face this black-robed killer. He had no weapons of his own, his lack of a military rank preventing him from bearing arms in the presence of the Tzarina. He crawled as fast as he could to the fireplace, realising that his only hope of helping lay with giving the Tzarina's guards a fighting chance in this unequal struggle.

The second guard was down, the assassin's blade deep in his chest and Kaspar watched as the Tzarina's last guard yelled a fierce oath and leapt to the attack. The boyarin were finally overcoming their confusion and panic, cries of alarm sounding as they saw the danger to their queen. They were arming themselves, but Kaspar knew that by then it would be too late and the Tzarina would be dead.

He reached into the fire and dragged out a blazing brand, feeling the flames burn his skin, but gritting his teeth against the pain. He surged to his feet as the assassin spun beneath a beheading stroke and opened the Tzarina's warrior from groin to sternum with his sword.

Kaspar had seconds at best. As the killer fought to free his blade from his victim, Kaspar hurled the fiery missile at his back.

Fat orange sparks flared where it hit and the black robed figure shrieked as its robes caught light.

'Kaspar, down!' shouted a voice he recognised as Pavel's.

He ducked as something flashed over his head and saw a glass bottle shatter upon the murderer. Flames engulfed the killer, spreading wildly over his body and transforming him into a blazing torch. He lurched around the room like a drunk, ablaze from head to toe, and his shrieking squeals rose to new heights, sounding for all the world like a wounded animal.

The doors to the hall burst open and more warriors burst in, men with spears and long muskets. The black powder weapons boomed and the blazing figure was blasted from its feet, landing in a thrashing heap in the centre of the crater its mysterious sphere had blown.

The warriors with spears ran to the blazing body and stabbed it repeatedly with the iron tips of their weapons until at last it was still.

Kaspar rolled onto his back and said, 'Kvas?'

Pavel nodded as the flames consumed the killer's flesh and filled the room with its sickening stench.

'I not have any need for it any more,' said Pavel, offering his hand to Kaspar.

'Good,' said Kaspar, accepting Pavel's hand and climbing to his feet.

He saw that the Tzarina was no longer in danger, her warriors gathered about her as the boyarin took stock of their losses and shouted great oaths of vengeance to Ursun, Dazh and Tor.

Kaspar limped over to where the shaken boyarin gathered around the smouldering corpse, spitting on its charred remains. Much of the flesh had been seared from its body and the charred remains were twisted and deformed, but the skull was strangely elongated and possessed more than a passing resemblance to...

Kaspar turned away from the corpse, unwilling to believe that what he had seen could be real. It was a man, deformed and obviously disfigured, but a man. It surely could not have been anything else, surely...

The boyarin parted as the Tzarina walked stiffly to the edge of the crater in the floor. Her face was a mask of controlled rage, glittering blood coating one side of her face and a mist of sparkling ice crystals forming in the air around her. As the crystals fell to the floor around her and shattered musically on the floor, Kaspar and her boyarin backed away from a fury that burned the air with its frozen heat.

'Get me Losov,' she said.

CHAPTER NINE

I

FINDING PJOTR LOSOV took longer than expected, but eventually he was brought before the Tzarina, his face lined with concern and worry. The West Hall was no longer the bloodbath it had been half an hour ago, the bodies of the dead having been removed and the wounded taken to the Banqueting Hall, where Sofia and other hastily gathered physicians were caring for them as best they could.

The Ice Queen stood with the mighty sword Fearfrost drawn, holding it by the pommel so that the tip of its shimmering blue blade rested on the floor. The dead assassin's sword lay on the floor in front of her.

Kaspar sat on a wooden bench near the fire and sipped a mug of kvas, his nerves still unsettled after the horror of the killer's attack. He could not rid his memory of the sight of the charred, deformed corpse and, most of all, the hideous, crawling sense of insignificance and misery he had experienced while lying next to whatever damned realm the killer's brass sphere had opened a gateway to.

'My queen,' said Losov, dropping to his knees before her. 'You are hurt!'

'I will live, Pjotr, it–'

'Oh, it gladdens my heart to see you,' interrupted Losov. 'When I heard that there had been an attack I feared the worst and set out to double the guards on the gates. Ursun bless us, but I am so glad you are alive.'

'Spare me your lies, Pjotr,' said the Tzarina, her voice like a dagger of pure ice. 'It is your own hide you should be more concerned with now.'

'Lies? I don't understand.'

'Come now, Pjotr... did you really think you could have betrayed me for all this time without me knowing?' asked the Tzarina, a mist of sparkling cold forming around her.

'Betrayed you? I swear I am loyal!' protested Losov.

The Tzarina shook her head. 'Stop it, Pjotr, you only diminish yourself further now. You of all people should know that the *Chekist* have eyes everywhere. I know all about your sordid little visits to the Lubjanko and what you do there. Your deviant practices disgust me, and you will pay for all the suffering you have caused. But to think you could fool me for so long, that is just insulting.'

Despite the icy mist that reached out from the Tzarina, Kaspar could see that the kneeling Losov was sweating now and relished the man's discomfort.

'No, no, you are mistaken, my queen!'

'It was useful and amusing for me to keep you around, to listen to your prattle, your pathetic attempts to manipulate me and manipulate you in turn, but now many of my finest warriors are dead or dying and the commander of my allies is vanished. You are no longer useful or amusing, Pjotr.'

Losov spun, seeking supporters around the hall, but finding none. Kaspar saw the fear in his eyes and raised his mug of kvas in mocking salute.

'Now all that remains is for you to tell me who you have been collaborating with, for I know a man as foolish as you could not be working without a more cunning master. Tell me, Pjotr, who else is involved in this conspiracy to kill me and destroy my land?'

Kaspar and Pavel listened intently, both eager to hear more of Losov's disgrace. Kaspar desperately wanted to know why

Losov had paid to have Anastasia's husband killed, sure that the name the Tzarina would get from the traitor would be his answer.

'It is of no matter now, Pjotr,' continued the Ice Queen when Losov did not answer her question. 'One way or another I *will* find out what I want to know. You have seen the *Chekist*'s gaol and you know that there is no man alive who can withstand their tortures. Tell me what I want to know and spare yourself that agony.'

Final desperation flashed in Losov's eyes and Kaspar saw him snatch for the assassin's fallen weapon. Losov surged to his feet, the blade stabbing upwards for the Tzarina's stomach.

Kaspar saw a flash of blue steel and a spurt of red, and Pjotr Losov was falling, his sword arm severed at the elbow and his torso cleft from pelvis to collarbone by the freezing edge of Fearfrost.

The Ice Queen held her sword before her, frozen icicles of blood dripping from the blade.

Boyarin Wrodzik kicked the dismembered body into the crater along with the charred corpse of the black robed assassin and spat on Losov's remains.

'Such is wrath of the Khan Queens and the fate of all traitors,' said the Tzarina.

II

DAWN WAS ALREADY lightening the sky by the time Kaspar and Sofia were able to finally return to the embassy, carried back in one of the Tzarina's lacquered, open topped carriages driven by an uncommunicative driver in a square red cap. They were swathed in furs and though it was nowhere near as cold as it had been in previous months, they huddled close to one another beneath the thick furs for warmth and comfort, the fingers of their hands laced together.

Neither of them had said anything on the way back, still in shock at the bloody events of the night and the cold anger of the Tzarina. Far from the regal, aloof monarch the Tzarina usually appeared to be, her execution of Pjotr Losov had recalled the wild ferocity of the first khan queens, and Kaspar shivered as he remembered how he had shouted at her several months ago.

Surgeons more qualified in battlefield injuries had taken over from Sofia, and she had only reluctantly allowed herself to be led away where she could clean her bloody hands and change from her gore-smeared dress.

Seventeen men had lost their lives in the attack. Clemenz Spitzaner and most of his staff officers had survived the violence, but General Pavia and his senior commanders had not. In the context of the loss of life suffered at Krasicyno and Mazhorod, such numbers were slight; they represented the upper echelons of command in the Stirland army.

Seven boyarin were dead, obliterated like the general by the terrible weapon the robed assassin had used, and six others would never fight again.

Kaspar had immediately volunteered for a field rank. Of course Spitzaner had protested immediately, but Kaspar had seen that the idea appealed to the remaining officers of the Stirland army, his reputation as a fine commander well known to them. Kaspar had arranged a meeting with them in the morning, giving everyone a chance to recover from the night's slaughter before speaking of such weighty matters.

Despite the bloodshed of the evening, the thought of leading men into battle once more gave him a satisfying feeling that he would be able to play a part in the coming war. He could see that Sofia was unhappy with his decision to volunteer for command, but he could not take it back now.

Before leaving the palace, Kaspar had approached Pavel and said, 'I never thanked you properly for pulling me away from that vile darkness. I think I would have died there if not for you.'

'Is of no matter,' said Pavel lightly, but Kaspar could feel the gratitude in his words.

'No,' said Kaspar. 'It is of some matter. You and I have been through much together and I counted you as one of my truest friends, but too much has happened in Kislev for me to forget the things you have done since I saw you last.'

'I know,' said Pavel. 'There nothing can undo what I did, but I wish…'

'Wishes are for songs, Pavel, and neither one of us can sing worth a damn. But know this: if the fates see fit for us to fight alongside one another again, I will do so gladly. I think our friendship has died here, but I will not be your enemy.'

'Very well,' agreed Pavel. 'A man can ask for no more than that.'

Kaspar nodded and offered his hand to Pavel. 'Fight well and try not to get yourself killed,' he said.

'You know me,' grinned the big Kislevite, shaking the ambassador's hand. 'Pavel Korovic too stubborn to die. They will tell tales of my bravery from here to Magritta!'

'I am sure they will. Farewell, Pavel,' said Kaspar as Sofia led him to the carriage that would carry them back to the embassy. The journey passed in silence until the driver halted before the embassy, stepping down from his seat to open the door for them. He accepted a copper coin from Kaspar before climbing back and driving off in a clatter of hooves.

Red and blue liveried guards opened the gates for them and as they walked arm in arm to the embassy, Sofia asked, 'Do you really mean to take a field rank if they offer you one tomorrow?'

Kaspar nodded. 'Yes, I do. I have to.'

'You don't, you know. You have done your duty to the army and there are others who can do it,' said Sofia.

'No, there aren't and you know it,' said Kaspar softly, seeing the worry in Sofia's face. 'Spitzaner cannot command two armies and I am the only other man who has experience of leading such numbers of soldiers.'

'Surely one of the boyarins could command?'

'No, the Empire soldiers would not accept a Kislevite as their general.'

'But you are too old to go into battle,' protested Sofia.

Kaspar chuckled, saying, 'Very well, there you might be correct, but it changes nothing. If they offer me the rank, I will take it, things are moving too fast for me to refuse.'

'What do you mean?'

'Don't you feel it, Sofia? History is unfolding before us,' said Kaspar. 'I remember once the Ice Queen told me that I had the soul of a Kislevite, that the land had called me back here to fight for it and that I had something to do here. "Come the moment, come the man", those were her very words. I didn't understand what she meant then, but I think I am beginning to.'

'Damn you, Kaspar, we had no time,' said Sofia, tears gathering at the corners of her eyes. 'Why did this have to happen now?'

'I don't know,' replied Kaspar, stopping and turning her to face him. 'But it has, and sometimes there are things we have to do, no matter what our heart tells us.'

'And what is your heart telling you to do?'

'This,' said Kaspar, leaning down to kiss Sofia on the mouth.

They kissed until a booming laugh sounded from outside the embassy gates and Vassily Chekatilo said, 'This all very touching, Ambassador von Velten. I think I right when I ask you if you in love with Madame Valencik.'

'Chekatilo,' snarled Kaspar turning to see the fat Kislevite lounging beside the embassy gates in a thick cloak of black fur. 'Get out of here, you bastard.'

Chekatilo chuckled and shook his head. 'No, not this time, Empire man. This time you will listen to me.'

'You and I have nothing to say to one another, Chekatilo.'

'No? I think you wrong. You still owe a debt to me and I here to collect.'

Sofia opened the door to the embassy and more guards appeared, their halberds bright in the first rays of morning sunshine.

'And I will tell you again that I will not give you what you want. I know about what you had Pavel do, so you can forget about getting him to do your dirty work any more. Get it through your thick skull, Chekatilo, I will never help you!' shouted Kaspar. He felt his temper getting the better of him again, but had seen too much pain and suffering tonight to be browbeaten by a common criminal.

'I think you will tonight,' promised Chekatilo.

'And why is that?' asked Kaspar, not liking Chekatilo's cat-like grin one bit.

'Because if you do not, Anastasia Vilkova will be dead within the hour.'

III

REJAK YAWNED, FLEXING his shoulders as he watched the house come to life. Servants filled pitchers of water from the well and opened shuttered windows to let the weak morning sunlight in. He cracked his knuckles and rapped his fingers against the iron pommel of his sword with a predatory smile.

He sat resting his back on the wall of the building across the street from Anastasia Vilkova's house, his sword concealed beneath his cloak and features obscured by a furred hood. He did not think that the Vilkova woman knew him or would recognise him, but there was no sense in taking chances.

He knew she was home, having seen her return less than an hour ago. Where she had been he didn't know, probably enjoying a tryst with the ambassador and returning before morning to avoid scandalising her prettified society.

Reasoning that enough time had passed for her to have gotten herself cleaned up and perhaps even undressed, he pushed himself to his feet, wincing as the injuries to his shoulder and stomach pulled tight. He had always healed fast and the weeks since his wounding by the black-robed killer had been hard for him, unused as he was to enforced inactivity. But the wounds had healed well and though he would never be as supple and fast as he once had been, he was still as quick as any man alive he knew of.

Rejak strode across the street, his excitement growing at the thought of violating such a beautiful and respected woman. Normally his conquests were weirdroot whores from Chekatilo's brothels, and the idea of this influential woman beneath him and begging for her life as he took her hurried his steps. He thought of her soft mouth, long dark hair and full breasts and licked his lips. Yes, he would enjoy breaking this bitch.

He entered the grounds of her house, marching up the gravel incline and passing the pathetic specimens of humanity she had granted shelter within her walls. Scores of people camped within her grounds, hardly any of them sparing him a second glance as he made his way to the front door.

The main door was lacquered black wood with a brass knocker at its centre. He gripped his sword handle and rapped the brass ring hard against the door. Best to give the impression of civility, he supposed.

Rejak heard the tumblers of the lock turn and a click as the door eased from the frame. He hammered his boot into the timber, slamming the door back on its hinges and sending the old servant woman behind it sprawling with blood streaming from her face.

Swiftly he crossed the threshold, entering a marble-floored hall and seeing a curved flight of stairs with a brass balustrade rising to the upper floor ahead of him. Twin suits of armour flanked the bottom of the stairs and a family crest bearing two crossed cavalry sabres hung from the adjacent wall. An incongruous door of iron was set on the curve of the stairs, partially obscured by a leafy potted evergreen, but Rejak ignored it as he heard a door slam upstairs.

That would be her, reasoned Rejak, shutting the front door then locking it and pocketing the key. He sprinted for the stairs, taking them two at a time. Upon reaching the upper landing he drew his sword and made his way down a long, carpeted hallway. Heavy doors lined one side of the corridor and he began kicking them down one by one.

'Come out, come out, wherever you are!' he yelled.

He saw a flash of colour from ahead of him and grinned as he saw Anastasia in an emerald green nightgown running for another set of stairs at the far end of the corridor.

'Oh, no, pretty one, you won't get away from Rejak that easily,' he shouted, sprinting after her. She was quick, but Rejak was quicker, catching her as she reached the top of the stairs. She spun, lashing out with her fist at the side of the head.

He laughed, catching her wrist and backhanding his sword hand into her chin.

She screamed and fell against the wall, blood streaming down her chin.

'You bastard!' she shouted, aiming a kick for his groin. Rejak twisted out of the way and slapped her hard with his free hand. His excitement was growing and he pressed himself against her, tearing her nightdress from her shoulder. 'Careful there, my beauty. Don't want to hurt me there. Not when I've still got things to do to you.'

To her credit she kept on struggling, even though she must have known it was useless against his superior strength and only served to arouse him more.

'I can see why von Velten likes you,' he hissed in her ear. 'I hope he doesn't mind spoiled meat, because that's all you're going to be soon.'

Rejak pinned her against the wall and pressed a hand to her breast. He squeezed hard, grinning lasciviously as it drew a cry of pain from her. Her chest heaved in terror and he laughed. 'That's it... struggle harder!'

He lowered his head to lick her cheek.

She slammed her forehead into his face and he cried out in pain, releasing her as his hands flew to his face and blood burst from his nose.

'Bitch!' he yelled and hammered his fist into her jaw.

She fell to the floor, but rolled quickly to her feet as he shook his head clear of the headbutt's impact. He turned his bloody face towards her as she lurched along the corridor towards the stairs that led to the main entrance and shouted, 'That's it, you bitch! I'm really going to hurt you now!'

Rejak set off after her, his anger hot and urgent.

He caught her at the top of the stairs, grabbing her by the arm and twisting her around. She spat in his face and he hit her again, sending her crashing downstairs. She tumbled all the way to the bottom, landing awkwardly and he followed her, no longer caring about having her, just about killing her.

She scrambled back from the bottom of the stairs, running to the front door, tugging ineffectually at the brass handle.

Rejak lifted the key from his pocket and grinned. 'Looking for this?'

She edged away from him around the walls, but there was nowhere to go.

'You die now,' he said.

IV

KASPAR RIPPED A halberd from one of his guards and ran to the iron gates of the embassy. Chekatilo backed away towards the gurgling bronze fountain in the centre of the courtyard in front of the embassy, his hands raised in theatrical terror.

'You kill me and she dies,' he promised. 'If Rejak not hear from me in one hour, he is to treat her like whore and then cut her into pieces. He do worse than Butcherman, that one, I think. Loves to kill, too much maybe.'

Kaspar forced himself to stop moving, to lower the halberd and think clearly. He felt his hate for Chekatilo threaten to overwhelm his judgement. He cried out in anguish and threw the halberd aside, taking several deep breaths as he fought for calm.

'What have you done?' he demanded. 'As Sigmar is my witness, if any harm comes to her, no force in the world will stop me from hunting you down and killing you.'

'She not be harmed if you honour debt to me and give me what I want,' said Chekatilo.

'How do I know she is still alive? For all I know, she's already dead.'

Chekatilo looked hurt at Kaspar's accusation. 'I many things, ambassador, but I not a monster. I hurt people because sometimes that the only way to get what I want. So now you will give me what I want or I have Rejak kill her in such painful, degrading way that people will talk of it for years.'

Kaspar wanted to run through the gates and strangle Chekatilo with his bare hands, to choke the life from his miserable, filthy body and spit in his eye as he died. But he could not, and from Chekatilo's smug expression, he could see the bastard knew it too.

'Damn you, but you are wrong, Chekatilo. You *are* a monster,' he said.

Chekatilo shrugged. 'Maybe I am, but I get what I want, yah?'

Kaspar nodded. 'Very well, I will give you what you want,' he said slowly.

Chekatilo laughed as Kaspar turned and entered the embassy.

V

ANASTASIA EDGED AROUND the hall, her breathing ragged and laboured. Rejak could feel his arousal growing again as he saw the curve of her breasts exposed where he had torn her night-gown.

'Nowhere to go,' he said, wiping blood from his chin.

'No,' she agreed, continuing around the edge of the hall and looking at something beyond his shoulder. 'There isn't, is there?'

'Best not to fight then, eh? Might not hurt as much, but I can't promise.'

He moved left, cutting her off from reaching the stairs as she reached the family crest bearing the two crossed cavalry sabres. She quickly reached up and tore the weapons from their hangings, turning to face him with them held awkwardly before her.

'You think you can use one blade let alone two?' laughed Rejak.

'They're not for me,' said Anastasia, throwing the swords across the room.

The swords sailed over his head and Rejak followed their spinning trajectory until they were plucked from the air by a man standing beside the iron door he had noticed earlier.

The man was thin and wasted, his skin blotchy and scabrous, and Rejak relaxed.

Until the man spun the swords in a blindingly quick web of silver steel and dropped into a fighting crouch. The man's movements were sublime, his every motion honed to perfection, and there was only one man Rejak knew of who could move like that.

His features were sunken and hollow, and only when Rejak looked deep into the man's violet eyes, did he finally recognise him.

Sasha Kajetan.

The *Droyaska*. The Blademaster.

VI

KASPAR WHIPPED HIS horse to greater speed as he and the Knights Panther rode desperately through the streets of Kislev towards the Magnustrasse and Anastasia's house. The streets were thronged with people and he shouted fearful oaths to try and get them out of his way.

His heart was heavy with black premonition, but there was nothing he could do except ride harder, pushing Magnus to more reckless speeds as they thundered towards the wealthy quarter of the city.

Kaspar prayed he was not riding towards more grief.

VII

REJAK FELT HIS momentary flutter of fear fade as he saw the ruin of the legendary swordsman's form. The man's limbs were thin and wasted, the flesh sagging from his bones, and his ribs were plainly visible through the skin of his chest.

He looked no better than a beggar and Rejak grinned through his mask of blood.

'I have always wanted to fight you,' said Rejak, circling the room with his blade aimed at Kajetan's heart. 'Just to know who was the faster.'

'You hurt my matka,' hissed Kajetan, circling in time with Rejak.

Rejak glanced over at Anastasia in confusion. What in Ursun's name was the swordsman talking about? There was no way she could possibly be Kajetan's mother.

'That's right, my handsome prince,' said Anastasia. 'He did. He hurt me just like your father, the boyarin, did.'

Kajetan screamed, 'No!' and launched himself at Rejak. Their swords clashed and Rejak spun away from the attack, his own weapon sweeping low to cut the swordsman's legs out from under him, but Kajetan was no longer there, somersaulting over the blade and landing lightly on his feet.

'Kill him, my prince!' screamed Anastasia and Kajetan attacked again, his twin swords slashing for Rejak's head. Chekatilo's assassin parried swiftly, launching a deadly riposte and slicing his blade across Kajetan's thigh next to a scar on his leg where he had obviously been recently wounded. The swordsman stumbled and Rejak kicked him in the balls.

Kajetan grunted in pain and dropped to one knee, vomiting across the floor. Rejak jumped back in horror as the black, gristly liquid bubbled and hissed, eating away at the marble flagstones.

Overcoming his revulsion, he closed to deliver the killing strike, slashing his sword at Kajetan's neck. The swordsman rolled beneath the blow, vaulting to his feet in time to block Rejak's return stroke.

Kajetan recovered quickly, his swords drawing blood from Rejak's arm, and the two swordsmen traded blows back and forth across the marble floor of the hall, fighting a duel the likes of which had never been seen before. Kajetan was by far the better bladesman, but his strength was a fraction of its former self and Rejak could see that he was tiring rapidly.

But Rejak was tiring too, his sword arm burning with fatigue and the wound in his belly stabbing hot spikes of pain into his body with each lunge and parry.

The two men warily circled each other once more, exhausted by their furious exertions and knowing that only one of them would walk away from this fight.

Rejak attacked again, a blistering series of slashes and cuts designed to keep an opponent on the back foot. His bladework was faultless, but nothing could penetrate Kajetan's twin sabres and Rejak realised with sick horror that he had no more to give.

Kajetan's blades caught his sword on his last downward stroke and with a twist of the wrist, Rejak's blade was wrenched from his grip, skittering across the floor and coming to rest at the bottom of the stairs.

Rejak leapt backwards, diving across the floor towards his sword.

His hand closed on its leather-bound hilt and he rolled to face his opponent again.

Kajetan was before him, his crossed blades resting either side of Rejak's neck.

'You want to know who is faster?' snarled the swordsman. 'Now you know.'

Kajetan slashed both blades through Rejak's neck and he toppled backwards onto the stairs, his head almost completely severed.

His last sight was of Anastasia Vilkova staring down at him with undiluted hate.

She spat in his eye and said, 'Tchar take your soul.'

VIII

THEY RODE THROUGH the open gateway of Anastasia's home, Kaspar vaulting from the saddle before his horse had stopped moving. He ignored the flare of pain in his knee, running for the black door and drawing both his pistols. The door was locked, but a few heavy kicks from the armoured boot of Kurt Bremen soon smashed it from its hinges.

Kaspar bolted inside, moaning as he saw a body lying at the foot of the stairs in a lake of blood. He ran over and knelt by the body and felt his heart lurch in surprise and relief as he recognised Rejak's dead-eyed features. The man's head hung slack on his shoulders, attached to his body by a few gory scraps of severed muscle and sinew.

Kurt Bremen joined him as the knights fanned out through the house to search for Anastasia.

'I don't understand,' he said. 'What the hell happened here?'

Kaspar did not reply, his eyes falling upon a pair of bloody cavalry sabres lying beside the body and a pool of glistening black liquid in the centre of the marble floor. He left the body where it lay and bent to examine the black pool and the floor beneath it. The marble flagstone had been eaten away by the stinking substance's corrosive properties and Kaspar knew he had seen something like this only once before.

Below the Urskoy Prospekt as it turned an iron breastplate to molten slag before his very eyes.

'Is that what I think it is?' asked Bremen.

Kaspar nodded. 'I think so.'

Bremen looked back at Rejak's body and the cavalry sabres. 'But that means...'

'Aye. That Sasha Kajetan was here. He killed Rejak.'

'But how?' asked Bremen. 'It doesn't make sense, why would Kajetan be here?'

Kaspar wondered the same and felt a creeping horror overtake him as the significance of Rejak's death and Kajetan's presence in this house settled on him like a sickness. Kajetan had been a broken man, a virtual catatonic, and Kaspar knew that there was only one thing that roused the swordsman to such violence. Matka.

'It does, Kurt. Sigmar, save me, but it does,' said Kaspar sadly as the veil finally fell from his eyes and he saw how masterfully he had been manipulated.

'Sigmar's blood, do you think Kajetan has Madame Vilkova?'

'No,' said Kaspar, shaking his head. 'And your knights will not find her here either.'

'What do you mean? Where is she?'

'It's been her all along, Kurt. It all makes sense now,' said Kaspar, as much to himself as to the Knight Panther. He sank to his haunches, dropping his pistols as his heart beat wildly at the scale of this treachery.

'What does? Kaspar, you are not making any sense.'

'She has played us all for fools, my friend. The woman no one could describe who freed Kajetan? The woman in the sewer who took delivery of the coffin? Our unseen adversary who knew everything we discovered? The woman who tried to discourage me from even looking in the first place? Losov's collaborator? It was her, it was all her.'

'Anastasia?' said Bremen, incredulous.

Kaspar nodded, cursing himself for a fool. 'Damn it, Kajetan told us as much. "It all was her for", he said. I didn't realise he meant those words literally. It was her directing Kajetan's murders all along. No wonder she tried to have him killed before we could hand him over to the *Chekist*.'

'I can't believe it,' whispered Bremen.

'All the things I told her,' said Kaspar, rubbing his eyes and fighting back the hot flush of shame. 'All the times we lay together in bed and talked of the boyarins, the forces of the Empire, where they were massing, how they would fight and about the men who commanded them. And like a bloody fool I told her everything.'

Kaspar slumped to the floor, holding his head in his hands. 'How could I have been so stupid. Her husband... she had Losov pay to have him killed so she could take his wealth. All this time...'

'I still find this hard to accept, but assuming you are correct, where do you think she and Kajetan are now?'

Kaspar rubbed his face and pushed himself to his feet before bending to retrieve his pistols. 'That's a damn good question,' he said, his anger now beginning to push aside his hurt.

'She must have known that when we found this mess, she would be unmasked,' said Kaspar, heading for the front door and marching towards the scabrous refugees camped throughout the grounds of Anastasia's home.

'Speak to these people, Kurt,' ordered Kaspar. 'Find out if they saw where she went and don't stop asking until you get some damn good answers.'

Kurt Bremen made his way around the refugees, shouting in fragmented Kislevite as Kaspar walked towards the gateway in the wall, confused thoughts spinning around inside his head.

He had ridden here to save Anastasia, but it appeared that she had needed no rescuing, what with the deadliest bodyguard in Kislev to call her own. He wondered if she had ever really cared for him, then chided himself for such selfish thoughts when much deadlier matters were afoot.

He leaned against the gatepost, his eyes idly following the profusion of tracks in the slush that ran through the gate.

Most of the slushy mud had been churned by the passage of their own horses, but one patch of ground retained tracks other than theirs; cart tracks...

Cart tracks with a cracked rim on one of the wheels that left a V-shaped impression with every revolution.

It took Kaspar a few seconds to remember where he had seen similar tracks.

In the sewers beneath Kislev.

Made by a cart that had been driven off laden with a strange coffin.

Kurt Bremen approached him. 'They say the White Lady left here not long before we arrived, that she was driving a cart with a long box on the back. No one mentioned anyone else, so I don't believe Kajetan is with her.'

Kaspar felt a terrible fear as he looked up at the sky.

Dawn was hours old and he knew exactly where Anastasia would be heading now.

For months people had seen the White Lady of Kislev drive carts of supplies and food to the armies camped beyond the walls. She was a vision of hope and had been a welcome sight to the soldiers of Kislev and the Empire.

So no one would bat an eyelid to see her driving a cart into their midst today.

'Sigmar save us,' swore Kaspar, running for his horse. 'Everyone mount up!'

'Kaspar, what is it?' shouted Bremen.

'We have to stop her, Kurt!' replied Kaspar, pulling himself into the saddle and guiding Magnus towards the gateway. 'I don't know exactly what it is, but I think that whatever is in that coffin is some kind of terrible weapon. She means to destroy our armies before they can fight!'

IX

SHE WHIPPED THE horses, pushing them as fast as she dared through the breaking morning towards the Urskoy Gate. People huddled at the side of the road waved to her as she passed, recognising her distinctive white cloak edged with snow leopard fur. Anastasia ignored them, too engrossed in reaching the city gate before anyone stopped her.

How could she have been discovered? The man who had come to murder her, who had sent him? The ambassador? Had the fool finally realised how he had been deceived and sent this man in a fit of one of his tempers? No, from her would-be-killer's words she felt sure that Kaspar had not sent him, but who?

Chekatilo? The Ice Queen? Or had it been mere happenstance that had sent a killer to her home – this morning of all mornings – when she was on the brink of fulfilling her destiny to her dark lord?

She allowed herself a tight smile as she remembered that in the works of the Great Tchar, there was no such thing as happenstance. Everything that had happened had unfolded according to his great, unfathomable designs, and no mortal could hope to divine his true purpose.

It angered her that she could have so nearly been undone by such a brutish foe. That an initiate of Tchar such as she had so very nearly been killed by a piece of filth like that...

If she had not already spent much of her power on holding the deadly corruption secure within the bronze coffin, she would have had no need to rely of the protection of Sasha Kajetan.

And it pleased Anastasia to know that her decision to free Kajetan had been proved to be part of Tchar's plan all along, though thinking of the swordsman brought a sharp frown to her face.

When Sasha had killed the other swordsman, he had dropped to his knees beside the corpse and sobbed like a baby. She had put her hand on his shoulder and said, 'There, my handsome prince. You have done your matka a great service and–'

'You are not my matka!' he had screamed, dropping his swords and surging to his feet, his face alight with anguish. His callused hands had gripped her shoulders and she saw with a shock that his normally violet eyes burned with an inner radiance, both orbs flecked with blazing winter fire.

'Oh, please no, not again...' he wailed, sliding to his knees and weeping as he saw the blood spreading from the man he had killed. 'This is not me, this is not me...'

'Sasha,' said Anastasia. 'You have to help me.'

'No!' he screamed, scrambling away from her. 'Get away from me. You are *Blyad*, woman. I see you now.'

'I am your matka!' roared Anastasia. 'And you *will* obey me!'

'My matka is dead!' shouted Kajetan, climbing to his feet and slamming his fists against his temple. 'She died a long time ago.'

Anastasia had stepped forward, but Kajetan had fled deeper into the house and she had no time to hunt him down. Whoever had arranged this morning's violence would soon realise their assassin had failed and wheels would be set in motion that would drive events beyond her control.

There was no time to waste, and so she had immediately gone down to the icy cellar through the iron door in the hallway and awkwardly dragged the coffin up the curling stairs. The coffin was heavy, but eventually she was able to haul it into her house's rear courtyard and lift one end onto the back of a cart. Gasping in exhaustion, she finally loaded her deadly cargo onto the cart and leaned against its iron-rimmed wheel.

When she had her breath back, she led two of her horses from their stalls and hitched them to the trace. One horse was missing from the stalls and she shrugged, guessing that Sasha Kajetan must have taken it.

Where would he go, she wondered, but dismissed the thought as irrelevant? She could not worry about that now. Kajetan was a rogue element best forgotten, and, pausing only to retrieve her white cloak from the house, she set out into the streets of Kislev.

At last she saw the high towers of the city walls ahead of her and turned from the Goromadny Prospekt into the main esplanade of the gateway. The gates were open and she hauled back on the reins as she approached, the armoured men standing with their long axes bared smiling and waving to her as they saw her brilliant white cloak.

Anastasia forced herself to smile back as they wished her a good morning, hearing herself mouth banal pleasantries in reply as she passed beneath the shadow of the gateway to emerge onto the crest of the hill upon which Kislev sprawled.

The cart rumbled across the timber bridge over the moat and she turned off the main roadway onto the rutted tracks that led towards the encampments of the allied armies. Hundreds of morning cookfires and thousands of tents filled the steppe plain before Kislev and she felt a thrilling excitement build inside her at the thought of the charnel house this place would soon become.

Nearly twenty-five thousand soldiers and perhaps another ten thousand refugees were camped around the base of the *Gora Geroyev*, the Hill of Heroes.

Soon it would be known as the Hill of the Dead.

The track angled downwards and she leaned back on her seat, hearing the good-natured shouts of welcome from hundreds of soldiers' throats as they recognised her. The sounds of the camp surrounded her, the clatter of pots as cooks prepared food for the hungry soldiers, the wailing of children, the barking of dogs and the whinny of horses.

Soon there would be nothing but the silence of the grave.

An ad hoc square had been cleared at the base of the hill, where generals and boyarin gave speeches to rouse their soldiers, and it was at this spot she finally halted the cart.

Anastasia pulled on the reins and climbed down to the mud, digging a rusted bronze key from her cloak and making her way to the back of the cart.

She slid the key into the first padlock that secured the coffin shut. As the key turned, the padlock crumbled to umber dust and a breath of corruption, like the death rattle of a thousand corpses, sighed from the coffin.

Taking an instant to savour the moment, Anastasia smiled as the sun finally began breaking through the early morning clouds and burning away the low ground mist.

It was going to be a beautiful day.

* * *

X

KASPAR DRAGGED ON the reins, swerving to avoid a burly Kossar waving his axe as they approached the gates. He and the Knights Panther had ridden their horses almost into the ground as they raced through the streets of Kislev. Kaspar prayed they would be in time to avert whatever terror Anastasia planned to unleash.

The Kossars waved at them to stop, but Kaspar had neither the time nor the inclination to waste his breath on them now. He rode past the Kislevite soldiers, galloping hard for the open gateway, his knights following close behind with wild yells at the confused Kislevites.

They rode out onto the cold, windswept expanse of the *Gora Geroyev* and Kaspar stood tall in the stirrups, desperately seeking any sign of where Anastasia might have gone. He turned the air blue with his oaths, unable to see her and felt a terrible powerlessness.

Kaspar kicked back his spurs and rode over to a group of red and gold liveried arquebusiers who sat beside a flickering cookfire brewing some soldiers' harsh-tasting tea.

'The White Lady of Kislev! Have you seen her?' he shouted.

'Aye,' replied a Talabecland sergeant, pointing to the base of the hill. 'The good lady headed down that way, sir.'

'How long ago?' demanded Kaspar, wheeling his horse.

'A few minutes ago, no more.'

Kaspar nodded his thanks and raked back his spurs, risking life and limb as he thundered downhill, barely avoiding pockets of soldiers, camp followers and rocks in his mad rush. He shouted at people to get out of his way and left angry yells and curses in his wake as the knights followed him, their passage made easier by the ambassador's frenetic ride.

He reined in Magnus and again stood high in the stirrups, twisting left and right.

Kaspar's heart raced as he finally saw her, a few hundred yards away, her white cloak a beacon amidst the muddiness of the campsite. She stood at the back of a small cart, a coffin of bronze glinting in the sunlight.

'Kurt!' he yelled, pointing to the bottom of the hill. 'With me!'

He whipped Magnus hard and leaned low in the saddle as he guided his mount through the crowded camp towards Anastasia.

She turned as he drew near, hearing the thunder of horsemen approaching her, and Kaspar was left in no doubt that she had been the architect of his woes as she smiled at him with a predatory coquettishness.

'I knew you would come,' she said as he dismounted from his panting horse.

'Whatever that thing is,' begged Kaspar, pointing to the rusted coffin, 'I beg you not to open it.'

There were only two padlocks securing it shut and Kaspar could feel a terrifying threat emanating from within.

'Begging, Kaspar?' laughed Anastasia. 'I thought that was beneath you. You were always so proud, but I think maybe that was what made you so easy to manipulate.'

'Anastasia,' said Kaspar as the Knights Panther dismounted and a crowd of curious onlookers began gathering around the unfolding drama. 'Don't do it.'

'It is too late, Kaspar. This is corrupting entropy given physical form and such a beauteous thing cannot be kept confined for long, it must be allowed free rein to do what it was created to do.'

'Why, Anastasia? Why are you doing this?'

Anastasia smiled at him. 'These are the last days, Kaspar. Don't you feel it? The Lord of the End Times walks the earth and this world is ready to fall to Chaos. If you knew what awaits these lands at the hands of Lord Archaon, you would drop to your knees and beg me to open this coffin.'

'You would kill everyone here, Anastasia?' asked Kaspar. 'There are thousands of people here. Innocents. Women and children. Are you really such a monster?'

'I would kill everyone here a dozen times over for Tchar!' laughed Anastasia and turned her back on him, slipping a key into the coffin's penultimate padlock.

Kaspar dragged out his pistols and aimed them at her back.

She cocked her head as she heard the click of the flintlocks.

'Anastasia, please! Don't do this.'

Kaspar saw her turn the key and the padlock crumbled to powder. Seething horror seeped from the coffin lid and the crowds surrounding them began muttering in fear as they felt the malign power strain at its confinement.

'Stop. Please stop this,' pleaded Kaspar, the pistols trembling in his hands.

'You cannot do it, can you?' said Anastasia without turning. 'You're not able to murder me in cold blood. It is not in your nature.'

She placed the key in the last lock.

And Kaspar shot her in the back.

Anastasia sagged against the coffin, a neat hole blasted through her cloak.

She gripped onto the cart and struggled to face him, her face twisted in pain and disbelief.

'Kaspar...?' she gasped, and he felt something die inside him as a hateful rose of bright blood welled on her white cloak. She put a hand to her chest, her fingers coming away stained crimson.

Kaspar fell to his knees, tears blurring his vision as Anastasia fought to stay upright.

She reached for the key and Kaspar fired his second pistol into her chest, the bullet slamming her against the side of the cart and pitching her to the ground.

She dropped to the mud, her eyes glazing over in death.

And Kaspar saw that he was too late.

The last padlock fell from the coffin as a fine dust, blowing away in the deathly gust that seethed from the unlocked lid.

[illegible]

[illegible] Dun [illegible]

Kaye [illegible] his [illegible] and the [illegible]

[illegible]

[illegible]

[illegible] Kaye [illegible]

[illegible]

[illegible]

[illegible] the [illegible]

[illegible] his [illegible] pain and [illegible]

[illegible] and [illegible] something [illegible]

[illegible] piece of broken [illegible]

[illegible] hand [illegible]

[illegible]

[illegible] Kaye [illegible]

[illegible] and [illegible]

[illegible] the [illegible]

[illegible] ground

[illegible]

[illegible]

[illegible] from the [illegible]

[illegible]

CHAPTER TEN

I

LIKE THE SOFT exhalation of a drowned corpse, a low moaning issued from the coffin and wisps of a sparkling mist seeped from the gap between the lid and sides. The coffin rattled and shook with unnatural life. Snaking tendrils of iridescent mist whipped from its corrupt depths as the lid flew open and a sparkling jet of coloured light and vapour fountained from inside.

A Stirland pikeman was the first to die, the spectral light wreathing him in glittering mist that ripped the flesh from his bones as he was turned inside out by its mutating power. His scream turned to a gurgle as the collection of disembodied muscles and organs he had become collapsed in a steaming pile. Another man died as the light enveloped him and he sprouted appendages from every square inch of his flesh: arms, hands, heads and legs bursting forth from his skin in a welter of blood and splintered bone.

Everything the spreading mist of corrupt light touched warped into some new and bizarre form, men reduced to boneless, jelly-like masses of flesh, women bloating into fat, glossy skinned harpies with distended, vestigial wings. The ground itself writhed under its touch, brightly patterned grass and outlandish plants springing forth from the unnaturally fecund earth.

Kaspar backed away in horror from the coffin, which was now almost obscured by the multi-coloured spume that spread further with every passing second. Screams and cries of terror spread before its mutating power and he cursed himself for not firing sooner.

He and his knights ran for their horses, but Kaspar had no intention of riding away from this hellish power. He knew what he planned would destroy him and just hoped that more people would be able to outpace this daemon-spawned power before it killed every living soul.

The knights climbed into their saddles and Kaspar watched them ride off with heavy heart. They had served him faithfully and he had not had time to tell them how honoured he had been to have them with him in Kislev. The corrupting light was almost upon him and he wondered if he would even be able to reach the coffin and close it before its power turned him into some hellish abomination. Would closing it even stop it?

He didn't know, but he had to try.

Shapes writhed in the misty light and Kaspar gave thanks that he could not see them clearly, their piteous cries of agony tearing at his heart. Monstrous silhouettes thrashed in their agonies and mutated beasts that had once been men gorged themselves on the flesh of the dead.

Kaspar reached his horse and climbed into the saddle, twisting as he heard the beat of hooves coming towards him and someone shout his name. He searched for the source of the shout and saw Sasha Kajetan riding around the colourful light towards him. He grabbed for his pistols before realising that he had fired both of them, and reached for his sword.

Kicking his feet from the stirrups, Kajetan leapt from the saddle and crashed into the ambassador. The two men slammed into the ground, the breath driven from Kaspar's lungs by the impact. He rolled onto his side and tried to pick himself up, but fell as his knee gave out under him.

Kajetan stood above him, and Kaspar could not help but shudder at the ruin of a man he had become. Gone was the fierce, proud swordsman and in his place, a wasted, desperate creature of pain and misery. Kaspar managed to pull himself to his knees with a grunt of pain and unsheathed his blade, saying, 'Stay back, Kajetan,' as the dazzling mist crept forwards.

'Ambassador von Velten...' hissed Kajetan, and Kaspar could see that the swordsman was badly injured. Rejak obviously did not die without a giving a good account of himself.

The swordsman stared at the rainbow-streaked froth that bubbled from the coffin and said, 'I told you there was thing I was yet to do.'

'We don't have time for this, Kajetan. I have to stop this,' said Kaspar, brandishing his sword before him.

'I told you there was thing I was yet to do,' repeated the swordsman, as though Kaspar had not spoken. 'And I told you that it involved you.'

The swordsman looked away from the ambassador as he heard an approaching horseman. 'No time,' he said and reached for Kaspar.

Kaspar roared and thrust with his sword, the blade plunging into Kajetan's belly and ripping from his back. Blood burst from the wound and the swordsman grunted, hammering his fist against the ambassador's jaw. Kaspar dropped, but Kajetan dragged him to his feet and thrust his unresisting body towards the knight who galloped towards him with a roar of fury.

Kurt Bremen had ridden back as soon as he had realised that the ambassador had not fled with them and reined in his horse with his sword raised to strike Kajetan down.

'You!' gasped Kajetan, 'take him and get him out of here!'

Taken aback, Bremen lowered his weapon when he realised what Kajetan was planning. The knight sheathed his blade, taking the ambassador from the swordsman and hauling him up behind the neck of his warhorse. He nodded his thanks towards Kajetan, watching in amazement as the man climbed into the saddle of his own horse, Kaspar's sword still lodged deep in his belly.

'I said go!' shouted Kajetan before riding hard towards the hellish epicentre of the brightly coloured nightmare.

* * *

II

THE PAIN THREATENED to overwhelm him, but Sasha held it in check as he rode through the scintillating fog of light. Creatures that had once been human thrashed and mewed piteously all around him; wild fronds of ever-changing plant matter whipping from the ground and a breathless fertility saturating the air itself.

His breath writhed with life as the power of change seized it, flickering like tiny fireflies in front of him. Briefly he wondered what black miracles and dark wonders might be worked with his other bodily fluids: his spit, his blood or his seed.

He could feel his horse stagger beneath him as the corrupting power overtook it. Rippling bulges seethed from the beast's flanks and it screamed as ungainly, feathered wings burst from its body, malformed and gelatinous. The horse tripped and fell, throwing him from its back as it thrashed in pain. He hit the ground hard and rolled, crying in agony as the sword blade jammed in his body twisted and cut him wider.

Sasha ripped it free and hurled it aside, falling to his knees as the pain surged around his body. Blood flooded from the wound and he knew he had only moments at best. Obscene flowers rippled from the ground where his blood fell, each one with the face of his matka, and he pushed himself upright.

He swayed and limped towards the cart bearing the coffin, dazzling lights bursting before his eyes, but he couldn't be sure if it was death reaching out to finally claim him or the power within the coffin. A blinding corona of light surrounded it and he had to shield his eyes as he climbed onto the cart and stared into its depths.

He was not surprised to see a body in the coffin, but this was one with veins that ran with fire and eyes shining with the light at the centre of creation. He felt the powerful magicks that had gone into this thing's creation: the fell, arcane science of the underfolk and the dark sorcery of Chaos.

The eyes rolled in their sockets, fixing him with a gaze that contained everything that had or might one day exist in the world. He felt himself stripped bare by its power, the flesh blackening on his bones as it consumed him. But he had one last gift for this world, one last way to achieve the atonement he craved.

His stomach heaved and he leaned forward to stare into the burning eyes of the writhing corpse of light. Its slack jaw opened and its breath was creation itself.

But if its breath was creation, his was destruction, and he spewed a froth of his deadly black vomit across its face. The light was blotted out as the viscous black liquid ate away at the corpse, burning it and melting it to stinking matter. Its malice screamed in his head, but he knew it was powerless to prevent its ending.

Sasha's world was pain as his body burned with the power of raw magics fleeing the corpse's dissolution, but he kept the black vomit coming, emptying himself before finally collapsing onto the sloshing remains.

His chest hiked and he tried to move, but there was nothing left of him.

The swordsman smiled as he saw a vision of radiant light growing from behind a slowly opening gateway. He reached out to touch the light.

And all the pain and the guilt and the terror and the anger and the trueself were swept away, leaving nothing but Sasha Kajetan, his matka's handsome prince.

There was nothing left to do.

He could die now.

III

THE DEVASTATION UNLEASHED by Anastasia Vilkova accounted for three hundred and seventy souls, most of whom were lucky to have perished in the opening moments of the swirling maelstrom. Other, less fortunate victims, were later shot down by weeping arquebusiers or otherwise put out of their misery by horrified pikemen.

Still other creatures, vile mutated abominations fled to the steppe to howl at the moon and stars in loathing for what they had become. The site of the carnage became a reviled place and within the hour that part of the camp had been forsaken, its tents left standing and every possession abandoned. No one had dared approach the wrecked cart that lay at the centre of the abandoned place, and during the night a freak ice storm of terrifying magnitude swept across the blighted ground, obliterating everything still alive, the grass, the unnatural plants and wiping away the taint of Chaos.

By morning, only a crystalline wilderness remained, and whatever had begun the terrifying events of the previous morning was now buried forever beneath an unyielding layer of imperishable ice.

It was a fitting tomb for Sasha Kajetan, thought Kaspar. A place where he would never again be tormented by the daemons of his past or those conjured within him by others.

Despite all that had happened, he could not bring himself to hate Sasha – a man who had twice saved his life. Sofia was right: Kajetan had not been born a monster, but made into one, and if his last act as a human being had been to save thousands of lives... well, that was redemption enough for Kaspar.

As to how that redemption balanced with the atrocities he had committed as the Butcherman, he didn't know, but Kaspar hoped that Sasha had at least earned a chance at absolution in the next world.

He turned away from the icy graveyard, knowing that Anastasia's body was also buried beneath the ice forever and felt the peculiar mixture of anger, sadness and guilt that came whenever he thought of her. She had been about to kill tens of thousands of people, but that didn't make the fact that he had shot a woman in the back any easier to deal with. Kaspar knew he had done the right thing, but he would never forget the look of hurt and disbelief in her eyes as she fell to the ground.

Though Kaspar had not seen the swordsman's last ride into the deadly mist of light, Bremen had told him later how there had been a final blaze of energy in the midst of the shining fog before it had quickly faded away to nothing. Whatever

Kajetan had done to stop it from killing everyone was a mystery that Kaspar supposed might never be solved.

He guided his horse towards the city, riding slowly through the mass of soldiers preparing to march northwards to meet a terrible enemy. Soldiers saluted as he passed, word of his new rank having spread quickly through the regiments. Though he still wore the black and gold of Nuln, he had caparisoned Magnus in the green and yellow of Stirland to show his men that he was now one of them.

At a gathering of the senior surviving officers of the Empire forces, he had again made his offer to take command of the leaderless Stirland army. Spitzaner had made his objections plain, but with no one else capable of handling a force of such size, his words carried little weight.

It was a simple fact of war that there were those who made brilliant regimental commanders, but floundered at higher levels of command, or men who could direct the forces of an entire province, but who had no idea of how to give orders to a battalion. Within the armies of the Empire, it was common for most men who attained command to settle at their level of competency and thus far, no one but Kaspar had volunteered to take the reins of command.

The idea of leading men into battle once more sent a thrill of anticipation through him, and though he knew it was foolish and he would regret it the moment the first blood was shed, he found himself – like a new recruit – eager for battle. To reach Urszebya before the High Zar, the allied forces marched at dawn the following day; the Stirland army, which he would lead, the Talabecland army of Clemenz Spitzaner and the Kislev pulk that would fight with the Ice Queen at its head.

Twenty-five thousand fighting men, now known by the soldiers as the Urszebya pulk, to face a rumoured forty thousand. Boyarin Kurkosk was marching east with nearly twenty thousand warriors, but it was unlikely he would arrive before battle was joined, and there was no time to wait for him.

If they defeated the High Zar's army, it would be the most spectacular victory since the Great War against Chaos. But if they lost…

Kaspar still did not fully understand what power might rest within the standing stones at Urszebya, but the Kislevites obviously felt they were important enough to risk open battle with much larger force.

There was a glorious madness to all this, but Kaspar knew full well the reality of what they were marching towards. Blood and death, horror and loss. Cyenwulf had defeated every army that had stood against him and his force had grown larger with each victory.

It had never known defeat and stood poised to destroy them.

Kaspar was under no illusions concerning their chances of defeating the High Zar.

Pavel had said that people would tell tales of their bravery as far away as Magritta and Kaspar believed him.

He just hoped they were not tales of lament.

IV

THE ENTIRETY OF the embassy guards stood to attention outside the iron fence, ready to march to the city gates and join the Urszebya pulk. None of them were obliged to join the pulk, but upon returning to the embassy the previous evening, Kaspar had been met by a determined Leopold Dietz, who had spoken of his men's desire to march north with the ambassador. They had sworn an oath when they accepted the posting to Kislev to protect the ambassador's life, and they could not very well do that by remaining in the city, could they?

Kaspar had proudly accepted their offer and in turn allowed Leopold Dietz the honour of carrying the ambassador's banner. They had shaken hands, and together, his guards and Knights Panther awaited the order to march. The knights were glorious, their armour polished to a mirror sheen and their purple and gold gonfalon raised high by Valdhaas. Their mounts were fresh and clean, their caparisons bright and colourful. It was an honour to command such fine warriors.

He himself wore a practical quilted jerkin in the gold and black of Nuln with an unadorned breastplate, vambrace and cuissart. His clothes were fresh and practical, for at least a ten day march lay ahead of the Urszebya pulk before it would reach the valley of Ursun's Teeth. Wrapped in a red, gold and black pashmina of thick furs, Sofia was quiet as he tightened Magnus's girth. Her auburn hair hung loose around her shoulders and she wore an expression of barely-controlled anxiety.

'In Kislev it is customary to mourn those who ride to war as already dead,' she said as Kaspar finished preparing his horse.

'I'd heard that,' said Kaspar. 'A rather morbid practice I had always thought.'

Sofia nodded. 'Yes, so that's why I am not going to do it. I will pray for your return with each morning.'

'Thank you, that means a lot to me, Sofia,' said Kaspar, taking her hand.

She dropped her head and said, 'We never had any time, did we?'

'No, we didn't,' agreed Kaspar sadly. 'But when we defeat the High Zar's army, I will return for you.'

'You truly believe you can defeat him?' asked Sofia.

'Yes, I do,' lied Kaspar.

The lie came hard to him, but he could see the need for hope in her eyes and though it went against everything he believed in, he told it rather than spoil this last moment.

Sofia nodded and the relief in her eyes made Kaspar want to weep. She reached up and unclasped her pendant, taking Kaspar's hand and placing it in his upturned palm.

She had worn it at the Tzarina's victory dinner, a smooth blue stone wrapped in a web of silver wire, and Kaspar was touched by the simple affection of the gesture.

'Keep it next to your heart,' she said.

'I will, thank you,' he promised. He wanted to say more, but could not think of anything that would not sound trite or overly melodramatic. He could see Sofia was on the verge of tears and ached to take her in his arms and tell her that he would be fine, that he would come back and see what they might have together, but could not force the words to come.

Instead he simply embraced her and said, 'I will see you in my dreams.'

She nodded and wiped her eyes on the hem of her pashmina as Kaspar turned and climbed into the saddle.

As he lifted the reins, Sofia said, 'Promise you will come back to me.'

'I promise,' he said, though he wondered if this was a promise he could keep.

Sofia smiled sadly and stepped back as he rode through the gate to the head of the Knights Panther. He saluted in proud respect to the warriors assembled around him.

He raised his arm and signalled the advance, turning for one last look at Sofia, but she was nowhere to be seen, the door to the embassy already closed behind her.

V

THE TRIP NORTHWARD into the oblast was much easier than the last time Kaspar had made such a journey. Winter was in retreat, though snow still lay deep on the ground and the wind cut though even the thickest furs. The Urszebya pulk made good time through the wilderness, wild Ungol horsemen riding far ahead of the soldiers, scouting for any signs of the High Zar's army.

They marched through the vast expanse of the oblast, the sky a wondrous, stark blue and the hardy steppe grass providing patches of colour amid the patchy whiteness of the landscape. The sense of a land coming to life was palpable, thought Kaspar, as though it had lain dormant through the long, dark months of winter and was now waking to flaunt its savage beauty. This was wild country, saturated with a sense of ancient passions and primal emotions, and, coming from this untamed land, Kaspar found it easy to imagine how the Kislevites had become the people they were.

Over the course of their march, Kaspar had made a point of getting to know the officers who would be serving under him, needing to know their strengths, their weaknesses and their character. They were men of quality, men with the look of eagles, who he would be proud to fight alongside when the time came. They had fought two major battles recently and were hungry for more.

Some officers talked of the Ostland halberdiers and how its men were lucky to be going home, but that they would envy the honour to be won on the field of battle. Each time Kaspar heard the missing regiment mentioned, he felt a great guilt weigh heavily upon him, for that had been the regiment he had signed over to Chekatilo when he had thought Anastasia's life was in danger. He had chosen them because there was barely a hundred of them and they had been in Kislev for nearly a year, trapped in the north following the massacre at Zhedevka. Kaspar imagined that they would have been only too glad to be able to return to the Empire, but that did not assuage his guilt.

After the chaos of Anastasia's attempt to destroy the Urszebya pulk, Kaspar and Bremen had ridden to the *Chekist* and told Vladimir Pashenko every detail of the past six months. Together, they had scoured the city for Chekatilo, but to no avail. The giant Kislevite was gone. The Ostland halberdiers were gone with him and every one of his haunts the *Chekist* knew of was abandoned.

No men could be spared to hunt Chekatilo down and Kaspar was forced to accept that the bastard would probably escape the executioner's axe he so richly deserved. It irked his sense of honour that Chekatilo would not pay for what he had done, but he knew there was nothing he could do about it any more.

Every night as the pulk camped, Kaspar went round the fires of the soldiers, telling them tall tales of his previous battles and sharing food and drink with them. It was exhausting work, but his men had to know him, to get a sense for the man whose orders might well send them to their deaths.

On the morning of the twelfth day of march, as winter's last gasp of snow began to fall, the outriders brought word of Cyenwulf's army. If they were to believed, and Kaspar had no reason to doubt their word, the High Zar was less than two days from the mouth of the valley.

A nervous anticipation spread throughout the pulk as word of their foe spread, but on his nightly tour of the army, Kaspar was pleased to note the quiet courage his soldiers displayed. These men had fought and defeated the armies of the dreaded northmen before, and they would do so again. Kaspar told them he was proud of them and that the storytellers of Altdorf would tell tales of them for hundreds of years.

The snow continued to fall throughout the day and as the sun climbed to its zenith the Urszebya pulk reached the valley of its name. The land hereabouts was harsher than the steppe and in the distance through the snow, Kaspar could see twin scarps of rock rising sharply from the ground, forming a wide cut in the landscape.

A deepening valley sloped into the steppe, it sides steep and composed of a dark, striated rock. Distant cheers filtered back to him from the vanguard as they reached the valley mouth and Kaspar's gaze was drawn up to the summit of the valley sides.

Though still many miles away, Kaspar could see a jagged black spike of rock, the first of the tall menhirs that ran the length of the valley and gave it its name.

Urszebya. Ursun's Teeth.

The rugged beauty of the land was stunning and Kaspar knew he had never seen anything quite like it. But his wonder at its splendour was touched with regret for he knew that this was the last time he would look upon the valley in this way.

Today it was beautiful, but tomorrow it would be a hateful blood-soaked battlefield.

VI

THE SKY WAS turning to a bruised purple as Kaspar and Kurt Bremen made their way to the billowing, sky-blue pavilion of the Ice Queen. Despite the bitter cold and lightly falling snow, the Tzarina's guards who surrounded the giant tent were bare chested, displaying no outward signs of any discomfort. They collected weapons from every man who entered the pavilion, taking no chances with their queen's safety after the attack at the Winter Palace.

Kaspar surrendered his pistols and sword and Bremen unbuckled his sword belt. A giant warrior with long daggers sheathed through the skin of his pectoral muscles and a tall coxcomb of stiffened hair pulled back the pavilion's opening to allow them entry.

Inside, Empire officers and Kislevite boyarin were gathered around a roaring firepit where another of the Tzarina's guards turned a roasting boar on a long spit. Sweet-smelling smoke was vented through a central hole in the roof of the pavilion, and the crackling aroma of roasting meat made Kaspar's mouth water.

Tables and chairs formed of rippling waves of ice rose up from the ground and the supports for the pavilion were tall columns of fluted snow. The Tzarina sat on her golden throne, regal in a sparkling gown of icy cream. Despite the rigours of a twelve day march, the Ice Queen looked as immaculate as ever, and Kaspar wondered how much effort it took her to maintain such appearances.

But as he looked at the adoring faces of her boyarin, he knew it was not mere vanity that made her appear so ostentatious, but necessity. To her subjects, the Ice Queen was a beloved figure of aloof, regal majesty and to see her in anything less than the most delicate finery would be an anathema to them.

Clemenz Spitzaner and his coterie of staff stood as close as they were able to the Ice Queen, and Kaspar nodded in acknowledgement to his fellow general. Spitzaner bowed stiffly, still unhappy with Kaspar's presence, but having enough presence of mind not to create any kind of fuss about it.

Kaspar greeted his fellow Stirland officers and accepted a glass of Estalian brandy from a passing servant. He sipped the brandy, enjoying its fiery warmth in his belly.

'This is a civilised way to fight a war,' he said, raising his glass to Kurt Bremen.

The knight nodded and poured himself a glass of water from a jug shaped from sparkling ice. Boyarin of all description milled around the tent, helping themselves to meat cut from the boar and making loud boasts of the glory they would earn on the morrow. Kaspar saw the Tilean, Albertalli, across the fire and raised his glass in salute.

The mercenary general smiled broadly and raised his own glass, making his way around the fire to stand beside Kaspar and Bremen.

'General von Velten,' he said. 'It is good to see you again. It fill me with hope to know a man of your reputation fights alongside us.'

'My compliments to you, general,' replied Kaspar. 'I have heard good things about your soldiers while marching here. They say your men held the line at Krasicyno for five hours against the Kurgans.'

Albertalli smiled modestly. 'Actually, it more like three, but, yes, my soldiers are good boys, fight hard and well. They will do same tomorrow, count on that.'

'I will,' promised Kaspar. 'We will have need of warriors who can stand fast in the face of such brutality as the High Zar will unleash.'

'Yes,' agreed Albertalli. 'It will be grim work tomorrow.'

'Isn't it always?' said Kaspar as the Ice Queen rose from her throne and began circling the firepit. Conversations died away and all eyes turned to face her as she spoke.

'Kislev is land and land is Kislev,' she said.

'Kislev is land and land is Kislev,' repeated the assembled boyarin.

The Ice Queen smiled and said, 'Look about you, my friends. Look at the faces of the men around you and remember them. Remember them. Tomorrow these will be the men who you will be fighting alongside and upon whom all our fates depend. For we are about a great and terrible business now. I can feel the ebb and flow of the land beneath me and it cries out against the touch of Chaos. If we fail here, then the land we hold dear will pass away, never to return, and all that we once knew will be destroyed.'

Every man in the pavilion was silent as the Ice Queen passed, the crackle of sizzling fat as it dripped into the fire the only sound that disturbed the silence. The chill of the Ice Queen's passing prickled Kaspar's skin as she spoke once more.

'Tomorrow we stand before a foe many times our number. The High Zar brings warriors drunk on slaughter and victory, monsters from our worst nightmares and a creature from the dawn of the world. I have felt its every tread on the land and now it comes here to destroy us all. And make no mistake, without your courage and strength, it will succeed.

'The strength of Kislev lies in you all. The land has called you all here and it is here that you will put that strength to the test in defiance of Chaos. There is power in this land and tomorrow it will run in all of your veins. Use it well.'

'We will, my queen,' said a Kislevite boyarin solemnly.

Clemenz Spitzaner spoke next, saying, 'Tomorrow we will march out from this valley and together we will destroy this barbarian,' and raising his glass in a toast. Heavy silence greeted his words and the Ice Queen turned to face the Empire general.

'General Spitzaner,' she said. 'I think you must have misunderstood me. March from the valley? No, we will not be marching anywhere, we will make our stand right here at the end of the valley.'

'What?' spluttered Spitzaner. 'Your majesty, I would counsel against such a stratagem.'

'It is too late for any other plan, General Spitzaner. The decision has been made.'

Kaspar frowned, seeing that some of the boyarin were equally unsettled at the prospect of fighting within the rocky valley. He stepped forward and said. 'Your majesty, I think General Spitzaner's belief that we would fight the High Zar on the steppe is shared by a great many of us. While it is true that this valley has a number of tactical advantages, it has one flaw that perhaps you have not been made aware of.'

'Not aware of, General von Velten?' said the Ice Queen. 'Then pray enlighten me.'

'There is only one way in or out of this valley,' said Kaspar. 'If we are defeated, there is nowhere to retreat to. We would be destroyed to a man.'

'Then we must endeavour not to be defeated, yes?'

'Of course, but the fact remains that we might be.'

'Do you trust me, General von Velten?'

'It is not a matter of trust, it–'

'It is *all* about trust, Kaspar von Velten. You of all people should know that.'

Kaspar felt her icy gaze upon him and realised that she was right. In battle, everything came down to moments of trust. Trust in the steel of the man next to you, trust that the officers beneath you carry out their orders, trust that the courage of the army will hold and trust that those who commanded knew what they were doing. This was such a moment, and Kaspar willingly surrendered to what the Ice Queen planned, feeling her acceptance of his trust as a cold, but not unpleasant shiver.

'Very well,' he said solemnly, 'if the Ice Queen of Kislev wishes to make her stand here, then the army of Stirland will do so as well. We will not fail you.'

The Ice Queen smiled and said, 'I have faith in you, General von Velten. Thank you.'

Kaspar bowed as General Spitzaner said, 'Your majesty, please. Regardless of what Herr von Velten says, I have grave doubts concerning this plan.'

'General Spitzaner,' said the Ice Queen. 'The decision has been made and there is no other way. We will fight together or we will be destroyed. It is that simple.'

Kaspar could see Spitzaner was angry at having been so manoeuvred, but to his credit, he knew not to cast further doubt on the Tzarina's plan in front of brother officers.

He bowed stiffly and said, 'Then the army of Talabecland will be proud to fight alongside you.'

'Thank you, General Spitzaner,' said the Ice Queen, as a servant handed her an icy glass of brandy.

'To victory!' she shouted, draining the brandy and hurling the glass into the fire.

Every man in the pavilion bellowed the same words and threw their glasses into the fire. Flames shot high into the air, mirroring the passion burning in their warrior hearts.

'Death or glory,' said Kurt Bremen offering Kaspar his hand in the warrior's grip, wrist to wrist.

'Death or glory,' agreed Kaspar, taking Bremen's hand. 'Is of no matter...'

CHAPTER ELEVEN

I

KASPAR WATCHED THE sun climb higher into the dawn sky, wondering if this was the last morning he would see. The screams of the Ungol horsemen captured by the enemy during the night had mercifully ceased, to be replaced by the braying of tribal horns.

Scraps of mist clung to the ground and Kaspar could see that the leaden sky promised more snow. His knee ached with the cold and he was glad that his rank gave him the right to go into battle on horseback. From his position at the end of the valley he could see the awe-inspiring sight of thousands of soldiers filling the valley before him: pikemen, halberdiers, archers, Kossars, swordsmen and knights in silver and bronze armour. Colourful banners flapped noisily in the cold wind blowing from the valley mouth and Kaspar felt proud to be leading these fine men into battle.

Hundreds of horses whinnied and stamped their hooves, aggravated by the presence of so many soldiers and the scent of the terrible creatures that marched with the army of the High Zar. Knights from the Empire calmed their steeds with stern words while Kislevite lancers mounted on horses painted in the colours of war secured feathered banners to their saddles. Black-robed members of the Kislevite priesthood circulated amongst the soldiers, blessing axes, lances and swords as they went, while warrior priests of Sigmar read aloud from the *Canticle of the Heldenhammer*.

He could hear a distant vibration through the cold ground, the tramp, tramp, tramp of tens of thousands of approaching warriors. The morning mist conspired to hide them from view for now, and Kaspar just hoped that it would lift soon to enable the cannons and bombards placed on the crest of the valley to fire. He yawned, amazed he could feel so tired and yet so tense, and thought back to his dream of the previous night.

He had seen a twin-tailed comet blazing across the heavens and a young man fighting a host of twisted creatures that bore the bestial features of animals yet walked upright like men. With a pair of blacksmiths' hammers, this young man had smote the beasts and Kaspar's heart had swelled with fierce joy.

But then his dreamscape had moved on, and he had seen the Empire in flames, its cities cast to ruin and its populace burned to death in the fires of Chaos.

It was an omen, of that he was sure, but for good or ill, he did not know.

Kurt Bremen and the red and blue liveried embassy guards surrounded him, his gold and black standard carried by Leopold Dietz. A dozen young men on horseback waited behind him, runners who would carry his orders to the regimental captains on the front line.

A magnificent-looking troop of Kislevite lancers, their feathered banner poles whistling in the wind, rode past and Kaspar saw Pavel at their head, his vast frame carried on an equally massive steed. Red and white pennants fluttered from their lances and each carried a quiver of iron-tipped javelins slung from their saddle horns.

He had shared a mug of tea with Pavel this morning to say their goodbyes and silently wished his former comrade luck as he passed out of sight behind a block of Kossar infantry. The tall, burly men were laughing and joking while smoking pipes and resting on their axes. Kaspar admired their calm.

Regiments of infantry covered the gently sloping plain before him, the Empire armies holding the centre of the line, thousands of men in huge blocks sixty wide and forty deep. Kaspar and Spitzaner had arranged their forces in a staggered formation, each regiment able to support another, with smaller units of arquebusiers and spearmen attached to every one. Individually, each regiment was a strong fighting unit, but working together, they were amongst the steadiest soldiers in the world.

Knights of both Kislev and the Empire sat on the flanks of the army and ahead of them, galloping groups of yelling Ungol horsemen and the light cavalry of the Empire were strung out in front of the main body of the army. When the time came to unleash them, they would harry the flanks of the enemy in an attempt to draw off warriors from the main attack.

High on the ridge behind him, braziers smoked behind gabion-edged firing pits, dug from the frozen ground by Imperial pioneers during the night. The bronze barrels of the mighty cannons and bombards of the Imperial Gunnery School protruded from the emplacements, frustrated engineers wandering along the edge of the ridge, desperate for the mist to rise.

The Ice Queen herself rode a white horse with shimmering flanks of sparkling ice and eyes like the bluest of sapphires. Her loyal guards surrounded her and she carried Fearfrost already drawn. Her cloak of swirling ice crystals hugged her tight and a ghostly mist gathered around the feet of her mount. She turned to Kaspar and raised her sword in salute to him before looking expectantly at the tall black stones atop the valley sides.

Kaspar followed her gaze, seeing the great standing stones that gave this valley its name and hoped that the Ice Queen was right to risk everything for them.

A swelling roar built from the mouth of the valley, guttural chanting from the High Zar's warriors that echoed in time with the clash of their swords and axes on iron-bossed shields.

'So it begins...' said Kaspar.

* * *

II

THE WIND PICKED up as the sun climbed higher and within minutes of the Kurgan horns being blown, the morning mist vanished and the enemy they had been preparing to fight all winter was suddenly revealed.

A line of armoured warriors stretched from one side of the valley to the other, their black furs, horned helmets and dark armour making them look more like beasts than men. They marched in a loose line, no discipline to their advance as screaming horsemen wearing nothing but furred britches and swirling tattoos streamed forwards. Packs of snapping hounds with long fangs and furry hides stiffened with matted blood ran forwards with the horsemen, their baying howls chilling the blood.

Wild horns skirled in time with their screams, but were soon drowned out as the Imperial guns opened fire. Kaspar watched as a cannonball slammed into the ground before the enemy and slashed a path through the densely packed warriors. Blood sprayed as men were smashed to a red mist by the missile, but within seconds, they had closed ranks and continued onwards. A rippling series of booms sounded and yet more bloody furrows were torn through the enemy warriors.

Kaspar felt a great pride in the men of Nuln as they loaded and fired again and again, sending iron cannonballs slashing into the enemy and huge shells that exploded in the air and sprayed them with lethally sharp fragments of red hot shrapnel. Men and horses screamed as the fearsome Imperial artillery killed them in their hundreds.

But Kaspar knew that guns alone would not win this fight as the artillery positions were once more wreathed in smoke. The wind was favouring the gunners, blowing the roiling banks of smoke behind their positions and allowing them to better target their victims.

'Those horsemen are getting too close,' he muttered to himself.

The tattooed riders galloping ahead of the enemy army stood high in the saddle, their trailing topknots streaming out behind them as they rode in close before expertly wheeling their mounts away. Each time, they would loose shafts from their powerful, recurved bows and each time a dozen men or more would fall to the ground, pierced by black fletched arrows.

They rode in again and again, tempting the warriors they fired on to charge them, but Kaspar and Spitzaner had issued clear orders that these horsemen were not to be engaged. Scattered gunfire from arquebusier regiments felled a number of the wild men, but they left behind few dead when they finally pulled away.

But as the horsemen retreated, the baying hounds hit the Imperial line. Few had fallen to the black powder weapons and they attacked in a fury of claw and fang. Those regiments attacked shuddered as men were torn from their feet, but the majority of the hounds were soon despatched by disciplined ranks of lowered halberds. Drummer boys began dragging the wounded back as the remaining soldiers closed ranks.

The black line of enemy warriors kept coming, hordes of them, and Kaspar felt a shiver of fear as he grasped the sheer scale of the High Zar's force. They came in a never ending tide of black iron and horns. Monstrous men in thick furs and brazen axes and swords. Hordes of armoured warriors on horseback rode alongside the infantry, their black steeds snorting and pawing the ground in anticipation of bloodshed. Their riders were giants of men, carrying huge-bladed war axes and pallaszes and Kaspar feared for when these awesome killers entered the fray.

A pair of massive totems on great, wheeled platforms followed them, dark idols dedicated to the terrible gods of the north. The bodies of a dozen men hung from their tops, their entrails swinging from opened bellies and feasted upon by carrion birds.

Shaggy creatures bearing enormous axes loped before these idols and hulking monsters with great clubs tramped amongst them. Three times the height of a man, these distorted creatures had oversized muscles and looked capable of tearing their victims apart with their bare hands. Something huge and dark marched before the idols, its shape indistinct and blurred, a dark umbra of lightning-pierced cloud wreathing its terrible form.

Its concealing cloud lifted and Kaspar could see the huge creature in all its terrible glory. Surely this must be the beast of ancient times the Tzarina had spoken of, a horrific monster with a dragon-like lower body of dark, leathery scales and the grotesquely muscled upper body of a man. Its torso and chest were scarred with ancient tattoos and pierced with rings and spikes of iron as thick as a man's wrist. A mane of shaggy fur ran from its crown to where its body became that of a monster. Lightning flickered around its grotesque head and huge tusks protruded from its enormous jaws.

'Sigmar preserve us,' whispered Kaspar.

'Amen to that,' added Kurt Bremen and Kaspar was surprised to hear fear in the Knight Panther's voice.

A host of armoured chariots rumbled through the army, the chanting warriors and beasts parting before their advance. Cruel, hooked blades protruded from the wheels of the chariots and Kaspar shuddered at the havoc he knew they would wreak amongst the Imperial soldiers.

He tore his gaze from the huge monster at the centre of the High Zar's army and turned to one of his runners, saying, 'Send my compliments to Captain Goscik, and order him to fire on those damned chariots as soon as he can. Tell him to aim low, I want the horses pulling them shot down.'

The runner nodded in understanding and galloped off as the distant crackle of musketry intensified. Arquebusiers fired rippling volleys of lead bullets into the advancing horde and soon the valley was filled with acrid, drifting smoke.

A huge roar went up from the High Zar's army and Kaspar watched the first wave of fur-clad warriors charge forwards. They came in ragged groups, huge swords swinging wildly above their heads and berserk screams echoing from the valley sides. With a disciplined shout, the pikes of the Imperial line lowered and the first of the enemy warriors were spitted on their lethally sharp points. Screams and shouts drifted from the fighting as men died, run through with Empire steel or hacked down with steppe-forged iron.

The Imperial line bent back under the weight of the charge, frenzied warriors hacking left and right with their massive swords and axes. But here, the very size of their weapons was their undoing. Each of the tribesmen needed a wide space around him to swing his weapon and thus avoid killing his fellow warriors, but the tightly packed ranks of the Empire allowed half a dozen men to fight a single Kurgan warrior.

The fighting was brutal and brief, and Kaspar watched the Kurgan warriors stream back from the struggle, bloodied and broken by the stout defences of his countrymen. Jeers and ululating trumpet blasts followed them as they fled, but Kaspar knew that this was but the tip of the iceberg.

The worst was yet to come.

III

General Albertalli wiped blood from his eyes and slapped the men nearest him on the back with pride as they shouted colourful insults at the retreating enemy warriors. Bodies littered the ground and he shouted at his men to close ranks. The wounded and dead were dragged to the back of the regiment and his sergeants shoved men forward with curses and the butts of their halberds.

'Are you alright, sir?' asked one of his soldiers as he wiped more blood from his eyes.

'Yes, lad, I'll be fine,' he said with a reassuring smile. 'I've had worse cuts shaving. Don't you worry about me, and anyway, I cut the bastard's head off who gave me this.'

The soldier nodded, but Albertalli could see the fear behind his eyes. He didn't blame him. For all his smiles and reassurance, that last attack had almost broken them. He and his sergeants, huge Tileans with great axes who protected the standard of Luccini, had led a brutal counterattack that had sent the Kurgans reeling back, but it had been a close run thing. Smoke drifted across the battlefield and he strained to see how the rest of the allied line was holding, but he could see nothing through the thick musket smoke and press of fighting men.

His men shouted a warning as yet more enemy warriors emerged from the smoke.

His men had courage, that was for sure, but courage could only last for so long.

IV

PAVEL OVERTOOK A fleeing Kurgan tribesman, sweeping his sword back into his face and splitting the man's skull wide open. His lancers chased down the remnants of a group of tribesmen that had broken from a clash with one of the Tilean mercenary regiments, but they were getting too close to the main body of the enemy and without support, that was not a healthy place to be.

He shouted over to his trumpeter, who blew a rising, three note blast, and hauled back on the reins. The lancers on their red-painted horses wheeled expertly and rode back to their own lines, confident that they could see off any threat that came their way.

V

THE KURGANS THREW themselves at the allied line for another hour, breaking against the disciplined lines of pikes, halberds and axes like a black tide. Each attack smashed home and killed scores of men, but was hurled back every time, leaving mounds of Kurgan dead in its wake. Dozens of heavy chariots had charged forwards, ripping into the flanks of a regiment of Kossars and scything screaming men down with their bladed wheels. Their drivers were skilled and wheeled their chariots around, driving across the front of their foes before being dragged down and hacked to pieces by the vengeful Kislevites.

Kaspar watched these men fight with pride, but knew that the battle could not continue in this way. They were killing hundreds of the Kurgans, but their own casualties were mounting rapidly, and in a battle of attrition, the High Zar had thousands more men than they did. The centre was holding, but only just. He had ordered two regiments of halberdiers forwards, men from the towns and villages around Talabheim, and they had eventually thrown the tribesmen back. Cavalry charged into the flanks of the Kurgans, cutting them down by the score, spitting them on lances or crushing their bones with heavy hammers.

So far the discipline of the Urszebya pulk was holding, but Kaspar could see that the High Zar had yet to commit his most terrifying troops to battle.

VI

ALBERTALLI SHOUTED, 'Now!' and his men lowered their halberds once again as the enemy came at them. They surged forward to meet the Kurgans, bestial men in horned helms and dark armour, and the two forces met in a brazen clash of iron and flesh. He swept his heavy sword, its edge dulled by the hours of fighting, through the neck of a tribesman and kicked another in the crotch as he clambered over bodies that lay on the ground.

An axe swept out at him and he ducked below its swing, thrusting his blade into his attacker's groin. The man screamed and collapsed, dragging the blade from Albertalli's hand. He swept up a fallen halberd and blocked a downward sweep of an axe, slamming the butt of his weapon against a tribesman's temple and reversing his grip to stab the point through his chest.

All around him, men screamed and yelled, all mores of civilization forgotten in the heat of battle. The air stank of blood and terror, ringing to the harsh clang of steel on steel and the deafening booms of cannon. He stabbed and stabbed with his halberd, sweeping it through yet another tribesman's ribs.

The standard of Luccini waved above him and he yelled encouragement to his men as the gold finial caught the sunlight.

And then it was over, the Kurgans retreating into the smoke once more, driven back by the courage and discipline of his warriors. Damn, but he was proud of them. He leaned on the shaft of his halberd to regain his breath, exhausted by the fighting, when another warning shout went up. Again, so soon?

He straightened as more shapes came running at them through the smoke, and his heart skipped a beat as he saw the monstrous charging shapes. Huge, horned and shaggy beasts with slavering jaws and powerfully muscled bodies loped through the mounds of the dead with crude axes and looted swords.

'Hold fast, men. We'll see these things off!' he shouted as cries of alarm spread from somewhere close. He couldn't see from where and had no time to check as the first of the beasts thundered into their line.

Braying monsters ripped men from their feet with huge sweeps of their weapons, snapping fangs tearing mens' faces off, clawed limbs rending limbs from bodies. The beasts gorged on flesh, hacking their way through his men with ease. Albertalli chopped his halberd through the arm of a dog-headed creature, shocked when it roared and turned to face him without seeming to notice its wound.

He stabbed with the point of the weapon, the tip snapping off a handspan within its belly. The creature roared, bloody spittle frothing at its jaws, and its clawed arm swept down smashing his halberd in half.

Albertalli stumbled backwards, dragging out his pistol, but the beast was on him before he could fire, its massive jaws snapping shut on his skull and tearing his head off with one bite.

VII

THE SCREAMS OF the Tilean regiment were piteous as the monstrous beasts devoured them, but Pavel forced himself to shut them out as he spurred his horse forward. Sixty lancers followed him, leaning forward in their saddles with their lances lowered. Smoke swirled around them, obscuring all but the closest men, but he did not need to see his prey to know where to find them – they could all hear the sickening sounds of snapping bones as the creatures feasted on human flesh.

They rode from the smoke and saw the remains of the Tilean regiment, butchered almost to a man. Many of the beasts had charged wildly after the fleeing men, but many more remained, tearing great chunks of meat from the corpses of their victims.

'Charge!' shouted Pavel, lowering his lance and placing his weight into the stirrups as he leaned over his mount's neck. The ground trembled to the thunder of hooves, the shrill, shrieking whistle of the wind through their back banners driving them forward with even greater fury. The horned beasts looked up from their monstrous feast, snouts bloody and teeth bared in hunger.

The Kislevites charged into the creatures with a furious thunder of hooves and splintering lance shafts. Pavel thrust his lance into the chest of a massive, goat-headed beast, the impetus of his charge driving the tip straight through its chest. Blood jetted around the lance and the creature howled as it was punched from its feet. The lance snapped under its weight and Pavel threw aside the now useless weapon, dragging out his curved sword.

Lancers circled their horses, butchering the last of the beasts, but the damage was already done. Pavel could see that the charge of these bestial monsters had broken through the Imperial right flank. Regiments were moving to plug the gap, but a fresh tide of Kurgan warriors were already charging forwards to exploit it.

'Lancers, with me!' shouted Pavel, dragging on his reins and wheeling his horse once more.

VIII

KASPAR SENT YET more runners to order his reserve regiments forward, fearful that the attack on the right might yet overrun his forces there. But his reserves were running low and there was only so long they could continue in this way. His practiced eye swept the portions of the battlefield he could see through the smoke and the snow that had begun to fall.

The cannons were punishing the enemy and the centre was still holding. Spitzaner's army of Talabecland was fighting magnificently, and Kaspar was forced to concede that perhaps his former officer had matured into a halfway decent commander. Terrible reports of monsters attacking the mercenary regiments on the right had filtered back to Kaspar and he had been forced to reposition soldiers earmarked for the centre.

'We're too weak on the right,' he said, running a hand across his scalp.

'Shall we send Captain Proust forward?' suggested one of his staff officers.

'Aye, send his men into the gap on the right between the Ostermark pikemen and Trondheim's men,' ordered Kaspar.

The noise of the fighting was tremendous: screams, cannon fire and the discordant clash of iron weapons. He heard screaming from somewhere nearby and twisted in his saddle, trying to pinpoint its location.

'You!' he shouted to one of his few remaining runners. 'Find out where that's coming from and get back here as soon as you know something!'

He felt a strange sensation crawl up his spine and glanced round to see the Ice Queen with her hands raised, shouting into the wind in a language Kaspar did not understand. Flickering mist gathered around her, sending questing tendrils of light into the ground and he briefly wondered what sorceries she conjured.

Such thoughts were banished from his mind as the cold wind blew again and the smoke cleared long enough for him to see further along the valley.

'Oh no...' he whispered, seeing the huge, dragon creature charging towards their lines accompanied by a huge mass of gigantic horsemen. His eyes were drawn to the massive warrior who led them. Even though he was some distance away, Kaspar could see he wore shimmering armour and a helm of a snarling wolf.

There could be no doubt about it.

This was the High Zar.

IX

THE CANNON CREWS sweated despite the cold, dragging their heavy cannon back to the covered embrasure once the blackened loaders had rammed the powder charge and ball down the barrel. As the rammer cleared the barrel, the master gunner kept his leather thumb patch over the touchhole lest a stray spark or smouldering ember ignite the charge prematurely.

For the men of the Imperial Gunnery School, the battle had become little more than a series of repetitions: lload, aim, fire… load, aim, fire. They could see nothing of the battle through the stinking smoke and simply kept firing towards the enemy.

The loader hauled aside the wicker gabion in the embrasure and ducked back as the master gunner lifted the long, burning taper to fire the weapon. He pressed the flame to the touchhole and the massive gun rocked backwards, filling the emplacement with noise and smoke. The crew began hauling the gun back when the master gunner was snatched from his feet in a spray of blood.

Deafened by the sounds of battle, the gunners had not heard the howls and roars of the charging beasts that swarmed over the ridge. Dozens of monstrous, bestial creatures overran the artillery pits, tearing the gunners apart with long, bloody claws and powerful, snapping jaws.

X

KASPAR WAS SUDDENLY aware of the silence of the guns and his worst fears were confirmed when he saw his runner's horse galloping back through the smoke, its rider's headless body still clutching the reins. He saw howling beasts rampaging across the artillery ridge, smashing aside wicker gabions and hurling severed body parts before them.

The monstrous creatures were drunk on blood, frenzied to the point of intoxication by the slaughter. The beasts smashed through the gun emplacements and ran downhill towards the Ice Queen, bellowing in ferocious hunger.

Kaspar dragged on the reins of his horse and shouted, 'Kurt!'

Kurt Bremen had already wheeled his mount and yelled, 'Knights Panther, with me!'

Kaspar and the knights galloped desperately across the hard ground to intercept the charging creatures. He knew he should not be exposing himself to this kind of risk, but the old instincts of a soldier had kicked in and it was too late to stop now. The howling beasts saw them coming and altered their charge, rushing to meet them head on.

The knights smashed into the beasts, their heavy lances skewering the fierce creatures on their points. Lances broke and horses lashed out with iron-shod hooves to stave in ribcages and smash bestial skulls. Dozens of the monsters were trampled to bloody pulp beneath the heavy warhorses and as the knights wheeled their mounts, there were only four still standing.

Kaspar blew out the back of a beast's skull with a well-aimed pistol shot as the knights surrounded the remaining three creatures and hacked them down with their heavy broadswords. As the last creature fell, Kurt Bremen rode alongside Kaspar and said, 'Ambassador, that was... unwise of you.'

'I know,' said Kaspar, breathless with exertion and exhilaration. 'Don't worry, it won't happen again.'

Bremen chuckled. 'We shall see.'

Kaspar reloaded his pistol before riding back to where he had been observing the battlefield. The allied line was bending back under the force of the enemy attacks and as he watched, he saw the massive beast of ancient times finally strike his men.

XI

THE MONSTROUS DRAGON creature smashed into a regiment of Talabecland pikemen, their weapons shattering against its thick hide. Swords bounced from its ancient flesh and in reply, its huge axe swept out and a dozen men died. Another score fell with every stroke of its blade and its huge claws crushed men beneath its weight with every step. Its roar cracked the earth and lightning flared around it, incinerating friend and foe alike. There could be no standing against such a terrifying creature and the men of the Empire turned and fled, their standard falling to be trampled by the vast beast.

Nearby regiments, already hard pressed by the Kurgan tribesmen, stepped backwards despite the shouted demands of their sergeants. Seeing this horrifying god of war amongst them spurred the Kurgans to insane heights of bravery and they hurled themselves at the men of the Urszebya pulk with unremitting fury.

As the courage of the men of the Empire hung on a knife-edge, hordes of armoured horsemen, led by the High Zar himself, charged through the swirling smoke and mist and hammered into their ranks.

Against such terrifying violence, the allied soldiers broke almost instantly as the ferocious warriors killed and killed and killed. Streams of men began sprinting away from the bloody horsemen, who pounded after them and hacked them down as they ran with great sweeps of huge swords and axes.

The centre had broken.

XII

KASPAR SHOUTED AT his runners to send word to the flanks of the army. The centre had broken and enemy warriors were pouring through the gap, butchering everything in their path. Snow was falling more heavily now, deadening the sounds of battle and misting everything in flurries of white.

Kaspar felt a chill seize him worse than the falling snow, a sickening feeling that Spitzaner had been right. Fighting in this valley with no retreat had doomed them all. Even as he shouted orders to try and plug the gap in the centre, he knew it was too little too late. Hordes of heavy horsemen were charging uphill and not even the quickest regiment would be able to prevent disaster.

'General von Velten!' shouted a voice behind him. He turned his horse to see the Ice Queen beckoning him and spurred his horse towards her. He rode close to the Tzarina, feeling the skin-crawling sensation of powerful magicks surrounding her.

'Your majesty?' he said hurriedly. 'The centre has broken and I fear we are defeated.'

'You give up too soon, general. Have faith in me,' said the Ice Queen, and Kaspar could see that her eyes burned with an inner radiance, both orbs flecked with blazing winter fire. 'As we defend the land, the lands defends us.'

'I don't understand,' said Kaspar.

'You will,' promised the Ice Queen. 'Just hold the enemy back for a little longer.'

'I will do what I can,' assured Kaspar, 'but they are amongst us.'

'You must hold them, von Velten, I need only a little longer.'

Kaspar nodded as she threw her head back and white lightning split the sky above her, swirling clouds boiling and snow spinning about her in a miniature snowstorm. Kaspar and her guards backed away from the incandescent form of the Tzarina as a low moaning, sounding as though it echoed from the very centre of the earth, issued from the ground.

'Go!' shouted the Ice Queen. 'Hold them!'

XIII

STREAMS OF MEN, both Kislevite and Empire, fled before the wrath of the High Zar and his chosen warriors. Huge, armoured horsemen on giant, daemonic steeds thundered through the centre of the Urszebya pulk, killing hundreds as they rampaged across the bodies of broken men. The giant beast followed, slower as it slew and feasted on the dead it left in their wake.

Kaspar knew they could not hope to defeat the High Zar's warriors, but the Tzarina had not asked him to defeat them, merely to hold them back for a time. Storm clouds gathered above her and, though he did not know what she planned, he vowed that he and his soldiers would give her whatever time their lives could buy. Kurt Bremen and the Knights Panther stood ready to ride with him and Leopold Dietz, holding the ambassador's banner high, shouted at the embassy guards to stand to.

Kossars and scattered groups of Imperial soldiers rallied to his black and gold standard as the ground shook with the approach of the High Zar. Kaspar knew that getting men to fight was the easy part of any battle, but getting men to go back into a battle they had already run from was next to impossible, so he was filled with a humbling sense of pride as more and more warriors flocked to join them, called by some unseen signal to defend the queen of Kislev.

The dark horsemen crossed the ridge before them and Kaspar could feel the fear of these mighty warriors spread through the gathered soldiers. But not one man took a backwards step.

A swelling roar built from the throats of the men of Kislev and the Empire, and Kaspar raised his fist. His hand swept down and the Urszebya pulk swept forward to meet the High Zar, man to man, blade to blade.

The heavy cavalry smashed into the massed soldiers, their swords and axes chopping through them with terrifying ease. Screams and blood filled the air and a score of men were dead in the opening seconds of the fight. Kaspar fired both his pistols, unhorsing an enemy rider, before throwing them aside and drawing his sword.

Kurt Bremen hacked down a Kurgan rider and beheaded another, fighting with desperate skill and courage. Kaspar chopped at an enemy horseman's back, but his sword bounced clear of the warrior's thick armour.

The warrior turned and swept his sword down, the blade slashing past Kaspar's head and cutting deep into his horse's flank. Magnus reared and lashed out with his hooves, caving in the warrior's skull. Kaspar tried to rein in the pain-maddened horse, but the Kurgan's weapon had bitten deep and it was all he could do to hold on, let alone fight.

All was screaming chaos as the High Zar's armoured horsemen slaughtered them, screams, blood, noise and death. Kaspar lost all sense of direction as his horse thrashed around in agony, but it was plain to see that this battle was lost.

Another blade lashed out and he screamed a denial as a heavy axe virtually decapitated his horse. Magnus collapsed and Kaspar was hurled from the saddle, sprawling in an ungainly heap in the midst of the swirling melee.

He picked himself up as he heard a shrill whistling, but was unable to see where it came from. Bodies jostled him as he stood, stampeding horses and fighting men. He raised his sword as a huge black horse reared up before him, a length of pikeshaft buried in its chest. The beast flailed as it died and its rider was thrown to the ground.

The warrior rolled to his feet and hurled himself back into the fray. Kaspar saw from his snarling wolf helm and iridescent armour plates that this was none other than the High Zar himself. The giant tore off his dented helmet and hefted his huge pallasz, brandishing it two-handed as he cut down enemies by the dozen.

Kaspar limped through the worsening snow towards the High Zar, knowing that he could not defeat such a terrifying warrior, but unwilling to lose this battle without having faced his nemesis face to face. Knights Panther and the embassy guards closed in on the High Zar, but he seemed unfazed by so many opponents.

His pallasz swept out and a knight died. A lance splintered on his breastplate and Kaspar could not believe that it had not penetrated. Another knight died as his horse was slain beneath him by the High Zar and the pallasz stabbed downwards.

Kaspar reached the Kurgan war leader at the same time as Kurt Bremen and the two men attacked the leader of the tribesmen with magnificent heroism. Bremen's broadsword clashed against Cyenwulf's pallasz in a shower of sparks and Kaspar's sabre slid from the High Zar's armour.

The giant tribesman backhanded his fist into Kaspar's chest and he collapsed, feeling ribs break beneath his armour. Hot pain stabbed into him as he fell and he saw Kurt Bremen stagger under a blow to his hip. Blood streamed down the knight's thigh where the pallasz had penetrated the mail links beneath his armour.

Kaspar tried to stand, but fierce pain flared in his chest. He pushed himself to his knees as he heard the whistling sound again and looked up in time to see a tide of red-painted horsemen thunder from the smoke, their feathered back banners and long lances glorious and heaven-sent as they charged.

Pavel rode at the head of the lancers, his sword raised high as he and his warriors charged home, lances punching the armoured Kurgans from their saddles in a crash of flesh and steel. Pavel struck left and right and Kaspar was suddenly transported back to the days when they had fought side by side as young men. His old friend was a force of nature, killing with every strike of his sword as his lancers broke through the centre of the High Zar's warriors.

Pavel's sword struck Cyenwulf's head and the mighty war leader staggered, blood streaming from his forehead. His pallasz slashed and Pavel's horse fell, its forelegs cut from beneath it. Kurt Bremen attacked as the High Zar's attention was elsewhere, but once again his armour defeated a stroke that Kaspar knew should have split him apart. As his horse screamed in its death throes, Pavel joined the Knight Panther as the battle swirled around them.

As Kurt and Pavel fought the High Zar, Kaspar picked himself up, gritting his teeth against the pain and went to the aid of his comrades. It was an unequal struggle and though they outnumbered the Kurgan chieftain, his strength and skill was vastly superior to theirs. His heart heavy, Kaspar knew they could not defeat him.

Kaspar thrust his blade towards the High Zar's groin, but his sword was easily batted aside and Cyenwulf's riposte tore into his belly. He fell, pain the likes of which he had never known before gripping his body tight, and slammed face first into the snow, rolling onto his back as blood poured from the wound.

Pavel screamed in loss and risked a high cut to Cyenwulf's head, but the High Zar was ready for him and Kaspar watched in horror as the Kurgan ducked and his mighty sword swept up and hacked into Pavel's side.

The huge pallasz shattered Pavel's breastplate and buried itself within his chest, but as he staggered under the massive impact, Pavel dropped his sword and gripped onto the High Zar's blade with both hands. Cyenwulf struggled to free his weapon from Pavel's grip, but the giant Kislevite held it firm, blood frothing from his mouth and flooding from his side. Time slowed and Kaspar saw the entirety of this battle captured in the faces of these two warriors, the brutal, unthinking hatred of the High Zar and the passionate heroism of Pavel.

As the High Zar tried to free his blade from the dying Pavel, Kurt Bremen's broadsword struck and buried itself in the centre of his face. Cyenwulf dropped without a sound, blood and brains spilling from the shattered fragments of his splintered skull.

The Knight Panther dragged his sword free of Cyenwulf's head and fell to his knees. His face was ashen and his breathing ragged as blood poured down his thigh.

Bremen smiled, content with this small victory amid such bloodshed and horror.

Then the world shook as the creature of ancient darkness stepped from the swirling snow and mist. Its massive form towered above them and lightning flared from its head as it bellowed its fury across the battlefield.

XIV

KASPAR TRIED TO push himself away from the massive creature but searing, white-hot pain seized him and he was only able to prop himself up against the flanks of a dead horse. Blood soaked his shirt and streamed from beneath his breastplate to pool in his lap. The beast towered above Bremen, easily triple his height, and as it lifted its huge axe, the knight struggled to rise, ready to fight even though there was no chance of victory.

Snow and ice lashed around the monster and Kaspar saw grooves of blood streak its massive body as the unnatural storm beat the creature back. The low moaning he had heard near the Ice Queen sounded again, much louder this time, and he looked up as the sky darkened and a rumbling tremor ran through the ground.

Whips of white lightning arced from the massive standing stones that ringed the valley, each one thrumming with barely-contained power. As he watched, the stones spewed a thick mist, venting a writhing smoke that seethed and coiled like a snake. Crackling with power, the swirling mist descended and spread across the valley floor.

His vision was blurring, but he saw shapes forming in the mist, indistinct forms fashioning themselves from the insubstantial matter into something else entirely.

All down the length of the valley the strange mist closed with the battling Kurgans and bellowed war-cries turned to shouts of panic as the tribesmen saw what approached them. Ghostly figures of mist charged them with shadow-formed axes and swords. Shaped from their most deathly fears, the mist warriors attacked the Kurgan warriors, and though their bodies and weapons were fashioned from mist and smoke, they slew whatever they struck.

Kaspar watched amazed as the shadowy warriors of the mist slaughtered the Kurgan warriors, one minute appearing as huge, bearskinned warriors of ancient Kislev, the next soldiers of the Empire and then again as primitive warriors wearing the pelts of wild animals. There was something primal and elemental about them and they drove the Kurgans back without mercy. He twisted painfully to watch the Tzarina, seeing her wreathed in a writhing snowstorm, tendrils of smoke and light stabbing through her and outwards into the land.

And Kaspar recognised who these mist warriors were in that instant, realising why the Tzarina had been so adamant that the battle be fought here.

As the Kurgan army disintegrated under the unstoppable assault of these warriors, Kaspar knew that the Tzarina had tapped into something ancient and deadly dangerous, the power of the land, the elemental energy that was the source of all her own strength. Called to defend itself, she had given the land a means to strike back at those who defiled it and sought to do it harm.

A bellowing roar of pain shook the snow from the valley sides and Kaspar watched as the misty warriors surrounded the enormous monster before him, driving it back down the valley. It may have been old when the world was young, but this land had endured throughout the ages and had a power that could not be denied.

The beast was soon lost to sight amidst the howling winds and screeching voices on the air, and Kaspar leaned back as the sounds of battle faded.

He cried out as he felt hands lift his head and groaned in pain, seeing Kurt Bremen kneeling beside him. The knight's skin was the colour of parchment and streaked with blood.

Behind the knight stood the Ice Queen, unsteady on her feet with a fading halo of winter's light surrounding her.

'Did we win?' asked Kaspar.

'I think so, Kaspar,' said the Ice Queen, her voice hollow and drained. 'The land of Kislev is unforgiving.'

'Good,' he said. 'I'd have hated to go through all this for nothing.'

'You have been a true son of Kislev, Kaspar von Velten,' said the Ice Queen, kneeling beside him and taking his hand. Kaspar expected her hand to be cold, but it was warmer than his and he smiled.

'Thank you, your majesty,' whispered Kaspar.

The Ice Queen leaned close and kissed his cheek and again Kaspar was struck by the fact that her flesh wasn't cold after all, but warm and soft. She stood and gave him a smile of thanks before turning and walking off into the gathering evening.

'Kurt,' said the ambassador, his voice little more than a whisper.

'Yes?'

'Will you do something for me?'

'Of course. You know I will.'

Kaspar reached beneath his breastplate and pulled out something from the pocket of his shirt. He held out his hand and said, 'Take this.'

'What is it?' said Bremen, opening his palm.

Kaspar placed a pendant with a thin silver chain and a smooth blue stone wrapped in a web of silver wire into Bremen's palm and closed his finger over it.

'Give this to Sofia, Kurt. And tell her…'

'Tell her what?' said the Knight Panther as the ambassador's words trailed off.

'Tell her… that I am sorry… sorry I couldn't keep my promise.'

Kurt Bremen nodded, tears coursing down his cheeks.

'I will,' he said.

XV

WITH THE DEATH of High Zar Aelfric Cyenwulf and the retreat of the Old One, the Kurgan army melted like snow before the spring thaw. As the survivors of the Kurgan horde fled the valley, the warriors of the mist faded, swirling in the spring breeze until there was nothing left of them save the distant echoes of ancient war cries.

The warriors of the Urszebya pulk watched the fleeing Kurgans, but did not give pursuit, too exhausted by the furious battle to do more than collapse and weep or give thanks for their lives.

Truly it is said that the only thing more grievous than a battle lost is a battle won. The men of the Empire and Kislev mourned together and gave thanks together as the night closed in and the pyres for the dead were built.

Too many had died and the loss was too near for there to be any thought of victory celebrations; those would come later. As night closed in, the only movement across the steppe was a lone knight riding sadly for the south.

Epilogue
Six months later...

I

After the great victory at Urszebya, the fighting in Kislev dragged on. The days of wars being settled in one great battle were long since past and there were many skirmishes and slaughters to take place before the final outcome of the war was decided at a place of ancient legend.

The accounts of these battles have since passed into the annals of history: the Battle of Iron Gate, the Relief of Zavstra, the Defence of Bolgasgrad, the Siege of Kislev, the Sack of Erengrad and countless others, but such are tales for a different time, and there were heroes made in these days who would live on in song for hundreds of years.

It was a time of heroes and a time of great sorrow.

Truly was it named the Year That No One Forgets.

II

Vassily Chekatilo halted his convoy of wagons at the top of a grassy rise on the slope that led down to the bustling city of Marienburg with its vast docks, sprawling mercantile houses and lively trading districts. The great forests of the Empire were behind him and he could see the glittering azure expanse of the Sea of Claws ahead of him. Tall ships with billowing sails crossed the seas here, bound for all manner of exotic ports and strange destinations. Marienburg was a wretched hive of scum and villainy, and now that he had arrived, it was time for the local criminals to watch out.

The journey across the Empire had been fraught with danger and risk, but the papers he had extorted from von Velten had seen him past the worst of it, as had the hundred soldiers he had been able to appropriate thanks to the ambassador's seal.

Most of those soldiers had since returned to the Empire, blind patriotism that Chekatilo did not understand taking them back to wars that would no doubt see most of them die in agony. It was of no matter though, he had coin enough to pay for mercenary soldiers and, since the money was good, they had protected him well enough.

The River Reik foamed downhill towards the city below, its red tiled roofs beckoning him onwards, and Chekatilo could sense nothing but possibilities opening before him. He cracked the reins of his horses and guided his wagon train downhill towards his bright new future.

But Chekatilo had not noticed the stowaway hiding in the rearmost cart of his convoy, concealed beneath an oiled canvas tarpaulin, a bloated, albino-furred rat with a strange triangular brand on its back.

Its hidden masters had marked this man-thing for death and such decrees were never disobeyed or forgotten. Fortunately the rat could sense the presence of many of its brethren below the man-city ahead.

It waited...

ABOUT THE AUTHOR

Hailing from Scotland, Graham narrowly escaped a career in surveying nearly five years ago to join Games Workshop's Games Development team, which, let's face it, sounds much more exciting. He's worked on loads of codexes since then, the most recent being *Codex: Space Marines*. As well as six novels, he's also written a host of short stories for *Inferno!* and takes on too much freelance work than can be healthy. Graham's housemate, a life-size cardboard cut-out of Buffy, recently suffered a terrible accident during a party and now keeps herself to herself in the spare room, scaring people who don't know she's there and plotting the best way to have her revenge on the miscreant that damaged her.

Coming soon from the Black Library

GUARDIANS OF THE FOREST

by Graham McNeill

A LOW MIST closed in around the riders, deadening sound and imparting a ghostly quality to the soldiers that followed Leofric as he rode ever eastwards. The road, which had never been more than an overgrown mud track, little travelled and little cared for, petered out to nothing more than a flattened earthen line, barely distinguishable from the rest of the landscape.

The lands of Bretonnia were rich and fertile, the soil dark and fecund, its landscape tilled by the peasants, the sweeping plains of its dukedoms open and green. Unlike the thickly forested realm of the Empire far to the north that embraced the new sciences of alchemy, astrology and engineering, the realm of Bretonnia kept to the ancient ways of chivalric conduct. The beloved King Leoncouer maintained the codes of behaviour set down by King Louis over a thousand years ago, held by the grail monks in the Chapel of Bastonne.

By such martial codes of honour did the knights of Bretonnia uphold their honour and defend their king's lands. To be a knight of Bretonnia was to be a warrior of great skill, noble bearing and virtuous heart, a paragon of all that was honourable.

Leofric felt his right hand slip from the emblazoned reins of his horse and grasp the hilt of his sword as he crested the misty summit of a low rise and saw a dark line of green and gold on the horizon.

Athel Loren...

For centuries this forest had lived in the dreams and nightmares of the Bretonnian people. Even from here, Leofric could feel the power that lay within the dark depths of the forest, a drowsy, dreaming energy that clawed its way into the landscape like the roots of a tree. Dark oaks stood like sentinels at the forest edge, their branches high and leafy, a mixture of greens and russet browns.

Cold mists hugged the ground leading towards the forest, a wild, scrubby heath of unkempt grasses and thorns with stagnant pools of water and lumpen, snow-covered mounds of earth. Here and there, Leofric could see a rusted sword blade, spear point or arrowhead and the occasional bleached whiteness of bone.

No matter how many times he had come to enact the traditional family ritual, the sight of this ancient battlefield always unsettled him, as though restless spirits of the dead still haunted this bleak landscape.

'It's not like I imagined it to be,' said Helene, her voice just a little too shrill.

'No?'

'No, it's... it's, well, I don't know, but I thought it would look different. Given what you've told me I expected something more... unnatural.'

'Trust me, my dear,' said Leofric. 'There is nothing natural about this place.'

'I don't like it though,' said Helene, pulling her cloak tighter about herself. 'It feels like death here.'

'Aye,' agreed Leofric. 'It is a place of darkness.'

'What are those?' asked Helene, pointing to raised mounds of earth and stone.

Riding alongside Leofric's wife, Baudel said, 'They say that those mounds are burial cairns, raised by the first tribes of men to come this way.'

'Really?' asked Helene, ignoring Leofric's disapproving gaze. 'What else do they say?'

'Well,' continued Baudel, warming to his theme. 'My old father used to tell us that an evil necromancer once raised the dead from their tombs and tried to destroy Athel Loren itself.'

'I know that story!' nodded Helene. 'His army entered the forest and was never seen again. Do you know what happened?'

'It was the forest, milady,' said Baudel, lowering his voice theatrically. 'My old father said that it was the forest what came alive and destroyed his skeleton army.'

'Hush, Baudel!' snapped Leofric. 'Do not fill my wife's head with such nonsense. If this necromancer existed at all, then no doubt he was killed by the elves of the forest. That's what they are good at, killing and stealing what is not theirs!'

'Sorry, my lord,' said Baudel, suitably chastened.

'Oh, come now, husband, surely it's just a story,' said Helene.

Leofric stopped and turned his horse to face his wife, his face drawn and serious. He shook his head and said, 'Helene, I love you with all my heart, but you are from Lyonesse, not Quenelles.'

'What has that to do with anything?'

'It means you have not grown up in the shadow of the faerie forest, not had to lock and bolt your doors on certain nights to be sure that elven princelings do not come and steal away your children. You have never had to spend days with every gate and shutter drawn as the wild hunt thunders through the sky, killing everything in its path. Trust me on this, we will find no welcome here.'

Helene opened her mouth to let fly a witty riposte, but saw a familiar look she had come to know all too well in her husband's eyes and the quip died in her throat. She nodded and said, 'Then let us be about our business.'

Leofric nodded curtly and turned his horse back towards the forest. The mist thinned as they drew near the forest's edge and within the passing of an hour he saw the familiar sight of the waystone. It reared up atop a flowering mound of grass, its smooth grey surface carved and painted with symbols and spirals, meaningless to him, but which nevertheless raised the hairs on the back of his neck.

He looked left and right, knowing that there were other stones spread evenly along the edge of the forest, but unable to see them due to the clammy mist that the day's sun seemed unable to burn away.

The knight guided his horse into a hollow depression in the earth with an icy pool at its base and a low cluster of rocks and bushes gathered around its ragged circumference. The top of the looming waystone was still visible, but the majority of its unsettling form was hidden from sight by the lay of the land.

'Halt!' he shouted as he reached the base of the hollow, dragging on his reins and bringing his horse to a halt. As he dismounted, he saw that the tasselled ends of his horse's bright yellow and scarlet caparison were muddy and stained, but it couldn't be helped. The gelding was named Taschen, standing seventeen hands high with wide shoulders and powerful muscles that could carry his armoured weight into battle without effort. King Leoncouer himself had presented the magnificent animal to Leofric after he had saved the king's life during the charge against the daemon prince at Middenheim...

Leofric pushed the thought away, unwilling to relive the terrible memories of the horrific days defending the great northern city of the Empire from the traitor knight Archaon.

He handed Taschen's reins to his squire, a boy whose name he hadn't bothered to learn after his previous squire, Lauder, had died screaming with a beastman's spear in his gut.

The rest of his soldiers drew up in a circle around their lord, dismounting and walking their horses before brushing them down and loosening their girths. Compared to Leofric's steed, the men-at-arms' mounts were poor specimens indeed, and did not bear any heraldic devices or caparison, their riders' lowborn status prohibiting them from doing so.

Leofric marched over to his wife's horse, which had a well-cared for reddish brown silky coat. He reached up and helped her dismount gracefully from the saddle, smiling as she hitched up her long red robes to avoid the worst of the autumnal mud.

'I warned you that your dress would get muddy,' he said gently.

'And I told you that I didn't care,' she said with a smile. 'I've grown tired of this gown anyway. My ladies tell me that red is very passé for this time of year and that you should be buying me something in lavender next season.'

'Oh they do, do they?' said Leofric. 'Then the peasantry must work harder next year to pay for it.'

'Indeed they shall,' said Helene and they laughed, not noticing the pained looks on the men-at-arms' faces at their overheard conversation.

Leofric turned from Helene and removed the canvas sack from his saddle, shouting orders to his men-at-arms and directing them to the ice-covered pool at the base of the hollow. The men began breaking the thinner ice at the edge of the pool with the butts of their spears, taking it in turns to lead the horses to drink.

Leofric and Helene's horses drank their fill first as was only proper.

The knight of Quenelles moved to the far side of the icy pool as his squire struggled to lift a gilt-edged reliquae box adorned with woodcuts from the back of his dray horse and carried over towards Leofric.

'Set it down there,' ordered Leofric, pointing to a flat rock before him and drawing his sword, a magnificent blade as long as the butt of a lance and fully three fingers wide. Though it was stronger than steel, the sword weighed less than the wooden swords the peasants trained with and could cut through armour with lethal ease. Its blade was silver steel and shone as though captured starlight had somehow been trapped in its forging. The sword had been touched by the Lady of the Lake herself many centuries ago and had been passed down the line of Carrard since time before memory. Leofric knew that it was a great honour to bear such a blessed weapon and that when he could no longer carry out his duty to defend his lands and people, he would pass it to Beren, his only son and heir.

Leofric's squire gently set down the reliquae before his master. The box was crafted from young saplings hewn from the Forest of Chalons and carved with stirring scenes that told the heroic battles of Gilles le Breton, legendary founder of Bretonnia.

Atop the box, an image of the Lady of the Lake, goddess of the Bretonnians, was picked out in silver and rendered with swirling golden tresses. Leofric dropped to his knees as his squire closed his unworthy eyes and opened the winged doors of the reliquae.

Inside the reliquae, the inner walls were painted with scenes of wondrous lakes and pools of reflective water, with the image of a breathtakingly beautiful woman rising from the depths. A deep cushion of sumptuous red velvet sat within the container, together with the broken hilt of a sword and the faded, tattered scrap of cloth, its golden edges frayed and torn.

Leofric closed his eyes, feeling the peace of the Lady's presence wash over him at the sight of such holy relics: the faerie flag, a scrap of shimmering material supposedly torn from the cloak of an elven princeling by Leofric's great grandfather after he chased him from Castle Carrard, and the hilt of a Carrard sword that had cut down the orc warlord, Skargor of the Massif Orcal.

Leofric reached out and ran his gauntleted fingers along the broken hilt and folded cloth as he began his prayers to the Lady.

'Lady, bless me your humble servant, grant me the strength to confront those who ignore the wisdom and beauty of your holy light. You, whose bounty is with me all the days of my life, grant the lands I defend in your name the peace that this appeasement might bring...'

* * *

As Leofric began his prayers to the Lady, Helene sat upon a rock at the edge of the cold pool, gathering her skirts beneath her to make it marginally less uncomfortable. She felt a coldness here, and not just the coldness of the coming winter – something deeper chilled her. She looked back over her shoulder, seeing the gently swaying treetops of Athel Loren and the very tip of the tall waystone that marked the edge of the elven realm.

Strange that the forest did not grow beyond the stones. Idly, Helene wondered why, but then put the thought from her mind as Baudel approached with a pewter plate laden with cuts of cold beef, bread and a wedge of pungent cheese.

'Some lunch, milady?'

'No thank you, Baudel,' she said. 'I'm not really feeling hungry at the moment.'

'I'd ask you to reconsider, milady. It'll be a good few hours before we get back to the castle. Nice cheese, fresh beef to keep you going till then?'

'Very well, Baudel,' said Helene, accepting the plate.

Baudel turned to leave, but Helene looked over at Leofric with a concerned expression and said, 'Sit with me awhile. I want to talk.'

'Milady,' nodded the man-at-arms and sat on a nearby rock, his spear still held upright.

'Baudel, does Leofric seem different to you?'

'I'm not sure I follow, milady,' replied Baudel, guardedly.

'Yes you do,' said Helene. 'Ever since he came back from the Empire and the battles against the northern tribes I've felt a distance between us. You were there too, Baudel, does he seem changed… after the war, I mean?'

'War changes a man, milady.'

'I know that, Baudel, I'm not some milkmaid from Brionne. He's gone off to fight before, but he's never come back like this.'

'Like what?'

'Withdrawn and unwilling to talk about what happened.'

Baudel sighed and glanced over the pool at Leofric who was still kneeling before the Carrard reliquae, deep in his prayers. 'It wouldn't be right, me speaking out of turn about my lord and master, milady.'

'It's all right, I give you leave to speak your mind.'

'I appreciate that, milady, but it still wouldn't be right.'

Seeing the defensive look in the man-at-arm's eyes, Helene nodded and said, 'Very well, Baudel, your loyalty to your master is commendable.'

'Thank you, milady.'

'If you won't tell me what happened, at least tell me about Middenheim, it sounds like a magnificent place.'

'Aye,' nodded Baudel, 'it's grand all right. You've never seen nothing like it, milady, perched on top of a great big rock they call the Ulricsberg, higher than the lighthouse of l'Anguille by a long ways. To look at it you'd think nothing could take it, not man, not monster or nothing. But them northmen had wizards, dragons and other flyin' things that tore the place up with fire and magic, and they damn near won.'

'But they didn't, did they,' stated Helene.

'No, they didn't, but it was a close run thing, let me tell you,' said Baudel, darkly. 'The king himself led a hundred knights in the charge that faced a great daemon lord. Leofric rode in that charge and only the king and a handful of his knights rode out from that battle and... and you're a clever one aren't you, milady, getting me to spill my guts like that.'

Helene shrugged, realising that she would get no more from Baudel this day. She nibbled on a cut of meat and broke off a piece of cheese.

'It was devious of me wasn't it?' she admitted with a smile.

'Downright cunning,' agreed Baudel, rising from his seat.

'One last thing before you go,' said Helene.

'Yes?' asked Baudel, warily.

'Why can't I hear any birds or animals here? It's all very quiet apart from us.'

'The forest sleeps milady. It's waiting, just waiting for spring. As for the animals, well I think that perhaps they're all getting ready to sleep away the winter.'

'Yes, that must be it, Baudel. Thank you.'

'You're most welcome, milady,' said the man-at-arms, making an extravagant bow before turning and making his way back down to the pool where the rest of the soldiers looked to their mounts or ate hunks of hard bread moistened by a thin gruel.

Helene watched him go, frowning and cursing herself for being too obvious. Baudel might be a peasant, but he was clev-erer than most and had seen through her, admittedly clumsy, gambit.

She shivered again, feeling a crawling sensation up her spine and the ghostly caress of something unseen. Nothing stirred the air or broke the unnatural silence around her, save the hushed conversations of Leofric's soldiers. The cold was seeping through her furs and she wished to be away from this place, back in the castle with little Beren clutched close to her as she read him tales of heroic knights who slew evil dragons.

She missed her little boy and hoped that this strange ritual of the Carrard family would not take too long.

Helene still didn't understand the full significance of the ritual Leofric was here to perform – something to do with planting a seedling before the waystone and making an offering to the faerie folk.

Apparently, the practice had begun eighty years ago when family legend told that a much loved ancestor of Leofric's had been taken by the elves as a young boy and had never been seen again. Carrards had been coming to the edge of Athel Loren every five years since then to enact its quaint traditions.

She knew that Leofric begrudged such entreaties to the elven realm, though understood that he would never think of leaving the ritual unperformed, as such a stain upon the family honour would be unthinkable to a knight of Bretonnia.

As she watched her husband pray, she smiled, feeling the love she had for him as a contented warmth in her heart. She remembered the sun-drenched tilting fields outside Couronne where she had first met Leofric, picturing the dashing young knight errant with his scarlet unicorn pennant streaming from his lance as he unhorsed Chilfroy of Artois, a feat none of the gathered knights and dukes ever expected to see in their lifetimes.

Leofric had had the pick of the ladies that day, all wishing him to carry their favour upon his lance, but he had knelt before her, Helene du Reyne, sweat-streaked hair plastered across his forehead and a mischievous grin creasing his face.

'It would honour me greatly if you would consent to grant me your favour,' he said.

'Why should I do such a thing?' she had replied, straining for a regal aloofness.

'Lady, I have unhorsed my opponent in the glory of the joust!' he said. 'None other than the Duke of Artois himself, I am the greatest warrior here!'

'You are arrogant, young man, and have not the humility of a knight.'

'It is not arrogance if it is the truth,' he had pointed out.

'How do I know that for sure?'

'Tell me how I may prove it to you, my lady, for I love you and would ride to every corner of Bretonnia if you would but grant me a kiss.'

'Only the corners of Bretonnia? Is that all?'

'Not at all, I would ride to far Araby and drag back the greatest sultan were you to but look favourably my way.'

'Just to Araby?' she had teased.

'Only to begin with,' he had continued with a smile. 'Then I would sail to the far jungles of Lustria and bring back the treasures of the heathen gods if you might consent to speak my name.'

'Impressive.'

'I'm only just getting started,' he said. 'I've the rest of the world to travel yet!'

Deciding she had teased him enough, Helene had laughed and handed him a silken blue scarf, edged in white lace, and said, 'Here, you may carry my favour, sir knight. Win me this tourney and I might let you attempt to make me happy...'

'I shall, my lady! I will unhorse every man here if it will make you happy!'

And he had. Leofric had defeated every knight at the tournament before courting her as diligently and as wonderfully as any young woman could want. They were wed in the grail chapel in Quenelles a year later, and ten months after that, Helene had borne Leofric a strong son, whom they had named Beren, after one of the heroic Companions of Gilles.

Beren was so like his father, proud and with the haughty arrogance of noble youth. Though since Leofric had come back from the Errantry Wars in the north, a knight errant no more, but a knight of the realm, he had lost much of his former boisterousness.

Such was only to be expected, for a knight of the realm was tempered in battle, the fiery impetuosity of a knight errant moulded into a dutiful warrior.

But there was more to it than that. Helene knew her husband well enough to know that something more terrible than a bloody charge had happened in the war that had engulfed the Empire.

What had turned her fiery husband into a melancholy warrior who saw the cloud rather than the silver lining, the rain, not the nourished crops?

She finished the last of the beef and cheese and set down the plate on the rock beside her, feeling a shiver ripple its way along her spine.

'Colder than a Mousillon night,' she whispered to herself, as the sound of a soft, mournful weeping drifted on the air from above.

Helene twisted around, wondering if she had perhaps imagined the sound when it came again... a barely audible sobbing that tugged at her maternal instincts. Unbidden tears welled in the corners of her eyes as she listened to the unseen mourner, the sound reaching deep inside her and touching something primal in her very soul as she realised that the sobs were those of a child.

She rose from the rock and turned her gaze towards the forest.

The sound of the weeping child came again, beguiling and wistful, and, without conscious thought, Helene began walking towards the edge of the hollow. She glanced over her shoulder, seeing the yellow-surcoated men-at-arms gathered at the base of the hollow while Leofric continued his prayers.

She considered bringing the unearthly sound to the attention of her husband and his soldiers, but even before the thought was fully formed it was plucked from her head and vanished like morning mist, replaced with an insistent, urgent need to find the crying child.

Helene climbed from the hollow, the full majesty of the forest stretching out before her. The thick trunks of the mighty trees seemed to lean towards her, their branches sad with leaves of autumn gold. Leaves lay thick and still about the trees' roots and blew in a soft wind that whistled between the branches like an ancient lament.

Coils of greenish mist crept from the treeline, but Helene ignored them, her attention fixed on the sight of a young girl kneeling at the edge of the woods, clad only in an ankle-length nightgown of pale cream. The child's back was to her, and her long black hair fell about her shoulders and reached almost to the ground.

Helene's heart went out to the child. 'Oh, my dear...' wept Helene as she saw the distraught condition of the child, feet stained green with grass, and twigs and branches caught in her hair.

Was this what had happened to Leofric's ancestor? Had he been snatched as a child and left to die on this bleak moorland before the great forest of Athel Loren? Was this one of those poor unfortunate children taken by the elves, never to be seen again?

Helene took a step forward, hearing the jingle of harness and whinny of horses from behind her, and the thought of fetching help once again came to her.

The little girl let out a grief-stricken sob and all desire except that of aiding this poor, wretched child were banished from Helene's thoughts.

'Hello? Child, can you hear me?' asked Helene, taking yet more steps forward, feeling a growing fear settle in her belly with each mist-wreathed footfall. Dim lights flickered at the periphery of her vision and she had the fleeting impression of haunting melodies of aching loss from far away.

The child did not reply and though Helene tried to stop herself, she felt her arm reaching towards the young girl and said, 'Please…'

Her hand closed on the girl's shoulder and Helene sobbed in terror, feeling the softness of her flesh as a mulchy wetness.

The child's dark-haired head slowly turned to face Helene, and the lady whimpered in terror as she saw that this was no innocent child, but a thing of horror.

In an instant, the blackness of the girl's hair thinned, becoming a whipping tangle of thorned barbs, her face a haggard crone's, full of heartless spite and wicked malice. The nightgown sloughed from the thing's body, its greenish skin transforming into lashing wood, its fingers stretching into razored talons.

The creature of the forest leapt upon Helene with snapping fangs and slashing claws that ripped and bit and tore.

Helene screamed and screamed as pain and blood filled her senses.

The adventure continues in *Guardians of the Forest*
by Graham McNeill.
Coming soon from the Black Library.

Read till you Bleed

Do you have them all?

1 Trollslayer – William King
2 First & Only – Dan Abnett
3 Skavenslayer – William King
4 Into the Maelstrom – Ed. Marc Gascoigne & Andy Jones
5 Daemonslayer – William King
6 Eye of Terror – Barrington J Bayley
7 Space Wolf – William King
8 Realm of Chaos – Ed. Marc Gascoigne & Andy Jones
9 Ghostmaker – Dan Abnett
10 Hammers of Ulric – Dan Abnett, Nik Vincent & James Wallis
11 Ragnar's Claw – William King
12 Status: Deadzone – Ed. Marc Gascoigne & Andy Jones
13 Dragonslayer – William King
14 The Wine of Dreams – Brian Craig
15 Necropolis – Dan Abnett
16 13th Legion – Gav Thorpe
17 Dark Imperium – Ed. Marc Gascoigne & Andy Jones
18 Beastslayer – William King
19 Gilead's Blood – Abnett & Vincent
20 Pawns of Chaos – Brian Craig
21 Xenos – Dan Abnett
22 Lords of Valour – Ed. Marc Gascoigne & Christian Dunn
23 Execution Hour – Gordon Rennie
24 Honour Guard – Dan Abnett
25 Vampireslayer – William King
26 Kill Team – Gav Thorpe
27 Drachenfels – Jack Yeovil
28 Deathwing – Ed. David Pringle & Neil Jones
29 Zavant – Gordon Rennie
30 Malleus – Dan Abnett
31 Konrad – David Ferring
32 Nightbringer – Graham McNeill
33 Genevieve Undead – Jack Yeovil
34 Grey Hunter – William King
35 Shadowbreed – David Ferring
36 Words of Blood – Ed. Marc Gascoigne & Christian Dunn
37 Zaragoz – Brian Craig
38 The Guns of Tanith – Dan Abnett
39 Warblade – David Ferring
40 Farseer – William King
41 Beasts in Velvet – Jack Yeovil
42 Hereticus – Dan Abnett
43 The Laughter of Dark Gods – Ed. David Pringle
44 Plague Daemon – Brian Craig
45 Storm of Iron – Graham McNeill
46 The Claws of Chaos – Gav Thorpe
47 Draco – Ian Watson
48 Silver Nails – Jack Yeovil
49 Soul Drinker – Ben Counter
50 Harlequin – Ian Watson
51 Storm Warriors – Brian Craig
52 Straight Silver – Dan Abnett
53 Star of Erengrad – Neil McIntosh
54 Chaos Child – Ian Watson
55 The Dead & the Damned – Jonathan Green
56 Shadow Point – Gordon Rennie
57 Blood Money – C L Werner
58 Angels of Darkness – Gav Thorpe
59 Mark of Damnation – James Wallis